Also by Alcaly Lo

Shine Eye Girl
Monkey Bread

BETTER WILL COME
a novel
ALCALY LO

This novel is a work of fiction. Names, characters, places, and incidents are either the product of the author's imagination or are used fictitiously. Any resemblance to actual events, locales, or persons, living or dead, is entirely coincidental.

ISBN-13: 978-0-9840798-0-3
ISBN-10: 0-9840798-0-7

Alcalylo.com
mail@alcalylo.com

Pour Matou,
Issa,
Nat,
Ngo,
& Paul

He dreamed his dreams, and doing is believing, but Jay wouldn't have gotten into the prophet business hadn't his brother Joe Babylon met both the Scientology girl and the P-Funk bum that day.

Part one of the revelation took place in front of the cult's midtown Washington headquarters as Joe was walking away from his marketing job and into the sunshine, this being the warmest winter on record in Empire and throughout the northern hemisphere. The girl was unclean, chubby, and probably phony like only phishing bleached beach blondes can be. Vacant eyes as she stood in Joe's path when he crossed R out of turn, Joe being Joe. Drugged, brainwashed or merely empty-headed, the girl. Sausage fingers, bitten nails, grimy teeth, lazy smile, rehashed pitch, yellow sweater, yellow flier: Come and learn to live a toxin-free life; 10 minutes to change your in-look and outlook; catch a matinee and take the complimentary stress test; yo, believe it or not we repair souls from 9 to 5. Joe took the piece of paper just to be nice and because he couldn't say no to blondes real or bottled, something about them, and he glanced over it as he walked toward the Nova. He knew there was nothing scientific about Scientology. No *logos* to be gathered by would-be converts, no prospect other than an empty bank account, no self-discovery down the artificially illuminated path except that of being the biggest dupe. Hubbard, that scoundrel posing as a guru, woke up one day and decided to found a religion as a moneymaking machine. Even joked about it in a lecture before getting down to business. Turned his slow-selling sci-fi fantasies into an out-there cosmology replete with fancy creatures, Shakespearean undercurrents, worlds at war, boutique concepts like "Dianetics," and New Age riffs. Mesmerized enough suckers with his trickster's bag of alternative reality and feel-good notions to open up shop. Made it in the blink of an eye. Left behind a thriving, international, murky, and much talked about powerhouse. Give it to Hubbard, the dirty crook.

It got Joe thinking all the way home. Shallow Joe, who hadn't proven much of a thinking man until then. A mantra ran around his head like the Devil's sizzling whisper: Start a church, man, start a church; start a church, man, start a church; start a church, I'm telling you. To hell with jobs. To hell with nickel-and-diming. If Hubbard did it, you can do it. All the dummies out there desperate for ideas and new ways and new salvation. Mainstream Christianity, old and musty and scandal-prone: drinking, drugging, clubbing, thieving and raping priests, flocks disappearing quicker than polar ice and polar bears. Islam, worst PR crisis since its inception--terrorists, extremists, fundamentalists, jihadists, Wahabists, Shiites, Taliban, bombers, hijackers, mollahs, Hezbollah, Hamas. Judaism? Ethnocentric and way too tangled with Zionism to go truly global. Buddhism? Hinduism? Give me a break. Voodoo: underground, misunderstood, most likely overrated. And Santeria, well that's for the poor and the Spanish- or Portuguese-speaking.

No, Joe thought decidedly, or was it the Devil speaking? We need vision, direction, new ideas. We need a fresh and appealing package for the masses. Sell, man, sell. A church. A church. A church. A chuuuch, those rappers with crazy hair and diamond teeth and bouncing cars and curvy-foxy-raunchy vixens with names like Eyecandi and Superhead would say. A chuuuch.

So something black, maybe? There's money in the ghetto, dude. Everybody knows. Money in the black bourgeoisie, too. Fresh buying power and all that good stuff. Itching to spend their newfound riches, dying to throw some weight around, rushing to prove their worth now that they've made it. Their houses of worship? Confusing denominations, much gesturing and testifying and confessing, kick-ass bands all around, We be dancing in the name of the Lord. They say an aging batch of Coltrane followers jump and scream and roll and holler and sweat it out somewhere up in Harlem to this day--to this day. "He sounded truly out of this world." "His saxophone soared to the heavens." "I do believe John was the reincarnation of Christ." "The music sent me straight into ecstasy." Coltrane. Can you imagine?

Whatever is really going on inside storefront churches or full-fledged temples, black preachers are getting by very handsomely. The suits, the hats, the furs, the Bentleys, the rings, the chains, the poses, the causes, the affairs.... Charm and chops matter more than the message.

3

Anybody's a pastor these days. Anybody with a life story, a decent set of lungs, a propensity to perspire profusely: "Lemme tell you how I got saved--ha!" "I saw Him in a dreeeaaaam--ha!" "He hepped me out--ha!" "I beat my murder conviction--ha!" "I beat the pipe--ha!" "I beat foreclosure--ha!" "The bay-bays needed new shoes--ha!" "They was gonna repossess my car--ha!" "The Man Upstairs showed me the way--ha!" "Be He praiiised--ha!" "Can I get a 'A-men!'--ha!"

Joe banged his fist on the steering wheel, laughing himself silly. Preaching ain't a thing, the Devil went on, his tongue slithering like a snake: Preaching ain't a goddamn thing.

It's all about tapping the source, Joe told himself. Find a way to get into the game and you might just hit the jackpot. Find a gimmick, a jingle that enough people can sing along to. These ugly times make for full pews, million-dollar operating budgets, chunks of land, and investment accounts. Pass the plate. Pass it around more than once. Pass it till we get enough. Pass it till we choke on the dough.

I do believe that the Devil was riding in the Nova with us that day. *Vade retro, Satanas.* Good thing he stayed in the car when Joe and I went into the house. Or did he?

Maggie was in the kitchen fixing lunch. Joe kissed her first thing after walking in. I flew to her and pecked her Baby-I'm-home, too, something I hadn't done in many, many years. Food was simmering on the stove. It seemed Maggie couldn't stop cooking and eating now that I was dead and gone. Out were her Foreman Grill, blenders, magic pills, diet books; in gravies, meats, sauces, mayonnaise, fatty snacks, pies, Cherry Garcia ice cream, Jamaican Me Crazy sorbet. Sniffing greedily, I peered into her fricassee. The aroma, like a gigantic hit after a crave, went straight to my head. My last meal had been a Cuban sandwich more than five months ago. Though I never felt hungry, I missed food and the act of eating immensely.

"You're here early," Maggie commented as she looked Joe over, not letting her nastiness out the box yet. She was back to wearing colors, to my great relief. No more of that gloomy, unbecoming, unforgiving black that made her look like the Michelin Man's evil big brother. She was finally done playing the inconsolable widow for our friends and family. People had praised her strength and her resilience. They had sympathized. They had witnessed her sorrow. I knew for a fact that her grief, if that's what the few tears she had shed in public can be called, was short-lived. Maggie had been more shocked than saddened by my departure--I would even say that she'd been relieved, God correct me if I'm wrong. How did I feel about that? It was her business if she found it appropriate to sing every morning in the shower before slipping on a big black sack. And I had nothing to say about her eating spree, last month's fly-by-night salsa lessons, and her clumsy but budding friendship with our neighbor Steve, that creep who flew model airplanes way too close to power lines no matter how many times you chided him. No, what I secretly lambasted Maggie for was being a hypocrite and shortchanging me when I couldn't defend myself. My funeral had been cheap, fake, hastily put together. My stuff was out of our bedroom closet before I even made it inside the grave, all of it currently packed in boxes, awaiting a yard sale. Worse, Maggie had yet to pay a single visit to my tomb. Those are offenses not easily put aside, even when such things aren't supposed to matter any more.

At least Maggie would dress with a little more taste from now on. She had bought herself a flashy and modern wardrobe. Today I found her definitely easier on the eyes. Her face was done. Her hair was brushed back. Her nails were painted. She had sprayed some Number Five on her wrists. Blue jeans replaced her trademark polyester jodhpurs. Well, well, I wanted to compliment her: Look at you. Wifey at fifty-five could still make men dead or alive stop and take a look, as long as amazons were their type. Maggie my bunny. If only she could be a little nicer. More often than not the atmosphere in the house was heavy, same as when I was alive. A little détente could go a long way. A new and improved Ma may just be what our sons needed.

A little détente, but not today.

"I quit my job," Joe announced merrily.

"Again?" Maggie barked.

"Again," Joe confirmed.

Maggie took a deep breath. "Let me guess..."

"No reason," Joe stopped her. "I just upped and left."

"Second time in three months," Maggie pointed out, her temperature rising, her voice hardening, her lips flattening into a pugnacious line. "Wanna talk about it?"

Joe stood against the sink and bit into an apple, not letting Maggie out of his sight. "Not really, Ma."

Maggie lifted her head, wanting nothing better than to slap the apple from Joe's hands. Did he think he was cool? Was that a self-congratulatory smile? What was there to laugh about? Think about your blood pressure, she told herself, and I loved her for exercising such control so early in the day. Her steely eyes searched Joe's. Having seen her lunge at him for lesser offenses, and well aware that age wasn't slowing his mother down the least bit, Joe put the apple down and raised his guard.

"What are you going to do?" Maggie asked.

Joe dropped his arms and spat a seed into the sink. "Take the time to think."

Joe went into his room, threw his briefcase on the desk, sat on the bed, loosened his tie and shoelaces, took his head into his hands, mulled over his latest and very brief corporate stint--that ignorant supervisor's nerve!--got back up, and walked into Jay's bedroom without knocking. "Stale in here," he said before pulling the blinds and opening the window.

Stale it was. And cramped, dusty, dirty, and ignobly messy.

Jay growled, shutting his eyes tight before hiding his head under the pillow. Darkness was his friend. It had been a while since he saw the light of day and it hurt, it hurt like a particularly resented and most unwelcome intrusion.

"So I'm unemployed again," Joe began, sitting at Jay's feet.

Jay curled into a ball of disinterest. "Leave me alone," he muttered.

"It's almost 2," Joe went on. "You should be up, depression or not. This just doesn't look good, man. Pushing thirty and hiding in your bed because of a girl.

What a joke."

"Ma!" Jay called.

"Stop lounging about," Joe said, mock-punching Jay on the shoulder. "You make me sick."

"You two stop fighting immediately," Maggie yelled from the kitchen.

"We're not fighting," Joe shouted back, hitting Jay a little harder.

"Ma!" Jay whined again.

"You little pussy," Joe went on, his fists searching for soft spots.

Jay roared like a cornered lion. "Leave me alone!"

Joe snatched the comforter away, getting serious. "Get the fuck up, man."

Fed up, Jay sat up and slapped Joe.

They tussled on the bed before falling to the floor, a tangle of arms and fists and legs and objects and grunts.

I went to sit on top of the armoire. Always at each other's throat, these heartbreakers. Never a kind word, never a moment of peace. When my mind was still preoccupied with such concerns I used to blame myself for not achieving harmony under my roof. Two boys only two years apart, you'd think they would have enough in common and enough common sense to be best buddies. But it got to be too much pretty quick, I think as early as Jay being four and Joe still in pull-ups. I gave up on them, letting Maggie out of her cage and giving her carte blanche, washing my hands off the ensuing carnage and looking the other way when things were happening that shouldn't have.

I snapped my fingers, counting my honey off: 3, 2, 1 ... boom! Right on cue, Maggie pushed the door with her belly and barged in, hitting both our sons with the ladle she'd been using on their heads lately, a kitchen fury disciplining disobedient and overgrown monsters. The ladle, just the last in a long line of instruments of torture, was made of stainless steel. Maggie liked that the handle fitted snugly in her palm. She considered it well worth the 10 bucks she'd paid for it--sometimes you just had to bite the bullet. She would hang it on a belt if she could find one her size, carrying it with her around the house to improve readiness and cut on her intervention time. Maggie's ability to turn even the most innocuous of household objects into deadly weapons never ceased to amaze. All these years and she still managed to improvise, coming at you with the unexpected.

Bang bang! Woof woof! From my perch, I howled like a circus dog. Blows flew as Maggie took turns serving the boys, sweat beading her upper lip. "Jay, up. Joe, in your room."

"He needs to stop freeloading," Joe groused, rubbing his head.

"Tell him to get out of my face," Jay countered, rubbing his head as well. "And easy with that thing, Ma."

At least she rinsed it this time, I hooted.

Something akin to hatred flashed in Maggie's eyes. She looked at Joe and Jay, lifted the ladle one more time, laughed when they shrieked, and slowly retreated to her kitchen, her back straight as a countertop, her mission accomplished.

I glided down to follow her. As I was leaving, Jay picked Lisha's picture from the floor, blew the dust off it, and put it back on his night stand. The reverence in the gesture made me hurt for him. Shouldn't have called her names, I mused. Then you wouldn't find yourself in the position you're in now, you moron.

"Just go ahead and ask her to take you back," Joe suggested derisively. "You know you want to."

Jay got up, closed the window, pulled the blinds shut, and got back into his bed for more naptime. "Get out," he told his little brother. "I won't ask again."

Joe didn't budge. "What if I don't?"

Jay reached for the revolver under his mattress. "Then I might just have to shoot you," he said.

"I got a gun, too," Joe claimed, looking at the barrel and thinking to himself, This thing is long, this thing is longer than a mug. "So what."

Jay stuck the gun under his pillow. "Consider yourself warned," he said.

It's true that they were all packing. I was the one responsible for the proliferation. Maggie hadn't known what to do with the gun collection I left behind. Couldn't just display it on the grass and have neighbors take their pick, could she? So she'd kept the bulk of it in her room after letting Jay and Joe choose one piece each. A police-issue Beretta stole Joe's heart. Jay took the Magnum he knew to be my favorite. The guns came with manuals, attachments, cases, and one box of ammo each. Bad idea, I told myself over and over. Not the smartest thing you've ever done, Maggie. Suppose these fools decide to duel out their differences? Suppose somebody gets hurt? My soul won't survive a bloodbath. That much I know.

Joe went into the living room and turned the TV on.

10

I sat at the table when the fricassee showed up. Nobody ever used my chair. Jay had tried, once, but Maggie had scolded him with a what-do-you-think-you're-doing look. Not a disrespectful kid, my Jay. Just a little out of it for the moment. Wouldn't recognize him if you didn't already know who he was. Glossy skin, hair down to here, beard all over the place, beer belly, witch's nails, pigeon's chest. Walked around in the clothes he slept in, didn't bathe for days, barely spoke, never stepped outside. We were all waiting for him to get over his hirsute hermit phase, whatever it was about.

I knew how much it got on Maggie's nerves. I wished I could tell her she wasn't alone. I wished I could find a way to alert her of my presence, let her see me seeing her. I wished we could talk and discuss things civilly, for once: the kids, the house, Cairo, anger management, bipolar disorder, our hellish 30-year marriage, Nicole, my death, this crazy weather, Empire's latest blunder.

It's me, these days--wishing and wishing and wishing. Not much else to do but float around trapped in whatever parallel dimension death has thrown me in--temporarily, I hope. Ben the paterfamilias. Constant witness to my family's every move and every thought. The shadow in their lives, the presence in their midst. No Flying Dutchman by any means. As ghosts go, I'm not particularly errant or angry or vengeful. I might get annoyed or upset here and there, but I hold no grudge, I turn no pranks, I'm not looking for a body to inhabit. I only travel close, and never by myself.

Maggie and Joe ate and watched one of her shows, after which he went to his room. Was he feeling bad about his job? Worried about the future? Pondering his next move already? Joe was Joe. Ambitious, impatient, as ready for the next big thing as ever. Joe Babylon. My boy.

He went running on his old high school track later that afternoon. Woodrow Wilson, off Wisconsin Avenue, predominantly white when he and Jay used to go, almost all-black now. Easy parking, quiet in the hour before dusk, not too many amateurs and power-walkers. It was the only place in the world where he felt comfortable sweating it out. No gym for Joe. Exertion got him red in the face quick, and he couldn't stand that people saw. We all have our little vanities.

I watched him from the bleachers. Narrow shoulders, a straight back like his mother, chicken legs, controlled breathing, good rhythm, okay style, and, yes, a red face barely five minutes into it.

The jog cleared Joe's mind right on time for part two of the revelation, which was kicked off by the beggar who approached him as he was getting ready to get back in the Nova. A big black dude with a cane, a wig, a baritone, a woolen goatee, taunting eyes, dark jeans, a navy-blue cap, and a hooded sweater he should have kept for later.

"I love my master!" the man said at the top of his lungs, looking straight at Joe. "I loooove white people!"

Shocked, Joe stopped and did a double take. I got close enough to the man to see his rotten teeth, smell the crack on his clothes, and taste the malt liquor on his tongue.

"What did you say?" Joe asked, still a little out of breath. It was feeling warmer as the sun went down, a D.C. specialty usually reserved for summertime.

"I loooove white people!" the man repeated with much conviction. "I'm gon' be a good plantation boy today!"

Joe looked around, finding it hard to believe his ears. The people nearby seemed not to have heard a thing. They were beating the sidewalk hard and fast, heading home or for tonight's margarita hangout.

"That's a new one," Joe commented as the bum dragged himself closer. "Original as hell."

The man stood on his cane and pushed a mug toward Joe, his eyes boring into Joe's. "Help me out," he pleaded, lowering his voice to draw Joe in. "I know you got it. Rich boy like you."

Joe laughed almost bitterly. Rich? Didn't he wish. "I'm not rich by any measure."

The bum winked and tapped one of the hubcaps with his cane. "This purple baby set you back at least 40, 50 grand, G. I'm supposed to believe you're not loaded?"

Joe shrugged, shook himself off the man's gaze, and moved to open the door. Was it just him or did he discern a vague threat here? "You believe what you want, dude."

The bum sensed he was losing his prey. It was getting late, crack and Steel Reserve were calling, there was no standing between these passersby and their evening plans. Joe would be the last catch--hit this one and call it a day. So he went for the kill: eye contact, slumped shoulders, tremolo, humility. "Come on, man.... Do some wit' me. I need help bad."

Joe hesitated. Funny-looking but well-fed beggar. Strands of color meshed into the long, surreal wig. Only things missing were square glasses, a robe, a stage, a band,

13

a grown man in oversized diapers, and the mother-funking Mothership. "Bet they call you George Clinton," Joe quipped.

The man lifted his cane and started to shuffle on the sidewalk. I watched his footwork with much interest, having recently discovered the joys of dancing. *"Make my funk the P-Funk,"* he sang off-key, *"I want my funk uncut!"*

Joe looked for change in the ashtray.

"Make my funk the P-Funk," the bum went on, *"I wants to get funked up!"*

"What's that 'love my master' stuff about?" Joe asked as the man, already out of breath, cut back on his clowning. "I'm intrigued, I have to admit."

"Sumthin' to let y'all white people know how I feel," the bum proclaimed, sticking to his script.

Joe sneered. "Can't be loving white people that much that you feel the need to trumpet it on every street corner."

"I have a big heart," the man declared. "You'd be surprised."

Joe laughed without meaning to. "Kind of controversial, don't you think? And none too politically correct."

The bum shrugged. "This the white man's world, dogg. I'm just livin' in it."

Jay handed him a few coins. "I'd tone it down if I were you. Your pitch sounds a little ... rough."

"Some of us do miss the good old days," the man insisted, forgetting to say thank you as he grabbed his meager earnings--hadn't he just performed on a bad leg for this cheapskate? "Believe it or not."

Joe nodded. "You're just more vocal about yours," he deadpanned.

The bum took offense. "Keep your change," he said, emptying his mug on the sidewalk. The coins rolled into crevices, under the Nova, and as far as the middle of the road.

Joe watched him walk down Wisconsin, the slighted man making a dignified exit. Walk. Stick. Drag. "I looove my master!" Walk. Stick. Drag. "I looove white people!" Joe shook his head. What had just happened here?

Another hustler with a fancy line, Joe thought on the way back, made uncomfortable by the encounter. The colorful hair, the busted sneakers, the rogue eyes, the foul breath, the blatant ass-kissing. Why had he given him money? White guilt, he decided. It was white guilt. You felt bad for what had been done to black people. You felt bad and so you gave it up. The bum had a captive audience in every white person he met. Bring out the ghost of slavery and everybody with a conscience goes straight for their wallet. Had he heard right? Had the guy really said "plantation boy" and "good old days"?

Joe took the long way to Military Road, maybe because there wasn't much waiting for him at home. Daddy dead, Maggie itching to sell and get out, Jay wasting away.... Joe needed a clean break from it all. It was time for a new life. A house of his own in a faraway neighborhood. Potomac would do just fine. Immaculate lawn, backyard for days, infinity pool, automatic gate, 8-car garage, unabridged view of the river, a wife. Make her blond and pretty and brainless and bedonkadonky like he liked them, like that

Scientology girl. And then give him blond and pretty and brainless little Joes. He smiled.

Rock Creek Park felt good and so did the Nova. All that power. A purple beauty indeed. What had P-Funk called it? A chunk of history. 50 grand was a stretch but I could sell it, Joe told himself. Here's seed money for you. Dump the Nova and start a business. Not just any business. Something new and foolproof. Something juicy. Come on, Villanova Boy, think. Think. I know you can come up with something. I know you can.

Joe parked in the driveway and took his time going in. I was grateful for the open-window ride with my feet on the dashboard, Rock Creek's trees and rocks and creeks, the speed, the gorgeous roar of the engine, the smell of burning gasoline. Night had fallen and the lights were on.

I flew inside the house. Maggie was reading. Jay was snoring hard. I flew back out and sat on the rooftop to look at the stars, occasionally peering at my boy inside the Nova.

Don't wanna be here, Joe mused again. And I'm not getting out of this car until I come up with something. This won't be just another day in the life. If I get off this seat it's because I will have found the idea of the century. If I go back in it's as a rich man in the making. Stay here and think until my brain bleeds I will. Stay here and starve to death.

He closed his eyes and thought about his day. Slamming the door with no regret whatsoever at his job; the Scientology girl; Hubbard; churches; "I looove my master"; good old days; black; white; guilt; money.

Images flew around Joe's head as if he were

watching a movie. Lights: he was on a stage. Microphones: he harangued. Flashbulbs and cameras: he transfixed. Open hands: he pleaded. Tears: he touched. Music: the masses were at his feet. A nave: he built a home for straying sheep and into it they came, onto him they flocked. Redeemer: he sowed, he reaped, he pushed on, he became famous. A private airplane: the world was his. Millions of dollars: everything he had ever wanted, everything he could imagine.

It took him just under 30 minutes. A revelation it was. Simple and unlimited in potential. As crooked as Scientology. As controversial as the P-Funk bum. Big, definitely. So big that Joe felt like the inspiration was coming straight from the sky. A revelation, indeed. A new religion. A new gospel. A new church. The Church of Retribution.

Joe got out of the car and danced on the gravel, kicking up dust in his running gear. "I got it!" he shouted at the stars, the moon, the bats, the world.... "I got it!"

Scared to death, I watched him moonwalk around the Nova. What on earth had I done to deserve such a greedy knucklehead for son?

Joe took his time before setting things into motion. Didn't want to blow it by rushing. Ideas this good came once in a lifetime. Better think it all over, look at every angle, draw a business plan. He strove to remember and implement the few sound precepts he had absorbed before getting kicked out of Villanova–an amalgam of common sense stuff, really: Do your research; know your target; identify your competitors; refine your product or service in order to make it the best in its category; come up with a friendly and easily identifiable logo or acronym; strategize; raise enough capital to get through the first couple of years; promote, market, and launch your product or service with a bang; begin small; keep your overhead low; don't expect quick returns; prepare for steady growth by increasing your customer base and hunting for new outlets.

Starting the day after the two-pronged revelation Joe sat among readers, writers, researchers, and homeless men and women in the Quiet Room of our neighborhood library to try and flesh out his project neatly on paper.

"I'm going to meditate," is what he told Maggie as we were leaving early that morning.

"Wonderful," she commented acidly, secretly relieved that, with Jay sleeping the whole day through, she'd have the house for herself. "Work on your attitude. All bosses can't be wrong all the time. Some of this negative stuff has to come from you."

"Thanks for the advice," Joe replied. "I'm sure you've put it to good use throughout your own life."

"I'm not the one living off his mama," Maggie reminded him.

Joe took the blow in stride, even managing a smile. "Hitting under the belt, as always.... And here I am trying to get started on a whole new path. What a sendoff."

"Will you be home for lunch?" Maggie asked, impressed by Joe's focus and sweetened by what she perceived as the moment zero of a major job search campaign.

"Don't think so," Joe answered.

"Make sure to grab a PowerBar or something."

"I will."

We both kissed her on the cheek.

The Nova roared.

Inside the library's Quiet Room I sat with Joe as he got going, facing only a blank partition so as not to be distracted. Pen in hand, he strove to detach himself from our surroundings. Fire that brain up, Villanova Boy. Pages being flipped, keyboards being tapped, lessons being whispered, comings and goings, gum being popped, candy being unwrapped--he walled himself from it all. Words began to fly, covering the piece of paper in front of us. I had a hard time believing my eyes.

Product or service or mission, **Joe wrote:** Fostering goodwill and understanding between the black and white races by

1) Formally apologizing for the sins and horrors of slavery, segregation, and discrimination.

2) Providing a concrete and viable outlet to white guilt in order to alleviate racial tensions, rectify a moral wrong, and change history.

3) Serving the black community at large by channeling the money obtained from the target audience through a formally constituted and duly registered entity called Church of Retribution, or Reparation, or Restitution--not quite sure which at the moment.

Target: Everyday white people, state and federal governments, small businesses, big corporations, white America.

Feasibility: To be seen.

Competition: None.

Startup money: The Nova.

Concerning the business side of things, that's as far as Joe got on the first day.

The spiritual approach was harder to lay out. Joe was confused about where to begin. Was it to be a religion, this project of his, or a simple movement? Why make it a church when a basic nonprofit could work just as well? How do you anoint yourself a guide of men? How does your message translate into a brand and the brand into hard and cold cash without raising too many eyebrows?

The cornerstone of the revelation was the assumption that white people felt sorry for what their ancestors had done. That they were appalled and mortified and wanted nothing better than to bury this particularly shameful part of history under the collective rug. Pluck other human beings from their homeland, whip them, chain them to the bottom of ships, take them across the sea, feed the sickly and the unruly to sharks, auction the survivors off, work them mercilessly from sunup to sundown, use and abuse them, free them a few centuries down the road without granting them equality--what had our ancestors been thinking?

So yes, there was matter for white folks to feel bad, and not just the liberal and the softhearted. Any compassionate, decent individual could see that America owed something to her black constituents. Look at them today: Disproportionately low-income and unwed and unhealthy and uneducated, always in the news, their children lost and confused and failing at everything but sports, street posturing, and trend-setting. Nobody publicly acknowledged it, but their situation was a direct result of racism and oppression and the horrors they'd been through. Uproot and enslave a group, discriminate against it and this is the end-result--this mess of self-hate and alienation and underperformance. Every white person in America had to feel a pang of guilt at some level. Had to. If somebody proposed white people a clear way to right the wrong, they would rush in. "Looove my master!" the P-Funk bum was yelling every day to every white passerby he saw. "Looove my master!" and they probably hurried to shut him up with cash the way Joe had.

You could formalize that reflex. You could put walls around it, a roof on top, a plaque on the door. Make the process discreet and efficient. Guarantee that the money the white community was ready to disburse in the name of

21

forgiveness went into the right hands, the perfect endeavors, the neediest cases. Joe's brainchild, as the trusted intermediary between the two races, could show a balance sheet and returns: This is how much we've collected, this is all the good work accomplished; we've apologized in your name and we're putting the money where we said we would. Who are we? The Church of Retribution, baby. Or Reparation. Or Restitution. Feeling bad for the descendants of good-old Selma, who was owned and put to use like a hardy cow by your great-great-grandpa Mitchell on his tobacco farm? We'll fix it for you, ma'am. Track down Selma's family and transmit your formal regrets along with a check we will. You'll sleep better at night, Selma's relatives will feel gratified, the bay-bays will get their shoes, we'll take our cut, everybody will go home happy.

Suppose they don't want to pay? Joe asked himself. Suppose every person or entity contacted goes, "Restitution my ass--I don't owe black people a dime!" Suppose the whole guilt trip is overrated? My dreams would crumble. No chuuuch, no future bright, no big time. If only I could find a way to test the waters, be methodic, be systematic, be scientific about this. After all, the idea of restitution is nothing new. It's been floated on the Senate floor time and again, to very tepid reactions. Holocaust victims have gotten their money and stolen artwork, but when it comes to blacks something in the mind of Republicans freezes. Maybe I'm plain wrong. Maybe America isn't ready to come to terms with this.

"Did we ever own slaves?" Joe asked Maggie

during dinner toward the end of the week, almost making her choke on a potato.

Maggie gulped down a full glass of malbec before looking up, flushed.

I stifled a smile. If only you knew, I wanted to tell her, what your son is up to.

"What's the matter with you?" Maggie shouted.

"Nothing, Ma. I just wanna know."

"The stuff that comes out of your mouth.... Who's 'we'? What slaves?"

"Our family. Both sides. Dad's from Virginia. You're a Marylander. You guys weren't dirt-poor, were you? So if your relatives were landholders four or five generations back chances are they had slaves, no?"

Maggie resumed eating. "Of course," she acknowledged. "It was the thing back then. Everybody was doing it. That was the only way to go."

"So the short answer is yes?"

Maggie nodded reluctantly. Every time we had seen horses while driving down 301 South or Route 4 she'd told me she wished that the fabled Upper Marlboro farm owned by her family for generations had remained in their hands. Her "Gone with the Wind" fantasies, I called it.

Joe put his fork down and inched forward, looking intently at Maggie before firing off his next salve. "How do you feel about that, Ma?"

Maggie fired right back. "How do I feel about what, Joe?"

She was getting heated, I could tell by the way she said his name. You came between Gung Ho Mag and her meals at your own risk. Everything in front of her, from the smallest spoon to the heaviest dish to the table itself could turn into a deadly hazard without warning.

If Joe realized how much danger he was putting himself into, he didn't let that stop him.

"Owning human beings," he elaborated. "Working them to the bone. Raping the women, killing the men, selling the babies."

Maggie didn't flinch. "I don't care one way or the other. Slavery was gone long before I was born."

"But not segregation," Joe went on. "What side were you on when all that stuff was taking place?"

"What stuff?"

"Gosh!" Joe said, "I really have to pull it out of you, don't I? Jim Crow, Ma. The sit-ins, the marches for voting rights, the bombings, the dogs, the lynching, the 'Whites Only' signs.... *That* stuff. Where were you when it was going down?"

Maggie switched her knife to her right hand. Here it comes, I wanted to scream. Look out!

"Where was I?" Maggie answered defiantly, her second chin trembling. "Living my life!"

Joe looked at the knife and lowered his head, preparing to duck. "You never felt concerned? Nothing that was going on bothered you? Caring and sensitive as you are, you mean to tell me the plight of those oppressed people didn't touch you?"

Maggie sighed and put the knife down. Joe couldn't tell if it was out of exasperation, regret, or sheer vanity.

"I guess I was in my own little bubble," Maggie conceded, resigned now that her food would get cold. "My parents sheltered me. And then, well, it all started to change very fast."

"How were things in D.C.?"

"Good until they tried to integrate the neighborhoods, the schools, the stores, the pools, the lunch counters at Woodies and People's, and just about everything else. I almost got caught in the middle of a bad fight twice: at the Anacostia waterfront and at the downtown skating rink. But in general Negroes lived their life and we lived ours."

"'Negroes'?"

"That's what my mom and dad used to call black people. And so did everybody else."

Joe's eyes shone: This was hot stuff. He got excited like a bloodhound picking up a scent. "Were grandpa and grandma racist?"

Maggie acquiesced. "He more than she."

"How bad?"

"Bad."

"Did you have black friends?"

Maggie shifted on her seat. "Of course not."

"Am I making you uncomfortable?"

Maggie grabbed her knife and fork, feeling hungry again. "In your dreams. What exactly are you getting at?"

Joe watched her hands. "Nothing," he lied. "Just saw a copy of 'Roots' at the library, and it got me wondering."

Maggie took a bite and chewed it carefully. Cold. She knew it. That damn Joe and his questions.

Joe kicked his chair back and crossed his arms. "If you had a way to take it all back, would you?"

"It's not possible to rewrite history," Maggie

snapped. "Now shut up and eat."

Jay walked in and helped himself to the meatloaf and potatoes in white sauce. His collar, ripped during the fight with Joe, hung low on his chest. His pants were smelling as if something was growing inside them. Both Maggie and Joe covered their plates with their hands when he scratched his head, sending flakes the size of cereals floating in the air.

"Shameless," Joe hissed.

"What are you two talking about?" Jay asked, saliva sticking to his yellow teeth like stubborn glue.

"How you stink," Joe said, disgust twitching his face.

"Slavery," Maggie answered, pinching her nose.

"Wicked," Jay commented before retreating to his room.

They watched him leave with unmitigated relief. Joe rushed to open the window. The night's cool air seeped in, along with Military Road's muffled sounds. Maggie reminded herself to purchase a 10-pack of Lysol on her next trip to Price Club.

"What about dad?" Joe pushed on. "Did he get actively involved into anything?"

Maggie's face registered something akin to distaste. You'd think the mention of my name was enough to make the food in her mouth turn sour. It hurt to see that.

"He was a sympathizer," Maggie said, the word burning her lips. "His family was more open-minded, I guess. Ben never marched or sat or rode on those freedom buses, though." As her smirk widened, I braced for the accusation to drop. "But of course," Maggie continued with self-righteous irony, "we know now just how much nigger love your father had in him, don't we?"

Joe laughed. "I'm with you on that one," he said, though his thought was, Watch me turn into a nigger lover, too, Ma.

I shook my head, walked through the wall, and took a few steps on the porch to cool off. Maggie could play the victim all she wanted. If I had one regret for what I had done it was not to have done it sooner. But these people and the N-word, let me tell you. Maggie and Joe had been using it liberally around the house for as long as I could remember. Nigger this, nigger that. No way to make them stop. Me, not a chance. Jay, never. Except, of course, that fatal once in front of Lisha. Nigger this, nigger that. It wasn't cute, man. It wasn't right.

A slight drone could be heard above the trees. I looked up. That damn Steve flying one of his toy airplanes at night.

The P-Funk bum came to Joe's mind in his first moment of doubt. The man was out there eating and drinking and smoking off his one-line hustle. Getting paid and getting by. So there definitely was hope. And if Hubbard could sell his cuckoo intergalactic package to Hollywood types and pop stars out of a red-brick fortress that stank of maleficence, surely there was room for a Church of Retribution in Washington. Everything in life depends on how you present things, and yourself. What America needed was someone like Joe to show the way. He would appear business-minded and efficient. He would prod consciences, handle the money, build bridges. He would take from one group to give to the other. He would help--"hep." He would heal.

Joe the messiah? Messenger would be more like it. Spread the good word, Joe. Go tell it everywhere: street corners, investor boards, conference rooms, shareholder meetings, cocktail parties, live stages, morning radio, late-night TV, the Internet. Go "get it said": This is the time to repair. We must atone, my white brothers and sisters.... Atone we must, and rip the poison from our hearts and minds. I said riiiip--ha! We must forgo hate and rekindle love--yesss! We must reach out and ask for forgiveness. We must go to the black man and the black wo-man and say, I'm here today.... Said I'm here todayyy.... I'm here--ha! (foot work, light jumps).... I'm heeere (high pitch).... I'm here to tell y'all I'm sorry for slavery (eyes closed).... Sorry for the rope and the whip and the chains (a shriek, a tear, fist on the heart, the other hand holding the mic).... I said the chaiiin (catch breath, wipe sweat off brow).... (Subdued, now) I'm here to pay for my sins, y'all.... Give back what my great-great-granddaddy owes.... Give back what *I* owe.... Give it back in full.... I'm here to (relaxed and repentant) ... to spread love (whispering).... See, great-great-grandpaaa (crescendo).... He was meeaaan and wild--ha!.... Thought he owned the Earth and every living thing--ha!.... So he went across the sea.... Hunted and trapped and took.... (Shake head left and right) But how can a man?.... I'm asking you to-day.... How can a man--ha!.... Own another man, huh?.... How can a man--ha!.... Say he's sup-e-rior, huh?.... And deny the other man--ha!.... Damn near evvverything! (shouting out loud, violent jumping, ripping shirt).... Great-great-grandpa was wroong--ha!.... He was insane--ha!.... Devil-prone--yesss!.... And uuugly, too!.... Sooo ugly!.... Look at the black man to-day--ha!.... No mo-ney--ha!.... No peace of mind--nooo!.... No jusssstice--ha!.... Reviled.... Cornered.... Vilified.... Stigmatized.... And the black bay-bays--ha!.... Nothing to eat!.... Nothing to doooo!.... No future! (calming down again).... (Mezzo voce) So we must fix this, my white brothers and sisters.... (Looking the transfixed audience straight in the eye) We're gonna repair, retribute, restitute.... In the name of brotherhood.... In the name of the human spirit.... So we can start anew.... A clean slate, my white brothers and sisters.... A clean start.... No more debt.... No guilt.... Justice, at long last (a humble nod. The collection plates are ushered among the rows of attendants).

Where was this stuff coming from? Joe saw himself possessed by the spirit, a shepherd haranguing his sheep. He had a hard time sitting still in the library's Quiet Room among the readers, writers, researchers, homeless men and women.

Tired of scribbling on paper, Joe brought his laptop early into the second week and began to bang away, giving free rein to the inspiration that came to him in disorganized spurs, sometimes blindingly and breathtakingly.

Visions crowded his head and filled his computer screen. Father Joe waking the people. Originator. Innovator. Trailblazer. Advocate. Conciliator. Facilitator. Peacemaker. Champion. Taking from whites to give to blacks, stirring crowds nonstop, his words tugging at hearts: Everybody on board now, the train to Canaan is leaving and you don't want to be late, wouldn't want to miss this one, oh no-no-no, for it's the big one. Corporate donors welcome. Sponsors and venture capitalists, too.

Why a church? Churches are tax-free, man. Tax-free. Then there's this zero-oversight, faith-based initiative giving subventions to religious groups for supposedly helping to advance the White House agenda on social issues. One-shack backwater zealots in places with names like Beyruth, Ohio, are receiving cash for programs that may only exist on paper. Free money is what it is. Infuse a zest of spirituality into any enterprise and it confers it automatic legitimacy and rakes in government subsidies.

"Church of Retribution" sounded damn good. So did "Restitution." Joe wasn't sure about "Reparation"--didn't want his house to be confused with a garage now. The address would be prestigious, or at least respectable: 16th Street smack in the middle of Worship Row, among the 50 other more mainstream denominations. No creepiness, shadiness, cheesiness, free stress tests, interplanetary B.S., coercion, robes, hoods, name tags, hierarchies, community living, free unions, group sex, mass weddings, chanting, or poisoned Kool-Aid. Easy on the preaching, overall. A racially mixed flock. Blacks and whites sorting out their differences. Same benches for everybody, no colored people riding the back or using separate toilets. Workshops galore. Sensitivity and diversity classes. Trust-building games and activities. Slogans like "We Are One," backed by new advances in genetic research and anthropology. They'd study the civil rights movement, pay tribute to all the fallen heroes, organize prayers at key sites of the struggle in Mississippi and Alabama and right here in Washington. All the whites in attendance could get up and say something like, "My name is so-and-so and I'm here to apologize for slavery, discrimination, and segregation." Then the blacks would get up in turn and go, "I forgive you." Everybody would hug and shake hands. Lovefest, baby.

Partitioned offices would occupy the sprawling upper floor. Glass doors, skylights, plants, cubicles, phones, computers. Blondes trained in guerrilla warfare and a take-no-prisoners approach to fund-raising would call every white-sounding name on the White Pages, every white-owned business, corporation, hedge fund, investment group, and country club. The Web site would accept all major credit cards. The church would publish a monthly updated list of donors and contributors, individual or commercial, to allow black people to check online and see who'd been apologizing and donating. Not only wouldn't whites be able to lie to one another or to their black friends about their true feelings and progressive inclinations, multinationals as well as businesses catering to minority shoppers would run the risk of mass boycotts and a public outcry if their names weren't prominently displayed. In time, the list would become the Church's most formidable weapon. It would make or break. It would turn into a cultural icon. It would take on a life of its own.

You had to know how to talk to people, Joe reckoned. Once you grabbed their nuts and put a squeeze on them, the dough piped in nice and easy. Then the real work could begin: Channel funds into worthy projects in D.C.'s neglected, i.e., black, neighborhoods. Lobby the mayor's office for better all-around services: more police presence, crime prevention, trash pickup, publicly funded recreational and vocational programs. Donate homes and cars. Finance free clinics and training sessions and employment seminars. House single mothers. Give refuge to abused women. Keep children out of jail. Set up a scholarship fund to send promising black students to college. Bankroll soup kitchens, homeless shelters, daycare centers, youth-oriented facilities, after-school programs. Better yet, build and run your own charter schools. Monitor group homes and halfway houses. Reach out to the brothers and sisters in jail. Help reinsert freed convicts into society. Replicate the experiment in different states. Make that *all* the states.

It wasn't clear to Joe just how a substantial enough chunk of the money would end up in his pockets. He could already tell that with the kind of hell he proposed himself to raise, outside scrutiny would be off the charts. The press, the politicos, the man on the street ... nobody was getting any dumber. They'd smell a juicy hustle and try to catch him in the wrong.

Nothing but the purest transparency would do as far as the church's operations were concerned--he'd hire the best managers and accounting firms and auditors to make sure of that. A generous monthly retainer for himself might do the trick. He was the boss, after all. The founder, the leader, the visionary. He deserved a substantial salary, a company car, paid accommodations and expenses, stock options, bonuses, and a parachute just like any other C.E.O. or bona fide pastor. Nothing outrageous, of course. Enough good would be accomplished in the name of the church for would-be complainers and dirt diggers to allow him his little perks and cut him some slack.

Look out for the black luminaries, Joe told himself.

Jesse Jackson, Al Sharpton and them. Steel yourself because they will poke fun and attack and discredit and try to bring you down. You're infringing on their turf. They're the ambulance chasers, the so-called superheroes, the go-to people, the coalition men, the grassroots guys, the megaphones. You're the little white boy on the block stirring stuff up, stealing their followers, showing them how it's done. Expect bad blood, jealousy, jabs, full-scale attacks, recrimination, maybe even a couple of lawsuits. Don't play their game. Bring them on board if need be. Co-opt them and allow them to co-opt you. Enough causes out there to go around. Let Jesse and Al handle the police brutality, work discrimination, and rape cases. You focus on the healing, the gap bridging, the community building, the unifying.

In the Quiet Room, running on an empty stomach, Joe was still typing up a storm on the 14th day and getting dizzy.

All in all, when you considered entering the political field, possibilities were unlimited. No president in or seeking office, no campaign advisor, no senator or congressman could afford to ignore an influential organization like the one the Church of Retribution promised to develop into. Washington loved muscle, clout, and a captive electorate. Joe would become a player.

The movement could even be enlarged, taken overseas, trumpeted on the global platform. Think about all the wrongs committed against Africans! There was another Holocaust nobody talked about. Yet that's where it all began, when you considered it: the slashing, gutting, burning, pillaging, assassinating, enslaving, invading, dividing, colonizing, conscripting.... Those people would have been fine had they been left alone. They didn't need the white man and his civilization. They were living the life they knew, thank you very much.

So it wasn't just America who should be hit in the wallet. Europe needed to pay, too. The looted gold, the manuscripts, the statues, the rubber, the timber, the oil, the diamonds, the coffee. Think of all the reparations that could be exacted for human cost, psychological toll, stress, emotional distress, and back pay. Europe owed. It owed like a motherfucker. Belgium alone should be sued for billions when you adjusted to inflation what King Leopold had taken from the Congo. (What would be the commission on that baby? Joe wondered feverishly.) The greatest scam in human history was how Europe had plundered its ex-colonies, putting them in the position they were in today only to turn around and increase their burden with so-called aid after granting them independence. I'll break your legs, bill you for the surgery and the medicine and the rehab, loan you money because you're incapacitated and unable to feed your family, charge you interest, forbid you to seek help or do business elsewhere, and laugh at you because you're such an underperforming weakling. How's that for an analogy of North-South diplomatic and economic relations?

There was work to do, for sure. The scope of what Joe had stumbled into went beyond his wildest, wildest dreams. Better take it easy at first, he told himself one more time, shutting the computer off. Better go slow, Villanova Boy. Start locally, grow steadily, and then you can expand.

Do it all by the book.

The lights in the Quiet Room flickered and the librarian walked in to kick everybody out.

"Productive day?" the man asked Joe.

"If only you knew," Joe answered, stretching and yawning. "If only you knew."

I prayed that he wouldn't crash the Nova, sleepy as he was. But he was high on nervous energy, my Joe, Joe Babylon, piloting us through D.C.'s night traffic with a sure hand.

Back home, he kissed himself in the mirror. "You're a genius," he said out loud, wondering what people saw when they looked at him. Always had the Italian thing going, Joe: curls brushing against his forehead, dark and deep-set eyes, firm chin, straight nose, small mouth--was that the face of a crusader or what?

"Am I too pretty?" he asked Maggie at dinnertime.

Maggie stopped eating, preparing herself for the worst. "What do you mean?"

"I don't know," Joe said. "What would you think of me if you met me for the first time? What's my face value?"

Never one to miss a ball-busting opportunity, Maggie smiled benevolently. "Handsome, probably...."

"And?"

"A little too slick."

Joe sat back. "'Slick'?"

"Slick."

"As in?"

"Not to be trusted. Like you've got a trick upper

sleeve."

Joe's palms started to sweat. This supposed slickness of his was exactly what his last girlfriend, a petite lawyer named Rima who liked high heels and workout sex (that thing, that move she'd pulled with a cup in a motel room one afternoon!), had advanced for a breakup reason. "I feel like I gotta watch my back all the time with you," was what she told him that day, the lips he used to find so attractive forming a dismissive pout. "And I have enough of that at work, believe me." "That's all right," Joe had answered. "You're not my type anyway." "No love lost, then," Rima had concluded, trying to have the last word. "Absolutely," Joe had agreed, before he snatched off the Tiffany piece he'd gotten her for Valentine's Day. "You cheap bastard!" Rima had shouted in the middle of the street, holding her neck. "Go back to Mumbai, you wannabe-white bitch!" Joe had retorted as he walked away, "Or wherever the hell you're from." Too stunned to answer, Rima just had stood there, frozen in the moment. Knew I'd shut you up with that one, Joe had thought with much satisfaction. He had promised himself to strictly stick to blondes thereafter--homebred, no accent, no pretense, no law degree.

"Did I hit a nerve?" Maggie asked, bringing him back to their conversation.

"A big one," Joe admitted.

Smelling blood, Maggie pushed on. "Is this about girls? The fact that you get them but you can't keep them?"

Joe shrugged.

"Pretty looks isn't all," Maggie sang, she who neared 250 pounds and had all but renounced diets, exercise, and weight-loss programs. "The inside has to match."

You're right about that, I wanted to tell her after seeing how crestfallen Joe suddenly looked. Ooo wee. Hit the nail right on the head, baby. This sucker's as empty and selfish as they come. About nothing else but getting over. Don't care who gets hurt in the process. Joe's just gotta make it.

Joe stopped eating. His eyes were stinging. It was all Maggie to be able to shake his confidence with just a few words. "So what are you saying, Ma? I give off a bad vibe or something?"

Maggie nodded. If Joe was going to interrupt her meals regularly she might as well try and enjoy herself. "Your aura," she explained. "It's kind of nasty."

"How can I change that?" Joe asked.

"Allow kindness into your heart," Maggie ventured gracefully. "Take it easy on naked ambition. Think of others. Take the time to get wherever you want to go."

Joe pushed his plate and got up. "Thanks for the clichés, Ma. You just killed my appetite."

"The truth always hurts," Maggie said.

"Always the weirdest conversations," Jay commented as he staggered in, the sight and the funk of him making both Maggie and me wince and turn our noses.

Luckily, he just picked up his food and left. This ain't a carryout, I wanted to tell him. You filthy jerk!

Maggie seemed strangely affected by the exchange with Joe, and the fact that he'd gone to bed early. Her mother's heart. She didn't really hate him. Of course she didn't. Joe was her baby. More so than Jay, himself his daddy's son. Maggie wished sometimes that she could be more affectionate. Meanness and distance just came naturally. She didn't know why.

There was a lot of work remaining to be done with both our sons. We used to think that freedom would come once they hit college age. Freedom both emotional and financial, along with a new lease on life for us. Before the whole mess with Nicole tore our couple apart for good we had discussed renovations for the boys' rooms: a home theater in Joe's; my books, records, and guns in Jay's. Maggie and I should have been living very differently right about now. Sharing our time between Military Road and an Ocean City condo with panoramic views. Hand in hand in the sand. Taking it breezy, taking it easy, taking it light. Maggie and Ben, the graying lovebirds.

Sorry I disappointed you, Maggie baby. Didn't mean to leave you hanging. But then again, not so sorry I disappointed you, Maggie. It was fun while we were young, I admit. I used to like me a girl who could put up a good, honest fight. You were as tall and as strong as me. A striking figure, "striking" being the key word here. A city blonde built like a farm hand. You bucked, you shook, you rode, you rocked, you rolled, you swung. The boxing matches didn't bother me the least bit. After fighting Empire's war in Southeast Asia I thought violence as normal as day--hell, I relished it. Those were our anything-goes times, remember? You hit me, I hit you, we sumo, we make up, we light up, we get stoned. Our 20s? Hungry, man. Parties, light work, heavy booze, friends. The 30s were still fun: two sons, a house, a store, a future. The middle of our 40s is when whatever is wrong with you started catching up. You became prudish, jealous, paranoid, obsessed with bourgeois respectability. Let loose the bitch in you. Ruled our house with an iron fist. I became the enemy. A man couldn't come home to a hot meal even though you knew the kinds of hours I worked. You were busy, you said--"Get one of those deli nymphs of yours to fix you a sandwich, Ben." Nothing pleased you, Maggie. Like me, the kids couldn't do anything right. You screamed, you punched, you terrorized. Frisbeeing with my mother's plates. Cutting my suits. Sugar in my tank. Embarrassing Joe in front of his friends. Giving Jay the silent treatment for weeks at a time. Maggie Bang-Bang. And don't let me forget the migraines. No sex after 46 despite the fact that I still felt strong as a bull and I desired you. What's more natural than making love to one's wife? The minute madam stopped wanting it, it was over. "Not tonight, Ben." "Get over it, already." "Go masturbate, Ben." "Don't you have hands?"

Your tongue of fire.... "Vermin," you called me once when I was shaving. Of all your insults, the one that stung the most, the one that's with me still. "Vermin." Was that what you really thought of me?

"*Try a little tenderness*," I used to sing to you. "*Oh, try a little tenderneeess*." Roses, dresses, perfumes, snickerdoodle cookies, trips, guitar serenades, Ben begging at your door. "Maggie." "Maggie?" "Maggieee!" Nothing. I hung in there as long as I could, baby. But stuff was piling up. It was piling up way too high for me.

So tell me, Maggie: How were we supposed to make it, huh?

Maggie sighed and considered her food. Cold again. She wasn't hungry any more. Eat, I prodded her. Eat while you are alive and you still can. No relishing food on the other side. Trust me, I know.

So this is what death is like, at least for now. Here but not quite. In limbo. In transit. Stuck between worlds. In my people's everyday but not of it. I'm waiting. For what, I don't know. There are no instructions, no signs, no menu, no precedents, no clues. Nobody's telling me a thing. I feel cheated. If this exists, surely there is more. Rapture, heralds, floods of light, inner peace overwhelming, God, Satan, triage, processing of some sort. Why have I been confined to this no man's land, going straight from taking a bullet and lying in the alley behind Cairo to assisting to my own funeral? What is this dimension I'm in? Is "dimension" the right word? Should I say "parallel universe" or something in the same vein? Why am I wearing a suit? Why can I see, feel, smell, move, but nothing else? This is what death is like: Many questions and no answers.

Am I afraid? Sometimes. The state I'm in is utterly alien to the earthbound human experience, yet close enough. Something Hubbard might have dreamed up, in fact. No physical constraints. A new consciousness, a different way of being. But the bottom line is I have no control over anything. Don't know what tomorrow is going to bring. No telling how long this will last and what's coming after it.

My back-to-back thoughts back at the funeral parlor, when I appeared out of nowhere to take a look at my cadaverous self: There is another life after all, and, My tailor is better than yours. For a moment it was just the rigid corpse and me in that cavernous room. Had I risen from it? Was I the soul detaching itself from the flesh? If so, why were my clothes different? How peaceful and ready to go I appeared resting there, hands on my chest, gut rising like a gentle slope, a vague smile on my lips as if savoring a final, exclusive joke. You couldn't guess from looking at me that I was a soldier who ended up selling liquor and sandwiches for a living, that I worked too hard and drank too much for way too long, that my wife and I viscerally hated each other toward the end, that I died at the worst possible moment.

Was I supposed to say my goodbyes? In one of those bizarre effects that, though never encountered in the first life, were to become quickly natural in the second, the scene's scope enlarged progressively to include Maggie, the kids, and a group of well-wishers. I expected them to jump with fright once they saw me hovering over the casket, but no. Not a shriek, not a stare. I was invisible.

My wife and my children appeared stricken, but not overwhelmingly so. Maggie dabbing her eyes and wiping her nose as she killed Kleenex after Kleenex, the ridiculous chair they'd given her sighing under her weight. The boys sitting on each side: Joe as sharp as usual, Jay with his first shave and clean cut in years. More than sadness, hurt, or distress, I felt their confusion. It had been so sudden. Here one moment, then gone. I had left for work around 8:30 just like I did every day. The next time they saw me was at the morgue. It's true that I wasn't planning to come back home that night. But I never wanted to travel this far, either. Talk about loose strings. Had I been able to speak, I would have apologized to my family: Didn't mean to leave like that, you guys. Guess it was my time. Wish I could change things. Stay strong. Stay together. Make me proud. God bless.

I rode with the three of them in Maggie's Marquis, random thoughts crowding my head. Where were my car, my wallet, my keys, my duffel bag? What would happen to Cairo? Who was working the register and stocking the shelves if everybody was on their way to the funeral? Why was the car stereo looped on "I will survive," of all things? When would the life insurance money kick in? What would Maggie blow it on? Why were we going to the cemetery when I could distinctly remember asking to get cremated? Had they forgotten? Did a man's requests for his last arrangements mean nothing?

I walked among the mourners. Should my worth be judged by the amount of people who came to pay their respects, I could boast about touching a decent share of souls in my lifetime. Harold and Reggie, two army buddies I hadn't seen in years, wandering in squeaky wheelchairs, wondering when their numbers would come up, the same notion in their war-weary eyes: Another one bites the dust. Old employees I hadn't parted with in the best of terms forgiving me for my shortcomings as a boss. Business contacts, salesmen, partners I hadn't always treated fairly taking advantage of the opportunity to gossip and curse me under their breaths. Rick, my debauched milkman. Curtis "Speedy Gonzales" James, the Canada Dry guy. Customers asking one another what would happen to their favorite watering hole. Neighborhood shop owners. My landlord, that pissy jerk. Lisha and her folks, the only black faces among the lot, feeling out of place and a little self-conscious now that the police had arrested a black man for the killing.

Hearing from my manager Chris that Maggie had gone cheap on me nearly spoiled my day. "That casket was from a big-box discount store," he whispered to his fiancee Yvonne. "That's fake mahogany from China. And the hall was rented for just under two hours. See how they rushed us out of there? The only thing old Mag couldn't save on was the mortician."

Yvonne was incredulous. "They sell caskets at Costco?"

Chris nodded. "Everything a person needs from the cradle to the grave. It's a one-stop shop, babe."

"Wow," Yvonne said.

I couldn't believe my ears. Costco? Two hours? Damn you, Maggie.

More vain than me would have done a head count--something to brag about later in Heaven, or wherever I was destined. Looking at all the faces in attendance, it just hit me that I had had no true friend, in the end. Conspicuously absent was Nicole. Her role in my last stretch on Earth, considered by both of us an unexpected gift, might well serve to seal my fate. Oh well. It pained me that she hadn't made it. It would have been good to see her one more time. She must have told herself that she didn't belong. Knowing Nicole she'd show up later, alone, and lay a rose on me. My baby is thoughtful like that.

The ceremony itself was beautiful. 105 degrees in the middle of August, global warming on everybody's mind. Peeping birds, buzzing bees, out-of-cycle flowers, the greenest green, Arlington's rolling hills, cookie-cutter plots, white crosses. The uniforms, the swords, the rifles' discharge, Empire's flag. Timeless and perfectly executed. Just not what I had asked for.

"I heard Section 60 is a mess," Harold told Reggie on the way out, carriages rolling and wailing side by side, gloved hands on double wheels.

"What you heard?" Reggie asked.

"They can't bury the kids from operations Iraqi Freedom and Enduring Freedom fast enough. People come in to pay their respects and end up staying for days. Mothers talk and sing to their dead. Whole platoons come by with beers and cigars and balloons."

Reggie shook his head. "Long as they put me far away from those kids, I don't care. Don't need nobody disturbing my sleep. Let me rot in peace. I earned it."

Harold nodded. "That's what wrong with this country now, Reggie: Nobody has any class any more."

Life went on without me. Maggie settled into widowhood rather easily, at least in private. I didn't witness a whole lot of changes in my people's routines for the better part of the following half-year, aside from an understandable bout of collective paranoia: It was the first murder in the family. Maggie had bars installed on all the first-floor windows. She condemned the basement's rear

45

entrance and reconnected the alarm system. Self-defense played as big a role as sentimentality in her decision to give weapons from my collection to the boys, who were only paying lip service to the purported menace. "Don't take the guns outside," she warned them, as if they were still little children and those were toys she didn't want them to lose or break. Maggie kept all the big pieces for herself, including the M-16, the Uzi, and the AK. Cabinets, cupboards, pantries, sofas, and the refrigerator's vegetable drawer became hiding places for loaded guns. Lead in the sugar, lead in the laundry, lead in the lettuce, lead under the seats, lead inside the car. Maggie drove to a Maryland range every day for two weeks to brush up on her shooting skills. She briefly considered taking Krav Maga lessons before settling on mail-order videotapes, shyness getting the best of her. It was quite a scene to see her sweat it out in front of the TV, practicing close combat moves with pachydermic grace. Bloody home invasion and carjacking scenarios constantly played in her mind. The intruder or carjacker was always black. Maggie was always quicker on the draw. The intruder/carjacker always died.

Handling heavy weaponry gave her a rush. She combined two shoulder holsters into one, cutting and rearranging the straps so the contraption would fit her frame. On days she felt particularly threatened she would wear it while tending to her chores, chrome sticking out of her armpits.

It would have been easy to unload a clip on Joe and Jay every time they fought. The impulse was definitely there. I was glad she reached for the ladle instead. And I'm sure Joe and Jay were glad, too.

46

More worrisome to me were the murderous fantasies Maggie harbored toward Nicole. She reread the file obtained from Derek Strange, her private investigator, and drew a red-ink target on all of my lover's breathtaking portraits, ruining them forever. "I know where you live, bitch. I know what you do." She mimed attacks around our bedroom, stripped to her underwear the better to move. She burst out of her closet. She rammed the bathroom door. She crawled on the carpet with the Uzi between her teeth. She ducked under the bed. She hid behind the curtains. She wished the M-16 were a grenade launcher, the better to shred Nicole and what she represented to pieces.

Was I worried by all this? A little. Did I feel responsible, once again? Touché.

Maggie relaxed a bit after Leslie, the young homeless man accused of killing me during a botched robbery, was convicted and sentenced to 15 years after a brief and very public trial. It didn't matter to the police, the prosecutor, and the jury that Leslie shouted his innocence, that nothing connected him to the crime scene, and that no gun had been recovered. It was one of those emotional cases where public outcry trumps the facts. I knew of at least three people aware of the truth: Leslie, myself, and the real killer. "We got that nigger," Maggie and Joe rejoiced as they walked out of the courthouse. But justice, as far as Leslie and I were concerned, had yet to be served.

When the insurance money rolled in Maggie did the smart thing and sat on it. My car was garaged because it was still too early to sell it. Jay ran Cairo for two more months before throwing in the towel after the breakup with

Lisha. Maggie, who hadn't set foot in the store for close to a decade, decided to get rid of it. Joe handled the sale to a young Korean businessman named Bobby Kim, getting a very good price but leaving in a basement secret compartment a stash of *grands crus* and vintage single malts, the loss of which had me fuming for days--couldn't take it with me but it would have made me happy to see it stay in the family. Maggie spread the proceeds of the sale between four banks, six accounts, and two safe-deposit boxes. She checked her balances every night before going to bed in order to induce soothing dreams. She stopped working entirely, ending her 30-year stretch with the D.C. school system. Things were decidedly on the up and up.

Retirement made her restless at first. Knitting, exotic cuisine, salsa, book club, yoga, investment seminars--anything went as long as nobody in our circle knew or heard or saw, for the sake of decency. Steve started popping in--he only lived across the street--to "check on things," knocking a certain way and announcing himself clearly lest Maggie shoot him through the door. What had begun as neighborly concern turned into a subtle courtship. Even I had to admit that they had much going for them: fresh widowhood, at-home children poisoning their lives, health worries, the lure of a sunny beach. Steve's world revolved around mechanical things. He was an engineer who owned a couple of patents and drove around in a very futuristic 1979 Citroën, maybe because he was really French and his first name really was Stephane. A poseur with many suits, if you'd ask me: everyman, millionaire next door, distracted inventor. A smartass who knew everything about everything. Nerdy to the bone. Belt always too tight. Highwater pants. Short sleeves. "I am a *breton*." Maggie found him endearing, of course. He was so small, so helplessly put together, so hopeless, so bright. She could have smothered him with just one breast. All she wanted was to snatch his glasses from his nose, pin him against the wall and kiss him with her eyes closed. I noticed with the slightest bitterness that emotions long disappeared where I had been concerned were on the verge of blooming anew. The house was neater and better organized than when I lived in it. Steve enjoyed a hot meal and argument-free conversations every time he came by. That crazed look in Maggie's eyes softened when she held him in her gaze.

The kids were mostly indifferent to Steve. A new man in their mother's life could only represent a blessing. They knew how long it had been since anybody rocked Maggie's world--they had seen me pacing the halls. Would Steve be the brave soul? Was he up to the task? They waited impatiently, believing it would get Maggie off their backs. Get her to smile, chill, take it easy. A little bit of love could go a long, long way.

More and more, Maggie's thoughts started to veer toward her longtime dream, that condo on the Eastern Shore. Enough of Military Road. Our whole life was inside those shabby walls. She gave herself 6 months to get the boys out, sell the house, and go. A revolution was brewing.

She tried to work Joe and Jay from the inside. Better cut them loose nice and easy. Joe, whom she felt closer to, was easier to talk to. They shared a special bond, though sometimes you couldn't tell their love from hate. With me gone, Jay out of commission, and Steve still warming up on the sideline, Joe and Maggie were each other's sounding board and sole companion on most days.

They started to take long walks every other morning before Joe went to work. "Do you want to go back to school?" Maggie asked him on one such occasion, knowing how bitter an aftertaste Villanova had left in his mind.

"Nope," Joe replied without even considering the option.

"I could give you a loan...." Maggie offered.

Joe said, "*Niet*, no way, that money's for you and you alone."

"Interest-free," Maggie added, feeling generous.

Touched more than he could say, Joe shook his head. "Very nice of you, Ma. But I'll hit it big one way or the other. It's just a matter of time. Forget school."

She looked at him. The hunger in his eyes had scared her since he was a child. Joe always wanted what he couldn't have. Toys we couldn't afford, schools that were out of reach, friends who looked down on our modest family. How many times had he banged his head against the wall? How many closed doors? What if, when all was said and done, he hadn't the means of his ambition? Maggie and I had talked about it at length without finding effective ways to change his outlook. Joe was no different on that morning than when he was 10 or 15 or 22.

"I have no doubt that you'll make it," Maggie told him gently. "Just do it the right way."

She turned her attention to Jay, who had taken to his bed shortly after Cairo's transfer into Bobby Kim's hands.

He seemed to be burrowing deep into a funk the rest of the family couldn't quite comprehend. Was it my death? Was it Lisha? Was it the "Great Depression" that hit a little before Jay turned 18 making a comeback? We didn't know. Jay slept, ate, and slept. I spent time by his bedside before the sadness and the smell chased me away. Jay had a heavy heart. He cried for me, for Nicole, for Lisha, for the whole world.

The same bad dreams that had tormented him his whole life through wouldn't allow him a single moment of peace, I guess because he slept so much now. In those dreams, weird creatures came and went. They had human form but a different consistency, if you can call it that. They seemed made of pure energy, positive or negative. Not unlike me, they appeared out of nowhere by flying, teleporting, and crossing walls. The negative ones stood above Jay's head, meaning him harm. Though they didn't so much as touch him, Jay would get alerted of their presence. To open his eyes, move, or talk, would prove all but impossible. Pressure would start building into his head and he would begin to suffocate. He would struggle to free himself from the spell, knowing that if he failed to stir a finger, take a deep breath, let out a sound, or open an eye, he would die. So far, he had always succeeded in pushing the bad creatures away. Sometimes they left on their own, chased by the prayers Jay recited in his head as soon as they approached. Always, they vanished the second Jay managed to break free by gasping for air or uttering a sound.

The positive creatures also stood above Jay's head, watching. Their goodwill would envelop him like a magnetic field. He would be at peace, reconciled with himself and the world. Those encounters would carry him until the next dream cycle. They would make him hope, they would make him dig deeper into the meaning of things, they would make him search for a grander purpose in life even as he kept on sleeping. Once, in a departure from the usual stuff, one good creature had guarded over Jay inside the reconfigured bedroom while an army of dead men marched in front of him. The place had become empty except for Jay's bed. Its walls had turned gray, its floor transformed into plain cement. The dead men entered from one door and exited through another. They wore shrouds over bare legs and feet. Jay didn't know who they were or where they were going. Only that they were destined to a harrowing fate, one which the presence at his side protected him from.

Good creatures and bad creatures never met. They didn't compete and they didn't fight, at least not directly. Their actions didn't have life-changing or pattern-altering impacts, since Jay always went back to sleep after they left him. It may be simplistic to call them angels and demons, but it does seem fitting. A dream was either good or bad, depending on who was visiting. The creatures moved in a dimension separate from mine. I saw them come and go but they never so much as took notice of me. The demons were fearsome because of the malevolence they radiated. They made my heart beat faster and the hair on my neck stand up. The angels weren't pure peace and joy. There was a martial quality to their goodness. They were fighters, recruits, soldiers. It seemed as though there was a war out there, a war in which Jay somehow played a part.

So those dreams really weren't dreams. They

happened at night but they happened all right. And they weren't new, since Jay had tried to open up to me about them through our time together. To be honest, I had never paid him much mind. "Lay off the comic books," I suggested when he was 12, and, "Try and cut back on the weed," a few years later. What did I know about parallel universes back when I was alive? What did Maggie?

She had much less empathy than me when it came to our firstborn. He was too dramatic and happy-go-lucky for her taste. All she saw in the recent sleeping stuff was a downward spiral. Jay was using my death or Lisha or whatever else as an excuse to cop out. If Maggie didn't intervene he would stay bedridden and wither away. She'd have to care for him forever. All her money would go into it. No condo, no freedom, no second life. Better act now, spend a little time and money to get him on his feet, inject more life into him, then push him gently toward the exit.

"What if I got you health insurance?" she proposed one evening, standing by the threshold so as not to breathe in Jay's stench--the stuff was lethal.

"I'm not seeing a shrink, if that's what you have in mind," Jay answered, his eyes blinking wildly. "I'm perfectly fine, Ma. Just don't feel like getting up every day."

"That's not normal," Maggie countered. "It bothers me to see you like this. No reason why you shouldn't be out enjoying life. I mean, I know it's only been a few months, but..."

Jay laughed bitterly. "Did you really say 'enjoy,' Ma?"

Maggie went for the jugular. "Don't do it for me," she suggested. "Do it for your father."

Jay shook his head, appalled. "Easy on the guilt tripping, all right?"

Maggie felt like punching him the way she had done a few times in the past--hitting hard, hitting to hurt, hitting to mark. If Joe still carried her maternal hopes valiantly despite his shortcomings, Jay seemed to have made his peace with an early defeat in the race. His case was hard to crack. I had been the only one to see merit in his easy ways. Jay never carried his wounds with abnegation–he just wasn't tough enough. Maggie thought it was all my fault: I had always been too soft with him, a thing no one could ever accuse her of. "I'll make a man out of him if it kills him," she used to say, revealing, despite her training as a schoolteacher, a blissful ignorance of the effects of abuse and early trauma in a person's development. Maggie changed the subject every time I intuited that part of the problem with Jay lay with us. It chipped at her self-esteem and sent her back to her own problematic childhood.

I could see that a major tempest with Jay was building. Refusing to get up every day was just not the way Maggie dealt with things. Because my death seemed to have hit Jay the hardest, she would cut him a little slack. No regrets for Lisha, though: As far as she was concerned, the girl wasn't a right fit and her departure was a blessing. So Maggie would swallow her frustration and try to be patient. She stopped short of giving Jay an ultimatum that day, but they both knew it would come.

Jay didn't hate his mother, though he had ample reason to. He saw her as she really was: a woman acting out

54

deep-rooted insecurities. It was his bad luck to have been a baby when her fuses started to blow. Maggie's rage and cruelty weren't personal. She didn't know what she was doing.

Wrong, I wanted to tell Jay: Your mother's fuses were already damaged when I met her. I should have known better than to have children with her. We all paid the price for my shortsightedness, you most of all.

"Just tell me when you're tired of having me around," Jay said to end the conversation, pulling the covers over his head. "I'll get out of your hair."

"Don't say stuff like that," Maggie chided him. Holding her breath, she ran toward the bed, kissed Jay on the forehead, and ran back out.

That's as far as Maggie got with the kids.

All things considered, she felt much better now than when I was alive. I had got that one thing right. A successful and very useful death, you could call it. I was one of those people who knew just when and how to go.

Did the three of them talk about me? Of course. Not always with fondness, but not with undue animosity, either, unless Nicole's subject came up, in which case the camps would be quickly and clearly demarcated: Maggie and Joe on one side, Jay alone defending me. I was like every other man, I think. Plenty of good and plenty of bad. As long as they somewhat equated each other I might stand a chance when the final Judgment came. And wishing it would come I often was, as I found myself bored out of my mind most of the time. My condition had more limits than possibilities. I could read thoughts, peer into hearts, and move unrestrained by gravity and physical obstacles, but essential things remained out of reach. I couldn't touch. I couldn't taste. I never slept. I had no reflection in the mirror. Though I longed to see Nicole, I could only stalk Maggie and the kids, and not even simultaneously. Worse still, I couldn't intervene in any of the events developing before my eyes. Had I been able to, I would have kicked Jay in the chin for being such a mope and I would have slapped Joe a good couple of times to purge that Church of Retribution foolishness out of his head while it was still in its infancy.

Not that I'm not having fun. I feel more alive than before my demise, to be honest. Gone are the back pains, the blood pressure, the constant thirst, the worries, the guilt. I'm a dance machine nowadays. Put on some music and my legs start moving effortlessly. Waltz, jerk, jigaboo, wop, twist, breakdance, go-go, smurf, tango, butterfly, boogaloo, and my favorite, the Devil's Hop. Being able to fly, well that's been a gas from day one. And ghostriding--a term I find wickedly appropriate--on the Nova's hood when Joe maneuvers the park's tricky roads at full speed, that's just a gas-gas-gas. Death is what you make it.

Maggie's remarks about Joe's physical appearance and less-than-holy or trust-inducing aura hit home. He doubted that she had meant to hurt him the way she did. Ma was just doing what she does: Give it to you raw. A force of nature she still was, a hurricane that sent you swinging and reeling. Maggie my walkyrie. How could Joe take offense? He knew she had his best interests at heart.

The moral of the story was: Don't rely on your looks to get ahead and don't expect people to embrace you at face value. Joe just didn't have what it takes to mesmerize, hypnotize, magnetize, stir deep feelings, provoke blind submission. He, in one word, didn't have charisma, that essential quality of messengers, heroes, guides, saviors, leaders, gurus, and prophets. Better than anyone, he knew his attractiveness had limits. Deep inside he was a shell, he was a sham, he was empty--no answer when you knocked. Nobody would follow him. People would see another pretty boy with a gimmick and they would walk away. MTV hunks had at least the advantage of a supporting cast, makeup, flattering lights, editing, and manufactured drama. Any prime-time bad boy with a face, big dreams, and a frail girlfriend would trounce him in the ratings and inside the public's heart. Father Joe's Sunday sermons on Channel 85 would be a no-go. So would the DVDs, CDs, books, and accompanying high-margin merchandise.

The realization that he would be unable to dupe an audience was a setback. Joe, who had thought his library days over, returned to the Quiet Room. I again went along, for lack of better things to do. The night before had been endless--endless. Nobody visited Jay. Maggie had her first wet dream in a couple of decades and it wasn't pretty. Joe jumped four times out of his sleep to run to the bathroom. I scared away a colony of rats that had made their way into the basement.

The Quiet Room was packed. Leaving Joe to his musings, I floated from table to table until I found a student with an interesting architecture book and peered over her shoulder in the hope of seeing Fallingwater. Were it possible to pick up objects now, with all the time I had in my hands, I would have become the best-read ghost in the universe. But what to do with all the new knowledge? How to put it to use? And where? Accomplishments are at the core of the human experience. With nothing to build, no future to prepare for, no one to defend, protect, feed, or nurture, including myself, it was hard to stay motivated. Could ghosts get depressed? I wondered.

When Joe got into the car to leave at the end of the day I tried something new and stayed behind. Sure enough, before he got more than a hundred yards away I found myself sitting in the passenger seat, good ghost on a leash.

It took Joe one more week to refine his plan. Why put yourself at the front? he concluded. You're setting yourself up for a fall. Every bump and bruise in your journey will be exhumed and dissected, as you well know. The Villanova thing, Jesus.... If that ever makes it to the 5 o'clock news it'll kill the movement before anything gets accomplished. So no spotlight. No close-ups, interviews, stages, or microphones. No preaching and jumping and hollering. Found the Church and run it from behind the scenes. Be the puppeteer, the mastermind, the godfather.

The fact wasn't an easy one to accept, despite its undeniable logic. The Church of Retribution was Joe's baby and, in his mind, he should have been the only one standing to reap the forthcoming publicity, his name readily associated with the edifice, his benevolent smile beaming from brochures, programs, front pages, portraits, posters, billboards, bed sheets, tablecloths, screens, digital marquees, T-shirts, clocks, pins, and buttons. By choosing the role of an eminence grise he essentially renounced his spot in history. Somebody else would achieve in the public's eye the greatness Joe alone had been instrumental in concocting. Life wasn't fair.

His vanity threatening to hold him back, Joe did the one thing that scared him the most since his shameful expulsion from campus: He Googled himself right there in the library's main room and read every link that came up. The fact that there weren't that many wasn't reassuring in the least. No picture, thank God, but his name and his age were there for everyone to see, and what little details were given about the rape case were damning enough. "No running away from this one," he muttered. "Jesse and Al will have the time of their lives."

Joe didn't waste a single minute being mad at himself. The past was the past. He had made a stupid mistake and this is how he paid for it, even though there had been no legal fallout: His private business was out there. No choice but to look ahead and work his way around the mess.

Joe didn't doubt that a figurehead, sincere or propped up, was needed. Every group that respects itself has one. The first thing that came to his mind was to hire an actor. Somebody who looked and behaved unmistakably like a prophet. Somebody with a clean background. Somebody with that most elusive of qualities: charisma.

The brainstorming started again in full effect. Organize a casting. Do a credit check. Get a detective on the case. Look into family history. No thieves or murderers. Slave owners a big plus--the bigger the plantation, the better. What about a woman? A blonde? Too much trouble. Ever heard of a female prophet? Women get supporting roles, at best: mothers, saints, prostitutes, virgins. So no blonde. Good credit. Good background--southerners preferred. Good looks, but the kind radiating from the inside out. Study the lives of Jesus, Mohammed, Che, and other crowd favorites. See what made them such revered figures. Copy everything down to the beards and the robes and the sandals and the poses. If any of those guys were alive today they'd get an agent and an attorney before embarking into anything. So draw a contract once you find your dude. Make yourself the sole beneficiary of his life insurance policy--prophets don't usually live that long, it's a tough profession. Put him on salary, give him full benefits, make one thing clear from the very start: He talks, he's dead. Same thing for all the extras, the group of first followers who'll be hired to adore, repent, go out into the world and spread the message....

Joe was satisfied with his progress until he realized one thing: Unless he found someone who had never gotten any work or even audited for a part, people would find out his protégé was an actor and the truth would come out. Think Milli Vanilli, he reminded himself. How did that one end up, huh? You would always have to worry about an old girlfriend or a greedy mom surfacing. Everybody comes with strings attached. As soon as a man is born he starts carrying baggage. Your guy will have to be the cleanest of all. Cleaner than clean.

But maybe that's a mistake as well, Joe reckoned. Nobody's cleaner than clean. That holier-than-thou stuff freaks people out. It's just not credible. Make him average, then. The usual mistakes: a little bit of pot here, a suspended license there.... A stabbing or two could be O.K., but no gun, larceny, assault, robbery, or distribution charges. Just harmless scuffles to prove that the guy is really real. Something like a sit-in, a hunger strike, a street protest. And absolutely no hard time.

Could he have a girlfriend? Joe went on. Should he be married, gay, black, white, tall, muscular, lanky, local, foreign, young, old, dumb, educated, working class, agnostic, religious?

A purpose-driven analysis quickly narrowed the profiling field. What the Church of Retribution needed was a tall white male in his mid- to late-20s with a college degree, work experience, one very minor and politically motivated offense on his rap sheet, a decent build, siblings, middle-of-the-road parents. He should be either single or in a serious relationship with a black woman--marriage and children a bonus. Nice voice. Handsome, but not too much. Friends from all colors and creeds. Wholesome lifestyle--no alcohol or drugs--but nothing extreme like veganism, either. Though not a polemicist or a demagogue, firm on issues like the wars in Iraq and Afghanistan, human rights, the living wage, abortion, universal health coverage, and the environment. Not an adept of any religion, modern, ancient, revealed, or manmade, but a definite believer in a Higher Power.

Joe got a library card and checked out several biographies. He started to pour over them at home each evening after dinner, sitting at Maggie's desk while she watched TV across the room.

"Jesus? Gandhi? Malcolm X? What's gotten into you?" she asked on the first night, baffled.

"Nothing, Ma."

"I've never seen you walk through this door with anything that wasn't required reading. And even then Jay had to do the homework for you. This is a miracle!"

Joe sighed, flipping through the pages in search of revealing photos and nuggets of wisdom. "People change.... What can I tell you."

Maggie eyed him suspiciously. "You're not going into religion, are you?"

Joe stopped reading. His heart was pounding, sweat started to trickle down his palms. "What if I was?"

Maggie turned the volume down. "I don't know. It

would be ... unexpected." She stifled a smirk.

Joe took the high road. "I'm not as stupid as you think, Ma. And I might just surprise you one day."

Maggie rolled her eyes. "Oh, you know I know you will."

Joe shook his head. It dawned on him that he would have a lot of new things to explain in the near future. Now was as good a moment as any to start preparing Maggie. "You don't believe in anything," he asked. "Do you?"

Maggie scratched her cheek with the remote. "Not me. That's why I never took your brother and you anywhere near a church. That's for suckers. Any inclination toward religion that I might have had was quelled my very first year of teaching. The stuff those kids put me through every single day.... If anybody had a design in that, I wish I could meet them to knock their teeth out."

Hearing her, I felt myself getting pale. Your big mouth, Maggie. Careful before you damn yourself.

"I've been thinking...." Joe went on.

Maggie raised aw-shucks-here-it-comes eyebrows, preparing herself for a good laugh.

The next sentences seemed fake to Joe even as he was mouthing them: "Things haven't been the same since dad passed, you know? I ... I find myself wondering about a purpose. I feel the need to make a change."

Maggie inched closer, making the couch shift and sigh. This promised to be good. The cushion on her right raised up from under her, revealing the black steel of a .38. "What kind of change, son?"

Joe lowered his head, put a tear in his eye and added a humble note to his voice "I don't know yet, Ma. I mean,

I'm searching right now. The next thing I do professionally will have a meaning. It won't just be about a paycheck. I want to help people."

Maggie stared at him with her mouth open.

Don't believe him, I screamed. He's conning you.

The sound of Jay's bedroom door creaking open provided Maggie with an answer. "As long as you don't take to sleeping all day and expect a hot meal when you wake up, you'll be all right with me," she told Joe.

Jay walked in with a yawn, hair all over the place, beard down to his chest. We all held our breaths. "Food in the kitchen?" he asked, staring at the empty dining table.

"I didn't save you any," Maggie said.

"Why?" Jay asked, crushed.

"Boot camp starts tomorrow," Maggie announced. "I want you out of bed by 10. That's 10 a.m. Clean your room, your bathroom, and yourself inside out. Keep busy, preferably far away from here, preferably looking for employment. Then sit to eat with Joe and me at dinnertime or eat not at all. You'll have to earn your bread from now on, my friend. Enough is enough."

Jay cocked his head back. The smell of beans and fresh-baked bread wafting from the kitchen made his stomach growl. I knew, because I could smell it, too. "Seriously?"

Maggie's eyes burned holes in his forehead. He burned clean, like gasoline. "Seriously."

Jay took a step toward the kitchen.

Maggie raised a finger. "Don't even think about it."

Better not risk it, I warned Jay. That .38 under the cushion? All she has to do is reach for it. Open plane, five yards at the most, clean shot, you're history. Dead over a plate of beans.

Jay turned around and walked back to his room. The door creaked shut.

We started breathing again.

"Bonehead," Maggie hissed.

"Creep," Joe echoed.

I floated into Jay's room out of a sense of duty and found him back in bed, his face against the wall. The odor of ripe litter made me rush back out. Tomorrow would be an interesting day. The deadline had been set sooner than I thought. It was all because of Steve, who had encouraged Maggie all through the afternoon. He had just gotten on his younger daughter Simone's case. She was a 28-year-old punk rock chick on crystal meth who looked more like a ghost than me. "I gave her two weeks to clean up or get out," Steve fumed. "You have to be tough with them if it breaks your heart."

"I know how to be tough," was Maggie's reply.

If Jay got up and showered and shaved maybe we could hang out and do something. I liked being around him, no matter what the other two said. Fun as the Nova rides were, Joe was too tense for me. He wore me out and scared me stiff with this new project of his. Jay was a good kid, and I'm speaking objectively here. I would have dug him if he hadn't been my son and we had met by chance. His highs, his lows, his smile, his spirit.... Jay always had that vibe about him, man. Hip without trying or pretending. Attuned to the world in ways most of us only dream of--its joys, its evils, its sufferings, its beauty. Jay seemed to feel all of it more intensely than the rest of us. Because of what happened to him as a child, he was extremely sensitive and strong and fragile at the same time. Capable of the best and the worst. Always one hundred percent genuine. On a good day, Jay's karma could appease the most restless soul. On the flip side, you wiped your feet on him as you stepped over. This recent bout of depression was as bad as it ever got. Jay stayed in the dark. His mind was empty, his heart bled, his body ached. He was scared.

I was anxious to see him get himself together. Been waiting long enough. Jay had promise, man. A promise still not kept. To see that day.... It would erase everybody's doubts. It would set things straight. It would make up for the way I failed him as a father.

Jay didn't get up the next morning, or the one after that. Maggie thought about evicting him purely and simply, but decided to keep on starving him instead. Jay came out of his room once or twice, found no food anywhere he looked even though his nose was telling him otherwise, and went back in. Not a word was exchanged between him and Maggie. He traded insults with Joe, but that was nothing new. Though he could have rummaged into the fridge in the deep of the night, he felt above such actions. He had pride, my Jay.

It wasn't the first time that Maggie had refused to feed a member of our family. Whenever she got angry with one of us she withheld food, words, attention, and affection. You were reduced to nothing in an instant. You ceased to exist. You became part of the furniture, an object of scorn. Maggie's brand of silent treatment was worse than the arguments and the blows she was famous for. She went all the way, talking about you as if you were invisible, tickling your nose with delicate aromas, dumping the rest of sumptuous dishes in the trash bin right in front of your eyes, showing the people in her good graces extra love and care, leaving your laundry untouched, hanging up on your friends--1,001 ways to disrupt your day. The boys and I had several names for the phenomenon, most of them Hollywood-inspired: "The Cuckoo's Nest." "The Ice Age." "All Cruella's Children." "The Bench." "The Iron Curtain." "American Apartheid." "Shaolin's Orphans." "The Last Warden of Alcatraz." "The Prisoners of Military Road." "Papillon." "Let My People Go." "The Wall." "Desaparecido." "Brother, Brother, Where Are Thou?" It was a tough position to find yourself in. You felt rejected, dejected, isolated, because of course nobody in the house could openly take your side, lest they, too, incur Maggie's wrath. It could last for weeks--weeks. There was no possibility to discuss the offense, real or perceived. The only way out of the doghouse was to apologize, to crawl back, to shed all dignity and to admit wrongs you knew deep in your soul you hadn't committed. After having thoroughly broken your spirit and made a crying violin of your heart, Maggie magnanimously forgave you and took you back into the fold. Your privileges were reinstated. Suddenly, home was home again. With Maggie, you lay down and stayed down.

I was forced to keep following Joe around, as Maggie did nothing now but sit in the house all day. She watched TV, cooked, and waited for Steve. They had started kissing and it seemed that things might go further

67

any day now. I certainly didn't want to be there to see it.

Joe's hunt for the perfect man started in earnest, the time factor kicking in as his savings started to dwindle. I tagged along, mortified that he would actually go and try to put his plan into motion. The Church of Retribution wasn't just a vague and crazy idea any more. It was taking shape, and the world wouldn't, couldn't be the better for it.

Joe scanned ads in the papers. He searched faces in the crowd. He went in malls, theaters, concert halls, gyms, even. He shook hands and networked at conventions, SBA fairs and Chamber of Commerce breakfasts. He struck conversations in all the bars, restaurants, clubs, pool joints, spas, and spots that used to be his scene. He swapped business cards and cellphone numbers by the dozen.

To my great relief, nothing seemed to work. Good luck finding a good man among the young professionals out there. D.C. was full of self-absorbed, money-oriented sharks/hedonists poised to conquer the world. They set no other agenda for themselves than living life to the fullest and enjoying spoils and bragging rights deemed well-deserved, even as the fallout from their excesses threatened to blow the planet and its less privileged denizens to bits. Such were the priorities of the "me" generation: Who went to the most elite school, who drew the biggest paycheck, who put together the craziest deals, who billed the most hours, who made partner first, who played the roughest sports, who drank the most, who spent more, who had all the girls, who drove the biggest car, who threw the most awesome parties. No vision, no all-encompassing intelligence, no sense of public service, no notion of sacrifice for the common good. They reminded

Joe of his former self, all these millionaires in the making, these scions of Empire, these men of the future. He found them depressing and a little frightening in their single-mindedness and sense of entitlement. To think that he had wanted nothing better than to join their ranks.... He thanked the revelation for making him a new man.

"What are you up to these days?" Rima, his most recent ex, shouted at him from the core of a stilettoed, bright-eyed, and juicy-lipped trio of lionesses.

"Running my own firm," Joe answered above the cloud, techno music, and chatter, lifting his glass toward the mirrored ceiling. He felt not even an ounce of regret that she'd dumped him. Gazuza was the incredible name of the lounge we were in. I was drifting among the international crowd, shaking my thing stupid to the beat, hands in the air, a ghost bustin' loose. "Fabulous!" was all you heard. The kids talked and talked but nothing was being said. Numbing themselves with alcohol before hooking up was the game plan, the very thing that had gotten Joe in trouble back in the day. I ended up behind the bar, feeling incredibly thirsty when I discovered a bottle of Lagavulin 16.

Rima caught up with us in the narrow stairs. We were on our way out, stuck in traffic. "FYI," she told Joe, "I'm from here. Had you taken the time to know me, you'd have found that much out. Don't know where fucking Mumbai is."

Fishing at the bottom brought no breakthrough. Plumbers, electricians, mechanics, construction workers, waiters, couriers.... No underdog caught Joe's eye in any of the industrial park hangouts, retail outlets, service stations, corner stores, and underground clubs we visited. Tattoos, muscles, cigarettes, swagger, class resentment, a certain crassness despite very developed survival skills and an obvious resilience--limited education and lack of exposure made for unimpressive candidates. The men Joe introduced himself to all had wives and/or kids. Overworked and underpaid, they were either beaten up by a hardscrabble life or extremely volatile. Those who hadn't resigned themselves to their lot dreamt beyond their means. Show them a way out and there's no telling how they would handle themselves, the money, or the fame.

So Joe started to look closer to him. The problem was, he had no friends. His frat buddies had cut him loose as soon as the rape allegations spread around campus. "You're a liability," one had actually told Joe point-blank, and he would regret for the rest of his life having been too shocked to react. Part of his coping process had been to stick to himself, to need no one. Fuck the pack mentality.

He started to get discouraged again. Joe the hungry one. Would his life ever change? When would things work out? When would he make it? Never wanted to be a loser, my Joe. Never imagined that he'd carry a stain. Never thought he'd lose his way. The wishy-washy stuff was good for Jay. Joe fancied himself a fighter. He had backbone. He dreamed big. He wanted to leave an imprint on this earth. Ego through the roof. Balls big enough to drag on the floor and walk bowlegged, just like all those rappers with crazy hairstyles and cars and girls. Deeez nuts. Deeez motherfuckin' nuts.

Believe, Joe told himself. You've got to believe.

Maggie, who thought Joe was still engaged in that gigantic job search, tried to cheer him up during one of their walks. "It'll come around," she told him. "You just be patient and make sure to do something you enjoy. Like you said the other night, money isn't everything."

"Let's go to church," was Joe's answer. "A black church. There's gotta be one nearby."

"What would we want to do that for?" Maggie replied, puzzled.

"Just to see."

Maggie was incredulous. "You're doing the black thing, too? After that black girl almost got you thrown in jail? After everything that happened in this house?"

Here we go again, I sighed with exasperation.

"That girl wasn't really black, Ma--I told you before. And anyway, I kind of care for black people," Joe ventured, trying to get more and more in character if only for his mother's benefit. "I wish I could find a way to help them."

Maggie stopped walking. "What are you talking about?" she asked, catching her breath as yesterday's roast, mashed potatoes and gravy all came back to haunt her.

A bird sang. The winter morning was feeling chilly, for a change.

Joe looked Maggie in the eye. "There's so much to do, don't you think? Blacks always get the short end of the stick. Isn't it time we did more for them?"

Maggie was dumbfounded. "Blacks." He had said "blacks," not "niggers." She felt betrayed. What was going on here? Why wasn't Joe talking and acting like Joe any

71

more? "Why, man?"

"To redeem all the wrong that has been done, Ma. To make things better."

Maggie raised her head to the sky. This took the cake. "Two crazy sons out of two," she shouted. "And a dead, crazy husband. Lord, I thank you!"

Joe took her hand.

We resumed walking.

The first thing we heard when we got home was the shower running. I went into Jay's bathroom, overjoyed. He was leaning against the sink, stripped to the waist, staring at the tiled wall through the vapor. Behind the tub's curtain the water was running freely.

Jay was thinking about the dream he had had a little before 6, still unsure about what it meant. It was the second departure from the usual stuff, after the one in which dead bodies had marched in front of his bed. Yesterday he had been driving his white Caprice, the old cruiser I bought him eight years back, when a cop, a black woman, pulled him over. She was neither friendly nor aggressive. After she checked his documents and let him go, Jay followed her into a two-story villa by the sea. Entering the house, Jay went into three rooms one after the other. In the first, Hugo, my old Budweiser delivery man, was watching porn on a computer with a little boy sitting on his lap. They didn't see Jay walk in. Though what he witnessed made him uneasy, Jay didn't intervene. In the second room, a spacious washroom full of natural light, Jay realized that the house's occupants knew our family. The patriarch, a black man, and I shared the same profession, and there were black and white pictures of Joe with the house's children on the wall. Entering a terrace overlooking a garden, Jay discovered that the cop he had been following was the guardian of the premises. She was nowhere to be found, but Awazen Ezber, Jay's middle school friend, appeared in front of him. He was the son of a Syrian diplomat. A waif with a big head, penetrating eyes, and a mop of hazel hair, Awazen was a star student and a gentle soul. Jay and he had lost touch after his father got reassigned. They talked, happy to be reunited. As Awazen and Jay stood facing the garden, a voice cut through Jay's dream. "Believer!" "Believer!" "Believer!" it called out distinctly, seven times altogether. Then, "Get up!" "Get up!" "Get up!" Startled, Jay opened his eyes and looked at the alarm clock. His heart was beating wildly. After turning the light on he sat on his bed, still in the dream's grip, the voice echoing in his head. "Believer!" "Get up!" He didn't know what to make of it. He didn't know if he should obey. At a little past 6, it was still early. Maggie and Joe would be out for their walk soon. "Believer." Believer in what? And what was there to get up for? Another day to think about Lisha and dad? He lay back down, keeping his eyes open.

I had drifted out of the room feeling sorry that Jay didn't heed the call. No creature had been paying him a visit but I could guarantee that the voice was real--I had heard it just as well as he had. Didn't know where it came from or who it belonged to. Didn't need to know. In my position you had no choice but to get used to strange things.

That was less than an hour ago. Now Jay was getting ready to take the rest of his clothes off and jump in the shower. I felt happier than I had in years. Yes! Finally!

73

Back in the living room, Maggie and Joe looked at each other and shrugged. Maggie spoke first. "Breakfast?"

Joe nodded.

"Set the table for three," she told him. "Your brother's back."

I've been trying a long, long time, still I
can't make it
Everything I try to do seems to go wrong
It seems I have done something wrong
Why they're trying to keep me down?
Who God bless no one curse
Thank God I'm not the worst
Better must come one day
Better must come
They can't conquer me
Better must come, yeah

Delroy Wilson is all Jay wanted to hear on the day of his comeback. It seemed fit, given that it's what he and Lisha had been jamming to last August when news of my death hit, this little gem of a tune with its defiant message of perseverance, resilience, and hope. After hearing it in a downtown bookstore and getting the name from the cashier, they had run to Melody Records and bought the last "Delroy Wilson: Best of the Studio One Years" copy from a chillout dude called Charlie. Then they had grabbed Peruvian chicken *a la brasa con papas y platanos y*

coleslaw to go, found refuge back in Jay's bedroom, eaten
with their hands, and played their new favorite song until
Maggie stuck her head, and then her ample body, in the
door frame--her no-knocking self. "Turn that shit down!"
she had hollered from the step. Jay had been too stunned by
the intrusion to move. Here he was lying on his bed, Lisha
on top, bellies full, burping in each other's face, sharing a
moment, chillin', doing what lovers do, feeling up, feeling
cozy, feeling nice, his greasy hands under her shirt, her
fingers drawing nothings on his neck, his mind wandering
he didn't know where. "Turn that shit down!" Why had he
forgotten to lock the door? What if they had been naked? It
was just like Maggie to burst in, her house-her rules, her
jealousy and lousy manners. One look was enough to make
you feel like the scum of the earth. Jay got ready to say
something smart but his mother beat him to the punch,
shouting, "Your father's just been shot!" Throwing it to
Jay's face, really, as if he were somewhat responsible, as if
it were all his fault, like everything that went wrong at the
house and in their lives. It was a little after 10 p.m., a
Wednesday, a perfect day to be off so far, just perfect. Jay
thought he had heard wrong. Still pinned under Lisha, he
stared at Maggie, transfixed. The crimson of her cheeks, the
anger in her eyes, her shoulders filling the space so
completely, her head almost touching the top, the flesh on
her cartoonish arms swinging left and right, her elbows like
trapped golf balls--"The Bogeyman of Military Road,"
featuring Maggie Wilson, now playing in a theater near
you. Her words were too disconnected from her body
language to make sense. This was bad news, sad news, ugly
news, horrible news, yet Maggie appeared more mad than

anything. Jay's brain went wild, taking him for a ride, System Error, System Error, and he found himself unable to react. Lisha, who knew they had both heard right, sat up, got off the bed, gathered her things, walked to the open window, and started to cry. *"I've been trying for a long, long time,"* Delroy sang again, once too many, perhaps, because like a crazed bull that had just heard red Maggie ran across the room and banged the stereo with both fists, cracking the amplifier's top, her biceps flying this way and that, her second chin trembling, her breasts ready to pop. "Shut up!!!!" Poor Delroy went silent.

Much as Jay played and replayed that memory in his mind, I knew it as well as if I had lived it.

Dust on the wires, dust on the knobs, dust on the dials, dust in the circuits. Jay was glad that his equipment still worked, as it had remained untouched since that day. Mid- to late-'70s "roots" reggae was his favorite music, "Better Must Come" his number one track. And today it showed. Jay played it 27 times while cleaning the room. He strummed it on his Yamaha after tuning it. He cranked it in my car after bringing the monster back to life. Better must come. Delroy had found his voice again, lifting Jay up with him, helping him get his mind right. Better must come one day.

Jay's bedroom looked like a totally different place with the sun allowed in and a nice winter breeze blowing through. I took my spot on the armoire, holding back tears of happiness while my son swept, mopped, dusted, washed, and wiped. The bed sheets and his pajamas went in the trash. The mattress was flipped. Lisha's portrait got a

Windex shine and a kiss. Bass bounced around the walls. How could it be, Jay wondered, that he'd gone without music and fresh oxygen for so long?

He could still fit his jeans and T-shirts, the recent hunger strike having brought to more reasonable proportions the stomach that had been steadily ballooning. It felt weird to put his Nike on. Weird, too, to look at himself in the mirror. Hair, hair everywhere. His head, his face, his nose, his ears--a blond, blue-eyed scarecrow. And God, was he pale. Not pale as a ghost, because ghost aren't pale at all unless shocked by some utterance or risqué scene they walk into, but pale-pale, sun-deprived pale, pale to the point of looking sickly. What would Lisha, she who teasingly called him "Whitefolks, My Whitefolks," and "Whitey on the Moon," what would Lisha say if she saw him today? Nothing, probably. Lisha wouldn't say a thing. She wouldn't tease. She wouldn't joke. She wouldn't laugh.

How long did people stay mad? Jay wondered. Was it the same as staying sad? Maybe six months-plus was enough to forgive and forget. Maybe he should call her. He sure wanted to, as Joe surmised every time they fought. Jay missed Lisha. He missed her kisses, her silences, her neat, color-coordinated outfits, her hairdos, her pride, and her clear, no-nonsense, straight-arrow mind. He had been dreaming about her often, whenever the visitors from other worlds gave him a break, in fact. He dreamed about me, too, but that's another matter. Just two nights ago he'd been trying to convince Lisha to fly home with him. They were inside an airport in the Tropics. It was hot, sticky, unbearable. Jay had passports, money, and tickets for him, Lisha, and her baby girl. Where that baby came from Jay didn't know, just that it was Lisha's and he loved her as his own. At the airport Lisha wasn't angry at all, though they hadn't seen each other in a while. As quiet as usual, maybe just a little distant. She didn't want to travel because she had a job and she was still in school. Jay insisted until she came around. He wasn't pushy or forceful about it, just very secure in his belief that he would prevail. He let his feelings show, the feelings that had never strayed from his heart; he held Lisha's hand and told her they needed to get on the plane and get to their destination, all three of them--it was the right thing to do. "We'll come with you," Lisha finally agreed, putting her head on his shoulder. "But not today." That was enough for Jay. He sneaked in a kiss, and Lisha kissed him back. Like a reel coming abruptly to its end, the dream stopped. Jay woke up in a good mood.

He felt like reconnecting with his old life, all of a sudden, picking it up where he had left it. It had been pretty easy, so far. Getting up, cleaning up, firing up the speakers.... But Lisha would be another matter altogether. "These damn niggers!" he had screamed in front of her in Cairo the last time he saw her, two days after the Costco casket-Arlington farce and five minutes after 3rd District homicide detective Melvin Lee confirmed over the phone that, "that homeless guy Leslie is indeed our man." Something had gotten stuck in Jay's throat, something raw and mushy and disgusting. He had pressed his thumbs on his temples, taken a deep, deep breath, and screamed at the top of his lungs to cough it out, screamed not at Lisha but in general, screamed just to scream, screamed out of nowhere, screamed out of grief--another one of his indirect ways of mourning, I guess, a totally primordial thing to do in any case. "These damn niggers!" as in, always fucking up shit, shooting and robbing and killing innocent people, destroying lives. "These damn niggers!" and Lisha had raised her head to look at Jay across the deli counter, her limpid eyes full of hurt behind her Buddy Holly frames, her precious little lips pursed in a line of disbelief. Jay? Her Jay? Talking like that? The apron flew from her neck. Her purple purse latched on to her shoulder. Her braids jumped from under her cap. She ran out of Cairo never to come back. Good thing it was after the lunch wave because Chris and Jay would have been in deep doo-doo. "I guess she quit," Chris said when Lisha didn't show up the next day. They put a sign up and hired the first person who came through the door, a chubby, overqualified, ultra-sensitive Mongolian named Bola who, when asked if he had deli experience, answered, "I make sandwiches every day at my house." Jay still held Lisha's last check in a drawer--$261.67, a little over half a week's wages. It was good for five more months and nineteen days.

Call her? Jay was afraid to. Some things you can't take back. He had apologized, of course. He had begged. He had cried. In letters, in flowers, in messages to her answering machine. Lisha hadn't deigned speak another word to him. Quit? She was as good as gone. Her Filipino godmother/mentor/surrogate mom/roommate Marina spelled it out for Jay when he dared show up at their apartment on 19th Street, a mere two buildings from Nicole's: "Lisha no wanna talk to you, Jay. Lisha say you bad man. You bad, bad man. Lisha say she shan't see you." Marina had tripped on the double s and triple sh of the tricky sentence before repeating herself more slowly.

"Lisha. Say. She. Shan't. See. You." Then, with a small smile of triumph, either because she thought she had outmaneuvered a language that caused her much frustration or because she'd never liked Jay: "You bye-bye, Jay. You bye-bye."

The funny part is, he had occasionally gotten angry at Lisha during these last few months. For not understanding him. For abandoning him when he needed her the most. He had just buried his dad, goddamn it! Didn't that count for anything? Of course he didn't mean the insult. Had he ever let such words slip before? He had a black girlfriend, hadn't he? And how many friends from other races, countries, nationalities? Jay, racist? Come on now. Not a chance in the world.

Oh, he had had plenty of time to think about it. The fact of the matter was that there was no excuse, no justification for what he had said. He couldn't blame it on Chris, Joe, or Maggie, the people in his life who thought it appropriate to pepper their language with nonstop slurs and disparaging comments. Blacks had it worst in the trio's twisted worldview. They were Tyrones and Leroys and Keishas and Tamikas and Shamikas. They were lazy, brutish, dishonest, and plain dumb. Hispanics didn't fare much better: Migos, hombres, Pedros, Marias, and Josés. They belonged in construction sites, overcrowded apartments, maternity wards, front yards, the Rio Grande, and cleaning trucks. Asians were, more than ever, the Yellow Threat taking over our best universities, buying all our stores, stealing all our names. Charles, Mikes, Andrews, Michelles, Sarahs.... "Just look at Bobby Kim," Chris once told Jay. "From dry cleaning to liquor and wine.

81

What do those people think? That life is just a long, uninterrupted stream of small businesses? That all skills are interchangeable? That Koreans are smarter than anybody on earth?"

That was Chris, Joe, and Maggie. Jay knew better than to think and to talk about people that way. So why had he lapsed so badly, and in Lisha's presence, no less? Why had he been laughing at all the comments and jokes for so long, for as long as he could remember, even as he knew deep down that it was wrong? To be like the rest of them? Because it was easier than to stand for what he believed? Because those were his people? Because a black homeless man named Leslie had shot and killed Ben?

No smoke without fire, man. Discriminatory words and attitudes don't just come out of someone's mouth. Somewhere inside of him he must harbor hatred or fear or, at the very least, indifference. They lurked on the fringe of his consciousness, ready to roar, ready to come out and show their ugly faces. He was at fault. Who was the real Jay? A decent dude or an occasional racist? A man of conviction or a laugh-along? He needed to take a lucid look at himself and reconnect. Bad thoughts, bad words, bad feelings must get purged. A new direction must be taken, a new path must be traced. Jay had a good idea where to begin. Today was day one of his period of atonement. Better must come. Better must come right here, right now. Better must come no later than this morning.

The cleanup complete, Jay charged my car's battery and let the engine run while he checked the levels. The Eldorado was good to go in ten minutes, like I knew it would.

"Need money to get around?" Maggie asked from the door connecting the garage to the house, her pink Sliperella slippers, army-green sarong, and maroon blouse straight out of Sasquatch country. She was trying her hand at different styles now that a new man was almost in her life, with more or less lucky results.

Jay averted his eyes so as not to laugh openly (wrenches were displayed a few inches from where Maggie stood). "I'll be all right," he assured his mother, though he didn't have a cent to his name. You had to be careful with Maggie. She didn't really know how to give, and what she took and the way she did it often left you in bad shape.

She did her best to appear contrite. "You're mad at me? Didn't say a word during breakfast."

That question, "You're mad at me?" was vintage Maggie. It was an inherent part of her madness, her dysfunction. She punished you and expected you to be a gentleman about it. No matter how far she went you must take it upon yourself not to show grief, you were supposed to take your thrashing and allow her back in as if nothing had ever happened.

Jay forced himself to smile before remembering the resolutions of a few minutes ago: atone, ask for forgiveness, get better, stop being a hypocrite. Didn't that include smiling when he really didn't feel like it? "I'm not mad, Ma.... I mean, yes I'm mad, Ma."

"I wouldn't have let you starve to death...." Maggie assured him. "I was waiting for you to give up or slip into a coma. I would have nursed you back to life quick. You have to understand, Jay: Something needed to be done in

83

order to get you out of that room."

Jay closed the hood and went to sit behind the wheel without acknowledging her remark. He didn't know what bothered him the most: Maggie's condescension or her utter belief that he was weak. Life was a cosmic soup and his mother and he particles that would never meet.

Maggie shrugged. "Where are you going?"

Jay put the car in reverse. "To get some air."

Maggie took a step back. "That'll do you some good. Look for a job while you're at it. Dinner's at 7."

She watched us pull out of the garage, praising herself for Jay's sudden resurrection. Who knows how low this depression would have taken him hadn't she stepped in? Tough love worked every time. She couldn't wait to tell Steve.

I can't describe my emotions as Jay and I drove away in the Eldorado. It was almost too much. My ride, a song, my favorite person, a beautiful 1st of February. It had been so long.

"Ain't it weird, Dad?" Jay said as we were going south on Connecticut. "I mean, feel this sunshine."

It's freakish all right, I answered.

"I can't truly enjoy it," Jay continued, "knowing there'll be hell to pay down the road.... We really fucked the Earth, man."

I nodded, wondering why he kept addressing me as if he knew for a fact that I was there, slumped in the passenger seat, my arm hanging out the open window, no seat belt required. Did he think I had been the one talking to him from the Great Beyond? Could he feel my presence?

For someone who'd spent a little over the past six months sleeping, and the past week or so fasting, Jay seemed rather upbeat. Must have been the voice in the pre-dawn. Get up. Believe. Get up. Believe. He had thought about it while Maggie, Joe, and I were out walking, and he had found the strength and the will to make today THE day. Good for him. Good for us.

It didn't surprise me that Jay didn't think to confide in either Maggie or Joe. Mine was a divided house. The acrimony was real, especially between the two brothers. Jay knew he was alone.

He was glad to be out. Everything looked fresh, inspiring, full of possibilities. The balmy air, the trees, the vibe you got from the avenue. Jay was back, in Maggie's words. Jay was baaaack!

I've been trying a long, long time, why I can't make it
No one to give me a helping hand, they're only tryin'
to keep me down
Who God bless no one curse
Thank God I'm not the worst
Oh, my people can't you see
They're tryin' to take advantage of me
Better must come
Better must come, yeah
Better must come one day
Better must come, yeah yeah yeah yeah yeah
Mmm hmm

It could have just as well been Joe's song, provided he were into such things. Joe heard only notes and melodies, he couldn't care less about the message in music. Why take the pain to study and retain lyrics? Cheap beats, easy harmonies and choruses were enough to please and satisfy. Mid-tempo techno, ambient, lounge, or trance were his thing. He found Delroy and what he represented distasteful: A bunch of islanders singing on empty bellies and ganja--Eddie Murphy had a famous Saturday Night Live sketch about it called "Kill All White People." Curiously, Joe hadn't asked Jay to turn the music down this morning. It was he who had stayed behind, locking himself in his room with the shades drawn the better to plot his next move. Though worried about what he might come up with while I was gone, I was relieved not to have to spend another day stressing over his phony church. Still, a little ubiquity would have been nice.

The Eldorado had a full tank (I remember gassing up on my way to work the day I died). Jay followed Connecticut all the way to Q. I was beside myself with anticipation when we parked in front of Cairo. This was my block, my part of town, 30 years of my life. We lingered on the sidewalk to take in the Valentine's Day window display. Pink, black, flowery, and illuminated, it was eye-catching but overwrought. "What do you think?" Jay asked.

So-so, I answered.

We went in. Morning was always the best possible time to visit. Right after 12, Cairo became a zoo: office workers lined up for lunch until 3; 3 to 5, delivery people and salesmen took turns crowding the narrow aisles; 5 to 9, residents and partygoers exiting the metro station made us their last stop. Cairo wasn't much to look at, but it had turned into a gold mine in recent years. Dupont Circle was mostly gay, young, and well-off. I missed my store. I missed the neighborhood. I missed the crazy people. I missed the brass band that turned the block into a New Orleans outpost every summer afternoon.

Bobby Kim was behind the register, talking on the phone. He was short, bald, and quick-tongued. Second-generation Korean, barely in his 40s, as American as you and me, sound business notions despite what Chris said behind his back. The transition from cleaning shirts and pants to buying and selling chiantis, rosés, vouvrays, viogniers, moscatos, muscadets, sancerres, sauvignons, sauternes, sherries, pinots, ports, liquors, and liqueurs hadn't been the smoothest, but that was to be expected. Bobby was ready to learn. He had ideas, he had youth, he had backup. He asked about everything he didn't know, he studied books on what he couldn't learn from the people around him, he remembered the answers, he followed his hunches. His input was already being felt around Cairo. A new entrance door and door frame had gone up. Healthy drinks outnumbered sodas in two spanking-new coolers. Single beers had disappeared from the walk-in lineup. Major structural renovations were on the way, including a re-shelving of the wine section and a redesign of the deli. Fliers and ads were promoting Cairo aggressively to all the hotels, private firms, embassies, and diplomatic missions in a two-mile radius. Where I had been satisfied with whatever walked through the door, Bobby went after business like a fox on a trail. Cairo's gross was up less than four months into his reign.

"Jay? Is that really you?"

"I think."

Bobby and Jay shook hands across the counter. I strolled the aisles before going over to the deli, drawn by the smell of frying bacon. Bola and Gana, the compatriot he had brought in as second hand, were slicing meats and prepping vegetables for the lunch rush, two people when Lisha had been running the show by herself with Jay helping here and there. (Had Maggie seen Gana she would have had a fit. Delicate and sophisticated, maybe too much so for a kitchen, the girl looked every bit like the nymphs I had been accused of hiring for my own evil purposes. Maggie hated Cairo, though she had had me name it after her favorite Woody Allen movie. It was the one place where she wasn't the boss.) The menu board was as appealing as ever. 24 sandwiches all named after friends and family, 15 combos, 8 different kinds of bread, *empanadas*, salads, sushi, sweets. One of my old customers, an accountant who'd finished second on the "Survivor" show two years ago, walked in and ordered a Ben's Best on toasted rye, no onions, extra chili peppers. I smiled and complimented her on her good taste.

"Chris around?" Jay asked.

Bobby nodded, his forehead shining under a Dogfish neon hung too low. Among the pints and miniature bottles displayed in wine crates behind him, a boxed Johnnie Blue caught my eye. "For now."

"Something wrong?"

"Different styles. Chris knows I'd be in a jam without him and he lets me feel it. Want your old job back?"

Jay shook his head. "Too many memories."

Bobby bowed gracefully. "I can understand that."

The red-brick basement was as small and dark as I remembered. Storage had been the one thorn in my foot: The supplies that came in every day had to be hauled down 16 narrow and crooked steps, carried through a bolted door and stacked on pallets or on the shelves lining the walls--only to be brought back upstairs as we needed them. No way around it. The building was too old and the basement too small for belts, rollers, or a shaft. It was backbreaking work, and the main reason why my turnover had been out of this world. Young men in their prime lasted about three months, even at $10 an hour with free meals and paid vacations. I had given up on outside help about two years ago, solely relying on Chris, Jay, and myself. All three of us ended up suffering from chronic muscular pain as well as cuts, blisters, and calluses. Yvonne, a natural-remedy buff, shipped us homemade unguents from Germany regularly. Nicole introduced me to massages and acupuncture. (When I woke up in the funeral parlor and found out I could fly and float, the first thing I did was pat my back carefully, expecting a jolt. It was supple as a youngster's and completely worry-free. My whole body felt brand new, in fact. I had consistency, I had mass, yet I was able to go through solid objects. Ah, the vast wonders of death!) We used to stack as many as 12 cases on a dolly going down, and up to 8 going up. Men being men, we played at timing ourselves with a full load, first with our eyes open, then with our eyes closed, then with one hand. We knew these stairs as if we had built them.

"Bobby's doing a good job keeping his inventory in

check, ain't he, Dad?" Jay said.

The boy knows his stuff, I agreed.

Chris came out of the bathroom with The Post under his arm. His already bulging eyes opened wide when he recognized Jay. "Look what the wind blew in! What's up, man?"

"Chris."

They hugged under the bare bulbs.

"What you been up to?" Chris asked.

"Resting," Jay answered. "Taking it easy."

Chris rubbed his own clean-shaven chin. "What's the ZZ Top beard about? Going rock 'n' roll on us?"

"A little hippie phase," Jay said. "But look who's talking."

Chris shook his mane. Wide of shoulders, hair cascading down his back, he looked like a more muscular Jay. Seven years he'd been with me, a Maryland redneck who had roamed the countryside with a death metal band for most of his youth before throwing in the towel after his father passed away, leaving him a house in Mount Pleasant and a decent chunk of money. Chris carried himself like a Viking. His back was always straight, he held his liquor, his grip was firm, he looked you in the eye, his girl was solidly built. On the flip side, he thought he knew everything about everything, he didn't know his place, his tongue was too sharp for his own good, and his conceit bordered on delusion.

They sat on beer boxes. Chris was the big brother Jay had never had. They talked girls, drugs, music, and politics. Same easygoing approach to life. Both loved America and loathed Empire, its more supremacist, pugilistic, evil-minded, meddling, dominating, and far-reaching early 21st century incarnation. A firm believer in doomsday, Chris always babbled about moving to Europe--getting out and blanking out was his solution.

"Anywhere but here, man. It's only a matter of time before these terrorists get us. All the people who can afford to are migrating. I'm looking at a small house in the Carpathian Mountains. Yvonne loves it up there. Beautiful and dirt-cheap."

Jay, optimistic against all odds, was in favor of working the system from the inside. "The terrorists will leave us alone once we stop messing things up in their countries. Whatever happens to America will be of her own doing."

"The terrorists will never leave us alone," Chris countered. "You know why? Somebody's gotta be on top."

"They'll never beat us, man. America will prevail no matter what. We're too strong as a nation, as a people."

"I'm with you on that. God forbid the turbaned win and enforce *sharia* all over the world. But a global *pax Americana* is decades away. You can't be at war and not expect civilian casualties. The World Trade Center was just the beginning. They'll bring the fight to our homes, our schools, our businesses. I don't want my ass to get caught in the crossfire. That's all I'm saying."

It went on and on. How many hours had they spent analyzing and reconstructing the world?

Chris searched my son's face. "How you holdin' up, man?"

"Hanging in there."

"We miss your father around here."

91

"I miss him, too," Jay admitted.

Chris shook his head. "That fucking nigger Leslie.... They sentence him yet?"

The word made Jay wince.

"What I say?" Chris asked.

Jay looked him in the eye. "'Nigger.' That makes me uncomfortable."

Chris cracked a smile. "You're funny."

It's gonna be an uphill battle, Jay told himself before saying, "Leslie plea bargained and got 15."

Chris grunted derisively. "Bet you he won't serve more than ten."

"Probably."

"We can bust his cap as soon as he steps a foot outside jail."

"That's an idea," Jay said without much conviction. The only time we'd seen Chris in action was when he chased a thief all the way to R Street only to come running back in the store when the man turned around, pulled out a knife, and started chasing him.

I left the two of them to go check on my stash of *grands crus* and single malts. They were still in the hollow panel between the champagne and liquor rooms, hidden behind the ancient ice machine I had inherited when I took over. The day Bobby decided to get rid of the rusty thing it'd be over. Better him than some wrecking ball a hundred years from now.

Hearing voices, I crossed the ceiling and a wall to get into the flower shop next door. The same three people had been working there for over a decade. Vladimir was as tanned as ever, the darkest Ukrainian you were likely to meet--darker even than Mary, who was Indian, and Monica, who'd run barefoot across wheat fields in Chile as a child. They were getting fresh bunches in, early daffodils among them, the cheap and bloodstained stuff from Colombia and El Salvador that they resold for a fortune. I faced Vladimir for the first time since that fateful night, my blood running cold, anger making my fists shake. I wished my arms were as powerful as when I was alive. Choke him with my bare hands I would have in front of his coworkers, squeezing him slowly while he wiggled in vain, his iron-pumper's arms overmatched. But I couldn't will myself back to life. Vladimir wouldn't die today. I cursed him, cursed him again, cursed him with all my might. I invited upon him the bloating, maggots, bursting, putrefaction, and rot that my body was suffering in Maggie's discounted off-mahogany coffin.

Jay and I left Cairo after he got $500 from Chris, who always carried a full wallet in order to make up, perhaps involuntarily, for hungrier times. "Got some of that green," Chris intimated. "You up?"

Jay thought about the voice, Delroy's song, and his new mind-set. Was this how he was supposed to start anew: with a fat spliff? "Not today, bro," he refused.

They hugged goodbye.

"'Preciate that," Jay said, patting his pocket.

Chris nodded. "You need more, you come see me."

Going up the stairs together felt like the good old days. Nobody had put in more sweat and time in Cairo than us three. It was a second home and much more. Chris and I had been open-to-close, six days a week. Jay had officially joined the team after dropping out of college, having already spent a good chunk of his adolescence helping me around. The place was awash in memories. It's here that Jay and I truly bonded. Here that Chris met Yvonne. Here that I met Nicole. Here that Jay met Lisha. ("We call it *droit de cuissage*," Steve told Maggie when she confided how I, and Jay, and Chris, had been "preying" on employees, saleswomen, customers, "and every long-legged thing that came through that damn door.") Here, in a sense, that I died. We had made Cairo. Cairo, in turn, had made, and unmade, us.

Jay and I got back in the Eldorado after he grabbed a bottle of water. I scanned the streets as we rolled past, hoping for a glimpse of Nicole. This was her neighborhood, too. Her place was only three blocks away, one of those immense lofts with raised ceilings, recessed lighting, exposed pipes, hardwood floors, stainless steel appliances, and glass for walls. The "Industrial Condo in the Sky," I used to call it. Lisha and Marina's apartment, though close by, was nothing like that. Still, it had felt for a good long while like Jay and I were fishing in the same waters, to the point of walking together to our honey spots after closing the shop, father and son, partners in crime. He ducked into his building and I ducked into mine, See you when I see you. Jay, like everybody who knew Nicole, had been in awe. Of her for being who she was; of me for being her man.

God, I wanted to see her. Somebody please find my baby and tell her Mackie's back in town.

"I'm taking you to her," Jay announced as if he had

heard my plea.

I relaxed in my seat, smiling.

We followed Q until we reached 7th, turning left. After it crossed Florida Avenue, 7th became Georgia Avenue and suddenly the name Chocolate City took on its full meaning. I sat cross-legged on the Eldorado's roof the better to enjoy the scenery. Car washes, Chinese parlors, nail salons, booze dives, seafood counters, barbers, drugstores, chicken shacks, Howard University, Banneker High, Afro-centric boutiques, table vendors, strolling bootleggers, Laundromats, record stores, dance halls, police cruisers, yellow police tape, drug corners, hangers-on, ripped phones, go-go bills, rowhouses, loudspeakers, fenced lots, pit bulls, babies, whitewalls.... Georgia shined, Georgia crackled, Georgia simmered, Georgia hustled. Smell, sound, vibration, pulse, people, soul. This was the real D.C. to me. So much more authentic than the White House, K Street, the Mall, and Capitol Hill. Life, not at its easiest, but at its most real.

"Here we are," Jay said as we parked in front of Happy Cuts, Nicole's salon, on the stretch of Georgia one block south of Kennedy Street. Happy Cuts was sandwiched between an old 7-Eleven and Macondo Lounge, a gentlemen's club of ill repute. A struggling shoemaker and the pink awning of Wings 'n' Things closed the strip. A towing company, a disaffected black-owned bank, a liquor store, a funeral parlor, and a gas station graced the other side of the avenue. Kennedy Street east of Georgia was the main attraction in this neighborhood, called Brightwood Park. It was home to KDY3 and KDY5, housing projects respectively at 3rd and Kennedy and 5th and Kennedy. Sprinkled among the crew members, their families, and their customers, were blue-collar people, Howard students, retired folks, immigrants from West Africa and the Caribbean. Though still rough by D.C. standards, it was a place where a white man driving a '69 Eldorado didn't cause a major stir.

Nicole saw Jay parking behind her BMW through the window. She welcomed him on the steps, apron around her waist, a braiding comb in her hand, a smile on her face. I hugged her as she hugged Jay, filling my lungs with her and holding her in, wanting to touch and rub and feel and lose myself a little more, crying like a baby, as overwhelmed by her presence as when I was alive. She, and the things we did together, had always been too much. Too much beauty, too much know-how, too much poise, too much youth. We used to joke, lying on her immense bed, that she'd give me a heart attack one day, riding me right into my death, the Horsewoman of the Apocalypse and her aging horse--if those Cairo steps didn't kill me first. Nicole. Feminine to a T, brown eyes on light-brown skin, short hair, made-to-order chest and ass that were breathtaking in their plump perfection. "I paid for them," she told me the first time she undressed in front of me, the afternoon light coloring her gold, cream lace coming off her skin faster than my eyes could see, her scent going to my head as I buried myself in her belly. "Nothing about my body is real, Ben. Just so you know."

"You got your money's worth," is what I answered from down below, knowing from that moment on that I was lost, my poor mind doing its best to keep up. Was I dreaming? Who was Nicole? What did she want from me?

Was this really happening?

You didn't so much look at Nicole as you blessed your eyes on her. And in many ways it's what our relationship had felt like to me: a blessing. Totally unexpected, probably undeserved, most likely wrong, too sublime for either one of us to stop and wonder and ask questions. I loved her. Not just until the day I died but way after, well into my death, right up to now.

Jay started to cry. I hadn't seen him let go until this moment. Not at the rented-out funeral hall, not in Arlington, not at the house. I had thought that he would forever keep it inside. But here, in Nicole's arms, on Georgia and Kennedy, he let it all come out as she held him tighter and tighter, patting his back, hushing him, crying just as hard. These are the two people who really care, I told myself. These are the ones who truly miss you.

"Sorry for your loss," Nicole whispered. "And sorry I didn't come. It was ... not my place, you know?"

"I understand," Jay said, pulling away.

They went in, walking all the way to the back.

The three other girls and the salon's customers acted as if they hadn't seen a thing. What more natural for a hippie who had just finished crying his heart out on the sidewalk than to walk in and get a shave and haircut?

"Sit right here and wait for me," Nicole told Jay after leading him into the shampoo room. "I'll be done in a little while. You eat yet?"

Jay shook his head.

"Chinese O.K.?"

He nodded.

She placed the call.

97

He ate his fried rice in a barber's chair.

There was something reassuring about the women's conversation and their laughter. Happy Cuts was a cozy little place. The walls were peach and green. Music was always playing. Pictures framed the biggest mirror: babies, friends, family, customers, and me.

Nicole tied a towel around Jay's neck and gave him a full wash. His hair was matted in places. At others, it fell in clumps. Appalled, she scrubbed his scalp raw. "What have you been doing to yourself?"

"Stopped cleaning. Stopped washing. Stopped eating. Damn near stopped living."

She tapped his forehead. "It sure shows, baby. You were about to lose it all."

Jay shrugged. "Least of my worries. What about you? How's business?"

She sighed. "One day at a time."

"Think you can help me find a job?"

She rinsed his head and covered it with a towel. I felt jealous. Nicole's touch. Nicole's hands. Nicole's warmth. Nicole's care. Oh, those massages.... "What are you looking for?"

"Something low-key," Jay said, looking at her in the mirror. "Like a little corner store. Preferably in an underserved area."

Nicole grabbed her heaviest clippers. "You mean the ghetto."

Jay smiled.

"Still hell-bent on saving the world, I see. It used to drive your father crazy, you know?"

"I know."

They paused to think of me, each in a different way. I was in 7th heaven.

Nicole sighed again. "How do you want your hair?"

"Real low," Jay instructed.

"That's about all you can get," she concurred, laughing. "Ain't no styling this mess."

She did his beard right behind it. It made Jay think of Clint Eastwood westerns.

"Still seeing Lisha?"

"She dumped me."

"Your fault or hers?"

"Mine."

"That's too bad. I really liked the girl."

"Me, too...." Jay said. "Me, too."

"Doing something about it?"

"I might."

He had a hard time recognizing himself afterward. He looked older. His cheeks had sunk, his ears were sticking out, his eyes had an edge to them. "Just what I needed. Thank you."

"How does it feel?" Nicole asked.

Jay ran a thumb across his skull, and then his jawline. "Liberating."

She wouldn't take his money, so he slipped a 50 under a clipper when she wasn't looking.

"I don't know how 'underserved' you like your areas," Nicole quipped as he was getting ready to leave. "But if Brightwood works for you, go to the bodega next door and talk to Nasro. His helper just quit. Little cutie named Alcaly who just got himself a major book deal."

"This store right next door?"

Nicole nodded. "Tell Nasro I sent you." She hugged Jay. I hugged her. "Come back and let me know how it went."

"I will."

Jay stood in front of the old 7-Eleven. We could see where the sign had been hanging. The layout was also typical, inside and out. Glass panel facing the sidewalk, small aisles, short shelves, long orange counters. Nasro was Middle Eastern or East African. 60s and showing every minute of it despite his jeans and checkered shirt. He had all his hair, a mustache, white teeth, piercing black eyes, a lean frame. Hard to judge how tall he was because of the elevated cashier station. Jay observed him ring two teenagers up, attentive and energetic, polite without being obsequious. The kids were dressed the same and smelled like weed. Their eyes were red. They talked and acted goofy. The one who bumped into Jay on the way out didn't apologize.

"Can I help you?" Nasro asked Jay after the teenagers had left.

Jay stepped forward. "I'm here for the job."

Nasro seemed taken aback. "What job?"

"The helper's job," Jay told him. "Aren't you hiring?"

"No," Nasro said.

"No?" Jay asked.

"No," Nasro repeated emphatically.

They stared at each other across the counter. I wandered away, looking at the items on the shelves. 7-Eleven would have never carried packs of synthetic hair, turbans, kaffiyehs, socks, Kootchie diapers, We R One and Madness Connection T-shirts, off-white knee-high stockings, So-Dry hygienic pads, children's toys, tortillas, noodles, Huggie juices, cheddar-flavored sunflower seeds, twisted donuts, beef patties, school supplies, "Back Yard Live at the Ibex-The Golden Years 94-96" go-go CDs, and "King of the Streetz" DVDs.

The silence in the store got heavy. It was Nasro who broke it. "I know why you're really here," he said, opening his palms. "I don't have anything to hide. You go and tell your people. I.R.S., F.B.I., Homeland Security, Customs ... whoever you work for. Tell them they don't need to send me a spy. Whatever they want to know about Nasro, they can come and ask Nasro. I'm an American citizen. I pay my taxes. I don't donate to Islamic charities. I don't support Hezbollah or Hamas or the Taliban. I don't build bombs in my back room. My daughters don't wear the hijab. I do pray five times a day, and, Allah willing, I plan to attend the next Haj in Mecca. So go in peace, brother. Tell your bosses I'm clean."

With the dignity and quiet outrage of a victimized king, Nasro crossed his arms and pointed at the door with his chin.

Jay let out a short laugh. "I don't work for anybody," he said. "I'm here for the job. Seriously."

Nasro looked him up one more time and shook his head. "No job."

Jay started to walk away. "I forgot to give you the password," he said, his hand on the door.

"What password?"

"Nicole."

Like ice melting under the sun, Nasro's face relaxed into a smile. "No white man has ever walked into my store asking for work. I thought you were looking for trouble."

He walked around the counter and joined Jay on the floor. "Welcome to Souk Number One," he said, offering his hand.

"What happened to your hair?" Maggie asked Jay at dinner--a lean salad and grilled steaks that a big cabernet would have complimented very nicely, but I guess that's just the sommelier in me talking.

"Trying something new," Jay said.

"Haven't seen you this clean in years," she approved, munching on croutons. "You look kinda cute."

"Thank you," Jay said.

He was clean for Arlington, I reminded them, wondering what was up with their notion of time. Maybe this was to be my true purpose in death: To record everything, to be my family's keeper of memories.

"He looks like a Marine," Joe intervened. "Like his daddy back in the day. Like he's ready for war."

"Thank you," Jay, imperturbable, repeated.

"Joining the army?" Maggie asked.

"Wouldn't dream of it," Jay assured her. "Not in this lifetime. Not under this regime. These people have no clue what a true superpower is supposed to do."

"Jay's only been awake for a day," Joe wisecracked. "Give the man time to find his bearings, Ma."

"Zzzzz," Maggie guffawed.

Here y'all go again, I muttered. Ganging up on my boy.

"Got me a gig," Jay announced evenly.

"What kind?" Joe asked.

"Already?" Maggie blurted out, impressed beyond belief. Maybe Jay wasn't such a loser after all.

"Souk Number One," Jay told them.

Maggie: "What's that?"

"A bodega," Jay explained.

Joe: "Where?"

"Georgia Avenue," Jay said.

Joe: "What part?"

"Uptown."

Maggie: "What kind of word is 'zouk'?"

Me: "souk," Mag. It's "souk." You used to be a teacher, for God's sake.

Joe: "He said 'sous,' Ma. 'Sous.'"

"I said 'souk,'" Jay corrected. "That's what they call markets in Arab cities: 'souks.'"

Joe raised an eyebrow when he heard the word 'Arab.'

A profound distaste twisted Maggie's lips. "Who owns that Zoo Number One?"

Goddamn it, I said loudly, seeing the argument coming from miles away, afraid that our nice family gathering would get irremediably spoiled. How many more times would we sit like this, all four of us around the table?

Jay kept his cool. "The owner's a Sudanese man called Nasro. Decent guy. Moved here in the mid-'80s to escape persecution. Seems like we'll get along fine."

Joe stopped eating. "Persecution? What kind of

104

persecution could a Sudanese man suffer in the mid-'80s?"

"That's Africa for you," Maggie answered. "They're always killing one another like dogs."

"Religious persecution," Jay said. "Nasro belonged to the Republican Brotherhood."

Joe: "What's that?"

Maggie: "What's that?"

"A small group whose leader was hanged for reinterpreting the Koran," Jay revealed. "Interesting, isn't it? But that's all Nasro would say."

"Google it," Joe suggested. "And watch your back. That Brotherhood sounds like a bunch of terrorists to me. Maybe there's a good reason why your dude Nassau ran. Maybe he was on his way to the scaffold like his boss."

Jay shook his head. "I'll wait to hear Nasro's side of the story."

"You and your underdogs," Maggie sighed. "Nothing moves you quite like a ragtag, ramshackle bio. Always need you some sheep to herd and a movement to champion. Like you're in any position to help."

Joe, who had started to drift off, snapped back to attention when he heard "movement," thinking his mother was on to him.

You know "ragtag" and "ramshackle," I told Maggie. But you've never heard of "souk."

"I don't care if you end up a Republican Brother yourself--" Maggie went on, "whatever that means. Just don't bring any trouble to your brother or me or this house. Your father broke my heart enough times already."

That's it, I said, jumping from my seat to the window, my dinner completely spoiled. Had I had the

105

power to, I would have flown far into space or deep inside Earth. But I knew, having already tried, that my upward boundary was the roof and my downward one the house's foundations. I had yet to tackle the deep sea, but I was hopeful.

"I'll Google that Brotherhood before going to bed, Ma," Joe assuaged Maggie. "Damn it if we're going to be as gullible as Jay."

"What's with you and Google?" Jay asked his brother.

"Google knows everything," Joe said. "That's what. If it exists, it's on Google. You should know that. Weren't you a computer science major before dropping out and running to stock Cairo's shelves like a good son?"

Jay felt his fists itch. "Better that than being a mama's boy," he said. "I quit school because I was depressed. That could happen to anybody. I'm not the one who got kicked out for roofying and raping a girl. And Google was founded way after I left."

Joe got agitated. "Who roofied and raped a girl? I never roofied and raped a girl!"

Jay went for the kill, shocking the hell out of me. "Google yourself and see what pops up, bro. Since you got so much faith in them."

I laughed at Joe's discomfiture.

Maggie raised a palm.

Jay and Joe caught themselves in midair.

"What's a corner store gonna do for you anyway?" Maggie asked Jay.

He smiled, knowing that whatever type of employment he chose, it would never be enough for her.

"It's a start, Ma. I know stores, from helping dad all these years. It'll be easy for me."

Don't justify yourself, I prodded him.

Joe, still smarting from the rape remark, jumped back into the fray: "One thing I like about you, Jay: You don't let ambition stand in your way. Going for the quick kill every time."

"Last time I checked you didn't have a job," Jay counterattacked.

Joe smiled sweetly. "Got something big lined up, bro. And you better believe it ain't no C-store."

"Kiss my ass," Jay said in a very Zen way, incompatible as it sounds.

Kiss his ass, I echoed.

Fed up, Maggie looked around for her ladle. It wasn't in the living room, and she couldn't remember leaving it in the kitchen. Maybe in our upstairs bedroom. There was a pearl-handle automatic scotched under the table a few inches to her right, in any case. "Don't start," she warned the boys. "Lest I squeeze a couple of rounds into each one of you."

"You wouldn't shoot us," Joe argued.

"Like hell I wouldn't," Maggie asserted.

Jay looked into his mother's eyes. "She would."

I bet she would, I said as well.

They dropped the matter.

Maggie, who was still hungry, surveyed the table. The meal had gone down nice and easy--maybe too easy. Mango sorbet would finish her off just right. She sent Joe to the kitchen. "Grab me that Häagen-Dazs and a big spoon, would you?" And to Jay: "I'm thinking about selling the

107

house."

"You want the pint?" Joe shouted, his head in the freezer.

"The half-gallon," Maggie shouted back.

"How long do I have?" Jay asked.

"Couple of months," Maggie told him. "That fair?"

Jay nodded. "I'll be ready. Can I go on using dad's car?"

Maggie smiled benevolently. "As long as you don't wreck it. That's going up for sale, too."

Jay and I both cringed. "Maybe I can buy it from you," he proposed.

"What with?" Joe said, placing the huge container in front of Maggie. "You don't have any money."

You stay out of it, I warned Joe.

Maggie scooped up a mountain of sorbet, marveling at how pretty it looked and how delightful it smelled. "That Caddy's a classic, Jay. I want 10 grand for it."

10 grand? I was appalled. Jay, who deserved to keep the car for free, appeared merely crestfallen. "Negotiable?"

Maggie felt her heart swoon. Delicious. The sorbet was simply delicious. "We'll talk," she told Jay.

He and Joe cleaned the table.

All of us went to sit in front of the TV.

Joe burped loudly. "Too much vinegar in that dressing, Ma."

"That's why they call it a vinaigrette. What do you guys want to watch?"

"Anything but sports," Jay, who was afraid to go to bed and hear more voices in the thick of the night, requested.

"No soaps, please," asked Joe, who felt wide awake after holing up in his room all day.

"You guys make it hard," Maggie protested, surfing channels at the speed of light.

"Right there!" Jay exclaimed after seeing Bob Marley in black and white and hearing the intro to "Exodus."

"Who's that?" Joe asked.

"That's Bob," Jay said.

"PBS," Maggie announced.

"Can we check it out?" Jay asked.

Maggie sighed. "Five minutes, that's all. You already know his story by heart."

"*I* don't," Joe told her, immediately drawn in by the reverential tone of the documentary's narrator and the near-sanctity of the grainy footage: Marley in concert, Marley as a shaman bathed in blue stage lighting, Marley as a prophet, Marley and women, Marley hitting spliffs, Marley and the press, Marley and Peter and Bunny, Marley and the Wailers, Marley getting shot, Marley in his Babylon exile, Marley playing soccer in Central Park, Marley in his Tuff Gong studio, Marley feeding thousands of destitute Jamaicans at 56, Hope Road, Marley soloing a heavenly and subdued "Redemption song" on a blue guitar. Asked bluntly by an interviewer what he did with his money, the star allowed a wide grin to spread across his face. "Me give it all away," he answered, mischief dancing in his eyes as if he had just been caught turning a good joke on the world. Marley the king: red Adidas track suit, thick locks framing his handsome face, his teeth sparkling like a lion's.

Joe was riveted. Riveted. To think that he had never

given reggae a second thought--no later than this morning, with Jay blasting that "Better Must Come" stuff. To think that he had dismissed Bob as another hairy island monkey without ever paying attention to what he had had to say. "Me give it all away." Simple as that. Here was a man among men, a glorious heart, someone who walked the walk, the archetype of the Church of Retribution's guide. "Me give it all away" as the one true philosophy. "Me give it all away" as the only thing to do.

They ended up watching the whole thing, down to Bob's untimely death at the age of 36 and the miles-long procession accompanying the casket to his native Nine Miles village. Little Ziggy danced at the funeral, smartly dressed in a suit and shiny shoes, backed by the Melody Makers and the I-Threes.

"I wonder how much they spent on that ceremony," Maggie mused.

"That's what we should have done for dad," Jay said, imagining himself dancing for his father, dancing in front of a crowd, dancing to celebrate a glorious spirit. "Something lavish. Something fun."

"Your dad was no national hero," Maggie shrugged. "Nobody would have danced for him. People barely showed."

"He was a hero to me," Jay said, filling my heart with pride. "Corny as it may sound. And people didn't show because that mortuary was a dump."

Yeah, I told Maggie: That mortuary sure was a dump.

"The cheat got the funeral he deserved," Joe told Jay, aligning himself with Mag--no surprise here.

110

"You guys are wrong," Jay said.

"*Time will tell*," the documentary's score went, all acoustic guitars, synthesizers, and percussion. "*Oh, time will tell/ Think you're in heaven but you're living in hell.*"

"Was he for real?" Joe asked as the credits rolled.

Jay was incensed. "Bob? Of course he was. Google him."

"I'm serious," Bob whined, not in a fighting mood any more. "The man seemed kind of powerful."

"Still is," Jay elaborated. "More than 25 years after his death. He's just been nominated Artist of the 20th Century."

"Joe's into that kind of stuff now," Maggie informed Jay.

Joe's into tricking the whole world, I said.

"Shut up, Ma," Joe pleaded.

He's into what?" Jay asked.

"Don't tell me to shut up," Maggie roared, rapping her knuckles on the top of Joe's skull.

"What kind of stuff?" Jay asked again.

"Prophets," Maggie said.

"Prophets?" Jay wondered aloud.

"Prophets," Maggie confirmed.

"Since when?" Jay asked.

"That's exactly what I said, "Maggie said: "'Since when?'"

"Since I feel the need to help," Joe announced with a crimson face.

Jay was incredulous. "You? Help?"

"That's what I said," Maggie said again. "My reaction, exactly."

"I can help if I want to," Joe affirmed. "It's my business."

Jay still couldn't believe his ears. Joe? His Joe? Pretty Joe? Selfish Joe? Joe Babylon? "Help who, bro?"

"The poor," Joe said.

"Niggers," Maggie said.

Don't say that, I told her.

"You can't say that," Jay told her.

"Says who?" Maggie said.

"It's wrong," Jay said.

It's wrong, I concurred.

"It's wrong," Joe agreed.

Et tu, Joe? Maggie turned the TV off. "What the fuck is going on in this house?" she hollered.

"What do you mean?" Joe asked.

"What do you mean?" Jay asked.

"You are *not* going to drive me crazy!" Maggie said.

Jay attempted to appease her. "Come on, Ma."

So did Joe. "Don't get upset, Ma--your blood pressure."

You're already crazy, I assured Maggie.

"Niggers everywhere I turn," Maggie started to ramble. "Ben boning that freak behind my back. Joe wanting to go to a black church. You, Jay, getting a job in the ghetto. And now I can't say 'nigger' in my own house?"

Jay's eyes popped. His jaw almost dropped. "Joe's going to a black church?"

Joe smiled meekly. "Not really. Not yet."

"What's going on?" Maggie shouted again, her hand looking for the gun under the cushion.

"Nothing," Jay assured her, looking at Joe.

"Nothing," Joe said in turn.

Maggie found the gun, aimed it at the ceiling, and pressed the trigger twice. The detonation deafened all four of us and punched holes above our heads, barely missing the chandelier that had always been such a bitch to clean.

"In your room!" Maggie shouted, a cloud of plaster enveloping her rapidly. "Now! Both of you!"

Their chests shaken by a sudden cough, the boys jumped from the couch and crawled in opposite directions.

Joe and Jay were left unfazed by the outburst. They knew it was only a matter of time before Maggie would succumb to the temptation and open fire. Just another milestone in the long road to complete dysfunction. The damage, as it was, was minimal. None of the neighbors called the cops. Steve, who thought he had heard something as he fiddled in his garage, phoned before coming over for a nightcap. "Is everything all right?" he asked with a concerned expression.

"Everything's fine," Maggie cooed as she let him in, the gun's discharge making her feel powerful and sexy. "You'll have to pardon the dust."

Steve was in shorts, T-shirt, and sneakers, his eyes blinking behind his glasses, his hands and nails full of grease. Maggie pulled him off the doorstep, slammed the door shut, pushed him against the wall, and glued herself into him mouth first and tongue out, her eyes closed, her palms feeling him up, her heart racing, blood sloshing through and through, something moving and calling and moistening down below, the old mechanisms snapping and clicking and oozing back into action.

"You taste like mango," Steve said when he managed to catch his breath. *"Ma petite chérie. Ma douce. Ma cocotte."*

Spurred by the words she couldn't understand but imagined totally endearing, Maggie moaned and rubbed her vast pelvis on Steve's crotch.

Jay and Joe had found refuge in Jay's room. Joe thought it funny that it looked so clean and smelled so good. "What a difference, man."

I went to sit on my armoire.

"So what's with you and prophets?" Jay asked.

"I've been having visions," Joe lied, saying the first thing that came across his mind.

"You, too?" Jay said.

"Don't tell me...?"

Jay nodded. They looked at each other. Brothers, enemies, competitors, opposites. How long since they had talked-talked, talked like the same blood, talked like civil and rational human beings? Jay invited Joe to sit at the desk. "You first."

I sneaked back into the living room and found it empty. Maggie had swept Steve off his feet and carried him to the top of the stairs. Could tonight be the night? She kicked the door and dropped Steve on the bedroom carpet. I thought she was going to let herself fall on him but he was able to get up quickly. Maggie put her back against the door, snatched off her plastic reading glasses and threw them across the room. "Come here."

Trapped. Steve was trapped. She pulled him by the collar. Steve crashed into her, his arms flapping helplessly.

114

His own glasses flew. Then his shirt, his belt, his shorts. I hooted with laughter when I saw his oversized boxers, but Maggie was on a roll. "My *petite chérie*," she murmured, licking Steve's left ear. Breathing hard, she kissed him again, neglecting to turn on the light.

I crossed back into Jay's room.

Joe was laying it think. Having declined Jay's offer to sit, he was standing in the middle of the room with his arms crossed and his head bowed, a carefully scripted version of his empty self, Joe as a more mature, I'm-so-over-the-whole-pettiness-of-a-little-while-ago little brother. "It's always the same thing," he was saying. "I see myself healing black people. Doing good deeds, you know? Like, helping them. Building rec centers, founding programs, lobbying the city for better amenities and services for their benefit. I don't know why, man. Never been that type of guy, and I'm sure you know what I mean. It's like somebody's trying to send me a message or something."

Jay nodded. "Dad, you think?"

"Could be, man." Joe wiped an imaginary tear for more effect. "I just want my life to have a real purpose from now on. I want to embrace everybody. I'm ready to make up for my mistakes."

"Like that rape?"

"I didn't rape that girl," Joe protested for the umpteenth time, with just the right dose of righteous anger, he hoped. "We drank, we went to my room, we had sex, we woke up, she cried wolf."

Jay wasn't convinced. "Nothing to do with you wanting to have a black girl, right? Nothing with you and your frat buddies donning Afro wigs and blackfaces on that very Halloween night?"

"I'll give you the Afros and blackfaces. Bad joke, even if we weren't the first. But, one, that girl was sleeping with everybody on campus, and two, she was passing herself off as white. She looks just like me and you, Jay. How many black girls named Rebecca who talk with a preppie accent do you know? If I wanted to rape a black girl I would have gone for the real thing, like one of my ex-classmates. Her name's Ebony and she's really black, black-black, pitch-black. Only white you see on her is in her eyes."

"You sound like you were thinking about it."

Joe threw his hands up. "I'm not a rapist, man. Bottom line."

You lying son of a bitch, I sneered before going back to Maggie and Steve, stopping mid-wall to wonder if I should, really, walk in on them. Must ghosts adhere to a code or do we pretty much have carte blanche? What of privacy laws? What of Maggie's right to get down behind closed doors? What about dignity, honor, morals? Did I really want to become the one who saw it all and heard it all? Would I be held accountable for snooping in on people? Ah, those damn uncertainties....

The sound of a slap made me throw all caution and self-restraint to the wind and run to the other side. Steve was holding his cheek, his boxers down to his ankles. "What the fuck is wrong with you?" Maggie admonished him, towering over him in her full naked splendor, her breasts like two extra arms, her back and stomach and thighs an outrageous festival of rolls, her face a furious scowl. "Couldn't hold it longer than that?"

"You pulled on it too hard," Steve apologized, tears in his eyes and in his voice.

Slap her back, I urged him. Slap her back or that's the end of you. Come on, be a man.

"I should rip your nut sack off," Maggie went on. "Just for wasting my time."

"*Non!* " Steve pleaded. "*Non!*"

Maggie grabbed his penis and his balls and squeezed hard. Steve didn't dare move, afraid she'd make good on her word, and he didn't dare shout, scared that the boys might run upstairs and kick his ass. Maggie gave her hand a twist. *Petite chérie* was enraged. Enraged. The buildup, the little niceties, the bits and pieces, the sweet nothings, the muted courtship, the French lover phantasms. Steve was supposed to take her to higher heights, not shoot off his load at the first caress. This isn't how she'd imagined their first night. She felt cheated. She felt cheap. She felt ashamed. What was she, Margaret Agnes Wilson, doing butt-naked in the middle of her bedroom with this sorry little man not even a year after her husband passed away--God bless his misguided soul?

She twisted harder.

Steve squirmed.

"Beg," Maggie told him.

Steve bit his lip.

Fight back, I pressed him. Do something. Throw a punch.

"In French," Maggie barked, her face very close to his, the Devil in her eyes and on her tongue.

Vade retro, Satanas, I chanted with wild

117

movements of the arms. *Nunquam suade nihi vana.*

"*S'il te plait,*" Steve murmured, tears rolling down his cheeks.

Sunt mala quae libas, I went on. *Ipse venena bibas.*

A cold smile stretched Maggie's lips.

I shook my head at Steve. You're finished, you little punk. You're done. Say goodbye to your life. Say goodbye to everything you hold dear.

Back in Jay's room, Joe was in the middle of his pitch. "I'm thinking of a church," he was telling Jay, wondering just how much he should say and whether Jay really needed to know it all--what if he stole his idea? "A place where everybody could meet and work out their differences. No talk of God. Just black and white men and women getting together to try and find a way to get along."

"Sort of like the Washington Ethical Society?"

"What's that?"

"Local people who've made a commitment to live ethically. They're registered as a religion and offer Sunday school for children, ritual weddings, baby naming and stuff like that. All creeds and races welcome. They've been around forever."

"Where?"

"Right here on 16th. I thought about joining after reading a Post piece on them a while back. They're expanding."

"I'd like that location for my church," Joe revealed. "Eventually."

Jay nodded. "Those visions," he asked. "How exactly do they come about?"

118

Joe adopted the enlightened-yet-modest air of a mystic. "They happen unexpectedly," he said. "When I drive, when I walk, when I study. I'm transported to a different place. I leave one state for another. The light is blinding. The sounds are intense. The colors are breathtaking." Joe touched his heart. "The feeling of peace is overwhelming. People in great numbers sing, dance, and rejoice."

"Do you hear a voice?" Jay asked. "Is anybody saying anything to you?"

Joe shook his head. "I'm the one doing the talking," he said. "I preach, I harangue, I suffuse."

Jay laughed. "You 'suffuse'?"

Joe kept a straight face. "I suffuse and infuse. Love and understanding."

"In your church?"

"On stage, on the phone, on the Internet, on TV, on the radio, door to door, office to office, town to town, parish to parish."

"Just how big is your church?"

Joe drew a circle with his hands. "Big, man. My church is big."

Jay thought about it for a moment. "Your visions sound nothing like mine," he finally told Joe. "But they're inspiring just the same."

To say that what Jay had just heard was unexpected would be the understatement of the century. So Joe was having an epiphany at the same time as he. Joe, of all people. Jay was shocked, but who was he to judge? At least he wasn't the only one seeing and hearing things any more--boy, was that a relief. Maybe it was meant to be a family thing. Could Maggie be next? Was now the time for all of them to change their ways and find their true calling?

Jay looked at Joe, who was staring at the rug under the desk as if in deep, deep thought. 20 minutes earlier they were bickering about Google and calling each other names. Now here they were at the edge of a breakthrough. This is my little brother, Jay told himself. Rough as our path together has been, I owe him something. I should set an example. I should be the better man and bury the hatchet. Give trust in order to get trust.

Joe, who knew not to oversell, kept his eyes on the rug and his stance humble. I don't think he had an inkling right then of just how important Jay would become to his plans. Maggie had dropped the ball at dinnertime and he had found it necessary to explain things. Perhaps he was just practicing, preparing Jay for the surprises to come, taking care of home before going out into the world with his message.

Jay was torn. Every time he had trusted his brother Joe had given him cause to regret it. He had come to accept the fact that they would never be close, the same way he strove to take Maggie as she was and not as he wanted her to be. What, exactly, did he owe Joe? Guidance? Assistance? Unconditional love?

Joe, his head in the rug's intricate design, was waiting.

Jay, finding it hard to bridge a decade and a half of rift, talked to his brother in his head. You always fought me, he told him telepathically. You never allowed me to play my part. You refused my tutorship, you ridiculed my initiatives, you snubbed my overtures, you took my kindness for weakness. I don't think I was ever good enough, dude. People look up to their big brother. You, Joe, looked down. Yet I did my best. I fed you, I bathed you, I got you ready for school. I protected you against bullies. I checked on you in the halls. I talked to your teachers. I taught you how to ride bikes and to skateboard and to approach girls. I cried when you fell and banged your head. I helped with your homework. It all changed before you turned 10. You stopped listening. You countered every command I gave. You spat on my extended hand. You did your best to get me in trouble with Ma. Cut your palm with a piece of glass and told her I did it. Provoked me until I lost my temper and hit you, only to run to her and have her trounce me. What did you want: my place? It's not like it was a sinecure. You know how Ma never gave me a moment of rest and how Pa was absentminded to the point of neglect. I couldn't figure you out, Joe. Why not be together, why not be at peace? You were very manipulative. It was always about you. And so it is that I learned to stay in my corner. The whole world thought of me as this cool dude, but rejection was all I got from my brother and my mother. Now here we are. Two grown men. One foot out the door. Daddy dead, mommy steadily losing it. You're telling me that we're really very similar, you and I. You're saying that we're on the same trajectory. You're ready to talk, discuss things, and maybe become a part of my life. You want me, without saying as much, to accept you.

Jay took a deep breath.

Joe looked up.

There was conflict in Jay's eyes, but his voice was firm. "Remember those strange dreams I used to have

121

growing up? Weird, human-shaped creatures standing in front of my bed?"

"I remember," Joe, who had long ago forgotten, affirmed with conviction.

"They never let up," Jay said. "I can count my nights of true, uninterrupted, restful sleep."

"Serious?"

"Serious. They're changing, too."

"Changing how?"

"Somebody talked to me yesterday at dawn. Called me 'Believer.' Told me to get up."

"What a coincidence," Joe said, feeling ambivalent. Voices? What if Jay was stumbling into something even bigger than the Church of Retribution? What if he was going totally crazy?

Jay looked at him intently. "You think I'm crazy?"

Joe smiled. "No more than me."

"I'm not into churches," Jay went on. "I haven't thought things out that far. I just know that there are certain things in me I'd like to get rid of. I'm talking condescension, racism, or plain carelessness. I, too, have been called into action. I, too, am in search of a purpose. But I don't want to guide or preach or 'suffuse.' I just want to help."

Well said, I approved from my perch.

"How do you propose to do that?" Joe asked.

"Souk Number One," Jay said. "I happened on it by chance, but that whole area is a disaster zone. Two major housing projects two blocks apart on Kennedy Street. I want to reach out to all the very young kids there and see what I can do."

Joe nodded. "Kind of using the store as a shoehorn. Like the C.I.A. does with the Peace Corps. That's brilliant."

"I'm not using anything or anybody," Jay recused himself. "I'll be working a regular job. And while I'm at it I'll try to put myself to use."

"Try not to get killed," Joe said. "Poverty isn't pretty."

How would you know? I asked, flying back into Maggie's bedroom after my sons shook hands and wished each other good night.

Maggie and Steve had progressed to the bed after Steve cleaned with a wet towel the mess he'd made on the carpet. Maggie was sitting at the edge. Steve was standing in front of her. Her fingers were juggling his privates a little more delicately now that her mood had swung back to lovemaking. From the dejected look on Steve's face, things weren't looking up. Giving her wrist a rest, Maggie decided to put her glasses on and venture her lips on him just to see if that'd wake him up. She let out a gasp as soon as she brought her face near. "You're circumcised?"

"Yep," Steve said, caressing her hair.

Maggie spat on the carpet as if she had just kissed a spider. "Don't touch me."

Steve was near tears once more. "Now what's wrong?"

Maggie's eyes bore into his. "You're a Jew? What's your last name?"

"Taubelman," Steve said.

"Oh yeah, baby. You're as Jewish as they come. Why didn't you tell me?"

123

Steve's voice got smaller. "Didn't think it was important."

Maggie leaned back. "You didn't think it was important? In these days and times? Are you out of your mind?"

"What do you care?" Steve asked.

"What do I care? Do I look like a Jew lover to you? You told me you were French!"

Maggie seemed more disgusted than angry. Steve gathered his wits and sat next to her on the bed. "I am French. Of Jewish origin. Couldn't help my parents circumcising me, but I'm not practicing anything. Never went inside a synagogue. Married a goy. No bat mitzvah for my daughters. No Manischewitz on holidays. No Maimonides in my library. Not a single Torah. That a problem for you?"

Maggie appeared dubious. "Not sure."

They stayed silent. The moon looked pretty through the window. Maggie started to feel cold. She couldn't hear any noise coming from downstairs. The kids must have gone to bed. What a night. She would have to clean up all that plaster tomorrow. Call it quits or go for it? She was already undressed, and it had been a long time.

"You'll have to put some goodwill into it if you're gonna keep me up," she coaxed Steve. "What, it's just dead for the night?"

"You're too pushy," Steve said. "I don't feel like it any more."

Poor you, I said.

"Ben never had a problem performing his duties," Maggie claimed. "I had to slow him down, if anything.

Now that was a man."

Steve stifled a yawn. "You slowed him down so much that he went and got himself a mistress."

Maggie stiffened. "You're not attracted to me?"

"Not when you act like this."

"I'm ugly? I'm fat?"

"I didn't say that."

"I don't know any man who wouldn't react to a naked woman."

"I'm not at fault here."

"So what is it?"

"I don't know."

Maggie gave Steve's penis one last, halfhearted tug. Nothing. "I give up," she sighed. "Get out."

She turned the light on. Steve scrambled for his clothes and made for the door with an expression that he wanted dignified.

Frustrated out of her mind, Maggie looked frantically for the ladle before pulling the M-16 from under the bed and taking aim. "Crawl out of the room," she ordered Steve.

"What?"

"Crawl," she repeated.

How terrifying she looked, standing there. Steve buckled his belt and got on all fours, shaking. It took him three attempts to work the lock. Maggie poked him on the ass.

"*Aïe!*" Steve shouted. "*Aïe!*"

"Don't come back," Maggie told him.

Try a little tenderness, I sang. *Try a little tenderneeess!*

Steve let himself out and ran across the street.

Maggie went in the shower. I sat on the sink. She was more confused than anything else now, my Maggie. All those contradictory emotions. She might have even shed a few tears, but I wasn't sure. The fiasco with Steve scared her for her future. It had taken a lot to follow her heart and reveal her desire, she who used to be so prudish, or at the very least self-conscious, about those things. She had had exactly two boyfriends before me. No other man had touched her after we got wedded (not even me, a few years into the marriage). She had been willing to try with Steve, but now Steve was gone. Would she ever find a companion? Would she end up alone? Who would be there for her 10 or 15 years from now when her body and her mind started to go haywire? Alzheimer's scared her to no end: It ran in her family. What was so wrong with her that she couldn't encounter love, true love? Was she a monster? Was she abnormal?

I felt sad for her. Had I put her in this predicament? No. Did I experience guilt all the same? Yes. Things are always more complicated than they seem. People don't know, they don't necessarily understand why they do the things they do. Maggie couldn't see herself for who she was. Who can? I wanted to wrap my arms around her, comfort her, tell her it was going to be okay. Nobody deserves to be without love and friendship and companionship. Nobody wishes for the constant swings and pain and paranoia and messiness of an unbalanced mind.

Maggie came out of the bathroom and threw herself on the bed. The mattress cried under her, exhaled loudly, held on tight. Realizing she was still aroused, Maggie reached for my side, where the M-16 lay in all its gleaming splendor. Pulling it close, she clutched the butt to her chest and lodged the nozzle between her thighs. I can't describe the things that ran across her mind as the metal touched her sex. I can't describe the things she did with that machine gun.

I spent the rest of the night levitating between floors. Pity was the order of the session. Pity for my wife and kids. Pity for Steve. Pity for all of us tortured souls.

Jay's first couple of weeks at Souk Number One were uneventful. He got into the groove quickly. I had to admit that he had been right about one thing: A store is a store. Nasro showed him how to work the register but mostly Jay was on the floor and in the cooler, where he liked to be. "We got a white boy working for us?" could pretty much summarize the clientele's reaction. Jay was at first an oddity, an object of curiosity. People stopped by just to see. Some stared so much that they bumped into things or forgot what they had come to purchase. Unruly customers suddenly went quiet. Little girls wanted to touch his skin. Little boys pointed, turned, and ran away. Grown men checked their attitude at the door. Young toughs, feeling unduly threatened or challenged by his presence, got overly confrontational. Young women smiled tentatively--a cutie's a cutie, and the crossover appeal that had worked with Lisha was still there. To most, however, Jay represented the Man, that reviled figure of oppression and authority, the fist in their throats, the hand choking their necks, the foot in their behinds, the nosy cracker, the dream crusher, the playa hater. "Some of these people have never seen a white man up close who isn't a teacher, a lawyer, a judge, a police or probation officer," Nasro informed Jay. "Some have never seen a white man up close, period. Give them time."

Once their suspicions about Jay's true motives for being in their midst abated, the cluster of regulars adopted him the way a team picks a mascot. Those were people who came in every day, day after day, and rarely to buy--neighborhood fixtures, men who had patronized Souk for years and who counted themselves among Nasro's dearest friends. They formed a core that Jay called the Loyal Three. They always stood by the coffee station. They always started talking by mentioning the weather. They never stayed less than a half-hour. They were Claude, a self-professed entertainment lawyer who favored dark suits, Ray-Bans, ascots, and alligator shoes and who worked out of his Upshur Street apartment; Ahmet, a diminutive traveling salesman who sold everything from umbrellas to carpets to mink coats out of a burgundy Mercedes S.U.V.; Hakim, known as the Go-Go Imam, a black man who ran a struggling nearby mosque.

"If Nasro says you're all right then you're all right," Claude told Jay.

"'Preciate that," Jay said in return.

"You'll have to come for tea one of these days," Ahmet, who was simply known as Gypsy, invited him.

"I will," Jay said after thanking him.

"This a good man you're working for," Hakim, who always dressed in a flowing black robe, assured him.

"Nasro's the best," Jay agreed.

Souk wasn't so big that two men couldn't run it properly. Hours of operations were 7 to 9, seven days.

Nasro and Jay opened together. Soon after, the Kennedy Street kids mobbed the place on their way to school. Working men, homeless men, drunks, drug boys, drug fiends, and stay-at-home single moms were in and out for little nothings during most of the day. The kids came back with a vengeance between 3 and 6. 6 to 9, foot traffic from locals or Georgia Avenue's northbound commuters. Nasro and Jay were out by 9:15, Jay acting as a lookout while Nasro rolled the curtain down and snapped two huge locks in place.

Jay was grateful for the routine and eager to learn. "Why no lottery?" he asked Nasro on the first day.

"Lottery is *haram*," Nasro explained. "Evil. Proscribed. Bad for you."

"Cigars? Rolling papers? Cloves?"

"Same thing. Those looking to get high or go broke can go to Midnight, the liquor store across the street."

"You're losing sales."

"Only the ones I don't want."

"Is money *haram*?"

"By no means."

"Then why?"

Nasro smiled. "A man has to be honest and harmless to others in his commerce."

"Is that feasible?" Jay asked after pondering the maxim. "In this country, to practice commerce is to get over."

"Money doesn't run me," Nasro said.

You pompous freak, I told him. You holier-than-thou. It's easy for you to spit on the rest of us small businessmen.

130

"My dad had a problem with selling alcohol sometimes," Jay revealed. "When some of his customers would start going downhill without warning, showing up every day after a professional setback or a personal tragedy, disintegrating right in front of him. He felt like he was helping them die."

I knew exactly who Jay had in mind. His name was Mark. Smallish dude, glasses, silver hair, Brooks Brothers suits. Purchased a bottle of red once a week when things were good. Moved to a daily diet of one half-gallon of Bacardi Light, one two-liter Coke, and one pack of cigarettes after losing his job. Six months into his binge he started to come in with a scraggy beard, shaky hands, and feces-stained pants. Not a word, not a flicker of life in his eyes. Barely able to count his money and carry his bag. The last time he walked in we refused him the sale and Jay escorted him back across the street. "Mark fell," he told me later. "He fell right on his building's steps, busted his glasses, and broke his nose." I'll never forget the look on Jay's face that day. It wasn't just pained: it was accusatory. I knew that if I ever went to Hell it'd be because of Mark and people like him, all my assisted-suicide cases. I was man enough to stand up to my sins. But why did Nasro have to know?

"Your dad," Nasro said, "had his heart in the right place."

"Indeed," Jay nodded.

I took to resenting Nasro early on because he promised to be for Jay exactly what I had failed to become: a clear-cut moral guide, a walk-the-straight-and-narrow father figure, a preach-by-example role model. Call it jealousy.

Or maybe it was the Islam thing. Nasro, though by far not the strictest by-the-Koran follower, adhered to the Five Pillars of his faith. "I've attested that there is no God but Allah and that Mohammed is his prophet. I pray every day. I fast during Ramadan. I distribute alms. I'm planning to go on pilgrimage to the holy city of Mecca." Those were facts he sounded off often.

I tried my best to catch him in the wrong. First of all, with his mustache, curly hair, and olive skin, he looked more Egyptian than Sudanese to me. Why had he been so paranoid the day Jay walked in asking for a job? What did he have to hide? Did he run out of his back room one of those terrorist cells Empire was always warning us about? What better cover for illegal activities than a store?

I got real close and smelled Nasro real good and real long to see if I could get a whiff of anything foul. Nasro, to my profound chagrin, only reeked of goodness. He didn't overcharge for all the stuff he got from his suppliers, mainly Century Distributors and a Chinese wholesaler operating out of a fortified warehouse off New York Avenue. Some items, like baby food and children's clothing, he sold at cost. Some, like his breakfast special (1 donut, 1 piece of fruit, 1 mini-carton of cereal, 1 small orange juice, 1 straw, 1 napkin, 1 plastic spoon), he took a loss on.

"Why not just give those away?" Jay asked.

"You have to charge something," Nasro answered. "Even if it's one dollar. You know why? People only care about what they buy."

Jay liked the sound of it. He liked it a lot. Souk Number One was exactly what he needed. He, who had always dreamed of finding a way to do good while earning a decent living, felt right at home. He wasn't after millions. He didn't want the mansion on the 50-acre estate. He had no use for a 10-car garage. A simple, unburdened life seemed to be the only thing worth aspiring for. I don't need much to survive, he told himself, Bob Marley's "Me give it all away" very present in his mind. I can take care of the basics, put a little away, and distribute the rest.

"That's the way," Nasro agreed. "Take little, give much, serve humanity."

I had my reservations. What if Jay decided to get married? How would he ever raise a family on half of a stockman's salary? What woman would accept that kind of life? "Serve humanity." What exactly did that mean? Was that the only future Jay saw for himself, "Serve humanity"? For a moment I couldn't help thinking, like Joe and Maggie, that Jay was prone to taking the easy way out every time. There was nothing intrinsically wrong with ringing sales and stocking shelves and mopping floors. I just thought Jay could do much better. What would it take to finish school or get a loan to start a business? Humanity could best be served from atop a pile of money. Philanthropy should start at home. You dig your foundations and you build your base. Only once firmly established do you set out to help others. It was easy for Nasro to speak. He'd had his start with four partners, each putting up $10,000 as a down payment for Souk. Nasro had bought out all his partners one after the other. He had lived in the tiny apartment above Souk with his family until he was able to afford a house in Silver Spring. That seemed to me like a very, very long shot at the American Dream.

But what could I do other than wish Jay the best? It has to be said that my son had a mystic streak--a messianic complex, even. He believed himself utterly imperfect and he longed for a way to achieve betterment, both spiritual and physical. The abuse he had suffered in Maggie's hands as a child, his crazy dreams, his seesaw relationship with Joe, his depression, my death, the breakup with Lisha, the long stretch in his room.... Everything that had happened to him had contributed to his somewhat detached and incomplete sense of self. Jay didn't live for himself. Needs, wants, hopes, wishes, aspirations, happiness, stability ... none of that mattered. At the end of his life he would measure his accomplishments by the nature and the quality of what he had been able to bring to the common table. His body, his mind were tools to conquer, refine, and put to use for the greater good. In order to obtain enlightenment he must first triumph over his defects, real or perceived.

Nasro agreed wholeheartedly. "The most valuable jihad is the one against oneself," he instructed Jay. "No war is holier, no victory more rewarding."

Jay nodded solemnly.

And who are you? I asked Nasro: Yoda? Khomeini?

In a sense, they had truly found each other. Jay wanted a guide. Nasro had always wished for a son. Working side by side, they took each other's measure and found a quick fit. When the shelves were full and the paperwork done and customers scarce, they talked. Though opinionated, Nasro was no polemicist or activist. With Jay or Souk's Loyal Three, he stood clear of certain discussions. Jay tried in vain to get him to condemn Empire and its global ambitions. Claude never elicited more than a half-smile with his Hollywood and music business gossip. Ahmet, humbled by Nasro's serious approach to a religion he himself had abandoned after fleeing his native Balkans, put a mute on his fast talk and crooked ways whenever he came around. Hakim, engaged in a fight for recognition with the area's richer and more mainstream mosques, never managed to obtain a stronger endorsement or commitment from Nasro past the occasional guest appearance for a Friday sermon.

Even the harrowing news of genocide and mass-migration coming out of Nasro's part of the world seemed to hold no lure. Asked what was the deal with Darfur, Nasro answered, "Same old stuff: Arabs against black Africans. So-called Muslims against animists. Nomadic herders against settled farmers. Government against rebels. Foreign interest groups vying for oil contracts. And when the time comes to share the spoils of war it will be Arabs against Arabs." Would he march? No. Would he take part in the protests sporadically organized to mobilize the public opinion and pressure Empire into humanitarian action? Not him. Nasro was a self-contained unit. He took care of his store, he took care of his soul, he held his tongue in check, he stayed away from trouble. Everything about him was controlled. He never raised his voice. He never showed real anger. He never laughed with complete abandon. He never talked bad about people. He never lost patience with his customers, slow, indecisive, disruptive, or downright broke as they might be. Wise, prudent, and positive: those were the terms in which Jay thought of him.

All that was fine with me. Whenever things turned boring I crossed the wall into Happy Cuts and hung around Nicole. May Jay be blessed to no end for taking the Souk Number One job. May he definitely triumph over depression. May he find peace and contentment in his heart. May he marry a voluptuous virgin who will satisfy his every wish, cook for him and make love to him every night, and bear him countless children. May he know riches that never end even if he thinks he doesn't need them. May the doors of Heaven open in all their majesty and let him in. May he, for allowing me to see Nicole every day, find everything he is after.

Happy Cuts, though separated from Souk Number One by only the tiniest of walls, was an altogether different world. No talk of transcendence here. No jihad. No African wars. It was all about hair, femininity, family, food, shopping, empowerment, health tips, R&B, blackness, men, children, beauty supplies, beauty secrets. I loved the peach and green interior. I loved the smell of shampoo and coconut grease. I loved the ease and nonchalance with which business was conducted. I didn't have to listen to anything unpleasant. I didn't have to think. I didn't have to worry. I could just sit in an empty chair or under a drying helmet, whistle "My Baby Must Be a Beautician," snap my fingers, tap my feet, wiggle my neck, and watch Nicole, breathe Nicole, live Nicole. O Nicole. O love. O happiness.

It appeared she was still single. "Go on," her employees encouraged her. "Pick somebody, anybody, and give it another try."

"I still love Ben," she would tell them. "I haven't let go."

"He'd want to see you happy," they told her.

Not true, I would tell them. Not true at all. I want her to stay mine. All mine. Nobody should touch her, go where I've been, see what I've seen. She's mine. Mine. Mine. Don't you go and tell her to start dating again. Keep your advice for yourself. Mind your business. *Vade retro*.

"I *am* happy," Nicole would invariably say. "I don't feel the need to meet people. You have to mourn properly. Those things take time. It wouldn't be good if I jumped out there only to find out I haven't healed."

I stuck my tongue out at all of them: the coworkers, the instigators, the well-meaning customers. Those words, "I haven't healed," were Nicole through and through. I had heard them often from her, in relation to her body. Nicole knew everything about the healing process. She knew, and she worried.

It was something else, that body. First of all, it cost a lot. Second, it was famous. Third, it was insured. Four, she was always afraid it wouldn't hold up. Like all things too beautiful to exist, it was inherently fragile.

Back to our first time, my very first trip to the white-on-white industrial condominium in the sky. The huge posters on the walls, shots of the same naked and faceless woman--Nicole? Nicole taking it all off. Me sitting wide-eyed and speechless on the bed. The gold of the sunlight filtering through. The gold of her skin. Nicole's breasts, Nicole's hips, Nicole's belly button, Nicole's lustrous triangle, Nicole's confession: "Nothing about my body is real." My answer: "You got your money's worth."

Her laughter. My own. Ben the droll lad about to get laid. Who cared if she had paid for her tits and her ass? They looked better that any I had ever seen. They felt as warm and as soft as any I had ever touched. They smelled good enough, they were big enough to eat. I wanted her, oh, I wanted her. My throat was dry. My body ached. This is no Maggie Wilson, bud. This is no wrestling match. The door is open. No need to beg, today. No roaming the corridors. You can have it all, Ben. There goes your tenderness--tenderneeess. Everything you're after. It's all for you. Go on and touch. Go on and grab, grope, feel, kiss, suck, inhale, lick, bite. Go on, Ben. Go.

I pulled Nicole to me and stuck my head right between her thighs. She put both her hands on my cheeks and made me look up. Brown. Her eyes were the lightest of browns. I saw myself in them. White man getting high off her scent in a sea of white sheets.

She spoke. "Don't you want to see my bill of health?"

I shook my head. See what? What for? Her taste was already on the tip of my tongue. See what? Now? I didn't want to stop. I didn't want to postpone anything. I wanted to dive in, go deep, drown myself in her. This Nicole. This woman. Seductress. Sorceress. Dive in. Drown. Liquid dreams. Now.

My voice, when I answered, was thick and raw. "Do you need to see mine?"

She nodded.

I dropped my hands and looked away. Little boy scolded, little boy blue. "Does that mean we're not doing anything? I can't have you?"

She kissed me and rubbed her thumb on my lips. Hushing me, quieting my fears, letting the sun in after a rainy day. Smile, little boy. Go ahead and smile. The Love Fairy lets love rule in early May. "You can have me. We just won't do everything. What we'll do, we'll do right."

She pulled a box of condoms from a drawer. Her hair, her neck, her back, her flawless legs, her waist, and that butt, that big ole, big ole butt. It bounced with every step. It spread and reassumed its shape. It rippled. It had a life of its own. A symmetry, a tone, a hue, a perfection unseen and unequaled. Nicole, Jinglin' Baby. O love. O destiny. O luck. I felt thirsty again.

Nicole held a condom up. "Strawberry?"

"Sounds good."

She unwrapped it and put it in her mouth. Kneeling, she rolled it on me all the way up, her lips not once directly touching my skin. I had never even heard of such a thing. You think you know it all and somewhere down the road a kid half your age shows you a new trick or two. "I took a class," Nicole whispered, pushing me on my back.

"What kind of class?"

"A pleasure class."

"How did you do?"

"Straight A's."

Out of the same drawer came a tube of jelly. I smiled when I saw her butt move again. Soon enough, I told him. Soon enough I'll get to you and it's gonna be me and you, just the two. When she walked back Nicole climbed and stood on the bed, her legs across my flanks. Her toenails were painted white. White! Her heels felt cool in my hands. I looked up, up, up the vertiginous highway of her thighs. O temptress. O woman. Watching me with an inscrutable expression, Nicole started to massage herself with the scented lubricant. What Nicole did, she did right. This is a vulvae, Ben. These are your labia. Up here in the cut, little ball sticking out, is the clitoris. Inside, more labia. Then your vagina. One finger, two fingers, three. It shines, Ben. It shines and moistens just for you. See it glisten. Watch it open. One finger, two fingers, three.

I felt my heart falter again. So much skin. So much flesh. So much woman. Shaking with desire, now. My parched voice: "Turn around."

She obliged. Hands on her hips, she hummed a go-go song and made her butt shake and do the butt dance. It rippled, it spread, it assumed its shape again. A pear, an onion, the juiciest Georgia peach. Nicole, Jinglin' Baby.

"Like what you see?"

"I like."

Nicole faced me. A smile parted her lips. "You shouldn't let me do that, you know?"

"What?"

"Walk all over you on the first date."

I pulled her by the hand.

She came to lie next to me. Her fingers ran across my face, my chest, my belly. And then tender traveling kisses, her tongue lapping me up one square inch at a time, her nipples setting me afire. I didn't dare move and break the magic. She kissed me again, this time closing her eyes.

She's the one who came on top and made love to me. Slowly, deliberately, sweetly. Pushing me deep into her. Keeping me in. Pushing herself out almost completely. Twining our fingers. Looking at me, looking through me,

140

looking far, far away, not looking at all. Talking softly. Keeping me down when I tried to switch sides. Rubbing her forehead on mine. Making me taste her sweat. Nicole's groove: up and down, back and forth, 'round and 'round. Nicole's School of Love. Nicole's knowing ways.

She held me for a long while afterward. I felt a deep contentment for the first time in years. It must be a dream, I told myself. Of course it's a dream. Who's this girl? What am I doing here? I was afraid that she'd be gone when I opened my eyes. I was scared that she would kick me out of her bed and out of her building. It was a mistake, Ben. A terrible mistake. We shouldn't have. Please leave now. Please. Now.

"You're still hungry?" Nicole asked.

I laughed, and she with me. A late lunch had been our excuse, our mating dance, my reason for leaving Chris and Jay in charge while I strolled the Dupont streets with this hot thing on my arm at 3 in the afternoon. More than a month ago I had allowed her inside Cairo after closing time--something I never do, and not just because it's against regulations. I had seen her around before that, of course. Not my best customer, but pretty and nice enough to leave an impression. "Sorry to bother you," she said behind the door that night. "But I have unexpected company and I'd appreciate it if you did me this one favor. I'll be quick."

"Let her in," I told Jay.

Grey Goose, Patron, mixers, and ice. "I'll make it up to you," she promised as I bagged her stuff. She had come again and again after that night. I had gotten to know her name, what she did for a living, and where she lived.

141

We flirted. We joked about her debt. "You owe me," I kept telling her. "You owe me big time. How about lunch one of these days?"

"Lunch it is," she accepted. "One of these days I'll leave work early and come get you. Will you be ready?"

"Try me," I said.

On that fateful Wednesday: "How about now?"

Me: "How about it?"

She bought a Clairette de Die and took my arm right outside Cairo. It felt natural, maybe because it was such a beautiful day. We were both in high spirits.

"Raku? Thai Chef? Circa? City Lights?"

She shook her head. "My place, Ben."

"You're cooking?"

Her laugh rang high and loud. "Definitely."

Her duplex was out of this world. So much space. So much white. There was a pole in the middle of her living room. A tall, gleaming, chromed-out pole.

I heard a crazy rhythm in my head. Hand claps, drum rolls, shouts, come-ons, whistles, ice cubes, the clickety-clack of high heels. I smelled smoke, whisky, cheap perfume, and musk. I saw muted lights, stroboscopes, pearl curtains, dollar bills. "You dance?"

"Occasionally."

The rogue in me, the soldier demanded: "Show me."

"Take a seat," Nicole said.

She fixed us drinks and put "Miss Black America" on. "A little slow," she admitted. "But it's my favorite song."

Her eyes in mine, she kicked off her espadrilles and

backed toward the pole. Her butt touched it first. She stretched her arms and encircled it. Her dress outlined her breasts and rose high above her knees. Her fingers grabbed the pole. Up she went, climbing before she swung and slid and climbed again, twirling effortlessly, a whirlwind of arms and legs and feet and exposed flesh and smiles. I emptied my glass, got up, caught her as she was coming down, kissed her as the stereo went quiet. Her lips were soft and minty.

"Upstairs," she said breathlessly.

I knew better than to stop and think. I knew better than to ask, "Why me?" "Why now?" "Why so fast?" or any other dumb question. You've got to take what life throws your way sometimes. You've just got to.

It felt right to make love to a complete stranger in a strange place in the middle of the day. It felt especially good because it had been such a long time for me. It also felt completely natural until Nicole told me that she had had a sex change at the age of 21.

We were sitting in the kitchen in our underwear, cold pasta and the Clairette on the table, the long-promised lunch at long last. I felt my stomach contract and my mind blank out and my chest go numb and the macaroni turn to ash. Hadn't my mother raised me better, I would have spat the food out.

"You had *what*?"

Nicole looked me dead in the eye. "A sex change, Ben. I wasn't born a woman. At least not on the outside." She said it almost defiantly, ready to detect and record my every reaction, and perhaps counteract as well--a knife was sticking out of her right hand as if by inadvertence.

I scanned her throat, her wrists, her fingers, her nails, and her cheekbones, half expecting her to shed her skin like a costume and show her true self, the Love Fairy gone for the day, the School of Love closed until further notice. Nothing of the sort happened. Nicole waited with unblinking eyes, the knife twisting and turning in her fingers. Accept me for who I am right here right now or leave, she seemed to be saying. Disrespect me, make a move too fast and I'll stab you.

It was the same girl who had been coming to my store. The one I had half-hopelessly/half-hopefully felt attracted to. The one on the pole. The one in the bed driving me crazy, driving me mad, driving me out of my mind.

"So this is what you meant by 'nothing about my body is real.'"

"Yes."

"If I laugh ... if I express outrage or just say the wrong thing, you're going to cut me? Is that why you're clutching that knife?"

Nicole shrugged. "I've had to defend myself right after coitus before. Some people just can't handle the truth."

The harsh tone, the big-girl stance. "Coitus." Not "sex." Not "making love." "Coitus." Who was she trying to impress?

At the same time, I felt a pang of jealousy. "Some people." Who? How many?

I looked at her long and hard again, still searching for the man in her, the man she said she used to be. If he had ever been there, he seemed long gone.

I took a swig straight from the bottle and resumed

144

chewing. "I must be blind, Nicole. You look like a regular woman to me. A very beautiful one at that."

"I'll take that as a compliment," she answered, still on the defensive.

"Still think your doctor didn't shortchange you," I added with a straight face.

Nicole laughed, but barely. "Doctors," she pointed out. "I had several. They collaborated on an article about me. Wanna read it?"

"Yeah. But please drop that knife first. You're making me nervous."

The article was in The New Yorker, no less. I glanced through the photocopied pages she handed me as one would distribute a press kit. Read too fast and she'd think me uninterested. Read too slow and it'd look as if I wanted to regain countenance. "So you're a celebrity."

"They didn't publish my real name."

"What makes you so special?"

She raised an eyebrow.

I winked. "Beside what makes you special."

She relaxed. "I had a lot of money to spend. I wanted the perfect body. I wasn't in a rush."

I fed her a forkful of pasta. "Was it painful?"

"Very. And still is, at times. I'll be in and out of doctors' offices all my life."

"Silicone? Saline implants?"

"Silicone. It's fleshier and more lifelike."

"And more dangerous, no?"

"I do M.R.I.'s annually."

"Grafts?"

She nodded. "And hormone regimens. And plastic

surgery. 10 years and a quarter-million dollars' worth. I have a DVD and countless pictures documenting the whole thing."

I grimaced appreciatively. The rogue, the soldier, Steve McQueen, Jimmy Dean, Empire's Finest. "Show me."

"Are you sure?" Nicole asked.

"Show me," I requested again.

She left the kitchen.

I made a point to eat heartily. The most important thing was not to say or do anything stupid. I didn't want to hurt Nicole. The kid had courage, the kid was honest, the kid was the best damn lover I had ever had. I didn't feel disgusted. I didn't think I had been duped or betrayed. Maybe those emotions, those feelings would come.

Nicole returned empty-handed. "It's too soon," she said. "I want you to get to know me first."

I finished the bottle and wiped my mouth with my hand. The ruffian, the alpha male, the long-deprived sex machine. "Can we go back to bed?"

Nicole took my hand.

I laid her down and looked at her from every angle, more carefully than when she had been standing above me. Head to toe, side to side, top to bottom, head and tail. She pointed out marks and scars that were all but invisible to the untrained eye. Who said plastic was dead? Who called it outdated and unfriendly?

My turn to pepper her with kisses and pick a flavor. "Pineapple?"

"Sounds good. Go slow."

It was easier said than done. Especially toward the

end, when all you wanted was to go as hard and as fast as you could, to pound-pound-pound, to plow the juicy and bountiful earth, to labor from sunup to sundown, to dig and sow and water the seed.

"That's why I like to be on top," Nicole reflected when we stopped. "Then I have full control. Then I don't have to worry about my insides tearing up."

She sat up and inspected her genitalia, pulling on her lips to explore her vagina with tentative fingers in a ritual she would never fail to repeat every single time we made love.

"How's it holding up?"

"It's fine."

We snuggled.

I asked her the million-dollar question: "Can you come?"

She bit my earlobe. "I just did."

Steve McQueen. Jimmy Dean. Empire's Finest.

I wasn't sure I would be back when I left the Condo in the Sky that day. A little peck at the door, a hug, a goodbye. No rendezvous, no promises, no appointment. I didn't know if I wanted to see Nicole again. Too much stuff to process. I had her card, she had mine. It could end right there.

No questions, no inquiries, no probing from Chris or Jay. They knew better than to ask or even say anything. Easy as I was to get along with, I wasn't their friend. Jay was my son, Chris my employee. It did occur to me that maybe they knew about Nicole's sex change. This, after all, was Dupont Circle. Nobody around was straight, nobody around had been straight dating from the '80s. Maybe Chris and Jay shared the one thought I was trying hard to suppress: You fucked a dude, Ben.

That one single thought did get my head spinning for a while. Was Nicole a man or a woman? What was I dealing with? Did I want that kind of mess in my life? How far could I take it? Where would it go? I knew next to nothing about transsexuals. (In that and many, many other things, Nicole would be my first.) Had I known beforehand, I wouldn't have gone along with the lunch thing. The pole would have left me cold. The dance wouldn't have titillated. "Miss Black America"? Please. The striptease wouldn't have teased. The condom-in-the-mouth wouldn't have excited. The highway, the jelly rub wouldn't have meant a thing.

Or would they?

I gave it a few weeks, more out of inertia than strategy. Nicole came by for a bottle of Clicquot. Low shoes, jeans filled to the seams, Mr. Butt in full splendor, white long-sleeves T-shirt, red baseball cap. Chris and Jay cleared the counter. Nicole smiled.

I spoke first. "Entertaining?"

"A graduation present."

"School of Love, Pleasure Department, Class of '07?"

She laughed. "Howard U, Fine Arts, my goddaughter."

"How 've you been?"

"Same old. You?"

"Same old."

She paid and left. I felt like running after her. There

was something sad about Nicole. Something endearing, too.

What do you want? I asked myself. What's the alternative? Maggie and that madhouse you call home? No love, no sex, no tenderneeess, no joy. For how long? Nothing will ever change between the two of you. The Mag you knew is long gone and she's not coming back. All this time you've never cheated, you've never strayed. What kind of life do you live? You work, you eat your deli sandwich, you guzzle your wine, you go to sleep alone. Let's face it, Ben: Maggie's a ball-breaker. And that kid Nicole? Best pussy in town and far from shabby to look at. Close your eyes, Ben. Listen to me: How did it feel when you were lying with her? Good, it felt good. Would you like to do it again? Yes, definitely. When she's around, do you react to her the way you would to a man? No. Are you a bigot? No. Are you a narrow-minded jerk? No. So Nicole is a woman, Ben. A woman. A woman. She's a woman and you should go for it, soldier. Sit her down, talk it out, see how it's gonna be. Hit her with a confession of your own. Tell her you're married. Tell her about Mag, the years of drought, the long and lonely corridor, the locked bedroom door, how you felt lost out there in the desert, how you had all but renounced companionship and romance until she came around. Give it to her straight, Ben. Don't be scared. If she rejects you, she rejects you. You'll survive. You're Steve McQueen. You're Jimmy Dean. You're a star.

I called. Nicole and I got together again. Took the time to talk and get acquainted. Fell in love and trounced each and every single law of attraction on earth. The white middle-aged baby boomer and the black transgender chick. What can I say. The kid was all right and there's such a

149

thing as dumb luck even for old fools like me.

I'm in luv
[I'm in lu-uv]
Wit' the other woman
[Hey, the other woman]
My life was fine
[Fine]
Yes it was
Till she blew my mind

It's not me who sent Nicole flowers for Valentine's Day. It's Youngin', Macondo Lounge's owner. The bouquet was big, beautiful, and expensive. It was delivered with a note--a bad poem, really. Youngin' was a 60-year-old hustler with literary pretensions. He carried hardcovers around, he kept a pen and a notebook handy, he had named his strip joint after the imaginary village in "One Hundred Years of Solitude," and he wasn't averse to backing the occasional book, CD, or DVD project from local artists, provided his name was prominently displayed on the finished product. Call him a patron of street arts.

Nicole had known him for as long as she had owned her shop. Youngin' was as much a fixture as Nasro in

Brightwood Park. On top of Macondo he ran Tows R Us and the adjoined used-car lot across the street. Legend had it that he owned 150 suits and as many hats and pairs of boots to match. His Benz was maroon on wheat, his rims were 26 inches, he liked his gold torsades thick and heavy. Tall, smooth-faced, square of head and shoulders, black as night, always impeccably dressed, he cut an impressive figure.

The only other person who had more pull in the neighborhood was a scarred druglord called Pepsi. People referred to him as the Absentee Owner, or sometimes just the Owner. Pepsi had been patiently taking over block after block in the city, from humble beginnings on Clifton Street to swaths of housing projects that were getting ever closer to the Maryland line. Kennedy became his after he exterminated the Jamaican gang that used to run it, bringing it back under home rule. He, too was a sharp dresser. He, too was a businessman with a signature corporate structure replicated in every venture. He, too had an eye out for Nicole.

So far, I'm happy to say, both men had been getting nowhere in their attempts. A strip-joint pimp? A big-time dope dealer? My beautician baby didn't play that.

I tested my freedom and hung out with both just to see what they were about, prowling the whole area when I didn't feel like staying in Souk or Happy Cuts. 13 walls north and I was in Macondo. 19 walls to the northeast and I arrived smack in Pepsi's territory: rowhouses, rooftops, gloomy high-rise apartments, vicious dogs. Why Youngin' and Pepsi? Because they were "it": complex, smart, nonconformist, one cut above. And because I could only witness so many strangers give in to poverty, drug or alcohol abuse, neglect, despair, illiteracy, and discrimination before feeling drained or numb. Georgia at Kennedy didn't have much to offer to a ghost looking to meet challenging people. Family after family appeared broken and struggling. Kid after kid was malnourished, undereducated, unappreciated, at risk. Woman after woman was used, overextended, and bruised. Man after man absent, unemployed, uncommitted, unresponsive, unsuccessful, and angry. The units? Crowded, filthy, unsafe. The lives? Empty, wasted, doomed, heartbreaking. Like Joe said, "Poverty isn't pretty." I walked in. I walked out.

So Youngin' and Pepsi. Two very different men, each interesting in his own way. Youngin' sprinkled every other sentence with a heartfelt "Bless you" or "Praise the Lord." He loved Jesus, money, and the ladies. The Macondo girls all slept with him sooner or later. The one dearest to his heart was Lola, a sculptural, dark-skinned Cuban who claimed that her mother had bedded Simenon and his wife in Havana in the '60s. Youngin' thought Lola brought to the place exactly the kind of cachet it aspired to, and he had made her artistic director after her first month with the house. Youngin's ambition for Macondo was to turn it into as fabled a destination as the mythic Colombian village it was named after. The girls were expected to don costumes and put on a show. The poles on Macondo's two stages were all removable. Props were rolled in and out. Some of the frills-and-thrills numbers like "The Wolfwomen," "One Night in Memphis," "Juke Joint

Annie," "Hottentot Venus," and " The Maid of Cadiz" were worthy of a Moulin Rouge revue. Each evening was themed, with Thursdays traditionally reserved for amateurs. Many aspiring dancers had had their big break on one such night, with movie or theater producers--or Youngin' himself--signing them on the spot. How many careers on the chitlin circuit had he helped get started? Littered with autographed portraits of celebrities, Macondo's crimson walls bore a permanent testimony to its cultural touchstone status.

A strip-joint pimp? Yes and no. Youngin' was in it for the money but he liked for things to be done within the confines of good taste. "Class" was another one of his favorite words. The cameras, the steep cover charge, the high price of drinks and food platters, the door frisks, and the No Athletic Gear policy kept most unsavory characters out. The house's strict etiquette forbid waving dollar bills and sticking money down G-strings or bra straps or pantyhose. People in search of cheap entertainment could always stagger south all the way to the Playground, where girls were made to crawl in cages and wrestle one another in plastic pools, and where unnameable things took place in the bathrooms and right on stage.

Youngin' packed a Derringer. Like Pepsi, he had killed before.

Mr. Absentee Owner was a little under 30. His most notable features were the scar on his cheek and his yellow pupils. There was a hardness to him that was almost inhuman. To stalk him was to walk with a panther. He was ruthlessness impersonated. A new breed, a bitter seed. Pepsi was no joke. He ordered murder after murder without losing a single minute of sleep. Cross him and you died. The main reason why his managers ran their little sections of the enterprise so well is failure meant immediate death. There were no reprieves or second chances on Pepsi's books. You did the job, you proved your worth or you went under.

It's thanks to him that the neighborhood was relatively quiet. After a plague of robberies nearly bankrupted Nasro and his partners early in the Souk venture, in the days when no insurer in town would bless them with a policy because of Brightwood Park's reputation, Pepsi himself had walked into the store to assure Nasro that the problem would be fixed. After that the place had only been the victim of random attempts from drifters who never realized the kind of danger they were putting themselves into. Pepsi didn't take no mess. He was all about order and expansion. Starbucks, the Pac-Man of coffee shop chains, was his model. His gurus were all corporate types. Wall Street was very much on his mind. Golf courses were where most of his time was spent.

What did these two guys want with my woman? Youngin' was looking for a brown sugar babe to sweeten his days. Nicole was just like he liked them: young, experienced, well-mannered, a body, brains, business sense. As for Pepsi, well, he wanted Nicole just to have Nicole. To have her, use her, and throw her away.

So far, she hadn't given either one the time of day. They were relegated to mere distractions, distant afterthoughts. Their attentions embarrassed her more than anything else. "I'm still mourning my man," is what she told them when they called or paid her a visit. I hoped the flowers and sweets that kept showing up at Happy Cuts would leave her indifferent for years to come. Nicole was mine. Mine. Mine.

It became commonplace for me to commute between Souk and Military Road. Across town, Steve was taking advantage of the general goodwill and romantic spirit spurred by Valentine's Day to plot a major comeback. I thought he'd be finished after that fateful first night with Maggie, but I guess that was counting without his genuine ingenuity, his mechanical prowess, his precocious attachment to my ex-wife, and, it must be said, his resilience. No heart-shaped balloons or fructose-infused cards for his damsel. Steve, a nuts-and-bolts guy, came up with a nuts-and-bolts idea inspired by his recent foray into the world of military contracting. Right when he was getting tired of flying custom model airplanes, he had stumbled upon a USA Today headline decrying the current supply problem with Predator, the drone utilized by Empire's armies in all its current battlefields. Demand, the article said, outpaced fleet inventory. Empire needed for its combat troops three times more Predator drones than the Air Force could supply. Predators were ideal for surveillance, missile-shooting, or bomb-dropping. They were convenient, they were safe, they were accurate, they were hard to detect, they were economical. *Merde*, tought Steve: *la voilà* my golden opportunity. So he set out to build his own drone in his own garage, improving on the Predator by keeping an eye on size, weight, and production times. His first prototype, lamely named "Maggie May," was first flown on February 20. It was small, metal-gray, hydrogen-propelled, and stealthy like an air submarine. It carried not a cluster bomb or high-definition cameras but a straw basket with a box of Amore gourmet cookies, a rose, a whip, and a paperback bestseller titled "S&M: Get Familiar, Get It Right, Get Started!"

Maggie May landed on our front lawn as its namesake Maggie, en route to the grocery store, was pulling the Marquis out of the garage. Maggie took a good look at the machine, thought terrorists were invading our neighborhood (she'd feared for years that devious Arabs might look to make an example of an American street named Military Road), searched frantically under the seats, grabbed the first gun she found, and started shooting through the window. The gun, security still engaged, refused to fire. The drone dropped the basket just a few feet from Maggie and immediately gained elevation. Afraid it was going to explode, Maggie broke into a cold sweat, jumped out of the car, threw herself on the lawn, and rolled back into the garage out of sheer will and adrenaline. Only when she reached the inside did she dare take a look.

"Happy belated Valentine's Day!" Steve shouted from across the road, waving the contraption's remote.

"You scared the shit out of me!" Maggie shouted back, holding her wheezing chest.

"Was that neat or what?" Steve hollered, beaming.

If Maggie dug the cookies (Amore were simply the best in the world. Steve's display of such esoteric knowledge and uncanny ability to divine her culinary tastes brought her to tears) and was overall well pleased with

Steve's initiative, she was more than intrigued by the S&M book and the whip. What a strange, strange declaration of love.

It all came together later that night as Steve and she were watching a documentary on the Iceman, that famed mob henchman who was such a psychopath that only the most extreme forms of torture, violence, or abuse could provoke emotional reactions in him. The very powerful footage of a screaming victim left in a cave for rats to gnaw at touched Maggie in a weird way. It wasn't the first time she had felt aroused by images or acts that her heart, her mind, and common morality deemed improper. The puritan backlash that punched the first hole in our marriage had been in a large part an attempt to control and eliminate those impulses. Such times, and our union, had come to pass. Tonight, with Steve--*Stephane*, I mean--Maggie found herself inclined to act upon her darkest desires for the very first time. Steve and she were alone. Jay was at work. Joe was out cruising the streets. The soufflé she had labored on all afternoon could wait. What was there to lose? Why be afraid?

Turning toward Steve, she made a fist, cocked her arm, took a deep breath, and hit him square in the jaw. Yanked out of his own reverie, Steve groaned and tried to get up. Maggie held him down and head-butted him.

"Aïe!" Steve shouted, grabbing his nose.

Maggie got up and dragged him off the couch by the collar. "Shut up. Get on your knees."

Happy like a hyperactive, overjoyed, and long-misunderstood puppy, Steve complied.

Maggie, who realized she had missed a step, made

him undress while she went looking for the whip. Shaking with anticipation, they made room by pushing the coffee table.

Steve kneeled with abject submission, awaiting his punishment.

Lord, have mercy on us, I prayed, turning away as the flogging began.

"You weakling!" Maggie hissed. "You scum!"

"*Oui*," Steve gasped. "*C'est vrai.*"

"You dirty Jew!" Maggie went on. "You circumcised pig!"

The whip cut the air in half. Steve moaned, bit his lip, and closed his eyes.

Maggie lashed him until he bled.

Both felt a rush like never before. She changed hands to make the session last longer, letting loose all her rage and frustration, letting go of her self-imposed restraint, following only her most basics instinct. Torture. Hurt. Humiliate. Control. Subdue. It was more than a rush: it was a liberation, a metamorphosis, a departure from everything she had ever experienced, the night of the baby butterfly. Maggie felt reconciled with her true, true self. Reconciled and at peace.

So did Steve. He had been equally repressed at home. His wife Christine had never accepted to play along and humor his fantasies. She'd been the meekest, weakest, dullest, most normal woman on earth. Hurt her husband, have him derive sexual gratification from pain that she, Christine, voluntarily inflicted? The thought was enough to send her crying to her psychotherapist.

When it was finished, when Maggie and Steve found themselves drained of their last strand of energy, when their screams and grunts stopped shaking the walls, they fell in each other's arms, Maggie almost crushing Steve under her weight. Love, love, love. They had found it, it felt good, they were happy.

"The soufflé's ready," Maggie whispered tenderly.

"Let's eat naked," Steve proposed. "My ass is on fire."

Maggie acquiesced. "I'll bring us towels."

A naked soufflé it was. They ate with one hand, holding fingers with the other. Their eyes never strayed from each other. They kissed between each mouthful, pushing food back and forth in each other's mouth with their tongues. Maggie spread salt and pepper on Steve's cuts, making him scream with delight. The fun was just beginning.

"I'll buy you a muzzle and a spiked choker," she promised. "Would you prefer leather, fabric, or metal?"

"Leather," he said. "Get some boots and a corset for yourself. I want you totally decked out."

She was excited just thinking about it. "How about handcuffs?"

Steve nodded. "Handcuffs sound good."

I shook my head and left the room, more saddened than sickened, once again. I had been aware of Maggie's sadistic tendencies almost as soon as Jay was born. He, as a baby, had taken the brunt. I, as a man, had refused to go down that route with her. Jay had suffered greatly. Joe had been spared. Our marriage could have been saved if I had done what Steve just now did--capitulate and let Maggie belt me; abandon my manhood to become her plaything. But I was no Steve. I had showed no interest in exploring that side of Maggie. It was enough to be in the know, to understand what I was dealing with. Some dark recesses are better left unexplored.

I sat in the front yard until Joe showed up. He had been driving around looking for his Church of Retribution man, again to no avail. A sense of urgency was creeping in. Following on the footsteps of the Virginia General Assembly, which a week ago had approved a resolution expressing "profound regret" for Virginia's role in the slave trade, the Annapolis City Council had just announced that it was considering a public apology for "our municipal government's past support and involvement in slavery and for our support of segregation for nearly 100 years." The State of Maryland was also said to be considering such an apology. Though he doubted that anything serious would come out of those efforts, Joe felt the need to hurry up. How long before somebody put two and two together? How long before his dream was snuffed right out of his hands? How long before some entrepreneur somewhere realized that reparations were big business? Damn politicians. Hypocrites, opportunists, and demagogues, all of them. The more noise they made, the more danger.

Maggie and Steve jumped as Joe parked the Nova on the gravel. The kids. They had forgotten about the kids. "Time these two fools move out," Maggie grumbled. Their clothes were on the floor. The whip was atop the TV. The coffee table was sitting at an angle.

Steve prepared to bolt. "Sit," Maggie told him. "I

don't feel like running upstairs. I won't hide any more. My sons, and the world, will have to take me for who I am starting with tonight."

Terror returned to Steve's face. "Let me at least put my boxers on," he begged.

One look from Maggie pinned him to his chair. He felt deliciously awful.

"Hi!" Joe said as he opened the door. Assailed by too many perceptions at once, he stopped and stood frozen with his fingers on the knob. The soufflé's delightful aroma, the living room in shambles, his mother sitting at the table naked, Steve the neighbor sitting just as naked by her side. "Bye," Joe said before turning around, slamming the door behind him.

Outside, shaken out of his wits, he stood by the Nova for a few minutes. Had he just dreamed what happened? Was he having visions? The look Maggie had given him--what was that? Defiance, scorn, resentment ... hatred, even. As if she wanted him gone. As if she wished never to see him again. What had he ever done to her? What was going on?

Surreptitiously, Joe walked to the nearest window. Sure enough, here were Maggie and Steve cleaning the table with not a single item of clothing between the two of them. Joe looked on as Maggie punched Steve while he had his hands full. Instead of defending himself, Steve smiled and kissed her on the lips. When he bent over to gather the utensils he had just dropped, she kicked him in the groin. An expression of pure beatitude illuminated Steve's face. Maggie picked him up effortlessly and carried him up the stairs, the ogre and its consenting victim. Tonight all bets are off. Tonight nothing is off-limits. Tonight the cave is on fire. Tonight we do everything and anything we want.

I watched Joe vomit on his mother's prized rosebushes, sure that the symbolism would escape him.

He got back in the Nova and started driving. His head was pounding. I sat on the trunk. We followed Missouri straight to Georgia and turned right. The avenue was all sound, light, and people. Where to go? Who to talk to? Joe had nobody. Nobody.

Leave Jay alone, I warned him. Don't you go and bother him with your problems. Stay away from my boy.

But Jay was precisely who Joe started thinking of. Seeing Maggie kick a man in the balls was sending him back down memory lane. During their childhood it had been fun to see Jay get thrashed for any reason, good or bad. A wrong look, a wrong word, any made-up accusation: "Ma, Jay pushed me"; "Ma, Jay was mean to me." The punishment was quick and out of proportion. Jay was smacked out of his head. He was slammed into walls. He was pinched, he was pushed, he was jacked, he was jerked, he was strangled, he was burned, he was hit with any massive objet that happened to lie around. Maggie had marked Jay more than once. Up to when he turned 17 she had fought him like a dude, *mano a mano*, holding nothing back. Black eyes, cuts, scratches.... Jay told me he was getting jumped at parties--this imaginary gang was always giving him problems for the most trivial reasons--and I acted like I believed him. Same story at school. Nobody ever suspected that home was the problem. Nobody knew that the gang lived with us.

Joe parked in front of Souk and walked in. He nodded toward Nasro, who nodded back. This would be the Republican Guardian, Joe told himself. Or is it Republican Guide? Don't look too much like an Arab to me, which is good.

Jay was standing by the cooler. He was surrounded by black kids. Three boys and a girl, 10 to 12 years old, all of them part of his newly extended family. Kevin, Mashey, Riri, and Shawn: zero father, 14 siblings, four empty fridges between the four of them. All dirty, skinny, and shabby. "After 9," Jay was telling them. "Y'all can meet me at the Chinese joint and we'll get some dinner."

"Cool," Kevin, who had a star outlined on the right side of his head, said.

Jay slapped fingers with all of them. Then he looked up and saw his brother. "Joe?"

The air of unhappy surprise on Jay's face crushed Joe. Holding his arms up, he went for a hug. Too stunned to move, Jay stood paralyzed while Joe embraced him. It was the first time ever. Something bad must have happened. Maggie. Lord, no. "Is Ma dead?"

Joe shook his head, refusing to let go.

Jay started to feel uncomfortable. What was that smell on Joe's clothes: bile? "You're choking me, bro!"

Joe took a step back and held his hand out. "I owe you an apology," he said, crying.

Jay thought something was wrong with his ears. "What are you talking about?"

"All these years..." Joe went on. "I haven't been the nicest little brother, I know. But..."

The words seemed to Jay wrapped in true

164

repentance and tentative tenderness. He felt each one directly and intimately. After everything he had suffered, everything he had endured, all the fights and misunderstandings and false problems, they came like a balm. "Don't sweat it, man. We're family."

Joe wiped his face. "Sorry."

Jay tapped his brother's shoulder. "Forgotten."

They walked to Nasro for a formal introduction. Both he and Joe smiled and bowed perfunctorily. No sparks here. Joe reminded himself to Google the guy.

It got close to 8:30. Jay emptied the trash, cleaned the floor, and started the lockup routine. Nasro stayed at the register. Claude the entertainment lawyer came by wrapped in a plastic sweatsuit, wearing his 1977 Wayfarers and carrying seven big jugs of wine from Midnight Liquors. Ahmet, who looked more and more like a New Jersey Italian to me, tried to sell Joe an umbrella even though the night was totally dry and nobody was calling for rain. "Everybody can always use an umbrella," he said over and over, sweat streaking his bald spot; "You need to keep one around as a preventive measure." Lola and another Macondo girl named Coco stopped by for replacement stockings and eyelashes. "You should come see us sometime," Lola, a good head taller than Jay, told him, caressing his cheek with her palm. "We'll improvise a number just for you."

"*Haram*," Nasro warned Jay.

"I wasn't talking to you," Lola, taking umbrage at the intrusion, told Nasro.

"I know," Jay told Nasro.

"What's that Nasro just said?" Joe asked.

"It means 'proscribed,'" Jay explained.

"Proscribed by who?"

"Allah," Jay answered.

Joe felt nauseous again. "You're converting? Already?"

"No," Jay affirmed. "That's just the way Nasro speaks."

Joe looked around. Diapers, sodas, Jamaican beef patties, rough kids, exotic dancers. Everything looked so ... cheap. "You should find something else. Really. This isn't you at all."

Jay smiled. "I'm happy here."

They turned off the equipment and all the lights except for the register area. Nasro dropped the locks in place after they pulled the curtain down. "Tomorrow, *insh Allah*," he told Jay. And to Joe: "Nice meeting you."

"Likewise," Joe lied.

The brothers walked to the Nova. "I'm buying dinner for the kids you saw earlier," Jay announced. "I kind of adopted a whole bunch of them. Meet you at the house?"

Joe was scared to go home alone. What would he see? What would he find? He knew he'd feel better if he stayed close to Jay and if they went in together. Jay's presence would protect him somehow, just like when he was a kid. Jay would help him make sense of whatever they stumbled into. "Can I stick around?"

Jay shrugged. "Sure."

They strolled up the block. The night was cool and the sidewalk empty. All the activity seemed concentrated on the other side of Georgia, around the gas station pumps and in front of the liquor store. Suppose we get mugged,

Joe told himself before the "For Lease" sign on the window between Happy Cuts and Macondo caught his eye. "What used to be here?"

"A shoemaker. Just went under."

"What shoemaker in his right mind would set up shop here?"

"The guy is Armenian. He fixes watches as well. One of those meticulous types."

"Bet you the spot stays empty for years."

Jay yawned. "Possible."

Facing the pink world of Wings 'n' Things, they crossed Kennedy. On their right, KDY3 and KDY5, the housing projects starting two blocks away and nestled two blocks apart, shone in all their concrete ugliness, illuminated by portable projectors powered by Humvees. People of all ages were coming and going, seemingly oblivious to the soldiers' presence. Muted and armed to the teeth, they monitored a checkpoint and harassed all would-be hangers-on. The scene was surreal, belonging more to post-U.S. invasion Baghdad than any of the streets of Empire's own capital.

"What's the army doing here?" Joe asked.

"Four murders in the past three weeks," Jay explained succinctly. "They're trying to quiet things down."

"You're not scared?"

Jay shrugged again.

They went inside the Chinese parlor. Cooking oil clung to the walls and floor. The only customers were the children waiting in front of the bulletproof partition. Their looks shifted from Jay to Joe.

"My brother," Jay explained. "You guys ordered

167

already?"

Kevin nodded. Joe was mystified by the star on the side of the boy's head. Empty bellies and designer hair. What was next? Black kids and their trends....

Jay addressed the pimply and lanky man behind the counter. "How much, Jimmy?"

"$34," Jimmy answered. "Same as yesterday, the day before, and the one before that."

Jay paid. The kids grabbed their food, two containers each, said thank you, and scurried out hurriedly.

"See you tomorrow," Jimmy wisecracked.

"Why two each?" Joe asked on the way back. "How much food do they need?"

"One for them, one to share with their families. The first time I tried to buy them dinner they wouldn't touch the stuff, insisting on taking it all home."

"You do this every night?"

"Pretty much."

"Why?"

"They're hungry. Their mothers don't care. It's close to 9:30 on a school night and here they are. Look across the street."

Joe saw them: Five more little boys in the gas station parking lot. Talking, sitting, wandering aimlessly. "What are they doing?"

"Hustling. Steering drug customers to the nearest point of sale. Pumping gas into cars for a few coins. Stealing from the little market. Waiting for some profitable mischief to come their way."

One of the boys waved at Jay. He waved back.

"Why didn't you feed this one?"

168

"Vaughn got his meal yesterday. Everybody's on rotation. They know to take turns."

Joe looked at the "For Lease" sign again. An Armenian shoemaker and watchmaker in the ghetto. Go figure.

The brothers stopped in front of the Nova. Jay and his causes.... Joe was afraid to say something that would alienate his brother. "I know you care about these people, Jay. I know you want to help. But there's gotta be a better way."

"Like what?"

Joe took a deep breath. "Like my church."

Jay laughed. "You're serious about that thing, aren't you?"

"Dead serious."

An old police Interceptor traveling north slowed down as it got to their corner. Both windows on the right side came down when the car stopped. Young men in dreadlocks stuck their heads out and admired the Nova. "Selling that joint?" one of them asked Joe.

"Soon," Joe said.

"What year is it?"

"'67."

The man took a drag from his Dutch and deliberately pulled a thick wad of bills out of his jacket. His nails were long and shiny. The rest of the car was too dark for Joe and Jay to peer into. I went in and found two more young toughs, a 15-year-old girl, three weapons, a stash of weed, a bottle full of suspicious pills, and a vial of PCP.

"Got 6 Gs right here," the young man said. "Deal?"

Joe shook his head. "No deal. I need about three

169

times that."

The young man spat on the asphalt, stuck the money back in his pocket, and rolled his window up. The Interceptor pulled away.

"Let's go home and talk," Joe proposed, spooked. "Where did you park?"

Jay gestured toward the corner. "The alley behind Souk."

Joe turned pale. "The alley? After what happened to dad? Are you crazy?"

Jay grinned. "Can't live in fear," he said before going to retrieve the Eldorado.

It hit Joe as he checked on Jay in his mirror after crossing 16th, making sure that the Eldorado was behind: Who better suited for the Church of Retribution front man's job than Jay? Who more qualified? Jay was white, young, and handsome. Jay was a thinker. Jay was casual of speech and manners. Jay was educated, if incompletely. Jay loved black people: He used to have a black girlfriend, he now worked in a black neighborhood, he fed black bay-bays every night. Jay was as straight as they come, in body and mind. Hard worker. Mr. Popular in high school and everywhere he ever went, any setting he walked into. All the charisma in the world. Nice as they come. Coolest white dude around. Blackest white guy you'd ever see. Sagged his jeans. Knew his reggae, hip-hop, jazz, soul, and funk. Compassion overflowing. Cause after cause after cause. Selfless to a fault.

Jay had something else: That famous quality of hurt present in all great men. That melancholy *je ne sais quoi,* the air of certain sadness that enveloped their persona, the buffer that seemed, if not to insulate them from hardships, at least to help them surmount them even-faced. It was in Jay's eyes and in his ways. It bespoke a gentle soul, someone who'd been through much pain and suffering at a very early age, someone who'd triumphed over obstacles big enough to crush common mortals. You saw, without knowing exactly when and how, that Jay had been to Hell and back. You sensed that he connected with you at the deepest level. Here was a man who would take on your ills and your scourges along with his own. A man you could count on. A man you could lean on. A man who would teach you everything he knew. A man you'd better stay close to. A man who'd lead you to better things, better places in this world and within yourself. A champion, in the medieval sense. A poet. A prophet. A guide. A revolutionary.

They're going to eat him up, Joe told himself, getting excited. The public, the press, corporations, TV networks, the man on the street, single mothers--everybody. They'll totally identify.

He's your guy, the Devil whispered, confirming Joe's hunch. It's him. It's him. Your own brother. You won't need a contract. You won't need to train him. You won't have to work that hard. Just keep him in check. Have him stick to the plan. Tell him only what he needs to know.

Joe smacked himself on the forehead and started laughing. What had taken him so long? Jay ... it was Jay all along! His own brother!

Leave my boy alone, I told Joe and the Devil. *Vade retro, Satanas*. Leave. My. Boy. Alone.

171

Joe went in first. The house was in the same state as he had left it. All the lights on, the coffee table turned around, clothes strewn across the floor, a pile of dirty dishes in the kitchen. He pushed the coffee table back in place and stuffed the clothes in a closet. When Jay walked in everything looked normal.

"Want some soufflé?"

"I stopped eating late at night," Jay said. "Tired of burping in my sleep."

"Mind keeping me company?"

"No."

They went in the kitchen. Joe fixed himself a plate, nuked it, and ate standing up. "My church is tied to the whole idea of obtaining reparations for slavery and discrimination," he began, jumping in the water with both feet. "I'm going to use white money to fight black poverty."

Jay's ears started to whistle. The blood ran from his face. His fingertips began to tingle. His heart jumped out of his chest and tried to run away. "What did you just say?"

"Take from whites to give to blacks. That's the vision. That's the idea."

"You're crazy. You're out of your mind."

Joe dropped his plate on the counter and faced his brother. "Why?"

"Because."

"Tell me why I'm crazy."

Jay laughed. "You're not a crusader. You're not qualified."

Joe shook his head. "I take that as an insult."

Jay held his hands up. "No harm intended, bro. I'd

172

stay clear of the race business if I were you."

"Why?" Joe asked again, feeling he was already losing ground.

"You can't handle it," Jay said. "It's gonna blow up in your face. That stuff's dangerous."

Joe lowered his head and squeezed a few crocodile tears from his eyes. "I just want to help," he lamented. "Broaden my horizon, build a bridge between blacks and whites in this city, in the whole country--all while making up for my own mistakes."

"By 'taking from whites to give to blacks'?"

"It's only fair. Everything we enjoy today originated from their sweat. America's might was built on black people's backs. Tell me that's not true."

Jay looked hesitant.

"What better way to come up with money to build neighborhoods, fund scholarships, set up empowerment programs?" Joe went on. "It's not only smart: it's fair. We owe them. We owe them big time."

Jay shook his head. "I don't know, man."

Joe capitalized on the advantage he'd just regained. "I've given it a lot of thought, Jay. It makes perfect sense."

"How?"

"All of us, each and every white person in this country is guilty. Guilty of instituting, condoning, profiting from, and perpetuating slavery, segregation, and discrimination. Guilty of considering black men and women as less than our equals. Guilty of mocking them, ridiculing them in public and in our hearts." Joe moved to stand in front of his brother. "Look into your soul and tell me I'm wrong."

173

Jay remained silent.

"I want to put it out there, Jay. I want to throw the race problem straight out into the world. I want to give it a public forum, a platform. I'm gonna build this church and invite all white people and black people of goodwill to come together. I'm gonna squeeze every dollar that I can out of every corporation on American soil and put it to good use."

Jay found his tongue. "What do you know about churches?"

"Everything. I was a business major, remember?"

"You didn't graduate."

"I know enough."

Jay felt dizzy. He went to lean against the refrigerator.

"You're O.K.?" Joe asked.

"A little vertigo."

"Scared?"

"Frightened stiff."

"Why?"

"Too heavy. Too many emotions involved. You put a stick into this kind of morass, God knows what comes out."

"It needs to be done," Joe insisted. "If only for shock value. If only to start a dialogue."

"You really think you can accomplish that, don't you? You really think you're gonna make a difference?"

"At the very least I can help a few kids here and there with the funds I'm going to raise. Kind of what you're doing, but on a bigger scale and with much more impact. I'm not talking shrimp fried rice or beef and broccoli here."

174

"What's in it for you?"

"I'll draw a salary from the church. Nothing extravagant. The purpose is reward enough. Better than your average 9 to 5, don't you think?"

Jay remained quiet for a moment. "Reparations, huh?"

Joe smiled. "That's right."

"It's been tried before."

"It hasn't."

"It has. With very limited success. Didn't you Google it?"

"Here you go again."

"I'm serious."

Joe shrugged. "Don't matter. I can do it better. Bring more palpable results."

Jay seemed taken aback by Joe's determination. "You've been working on this real hard, haven't you?"

"Ever since I got fired from my last job."

"I thought you quit?"

"Ever since I quit."

They laughed.

"I got it all mapped out," Joe revealed. "Seed money; how to register and incorporate a church; how to get our targets to listen; how to spend the money."

Jay sneered. "'Our' targets?"

"Join me," Joe pleaded. "I could use your help, you know?"

Jay shook his head. "Never in a million years."

Joe pushed on. "Not worth your time?"

Jay backtracked. "It's not that. The church itself isn't such a bad idea. I can see people of different races worshipping together in the hope of fostering understanding. I can definitely see that. But the money part...."

"Positivety only carries you so far," Joe argued. "I'm not planning on catering to the black middle class. They've made it, they're fine, God bless. I want to go where I'm needed, man: Barry Farms, Sursum Corda, Petworth, Potomac Gardens, Garfield Terrace, Kennedy Street, the whole damn Southeast D.C.... They're hurting, Jay. And I know you know what I'm talking about. Patting one another on the back in a storefront isn't gonna cut it by itself. Immediate help is required. Immediate and substantial help. I'm talking millions and millions. I'm talking life-changing programs, endowments, charities, scholarships...." Joe's eyes started to shine.

Again, Jay felt scared for his brother. "You're gonna get crushed out there," he warned Joe. "You're gonna get hurt really really bad."

"I'm a big man," Joe asserted. "I can take care of myself. Your help is more than welcome, though. I'll feel better with you around."

"This isn't your fight to pick," Jay said with certainty. "Black people don't need a white knight to come and fix their lives."

"We put them in this mess. It's only fair that we should work hard to try and get them out. An hour ago you were buying meals for a handful of kids. What made you do it? Why are you working in the 'hood? Why surround yourself with children in need?"

Pushed into the ropes, Jay took the time to answer. "I'm working on myself," he finally said. "Kind of like you,

I guess. There are certain things about me that I need to change. And you know I always wanted to help poor people. Kids, especially."

"Let's call it what it is," Joe intervened: "White guilt."

Jolted by the words, Jay took his chin in his palm. The debate was making him more and more uncomfortable.

"Here's our chance to do good," Joe continued. "Do good, do right, and absolve ourselves. And--who knows?--maybe bring about a better world. I say let's go ahead and do it, Jay. Me and you."

Jay sighed. "I don't know, bro."

Joe rinsed his plate and stuck it in the dishwasher. "Sleep on it," he suggested. "And get back to me."

"Got a name for your project?" Jay asked as they walked toward their respective rooms.

"The 'Church of Retribution,'" Joe announced proudly.

Jay felt his stomach contract. "Oh, boy."

"How about those dreams of yours?" Joe asked across the hall.

"Nothing since that night. You?"

"Every day," Joe lied. "That's how I know I'm right. It's like God wants me to do this."

The more he thought about it, the more Joe was convinced he had his man. No need to scout and phish and scan. No more running the streets. No wringing his hands as the clock ticked hopelessly. He could focus on recruiting Jay, bring him onboard, try and keep this one in the family. Don't mess it up, he told himself. There won't be another chance.

A delicate dance began. To woo Jay Joe started to play the perfect little brother, showing much deference, respect, and even concern instead of the jabs, jokes, and provocation that used to form the bulk of their interactions. It took no small amount of rearranging. For too long Joe had played the fortunate son and Jay the family idiot, with Maggie's benediction and my silent complicity. (Those roles were reversed outside the house, with Jay an easy favorite with the mainstream school crowd as well as subculture adepts like skateboarders, punk rockers, potheads, ghetto revivalists, porn addicts, surfers, car buffs, karate enthusiasts, computer geeks, self-declared schizophrenics, video game zombies, designer clothing freaks, and breakdancers, while Joe struggled with friendships, dating, and general interpersonal skills.)

Whenever Maggie mentioned our eldest child it was with a disheartened sigh, a roll of the eyes, a little laugh of derision, or full-fledged anger. Jay was no good. Jay would never amount to anything. Jay was hopeless. Jay was gay. What a bum Jay was.

So ingrained were those perceptions in his psyche that Joe had to resort to extreme measures in order to bring about the necessary changes. He found hypnosis a marvelous ally. At the beginning of each day Joe started to take the time to meditate and self-indoctrinate in the lotus position, repeating, "Jay is the man, Jay is good, Jay is beautiful, Jay is the greatest guy on earth, I would give my life for Jay," over and over at a very low voice, until he worked himself into a trance. Then, trying to bring loving and nurturing feelings to life by pressing his right hand on his heart, he would look intensely at the picture of Jay he had recently taped to his wall. "I love Jay," he would then whisper, wincing because those were words he had never spoken, or even considered to utter. It almost hurt to say them. They were heavy, they were loaded, they sounded unnatural, they felt contrived. Still, Joe forced himself. "I love my brother," he would go on saying. "I love my brother with all my heart and I pledge to be caring and nurturing and attentive to his needs from now on."

The feelings didn't come easy, if at all. Joe took to revisiting the past in order to make the connection, finding Jay easier to pity than to love. Just think of everything he's been through, man. Think of him as a victim, an innocent little lamb, Maggie's punching ball. The guy was so terrified he peed in bed until he turned 13, for God's sake. 13. Remember those early morning corrections? Maggie

179

would check his mattress, find it wet, order Jay into the bathroom, and make him stand under stinging cold water while she belted him. The more Jay shouted or cried, the more she hit him. Dad was blissfully asleep. Dad never knew anything about the shower atrocities, but you, Joe, you knew the truth. Jay wasn't wetting his bed because he was too lazy to get up. The stuff just happened. He would go to sleep at night and wake up in the morning in a pool of piss. Maggie never once asked. She just assumed he was doing it on purpose. One more indignity she had to suffer from the boy. One more reason to hurt, one more reason to hate. You felt sorry for him, Joe, remember? Part of you, anyway. Because Maggie didn't know her strength and Jay would let out those little wails and sobs. They did something to you, those cries. They anguished and pained you, too. Conscious though you were of your status as mommy's little pumpkin, you were scared. Scared of the blows. Scared of the shame. Scared for Jay.

What is a brother? Joe asked himself. What should I do for Jay? Who must I be? What can I bring to the table in order for him to accept me and pull his defenses down? How to make up for the past?

Being around seemed to be the first criterion. Being there, talking as often as possible, seeing each other, being aware of the goings-on. Support and loyalty were tied for second. Genuine affection seemed necessary--prevalent, even. It could easily be faked. Then there was empathy. You had to be able to look at your sibling's life and identify the problems, know what was missing, find out what was being done wrong, and come forward with solutions. And sometimes you had to cater to his needs before your own.

Brothers give their life for each other. They sacrifice. They have each other's back. They hide nothing. They share everything.

Jay used to be all those things for me, Joe told himself. I took everything he had to offer and never gave anything back. Maybe it's time.

It's eagerly that Joe took on the role of agent, impresario, and life coach, all unbeknown to Jay. He called or dropped in on Jay at work every other day "just to check on you," giving him a big hug as soon as he saw him. He bought him protein bars, energy drinks, steel-toed working shoes, and muscle shirts. He analyzed each and every aspect of Jay's life to see what could use improvement or what required intervention. He protected Jay from the bizarre new developments in Maggie's love life, wary of the trauma they might cause. (If what Joe had witnessed on the night of the soufflé wasn't cause enough for worry, there was the receipt he found from the downtown franchise of Pleasure Place, the sex toy chain: over $1,000 worth of harnesses, spanking boards, masks, sandpaper, men's electrified underwear, tattooing kits, Damocles swords, Taser guns, digital chastity belts, dog food, and accessorized leashes.) He subscribed to a fitness and nutrition magazine. He read parenting books and familiarized himself with the stories of Pygmalion, Rasputin, Fra Diavolo, and Svengali. He pondered the accomplishments of history's major fraternal teams: Romulus and Remus; the Wright Brothers; the Brothers Johnson; the Doobie Brothers; Van Halen; the Warner Brothers; George and Ira Gershwin; the Marx Brothers; the

Isley Brothers; the Brothers Kamarazov. On a more concrete level, he made himself a part of Jay's routine, waiting until Jay got home in the evenings to have dinner together, usually well after Steve and Maggie had disappeared upstairs or across the street. They ate and talked about any and everything. Joe was careful not to be the one bringing up the subject of the Church of Retribution. When, and if, he dwelled upon it, it was with the mastery and self-control of a ballerina, a pre-defection Baryshnikov.

Their talks were a lively back and forth.

"What you're proposing has been attempted before," Jay again warned Joe. "Plenty of people have tried."

"How come we never heard of them? Where are their results? Have you noticed any change in the way black people live? Have you seen any improvement in how they are perceived or treated?"

"Not in a long time," Jay answered honestly. "But it wouldn't be something we'd be aware of in the first place. We don't stand to benefit from those changes; we're not in the civil rights business."

"In these days and times you don't have to be. Something as big as reparations for slavery would make too big a splash to ignore. The press would pick it up and feed on it for months. Months. Personally I've only heard lukewarm, semiofficial expressions of 'regret' from a few states and local governments--and that's mostly at the initiative of some outraged, ultra-persistent black lawmaker. The field is wide open, I'm telling you."

"What about Jesse Jackson and Al Sharpton?"

"They were the first I thought about," Joe acknowledged. "But no, nothing. Both Jesse and Al work on a case-by-case basis. They don't do nationwide campaigns. You have a problem with a white man or a white institution, public or private, you go see them. They summon the press, drum up protests, start shaking trees, and cull the harvest. Not to say they're not doing an excellent job. Their profiling and police brutality cases are handled exceedingly well. It works both ways, too. Anybody on the white side of the fence who wants to reach out to the black community can go powwow with them. Every once in a while you'll have a white radio jock or TV personality go on damage-control mode after letting slip a slur or an offensive remark. Guess who gets the first phone call?"

"What about Oprah?"

Joe shook his head. "Thought about her, too. Nothing. Her TV show, her Broadway play, her magazine, her book endorsements, her woman empowerment projects, her Angel Network. Oprah's got her hands full--or completely tied by her white audience. Never heard her say a single thing about reparations."

"Those are the true heroes," Jay argued. "The black representatives. If they're not touching the reparations thing it's probably because it stinks."

"They're no more heroes than you and me, Jay. Otherwise they'd be at the frontline mobilizing the masses, organizing the movement, preaching and raising hell nonstop. I mean, don't get me wrong: Jesse and Al will threaten boycotts and go in the streets in a minute--all they do is march-march-march year round--and I would never in

183

a million years call Oprah a lightweight.... But when it comes to political and social advancement, their effort is lacking. Wide open, Jay.... The field is wide open."

"What's holding them back, you think?"

Joe took the time to think. "They don't have the fiber," he said dismissively. "They don't have what it takes. Martin and Malcolm.... Love them, hate them, or fear them, they were leaders. They gave their all. They turned their backs on riches, family, common pleasures, and everything that sweetens life and makes it more bearable. They were all about work-work-work and doing what it takes, doing your best, paying the price. They looked death square in the eye and accepted their destiny. But these guys here don't want to miss a thing. All about today, the right now. Big houses, women all over, nice suits, nice hairstyles, corporate boards, dividends, syndicated radio shows."

"A shame," Jay admitted, thinking about Kevin and all the Kennedy Street kids. "There's so much real work to do."

"Exactly."

The brothers did the sensible thing and Googled the word "reparations" on Jay's computer. Jesse, Al, or Oprah were nowhere near any of the links that came up.

"Told you," Joe gloated.

"Not so fast," Jay quieted him. "I see Farrakhan."

Joe immediately felt uncomfortable. He didn't mind invading Jesse and Al and Oprah's territory. He hadn't given them a second thought, to be honest. But the Nation of Islam was something else altogether. The bow ties, the bean pies, the fierce and divisive rhetoric, the fiery newspaper peddled by unsmiling, suit-clad troopers.... He found black Muslims confrontational and threatening. Didn't they keep some kind of armed faction called Fruit of Islam at the ready back in the day? What if they came after him just like the Iranians had done that writer, the "Satanic Verses" guy--what was his name again?--forcing him to hide and live in fear for many, many years?

Joe cleared his throat. "Farrakhan? I thought the man was dead?"

"Not yet," Jay informed him without taking his eyes off the screen. "He's ailing, though. Thinking about stepping down."

Joe wiped the sweat off his brow. "So what do you see?"

"Salaam Restaurant, Chicago. Farrakhan and several groups that have reparations as their core agenda had a 'great sitting-down' to tackle the issue."

"What groups?" Joe, feeling as though he was about to faint, found the strength to ask.

"Just about everybody," Jay said. " The Universal Negro Improvement Association..."

"Ain't that Marcus Garvey's old movement?"

"Not sure."

"Who else was at that restaurant?"

"The New Afrikan People Organization (N.A.P.O.)," Jay read diligently.

"Never heard of them."

"Me neither."

"Go on."

"The Republic of New Afrika, that's with a 'k.'"

Jay and Joe both took the time to shake their heads

185

and laugh a little. From the top of my armoire I did so, too.

"The Restitution Study Group," Jay went on; "The Kwame Ture Institute; the N.A.A.C.P..."

"I was wondering when they were gonna show up."

"The New Black Panther Party, and...." Jay paused a moment and looked at Joe.

"What?" Joe asked, worry twisting his insides.

"You're not gonna like this. The last group is called National Coalition of Blacks for Reparations in America (N.'C.O.B.R.A.)."

Joe put a brave face on his distress. "You mean to tell me that all those people are out there fighting for reparations as we speak?"

Jay took a deep breath. "That's what it looks like."

"No way," Joe exclaimed. "What's that you clicked on?"

"A newspaper article."

"What's the date on it?"

Jay found it on the top right corner. "August 9, 2003."

Joe felt a rush of fresh air power his lungs. "Almost four years ago," he declared. "They sat down at that restaurant four years ago and nothing came out of it. I knew it! I knew it!"

He slapped Jay in the back. They stopped for the night.

Joe had the Nova washed and detailed, leaving no spot untouched. She gleamed, sparkled and shone. He put her on sale for $25,000, advertising both in local newspapers and on the Net. It took an immense effort to come to terms with the pending separation. I wish I could say that Joe had felt half as bad when I left Earth. He loved his car more than anything in the world. She was his only possession. She was so much like him, he thought: classy, sporty, tough, intricate, dangerous, unique. She turned heads everywhere they went. Chicks loved her. Men were jealous. Nobody would give him a second look now. No one would double-check their mirrors when they heard him and saw him prowl. No one would freeze in terror or envy as he growled past. The church. It was all for the church, man. Joe braced himself for the loss, inconsolable in advance.

I knew, right then and there, that there would be no avoiding this thing. Joe selling his car meant that the Church of Retribution would happen, ready or not. It would come to see life, and change life as we knew it.

I understood, and so, levitating on my knees, closing my eyes and clasping my hands, I prayed. Dear God, I said, save the world from my knucklehead son Joe. Protect us, dear God, from the machinations of Satan. Keep my sons, my straying wife Margaret, and the rest of Your dutiful sheep from greed, stupidity, self-indulgence, and Evil. Forgive them, dear God, for they are flawed. Save us, O God.

Jay kept searching the Internet on his own through the following week, mostly out of a sense of duty. No matter what Joe decided in the end, he would help him get informed.

What he found seemed to validate Joe's claims. There had indeed existed a reparations movement, but it

187

seemed to have been short-lived. A flurry of declarations of intent, conferences, symposiums, and even a lawsuit or two back in 2002 and 2004. And then nothing.

"Forget about Farrakhan, the N.A.A.C.P., that N.'C.O.B.R.A., or even the New Black Panther Party," he told Joe one evening after work. Your true competitor is a lawyer called Deadria Farmer-Paellmann. Black woman married to a white guy. Dreadlocks. Early 40s. Went to law school with the specific intent to discover a way to wrangle from Uncle Sam a national apology and federal restitution for descendants of slaves. Changed focus after she realized that a victory over the government was unlikely. Identified about 60 corporations that profited directly from slavery. Got Aetna, the insurance giant, to apologize for covering slave owners against the loss of their human investments. Filed a lawsuit in the Brooklyn federal court in early 2002 against a handful of those corporations, seeking billions of dollars in reparations on behalf of 35 million African Americans. Suit still pending."

Joe's hands started to shake. He hid them behind his back and focused his will on keeping a straight and only remotely interested face. How could he have missed that woman? What kind of fool was he not to have done the most basic of researches? What did he have to show for the hours--no, the days--spent inside the library's Quiet Room? An amateur. He was an amateur. "I've heard about that Deadria," he affirmed. "She doesn't worry me at all. I'm not suing anybody. I have neither the means nor the time. That's not the way to do it."

Jay nodded. "She seems to be a tough cookie, but nobody's heard from her since. Same with..." Jay consulted his printouts. "Same with the Reparations Coordinating Committee, a group including a Harvard law professor called Charles Ogletree, Randall Robinson, of TransAfrica Forum, the recently deceased Johnnie Cochran, of 'if it don't fit, you must acquit' fame, and Cornel West, the black scholar. They were also building momentum for a class-action lawsuit back in 2002. Their committee also disappeared without a trace." Jay threw the papers on his desk. "My point is, those are all champs, Joe. If they failed so lamentably..."

"This battle is not one to be fought--or won--in a court of law," Joe declared. "The court of public opinion is the one that matters. The field of reparations is still wide open, as far as I'm concerned. Wide open!"

Jay handed him the stack of documents. "Some pretty interesting stuff in there. It makes you wonder about the very ground you stand on. Slaves, boats, and cotton cargoes were insured by firms like Lloyd's, of London. A company called WestPoint Stevens mass-produced garments that were designed to sustain extreme use while reflecting the slaves' inferior status. Railroad, tobacco, and mining interests used slaves on loan or bought their own outright. The original benefactors of some of the country's most prestigious universities, I'm talking Harvard, Princeton, Yale, the University of Virginia, and Brown, were wealthy slave owners. Newspaper publishers including Tribune and Gannett, the parent of USA Today, profited by running ads about auctions and helping owners track runaway slaves. Some of the names in these pages read like a Who's Who: the three brothers of Lehman Bros. owned slaves; FleetBoston's founder was a Rhode Island slave trader named John Brown; the investment bank Brown Bros. Harriman loaned millions directly to planters to buy slaves; besides Aetna, insurers like New York Life and A.I.G. sold life policies on slaves; JPMorgan Chase Manhattan has the dubious distinction of having slavery as well as Nazi ties: The Paris branches of both Chase and JPMorgan were bankers for the Third Reich. During World War II they froze assets and seized accounts and safe-deposit boxes belonging to Jews."

"Nice people. Didn't the Jews get their stuff back?"

"You bet. The U.S. government helped broker compensation deals between Holocaust victims and their families and the banks."

"Yet hypocrisy is the norm when it comes to black people," Joe said, righteous outrage getting the best of him.

"A few more noteworthy facts," Jay continued, "speaking of Empire: Even though slave labor was used for building and maintaining public infrastructures, legal challenges such as statutes of limitation and sovereign immunity prevent lawsuits against the federal government. Basically, you can't sue the government unless the government grants you permission to do so. That's why that lady Deadria switched objectives."

"I'm not planning to go after Empire," Joe reiterated.

"I'm glad," Jay said. "Don't take public support for granted, either. 9 out of 10 white respondents to a February 2002 CNN poll thought the government should not make cash payments to slave descendants. 55% of black respondents said yes. When the question was, 'Should corporations that made profits from slavery apologize to

African Americans?' 68% of blacks said yes and 23% said no. The numbers for whites were respectively 32% and 62%." Jay paused. "You okay? You look a little pale."

Joe smiled bravely. "I'm okay."

"There's more," Jay continued. "No company accused of profiting from slavery was breaking U.S. law at the time: Slavery was not a crime. Closer to us, the L.A. and Chicago city councils require every firm wishing to do business with those two cities to disclose any ties to the slave trade they or their corporate predecessors might have had. As you can guess, acquisitions and mergers make it hard to pinpoint culprits and assign blame more than 150 years after the facts. Some of these firms are already making amends. They fund college scholarships for African Americans, they pay for studies on racial disparities, they sponsor forums on race."

Joe clutched the pages Jay had handed him. "That won't wash away the blood on their hands," he said through his teeth.

"Perhaps," Jay agreed. "But where exactly do you come in?"

Joe, who was starting to get dizzy, took the time to answer. "Two angles," he said. "The first is the Church of Retribution, where whites and blacks will worship side by side, and where whites will be offered an opportunity to redeem themselves in words and actions, i.e., cold cash. The second is the guerrilla war I'm proposing myself to bring to all the white companies in the U.S., public or private, old or new. I'll make no distinction whatsoever. If you're white and American, you owe. No nit-picking here. We sinned as a group, we'll pay as a group."

Jay whistled softly. "You've got your work cut out for you."

Joe opened his palms. "Help me," he pleaded.

Jay shook his head. "I think it's pure folly, Joe. The craziest idea I've ever heard."

"Not an idea," Joe corrected. "A mission. God wants me--us--to do this."

"I'll believe it when I see it or hear it for myself," Jay declared. "So far, as I was telling you, my visions have been of a totally different nature. And what do you mean by 'guerrilla tactics'?"

"Grassroots campaigns. The power of the Internet. Flash-mobs. Robocalls. Public Relation offensives. Image busting. Reputation trashing. Propaganda. Name calling. Sidewalk hawking. Crashing shareholder meetings. Swaying consumers. Pulling African-American money away from the banks and the businesses that refuse to pay."

"Sounds like strong-arm tactics to me."

"Whatever it takes."

"Watch for racketeering charges."

"I'm no dummy."

"Well," Jay said with finality, "count me out."

Joe felt abandoned, and much worse: He felt heartbroken. Ben was dead. Maggie was falling head over heels for Steve and acting more and more irrationally. Jay was letting him down. The Nova would soon be gone. He wanted to cry. Cry. "You sure?"

"Positive. I'm not saying that your cause is without merit, mind you. You'll find plenty like-minded souls in the documents I just gave you. Over 500 of them."

"What do you mean?"

"Deadria had floated an electronic petition on the Internet back when she was gearing up for a fight. That database makes for interesting reading."

Like-minded souls, maybe not. Sharing common objectives, definitely. 529 petition signers, white and black, men and female, some with full names, phone numbers, and comments attached.

Marsha Cooper Stronman, Philadelphia, PA : "I trust the corporate companies that caused pain and suffering to many will try to extend some portion of a resolution."

Tyranus Blackock, AK: "Kill da white people! Make dem pay! I need some gold teef and a new Bentley."

Shelda Glover, PA: "My great-uncle was branded on the cheeks and flanks."

Derek Winnow, CA: "Show me da money."

Christopher Brieger: "Free African Americans of credit debt or reduce the debt by half so we able to pay it off and be able to do other things like buy a home."

Clayborn Williams, CA: "Just do it."

Laquinsa Williams, OH: "We deserve to be compusated."

I can sort the serious ones from the lunatics and call them when I'm ready, Joe told himself. They'll be my first followers, my core 500. I'm not alone. Lord, I'm not alone.

I had hoped--again against all hope--that Jay's refusal to join forces with Joe would slow Joe down. It did, but only until Maggie informed both of them of her decision to sell the house.

"I'm throwing in the towel," she wrote in an e-mail.

"Steve and I want to live together. We're getting rid of both our houses to buy a beach property jointly. The houses, and everything in them, will be simultaneously auctioned on eBay in exactly one month. Be prepared."

No flipping fixer-uppers for Steve and Mag. This wasn't a seller's market--hadn't been for over a year now. Their plan was to liquidate their homes "as is," following the rationale that there were people out there who wanted nothing better than to live somebody else's life. All the rooms would be left intact: beds unmade, pictures on the walls, food on the stove, in the refrigerator and pantry, dishes in the dishwasher, cars in the garage, music playing, all the lights on, the keys under the mat. The buyer or buyers could just walk in, assume a totally different identity, and start a whole new life.

Steve was to blame for that interesting concept. I was curious to see if it would work. "All around the world people want to live the American way," he told Mag. "U.S.A., Number One. They'd kill to come here and live like we live. Especially the French. Nobody wants to be French any more. The glory, the advantages, the competitive edge are gone. Soccer, wine, haute cuisine, couture, colonies ... everything has disappeared. To be *français* is so passé. I'll market us heavily on eBay Europe and I bet you that someone will bite quick. Provided there are no visa-related issues, a whole family will be able to travel to Washington and dive right into the American experience."

Maggie's e-mail upset the boys more than a little. Why hadn't she talked to them directly? Because she didn't trust herself enough to stay calm. Quicker and quicker on the draw as the days passed, Trigger-Happy Mama Maggie didn't want to risk shooting one of the boys before she could elope. She wanted a clean break. No tears, no phone calls, no recriminations, no hysterics. She was letting everything and everyone go except for her Steve. Jay and Joe she just couldn't stand any more. Couldn't do it. Had done enough, tried enough, been patient enough.

Joe had had the nerve to tell her about his plans--"Ma, I'm founding a church"--with the expectant air of a dog about to be let out to play.

"A church?"

"A church."

"What kind of church?"

"The Church of Retribution."

"Retribution for what?"

"For slavery."

"Where?" Maggie had inquired, not knowing what else to say, her mind hiding from her, her wits playing hide and seek, her palms playing the wringing game.

"How about the basement?" Joe had proposed as if it were the most sound and the most natural solution.

"My basement?" Maggie had asked, holding the wall as red dots danced before her eyes and palpitations started to make her chest contract.

She'd regained her balance after drawing a huge breath. Was Joe crazy? Was he on something? Maggie slapped him good and searched his pockets, his closet, and the Nova without finding any drugs.

It's a miracle she didn't kill him that day. A miracle. Her own son. Joe Wilson. Her little boy. The one she'd favored outrageously from day one betraying her like that, stabbing her in the heart. A church. A nigger church. In her basement. That was the last straw. The last straw!

"Put it on paper," Steve suggested. "That way, even if you end up killing one of them you'll have a trail, a body of evidence, something to show you were only responding to a most disgusting provocation."

And so Maggie dispatched the e-mail. One month was too much. She should have kicked them out purely and simply, effective immediately. Joe and Jay wanted to be black, let them be black. Let them get a taste of the full experience. No papa, no mama to care for them. Out of her house. Go struggle and fight like the people you love so much. Go sink or swim. Go and see if you can save even yourself.

"After everything I've done for them," she cried to Steve while choking him with the barrel of the M-16 one day, sitting on his chest in full policewoman uniform. "Such ingrates. Such renegades."

"Kids...." Steve managed to say in sympathy before his air supply went nil, bringing him more and more pleasure the closer he was getting to asphyxia.

"Joe's church was the lowest blow," Maggie continued after copiously spraying Mace in Steve's face. "'The Church of Retribution.' I almost had a heart attack. Can you imagine?"

Steve stuck a blue tongue out. In his eyes was the most beautiful expression of gratitude.

Life couldn't be better, despite Maggie's complaints. They were deeply in love. The sex was intense and fulfilling. The drone project was going great. He had gotten rid of his daughters by shipping them both to rehab. Maggie and he were due to look at a used Hummer later that afternoon, their first purchase together. Soon they'd start touring the area for a beachfront house where a secret dungeon could be built. Bouillabaisse was on the menu tonight. What more could a man ask?

Joe sold the Nova to a Japanese kid named Atsushi for $5,000 above the asking price. Atsushi traveled specifically for the transaction, shook violently when he test-drove the car, hugged Joe after paying him, took pictures, shrink-wrapped the Nova, took pictures, put her on a pallet, took pictures, got her towed to the Baltimore port, and shipped her to Nagoya, his hometown.

Joe fought the most insidious of depressions for the next couple of days. He'd never experienced such a loss. Never. It was as if his life were ending. Even the sight of Atsushi's cash left him cold. What was money compared to the void, the emptiness, the fracture? He had committed the ultimate sacrifice. Nobody could accuse him of not spilling his blood. No one could ever say he hadn't walked the walk.

The thought of his church kept him going. To keep his mind off the pain, he entered an online certification program that put him on track to become an ordained minister in his denomination of choice in a matter of weeks and for a little under $200.

"Let's shack together," he proposed to Jay.

"I'm taking Nasro's old apartment," Jay informed him. "The one above Souk."

"Can I come?"

"Too small," Jay refused. "I don't know how Nasro managed to live there with his wife and children. I'm sure it'll feel cramped just between me, my computer, and my guitar."

Joe looked on the verge of tears. "You don't want me to come with you, do you? I don't mean anything to you."

"You're my little brother," Jay assured him. "You mean the world."

It's true that those were very, very tight quarters. A studio apartment with an open kitchenette, a single closet, a bath, and three windows. Since he had moved to a house Nasro used it only to perform his daily prayers and to take precious refuge from Souk's nonstop grind. You gained access to it from Georgia Avenue through a small door and a flight of stairs that were all but invisible, sandwiched as they were between Souk and Happy Cuts.

"It's Spartan," Nasro warned Jay the first time he took him upstairs, a few nights before Maggie's ultimatum was to expire. "Completely empty. All the furniture went with us to Silver Spring."

A profound sense of peace enveloped Jay as he walked in and started looking around. The walls were white, the floors wooden, the kitchen equipped, if barely, the shower functional. Only two objects filled the living space: Nasro's prayer rug and a black and white portrait of Mahmoud Muhammad Taha, the founding father of the Republican Brotherhood. He wore a white robe and a

199

turban. His gaze was both direct and faraway. His forehead shone, appearing to let out a light from within.

Nasro moved to unhook the frame.

"Leave it," Jay asked.

"If you want," Nasro said. "I have several more at the house. One in each room."

"I could use the rug as well," Jay told him. "Unless you need it."

Nasro smiled.

"This is exactly what I was looking for," Jay remarked, letting the monk in him run free. "I already feel at home. I can eat pistachio nuts, dried figs, and dates, drink water from the sink, and sleep right on the floor."

"Perfect for a simple life," Nasro approved. "I spent whole Sundays here meditating. It's particularly pleasant on late summer afternoons, when the sun goes down and the breeze starts blowing through. I takes me back to Rufaa, my place of birth. I swear I can smell the Blue Nile and hear little children swimming."

They talked money. Nasro gave Jay the use of the apartment for a nominal sum. Hadn't it been against his policy, he would have given it to him for free.

They were getting to be more than good friends, having long ago crossed the restrictive threshold of boss-employee dynamics. A sense of kinship was developing. Jay was learning much just by observing the older man. His seriousness, his piety, his general goodwill, his good disposition. Jay had never met so peaceful, so disciplined, so content a person. Happiness, he saw, had nothing to do with accumulating things, heeding the call of unchecked ambition, and living in the fast lane. Happiness started with oneself, the conquest of one's desires and impulses, the shaping of one's beliefs and actions around a credo. For Nasro Islam represented that core, that center. He was a man of faith.

"Come on up to pray as many times a day as you wish," Jay invited him. "And when Ramadan comes around in a few weeks I'll fast with you to show solidarity."

Joe helped Jay move. Maggie checked each and every item Jay was planning to take with him. He gave back the keys to the Eldorado and the Magnum. "The Eldorado must stay because I'm throwing both cars in with the house," Maggie said. "But the gun is yours. Take it."

"Don't want it," Jay affirmed.

Maggie was dumbfounded. "Ain't you gonna be living on top of that Zook? Ain't that a black area? Why would you wanna walk around unarmed? It's your right to pack. The Constitution protects you. You're in your own country."

"'Souk,'" Joe corrected.

"You and Joe are the only two people I ever needed protection from," Jay declared.

"Now that's not very nice," Maggie protested.

"Not nice," Joe echoed.

"Keep it," Maggie insisted.

Keep it, I told Jay from the top of the armoire. Come on, don't be a fool. Keep it. Mag the Rag is right: You might just need it.

"I don't need it," Jay repeated. "But I'll take a few of dad's old albums, if you allow me to."

Maggie frowned. "Which ones?"

201

"Parliament. Darondo. Lee Perry. James Brown. Willie Hutch. Bobby Womack. Bill Withers."

Maggie nodded reluctantly.

Give him the damn albums, I intervened. All of them, if he likes. They're mine.

"The top two eBay bidders are Nepalese and Belgian," Maggie informed us. "Sanjib and Michel. Though I doubt either will be into that kind of stuff, I can only let you have 20 records. The house has to be as normal as possible when they walk in."

Jay smiled. "20 is plenty."

You petty you, I told Mag.

"When is the auction ending?" Joe inquired.

"3 days and 17 hours," Maggie said. "You better start packing."

"I'll be gone, too," Joe declared with much more courage than he felt in his heart.

The boys were putting a good face on the whole deal, but the notion that total strangers from across the world were to take over the house they grew up in had something creepy about it. You could look at it as a case of globalization gone awry, of course. But how bad were those people's lives if they must turn to such radical measures in order to make a change? Was this really what immigrants wanted most of all: To forgo everything they had been and all they had known just to become a Joe, a Jay, a Maggie, in the foreign street of a foreign country? Did Empire's culture and way of life really exercise such pull? What did Sanjib and Michel and their families hope to gain? Was that better than what they were turning their backs to?

On the other hand, leaving the only home they had known with the bulk of their stuff still in it was a fitting transition for Jay and Joe. They were done here.

All in all, Jay wasn't taking much. The computer, the guitar, Lisha's picture, a few pairs of jeans, white T-shirts, sneakers, the LPs he wouldn't be able to play but wanted for nostalgic reasons. I, before Chris, had got him hooked on a few things here and there. Even Joe, when he cared to remember, knew his Stax and Solar and Curtom and Island and Trojan and Motown and Atlantic.

The last night that Jay spent in his childhood room was rather eventful. The voice that had given him a break for so long made a major comeback around 6. Only, it didn't sound the same at all. "Work for me!" the voice said loud and clear. "Work for me!" seven times. It seemed to be coming from the sky. It had a distant crackle, the insistence, authority, brevity, and finality of a command--not unlike something Moses would have heard on the Sinai. Somebody from up above was barking orders. Soon lightening would strike, bushes catch afire, and stone tablets exchange hands. Jay jumped out of bed, got on shaky knees, and started to pray. "Lord," he pleaded, "please tell me what You expect of me. Here I am at Your service, O Lord."

No matter how much Jay strained his ears, no explanation, clarification, directives, or specification followed. The voice had retreated, leaving yet another enigma behind.

Had Jay turned on the light and looked up, he might have remarked on the ceiling a small object taped to the inside of the bulb cover. It was a NanoSnitch, a digital player/recorder that wasn't much bigger or thicker than a silver dollar. Joe had purchased it from a pawn shop the day before. After recording the short injunction he had set the playback function for 6 a.m., unscrewed the bulb's old-fashioned receptacle, and tucked the gadget right beside a fossilized cockroach while Jay was taking a shower.

"Had a good night?" Joe innocently asked Jay the next morning.

"So-so," Jay answered, his eyes red, his breath short, his head full of questions. "Work for me." Now what? Who was "me"? What kind of work? What was this new madness? Should he check himself into a mental institution?

"Does schizophrenia run in the family?" he asked Maggie at breakfast.

Maggie shook her head. "Alcoholism, bigotry, moral rot, and child abuse, maybe. Schizophrenia? We've never been that crazy."

They called Jay a cab right after eating. "I'll ride down with you," Joe proposed.

Maggie hugged Jay after all his stuff was loaded in the trunk. He looked so sad and helpless that she almost called the whole thing off. The poor little thing cried all night, she told herself, her mother's heart trying hard to pierce the calcified plaque that had been choking it for decades. But it seemed way too late to turn back, and way too hard. Jay and Joe's time was up. When kids started acting this crazy you had no choice but to let them go in the sake of sanity and prevention. Otherwise you ended up killing the little bastards. "Don't go and get yourself shot," she cautioned Jay.

A muffled sound filtered from the upstairs bedroom. Steve, tied to the bed since early last night, was getting impatient for his next beating. Maggie had booby-trapped the mattress after he complained about her latest habit ("Does the assault rifle have to lie with us every night? Suppose it discharges in our sleep?"). The loaded M-16 was standing between Steve's legs, cannon pointing at his crotch, strings connecting the trigger to Steve's big toes.

Maggie patted Jay's back and let go of him, literally and figuratively. "Love ya, sonny," she wanted to say, but the words didn't come out. They just couldn't. Too late to be sentimental. "Take care."

"You, too, Ma."

"Mission accomplished," Maggie announced after bursting into the bedroom. "One down, one to go. Joe should be out by tomorrow. And then either Sanjib or Michel is going to come take possession of this house. Yours should be gone by next week. After that it's freedom song, baby. You, me, the Hummer, and the castle in the sand."

She smacked the top of Steve's head. It rolled left and snapped back in place. Steve contracted his muscles in order to maintain the rest of his body in perfect immobility. His toes didn't move an inch. All around him the mattress was damp with sweat. He was on top of his game. "Good boy," Maggie said before smacking him again. Then, using the tip of her tongue, she proceeded to tickle the arch of his left foot.

"Everything all right?" Joe asked Jay as the cab was passing the old Ibex, the go-go nightclub turned into a furniture showroom turned into condominiums.

"Everything's fine," Jay answered, still too frazzled to share his pre-dawn experience.

Two trips were all it took to carry the stuff upstairs. Nicole came out of her shop to say hi. Joe, who knew about her but had never been formally introduced, got the shakes when she looked him in the eye and extended her hand. "Why do I feel this profound respect for dad all of a sudden?" he wondered aloud.

Because you'll never have a woman like this, I told him. Your blondes can't compare.

Then, as Jay showed him the place: "You were right. This is pretty small. Where's your furniture? Where are you gonna eat and read and sleep?"

"On that rug on the floor," Jay said, hoping that the voice wouldn't follow him here. Maybe there was something wrong with Military Road. Maybe the damn place was haunted. Here, with Taha watching over him, everything would be all right. He could feel it.

"Whose picture is that on the wall?" Joe asked.

"Taha," Jay, in deep contemplation, replied.

Joe let out a sigh of impatience. Jay and his riddles. "Who's that Tahoe?"

"Taha. The leader of the Republican Brothers."

"The one who got hanged? Nasro's chief?"

"Himself."

"Forgot to look him up. What was he accused of, again?"

"Treason. Apostasy. Are you familiar with the

Koran at all?"

Joe turned toward his brother. "You're joking, right?"

Lost in the picture, Jay started to speak. "It was revealed to Prophet Mohammed in two phases. The first comprises what are known as the 'Meccan verses.' They were dictated to the Prophet during the first 13 years of Islam, and they present it as the ideal religion. They convey a message of tolerance, gentle persuasion, peace, and equality between man and woman and among all races. According to Taha, those verses, though first in chronology, represent the 'Second Message of Islam,' one that had to be postponed until humanity reached a stage of development where it could accept its teachings."

Joe looked at the portrait. Under his turban, the man Taha seemed to peer straight into his Machiavellian soul. Joe looked away.

"The second phase of the revelation of the Koran constitutes the 'First Message,' Jay went on. Those verses were dictated to the Prophet and a cluster of followers in Medina, the VII century Islamic city-state, where they had taken refuge from persecution. They are called 'Medinan verses.' Their message is one of jihad, coercion, and threat. They form the basis of the *sharia*, or Islamic law, which was developed by scholars over the next few centuries."

Jay took a deep breath. Pulling Lisha's picture from his bag, he hung it next to Taha's on a nail that had supported one of Nasro's family portraits.

"Because they implied that the Koran was less than perfect and that it should be open to interpretation and critical revision, Taha's teachings amounted to subversion,

207

both religious and political. Those were the '80s. Sudan had become a radicalized Islamic state. Its rulers had no use for Taha's pamphlets and street-corner sermons, his egalitarian treatment of women and non-Muslims, his attempts to fuse dogma with life in a modern and democratic society. He died, in essence, because of his beliefs. His followers, who never amounted to more than a few thousand, were dispersed."

Jay stopped talking.

Joe's mouth was hanging open. "How do you know all this?"

"Nasro."

"You're scaring me, man."

Jay shrugged. "Nothing wrong with informing oneself, right?"

Joe appeared dubious. "I don't know, Jay. You're taking the need for information kind of far."

They went to Wings 'n' Things for breakfast. Again, seeing the "For Lease" sign on the shoemaker's window gave Joe pause. He tried to peer through the smoked glass and saw nothing but an old counter. He scribbled the number on the sign on an old receipt, called it from Military Road, made an appointment with a broker for the same afternoon, walked through the confined space, deemed it fit for the Church of Retribution, obtained assurances that it would pass the city-mandated health and fire inspections, and requested a 6-month contract, effective immediately.

"You're fast," the realtor, a sullen, bald, and very round man called Mofas, whose age and ethnicity Joe had a hard time placing, commented. "What kind of business are you in?"

"Religion," Joe answered after signing the paperwork, cutting his very first check as owner/guide of the church, and accepting the keys.

Mofas's eyes filled with tears as a wicked cough racked his chest. He spat in a cotton handkerchief, folded it in four, wiped his brow with one of the clean flaps, pushed the handkerchief back in his pocket, and handed Joe his card for the 5th time. "Have you incorporated yet?"

"Tomorrow."

Mofas looked Joe up and down and nodded. It took a fox to know one. "I'm a CPA as well," he declared. "Give me a shout. My nickname is 'Houdini.' I get people out of the most inextricable morasses. I can make money appear and disappear just like that."

Mofas smiled and snapped his fingers. He reminded Joe of someone, an actor, though Joe couldn't say exactly who. That Danny de something, maybe. "I know stuff about offshore shelters and compounded tax breaks that even Wall Street sharks can't dream up," Mofas went on boasting.

Joe dangled his new keys on his right index finger after Mofas left. He folded his arms behind his back and surveyed the place more thoroughly. Counter, display shelves, back room, busted floors, a rusted boiler, an archaic AC system, rudimentary toilets. The smell of leather, rubber, industrial glue, and honest sweat. The front window could easily be de-smoked. Joe closed his eyes and saw pews, a pulpit, a small altar--or should he call it a stage? He closed his eyes again and saw desks, computers, phones, and credit card machines. He closed them for the third time and heard songs, hymns, ka-chings, the sweet sound of money coming home to daddy.

Joe felt double his size. A gambler, a man of action, a shot caller. "It's beginning," he said loudly, scaring a family of rats. "It's starting."

"What are you still doing here?" Jay asked Joe when the latter walked into Souk in the middle of the 5 p.m. rush.

"We're neighbors," Joe announced. "You may congratulate me."

Joe's next move was the purchase of a bucket from Youngin's lot across the street. The 1999 Honda on special would have been the sensible choice, but driving foreign had never seemed right to Joe, or me, or anybody in the family for that matter, practicality and efficiency be damned. So Joe followed his heart and went for the $500 1984 Buick. Still, it was a huge step down from the Nova. If that wasn't a sacrifice, Joe didn't know what was.

He went to Home Depot for cleaning supplies and to Hudson Trail Outfitters for a sleeping bag and camping stuff, including a North Face "Summit Series" tent, a burner, a pot, a spoon, energy drinks, teriyaki pemmican, and powdered soup.

"I'm leaving," he told Maggie after packing all his suits and his toothbrush.

"Goodbye," Maggie said.

"You're not asking me where I'm going?"

"I know where you're going," she assured him.

"Where's that?"

"Perdition," Maggie said, dropping the word like a bomb. "That's the road you're on."

"Talk for yourself," Joe mumbled through his teeth.

Maggie looked around for a gun. "What did you say?"

"Nothing," Joe affirmed vehemently.

The first night was pure hell. Nervous energy kept Joe right at the edge of sleep. The dust choked him almost to death. Rats kept tripping over the tent's wires, forcing him to take refuge on the counter. Crackheads fighting over a lighter almost smashed the front window. Police cars and ambulances raced up and down the avenue, sirens ululating. During one stretch of fitful sleep Joe saw himself dressed in white, sporting a long beard as he healed a sea of black worshippers. One-hundred dollar bills were pinned all over his robe. More were glued to his mouth and to his ears.

Above Souk, Jay was just as restless. He dreamed of Lisha and woke up with an untamable and very painful erection, the kind he hoped would stick around when time came for live action. The dream was vivid, full of good feeling and pretty colors. He was buying Lisha flowers in the shop next to Cairo. She had a bunch of kids with her. "I love you," she told Jay before he and she went their separate ways.

"Wishing you were here," he whispered to the picture on the wall, missing her like never before, wondering if he'd ever see her again. Shouldn't he take that portrait down? Shouldn't he give in to one of the luscious Kennedy Street girls who stuffed his pockets full of phone numbers every day? Wasn't it time? Next to her on the wall, Taha seemed watchful and benevolent.

"What's up with the rats?" Joe asked Mofas after rousing him a little after 7. "They' re all over the place! You should have said something!"

"Those were thrown in free," Mofas assured him.

"Very funny," Joe said.

"I'll rent you a high-pitch sound machine," Mofas told him after he stopped laughing. "It'll take care of your problem in no time."

"What about tools?" Joe asked. "You have tools?"

"I have all kinds of tools," Mofas assured him.

Joe borrowed Jay's keys, took a shower in the upstairs apartment, hid the NanoSnitch behind the radiator, and made a copy of the keys before returning them. For the next seven consecutive mornings, Jay would be awakened by the "Work for me!" tirade coming from different places around the apartment: the toilet tank, the kitchen sink, Lisha's picture, the refrigerator. From inside objects, even: his computer, his guitar, his shoes, his clothes. It drove him nuts. It made him cringe and wince in dreadful anticipation. "Work for me!" "Work for me!" It made him beg and pray for liberation: "Lord, just tell me what to do and I'll do it. Lord, just point the way." Good or bad, the night creatures had never tormented him like this. Too troubled to think rationally, and plagued as he had been with nightmares and scary encounters since childhood, Jay never for one second suspected a machination.

Joe had the good sense to take the contraption off service at the end of that week. It was getting hard for him, too. Every time he got out of the shower and looked for a new place to hide the NanoSnitch he felt Taha's eyes on him. Following, accusing, damning. Those fierce eyes on the wall. Lisha he didn't mind. The girl was all right. He didn't think he'd exchanged more than two sentences with her the whole time she'd worked at Cairo and dated Jay. She didn't scare him in any way. Her portrait didn't radiate, it didn't swell, it didn't explode with moral rigidity. Taha was another matter altogether. "Fraud!" he seemed to be saying. "Cheat!" "Liar!"

Joe spent as much time with Jay as possible. He hung around Souk, taking in the scene. His respect for both Nasro and Jay grew. The men were saints--saints--there was no other word. To deal with thieves, addicts, drunks, paupers, and angered blacks day after day after day.... He didn't know how they did it. Boys and girls who should have been in school showed up every half-hour for the most trivial things. Mothers taught 5- and 6-year-olds how to steal. Young girls were ready to prostitute themselves for a pack of cigarettes. Teenagers walked in 15 at a time to loot the ice-cream box and the DVD stand. Frustrated customers hurled insults and objects across the counter. Fights broke out inside the aisles. Not a day without its share of incidents, high-flaring emotions, lost tempers, and heartbreak. "Poverty isn't pretty," Joe had told Jay once without knowing what he was talking about, but the words were proving prescient. The little children of Kennedy Street took the cake. Some of them were gray for lack of lotion. Some of them stank for want of soap, laundry detergent, and Laundromat money. Some of them were

213

already getting high. All were hustlers, their soft side coiled under a hardened shell. Kevin, Mashey, Riri, Shawn, and them. The bay-bays.

Jay, like Nasro, was doing his part. Buying dinners every night. Championing barely nubile single mothers (only 11 years old for the most precocious of them, Kamisha, an all-time record). Sponsoring newborn babies to the tune of 21 godchildren in his first month and a half of employment. From being called Whitey to becoming everybody's best friend on the block. There was a semblance of method to his madness: Every paycheck was partitioned as soon as he got it, with the smaller amount set aside for his expenses and the bigger chunk destined to his charitable enterprises. He walked around with cash ready to be distributed. Short on that honey bun or ranch sunflower seeds? Jay's got it. Shoes, book bags, notepads, diapers, beans, sugar, cereals, mixed vegetables, vitamins? Come see Jay. He was mobbed, he was bum-rushed, he was appreciated, he was loved.

"You're gonna get yourself killed," Nasro warned him. "Once all these people you're giving money to start expecting it, there's no turning back. They'll spit on you the day you stop."

"Look who's talking," Jay retorted.

"I only slash my prices," Nasro defended himself. "Giving handouts is a big mistake."

"So be it," Jay answered. "I gotta do something. Can't help helping others."

Giving wasn't always easy. It shocked Jay how people were unafraid to ask. Some who barely knew him came to him with hands outstretched. It hurt to see other human beings stripped of all sense of dignity and shame. Jay tried to help everybody. Only unrepentant addicts like Bowell, who had his face half eaten by a bad Lupus infection, and Brenda, who made her son Keith beg at the gas station all day for her dope money, got nothing but a polite no. (And Tricie, who tried to sell both her kidneys to Brazilian body parts brokers. [And Rob, who snatched Souk's microwave and tried to get Nasro to buy it back. {And John-John, who got severely disfigured and incapacitated by an 18-wheeler in an attempt to keep the crack nugget he had dropped in the middle of the road from getting crushed. And....}])

Though Jay worked a little over 70 hours a week, his money could only be stretched so many ways. As much as he could, he bought the coveted objects or foodstuff himself instead of giving dollar bills away. It pained him that, inevitably, some really needy people had to be turned away.

Some parents were suspicious of his motives from the go. "What are you doing with my daughter Erika?" a woman named Alina asked him one evening. "Why are you giving her money and pieces of candy?"

"So she can feed herself and feel a little special every day," Jay, imperturbable, answered. "Got a problem with that?"

"Maybe," Alina declared, hands on her hips. "How do I know I'm not dealing with a pervert?"

"All the Kennedy kids are on a 'good report card' and 'good behavior' compensation program," Jay went on. "They do well in school and at home, they get rewarded.

Erika made honor roll."

Alina seemed taken aback. "She did?"

Jay pulled out a pen. "Let's exchange numbers. You're one of the few mothers missing in my database."

Alina smiled and took the pen. Her next sentence was typical Kennedy Street: "Can I get $10?"

Nasro shook his head.

Joe stifled a smile.

I crossed the wall into Nicole's.

"How about some groceries?" Jay proposed.

"Me give it all away."

Joe saw that for people like Bob Marley and Jay the impulse went beyond money. It had, in fact, nothing to do with it. It was the act itself that held the promise of fulfillment. They gave and gave and gave. They gave just to give. They gave until there was nothing left to part with. Until they were all empty. Until they couldn't give any more. It was love they really wanted to share. Love. Experience. And time.

Maybe it was the white man thing. Maybe just the fruit of his kindness. Jay, with his blond hair and blue eyes, was becoming as much a Brightwood Park habitué as Claude, Hakim, Ahmet, Nasro, Youngin', Pepsi, and Nicole. People knew him. They knew him and they liked him. You saw it in the way he was greeted in the street, on the bus, at Safeway and around KDY3 and KDY5, where he started to venture out on visits to his godchildren. (His favorite, Mama, a little thing with heavy bags under her eyes, neat plaits, and an appetite for $1.29 Barcelona

216

peanuts in the shell, lived in a KDY3 high-rise with her 24-year-old mom and her six siblings. Jay went to KDY5 mostly to check on Pooh Bear, who had gotten two fingers eaten by the Woodley Park subway station escalator on a trip to go see Tai Shan, the Washington Zoo's baby panda.) Kids grinned and waved. Girls tried to hook up and get it on. Old-timers gave nods. The drug boys didn't harass or rob or beat him. Jay was on his way to ghetto superstardom.

That's the way I called it. Joe, for his part, saw ethno-bonding. Here they were, two brothers, the only two white men in the 'hood (Ahmet the Gypsy didn't count). Pioneers, explorers, missionaries. Gentrification had made great strides in the city in the past half-decade, and perhaps nowhere as much as a couple of miles down, around U Street, but this was still uncharted territory. Joe felt every stare, every question mark, every ounce of resentment. Unlike Jay, he had taken his gun with him and he carried it everywhere he went. Though he often accompanied Jay on his housing project expeditions, he felt excluded from the benevolence extended to his brother. Joe didn't have the platform of a store, a Souk Number One where people could come in and interact and get to know him. Kids didn't mob him. Girls didn't bury him under mountains of numbers (only Lola, Macondo's Cuban art director, kept asking him to come see her dance, but he suspected her insistence to be more business-related than an expression of interest or a simple social call). The drug boys gave him the cold eye, some going as far as to spit on the sidewalk as he walked past. Worse were the grocery or hardware store lines, where his impatience was frowned upon, his credit card greeted with here-come-the-white-man scorn.

217

So Joe sat back and watched. He observed the ways of ghetto people *in situ*, in habitat, in their own natural environment. And what an enriching social experiment it was. Day-to-day living; their own version of English; the high tolerance for noise; the reduced life span; the disappearing fathers; murder as a rite of passage; love as a mirage; commitment as a weakness; jail as a proof of manhood; low expectations; self-destruction and suicide; the esteem accorded to successful criminals; treating grown men with contempt, mothers like goddesses, and young women like garbage; sports, the army, music, and illegal enterprise as the only ways out; church and family; appearances; expensive cars, watches, and clothes before college degrees and self-owned homes or businesses; health care as a luxury; decent credit scores an unobtainable accomplishment; the police as the number one enemy; the high threshold for pain; the resilience; the bottomless, unending suffering; the heartbreaking struggle against impossible odds; a doomed generation's silent cries for help; the beauty of a people no less human than you and me.

As one of the regulars at Souk Joe became well acquainted with Claude, Hakim, and Ahmet. Claude, he had a hard time getting into. The man was just too mysterious, too contradictory. An entertainment lawyer who never seemed to go to work but pretended to write all the small print on all the latest major movie and record contracts. A Howard alumni who claimed to hobnob with Felicia Rashad, Roberta Flack, and Nona Hendryx ("I pinch her butt every year at homecoming in the middle of Main

Quad. She can't see me because of the crowd but she knows it's me"). A wine expert who drank cases of cheap Chilean import every week. A name-dropper ("I knew Miles." "The Gambinos called me on the day Sinatra died looking to buy my father's record collection." "My ex-girlfriend is Spike Lee's lawyer. Spike got screwed bad on his first movie deals. Bad!") who didn't seem to have much of a life outside Souk. No, Claude was decidedly shady. But Joe listened to everything he had to say just because this was the first black professional he had ever conversed with, and in case a few gems of legal advice transpired amid all the rubbish--one never knew when one would need a good lawyer. For some reason, Joe didn't doubt that Claude had indeed been--or still was--one.

Hakim was more down to earth, but barely. Joe suspected him of lying and putting up a front. The Go-Go Imam had played percussion for Chuck Brown back in the day. "I'm one of the original Soul Searchers," he told Joe. "I should have patented that drumbeat as soon as I came up with it. Guess who would have been nicknamed 'Godfather of Go-Go?' Wouldn't have to run around begging for money to build my temple today, no sir." As a Muslim, Hakim was as boisterous and in-your-face as Nasro was humble and low-key. He wore a full-length black robe and a starched turban year round. His beard sprouted from his ears and his nose and came down to his chest. He walked in a cloud of sickeningly sweet perfume. His speech was infused with Koranic verses. He made much of the fact that he had given up music and goods-peddling to follow his calling. Joe thought the man was a fluke, but Hakim was genuinely liked around town. His temple, big on hope and

219

small on money as it was, played a big part in the lives of a growing number of black men and women. His work with inmates at the D.C. jail and several group homes was publicly lauded. Hakim was, not unlike the way Joe proposed himself to be, on a mission to save as many young black men as he could. (In time, in fact, Joe would come to see him as a competitor. Saving black men was Joe's job, and his only.) On another front, Hakim struggled to gain acceptance from the area's more mainstream Muslim community: the professional and diplomatic classes of men of Middle Eastern descent who considered black Americans' brand of Islam lowly. Because he encountered no such snobbery from practicing African immigrants, Hakim was quick to shout discrimination. Familiarized with Taha's teachings through Nasro, he strove to change perceptions and bridge the cultural gap by "gentle persuasion."

Joe listened to the themes dear to the Go-Go Imam's heart. He visited his modest mosque. He went with him on fund-raising trips to the offices of Pakistani doctors. He watched him try to build a unified movement of believers of all origins, one that would put an end to the isolation of African-American Muslims. Joe sat back, listened, and learned.

It was Ahmet who endeared himself to Joe the most. Gypsy was helpful to a fault, a hustler and handyman all in one. Their collaboration began in earnest the day he invited Joe to his tent inside a three-story building on Decatur Street, one block away from Souk. All the walls in his second floor apartment had been knocked down to make way for the structure. It had a pointed top, pylons, and lace-like wings that were pulled back during the day. Sand, a plastic palm tree, and the dunes painted on the remaining walls made the oasis theme work. Inside, superposed rugs and *poufs* covered the floor. The tent was quite comfy once you found yourself lying underneath, elbow propped on a pillow, munching on grapes and roasted almonds while sipping on the green tea one of Ahmet's three wives served in small silver cups with just the right amount of foam. "You're not doing too bad for yourself," Joe intuited, and Ahmet accepted the compliment gracefully.

The tea party would have been perfect hadn't it been for the intrusive presence of a camera crew. Ahmet was the subject of a National Geographic documentary tentatively called "American Gypsy: Below the Radar." At least two people were following his every move. They witnessed his family life, his business dealings, his daily struggles and victories. Everything he did and said was recorded. More crewmen tagged his wives and his mother Gina as they hopped Metro train after Metro train to read palms, predict the future on the fly, or extort money from passengers by showing them pictures of Ze, Ahmet's supposedly autistic baby boy.

Everything about Ahmet seemed fodder for good TV: the fact that, unless you looked closely, he appeared no less white than your average Caucasian, albeit one down on his luck, a little rough around the edges, and in need of hair implants and a good dentist; his propensity to refer to a clan, bonfire dances, doe-eyed women, and wandering caravans you never actually saw; his tale of life in the Balkans; the hints that he may well be connected to some sort of east coast Gypsy Mafia; the fact that he, his wives, and his children were getting around without ever having learned how to read and write; his triumph over lung cancer; the preparations for his 15-year-old daughter Alexa's marriage to her 17-year-old first cousin.

Joe was wary of the cameras at first. Images are the hardest things to control nowadays. Once taken, they have a propensity to show up in unexpected and very public places. Joe relaxed after the documentary's director, a skinny and sickly-looking Macao native named Brian who wore his hair in his face, assured him that footage of him wouldn't be used without his express consent.

Soon, Ahmet and Joe were making plans for the shoemaker's shop. Their friendship was sealed the very first time Joe showed Gypsy around. The latter fell in love with the North Face "Summit Series," the very idea of planting a tent on a counter to tough it out. In Gypsy's eyes, such resolve and adaptability spoke volumes about Joe--volumes. They were brothers in the spirit. They belonged to rugged steppes, the wind, the tundra, the permafrost, rusted oil rigs, packs of wild dogs.

"Ready?"

"Ready."

They went to work after buying matching gloves, workman jackets, hard hats, protective glasses and masks, bandannas, boots, and hammers. Using Gypsy's mastery of the art of interior transforming, they made all the partitions disappear immediately after Mofas's high-pitch machine chased the rats away. Ahmet dislodged the counter and hauled it off in his S.U.V. The floor was raised a dozen inches to form a small stage where the counter once stood. They laid dark-red carpets and redid the toilets, installing a shower. The walls and ceiling were wired for video, sound, and high-speed Internet.

Brian enclosed his shooting equipment in Plexiglas to protect the lenses from sawdust. He was excited by the little that Joe told him about his project. "I could do a pilot on you right after we're done with Ahmet," he proposed. "If National Geographic accepts it we'll co-brand and cross-market the two pieces."

"I'll make my own movie when I'm ready," Joe refused. "And if you ever use any of this without my approval I'll sue your dysenteric ass." (Brian had fallen ill while shooting in Afghanistan. Ahmet was a welcome change after reporting on Empire's abuses in Kabul, Baghdad, and Guantanamo, the very much alive diamond rush in Sierra Leone, the nuclear threat in North Korea, Iran, and the former Soviet satellites, and the landmine problem in Angola. He was himself the subject of an upcoming documentary, "World Traveler," and pandemonium broke when yet more cameramen showed up to film him filming Ahmet.)

Given the high cost of revamping the AC system, Joe decided to go with portable fans. "We'll be out of here before the thick of summer," he announced wishfully. He did put in a retractable awning, a green one to go along with the facades of Happy Cuts and Souk, nothing nearly as fancy as Macondo's fully covered and carpeted walkway. The biggest problem was how to reconcile the space's dual use. Permanent pews wouldn't work since the church was to serve as an office during the day. Ahmet proposed folding chairs, plastic modular desks, and plastic plants. Next were five secondhand computers, phones, microphones, speakers, cameras, and a good digital video recorder from the pawn shop where Joe had found the NanoSnitch.

"Where are we installing you?" Ahmet asked Joe, seeing how they had forgotten to save room for Joe's North Face tent.

"On the desks after I snap them together," Joe answered. "You can have the tent. My sleeping bag will do."

"What a man!" Ahmet said, wiping a tear. "I'll cherish this gift for the rest of my life."

Brian made sure to capture the moment.

"Not without my approval," Joe reminded the filmmaker, his right hand's index and middle fingers pointing at his eyes in the universal I'll-be-watching-you sign.

"I know," Brian said.

Showing remarkable flair and no small amount of confidence, Joe finished his preparations by leasing a combination soda/chips/candy vending machine from Coke of Metropolitan D.C., opening a Citibank business account, wresting low credit card processing fees from Suntrust Bank, and taking out ads in The Washington Post, The Washington Times, and The City Paper describing the church and advertising its very first service, to be held two Sundays from now. Joe contacted a manpower agency and gave them his requirements: female ex-executives over 70, 100% white, distinguished voices, team-oriented, energetic, with their own health insurance. He screened 15 candidates, kept four named Hariet, Barbara, Christina, and Sheila, promised them $20 an hour plus commission, handed each a copy of Che Guevara's "Bolivian Diaries," got them started on guerrilla warfare and harassment tactics, and coached them on delivering the perfect pitch.

"This isn't for the faint of heart," he told the group, who quickly became known as the Grannies. "This is war. All you need to do is look around you. Nothing but poverty, destruction, discouragement, despair. People are dying every day just a flew blocks from here. Because they were never given a chance. Because of the trauma, the loss of self-love, self-knowledge, and self-confidence caused by decades and decades of the most wretched forms of oppression--y'all are old enough to have witnessed firsthand the events I'm referring to. We're here to remedy this situation, ladies. We're here to give back what was taken. We're here to save and uplift. Each and every one of you has a chance to become a hero, the opportunity to set things straight. It's in your power to do immense good. So I say let's go get 'em."

"Beats bridge, strip poker, and speed dating," Barbara, the most outspoken of the bunch, cheerfully exclaimed.

"I always felt bad for those nigra people," Sheila said. "I just never knew what to do for them."

Christina made her knuckles crack. "Just show me my first target," she demanded.

Hariet, an ex-general, gave Joe the salute. "Ready to serve," she affirmed.

Barbara raised her hand. "Corporations are almost

225

all entirely white-owned, so that's easy. But how do we know who in the White Pages is white? Do we narrow it down by neighborhood? Surnames don't mean a thing. I mean, blacks all got theirs from us, right?"

"I'll get you the most recent U.S. census I can find," Joe said. "How's that?"

Once the Church of Retribution was incorporated and all ready to go Joe wasted no time applying for a grant under the White House faith-based initiative. The amount of paperwork involved was ridiculously low, the forms' wording invitingly vague.

Joe called Bobby Kim at Cairo to have him recommend a good promotional company. "I'm supposed to know people in the T-shirt business just because I'm Korean?" Bobby shouted, unnerved by the request.

"You're a local businessman," Joe replied. "I just wanted to tap into your network."

"Tap this," Bobby told Joe before hanging up.

Joe drove to the wholesale district between New York and Florida avenues in Northeast D.C., parked in front of the first garment supplier that he found, bought two bales of T-shirts, one black, one white, from a chubby man called Mr. Wang, and cut a deal to have them printed and delivered at the church.

Vinyl lettering on the door and the front window represented the last touch. To see the name of his brainchild fully spelled out on glass brought tears to Joe's eyes. This was it. This was the moment he had been longing for. He felt wobbly. "All my life I've waited for this," he told Ahmet, who cried along. "My own business, my springboard, my American Dream, a chance to become a captain of industry. This means so much...."

Choked by emotion, surrounded by bright lights and lifeless microphones, Joe and Gypsy embraced each other and wept.

Joe made Jay the honors of the place. Jay was impressed. More than that, he was taken aback by Joe's speed, his determination, his resourcefulness. "Quite a bit you've already accomplished, bro."

"That's all God's work," Joe asserted. "That's what I'm doing. That's who I'm working for. God." Joe lifted his head toward the ceiling as if saying a silent praise.

Jolted by the words, Jay stood upright. "God's work." "God." "Work." "Work for me." Now he understood.

Joe turned toward him. "Something I've been meaning to tell you," he said. "In my latest vision you've become the man, Jay. It's you who runs this church. I'm just in the background helping you, smoothing things out. You're the leader of the Church of Retribution. This is yours. All of it. Command, and I shall obey."

Jay felt something strong and deep and urgent tug at his heart. He felt compelled to kneel and bow his head. "Lord," he said, "Thy will be done."

Joe smiled protectively.

Jay was an immediate hit with the Grannies. If Joe was their boss, his big brother became their sweetheart. He brought them little snacks from Souk. He swapped their cars every two hours in compliance with street parking limitations and he made sure their meters were always full of quarters. He reminded them to take their pills. He walked them to their vehicles at night.

Joe's acumen in choosing the type of employee perfectly suited for his business quickly became evident. Nobody hangs up on an old white lady who sounds educated, well intentioned, and frail. The Grannies had the ear of every white person and every corporation that they called: It wasn't just some skank trying to push something, Grandma was on the phone. Inside the office, pressure was kept at a minimum. The last thing Joe wanted was to be the cause of a heart attack. He did establish a reward system providing each month's top seller with extra days off, bonuses, and gift cards. A little competition could never hurt.

All six staff members of the church did the right thing and became the very first to contribute to the Retribution fund, i.e., the Citibank account. Joe gave a symbolic $1, Hariet, $100, Barbara, $75, Sheila, $150, Jay, $150, and Christina, $45.

They decided to go city by city, a move that prompted Joe to install a map of the U.S.A. right next to his freshly minted Master of Arts in Pastoral Science degree. (The other walls were covered with framed pictures of lynching picnics, public hangings, bombings, activists being covered with salt and sugar as they sat at lunch counters, crowds being hosed down and bitten and beaten up, "Whites Only" and "No Negro in Town After Dark" signs--so they all remembered precisely what and who they worked for.) Joe gave each of the Grannies a list to sift through at their leisure. The goal was to leave no name unchecked, no company off the hook.

Washington was the first town to get hit. The workload on the residential side was relatively easy, given that the majority of residents were black. On the business end, lawyers, consultants, brokerage firms, and lobbyists proved tough cookies. Joe collected the first dozen names for his black list, to be posted on the church's Web site as soon as Ahmet was finished designing it.

It was Sheila who brought in the first big fish, a technology company who had yet to donate to a single charity. The VP wanted to put $5,000 on her corporate Amex. Sheila and she had bonded over the phone: Both owned dogs and enjoyed tricot. "Ask her if she has a Visa or a Mastercard," Joe whispered, knowing that the fees would be a bitch.

"Visa," Sheila nodded.

"Go for it," Joe said.

They all held their breaths as Sheila entered the

digits on her terminal. The printer came to life, spitting a receipt out. Joe cried for the second time in two weeks. "We're on our way," he sang excitedly; "Lordie, Lordie, we're on our way."

Never had he felt so validated. His elation was nearly crushed to smithereens when he went back to work and dialed the next number on his list without paying attention, delivering his line without giving his interlocutor a chance to place a single word. "Hi ma'am how are you today I'm calling on behalf of a group called Church of Retribution we're a nonprofit representing the African-American community and we are calling to ask you to contribute to our Retribution fund which as you may have guessed proposes to compensate slave descendants for the abominations of slavery segregation and discrimination the money will promote black causes all over the country as well as improve black lives in your area there's no minimum it's a one time donation that gives you the opportunity to repair a moral wrong and make the world a better place your name will be prominently displayed on our list of donors and you will enjoy the priceless benefits of a clear conscience for the rest of your life I can go ahead and charge your credit card over the phone if you would like to get that done today ma'am...." Joe stopped and caught his breath.

The voice at the other end, when it came to life, was unmistakable. "Joe? Is that you?"

Joe started to shake violently. "Ma?"

"Is this some kind of bad joke? Please tell me you're not calling my house asking for money for your so-called church!"

Joe looked at the number he'd just dialed. Sure enough, it was Military Road. "Sorry 'bout that, Ma."

"Sorry nothing," Maggie yelled. "You're gonna make me come up there and blow the whole place up!"

Joe hung up, almost dropping the phone in his panic. He wiped the sweat from his forehead, waited until his heart was back to its regular pace, and carefully dialed the next number.

Past a few breakthroughs here and there, they weren't having much luck. Some higher-up at the Carlyle Group actually laughed at Christina. Laughed and slammed the phone. How unprofessional was that?

Joe received the promotional shirts from Mr. Wang and handed them out around the office, at Happy Cuts, Souk, Macondo, Wings 'n' Things, Midnight, the Low Price gas station, the Crossroads funeral parlor, the Chinese food joint, nearby public schools, and a couple of downtown homeless shelters. They came in all shapes and sizes, from toddlers' snap-ons to fashionably baggy. Women's were fitted and cut generously low at the collar. No more than a word or two on the front, the white shirts bearing black inscriptions, the black shirts stamped in white. Nowhere was the church mentioned, the message conveyed by the inflammatory words having been deemed informative enough: "Pay!" "Reparations Now!" "Restitution!" "Retribution!" "Reconciliation!" "Repent!" "Forgive!" "Slave Descendant." "Share!" "Apologize!" "Egregious Wrong." "New Covenant." "246 Years." "Redline This!" "Gimme Mine!" "America's Problem."

At the end of the first week, the drive's sluggish results ($14, 452) prompted Joe to organize an impromptu march on the White House. He rented a van, hired a few KDY3 crackheads, picked up hangers-on and loiterers on Georgia Avenue, took Ahmet, Jay, and the Grannies, and tried his best to get arrested for civil unrest and unauthorized demonstration at Lafayette Square. Brian shot a few frames, but the print press and TV networks, though informed in advance, all shunned the event. Maybe it was the church's lack of coordination, its shabbily assembled group, its hastily scribbled signs. No megaphone, no speech, no platform, no energy, no emphasis, no preparation, an April wind strong enough to redden knuckles and freeze brains--the protest barely made a dent. Tourists and Secret Service officers looked on in amusement. "Everybody's at the Cherry Blossoms Festival," Barbara consoled Joe in the van on their way back. "We'll do better next time."

So removed was I from Empire's day-to-day affairs and its ineffective, incompetent, and evil-minded rulers that the idea to wander into White House grounds while I had the chance didn't even cross my mind. The powerful interested me now even less than before (I had stopped paying attention after my tour in Nam). I knew for a fact that there were other forces at work in the universe and that we, from our caricature of a president on down, were mere pawns in a battle we didn't even begin to understand.

On Monday morning Joe received a phone call from a very strange woman who introduced herself simply as Imabelle. "I represent a group called 'Riots on Demand,'" she told him in a very lush, friendly, and suggestive voice. "We should meet, in your interest and ours."

"I'm busy," Joe told her before clicking over.

"We saw you down Lafayette Square yesterday," Imabelle announced after calling back. "We know what you're trying to achieve. We, at Riots on Demand, can help."

"Who exactly are you?" Joe asked.

"Not on the phone," Imabelle shushed him.

Joe was as intrigued by the pitch as he was by her voice.

"Let's do lunch," Imabelle proposed.

"Meet me in half an hour at Macondo Lounge," Joe, who hated to venture far from his headquarters during the day, told her.

They settled in a booth away from the stage. The numbers succeeding one another during their hour-long meeting, including "10,000 Turning Dervishes" and "Of Vice and Men," left them cold. So did the fries, bison burgers, and Looza passion fruit nectar. Youngin' himself checked on their table a few times. "Congratulations on your new business," he told Joe. "Much luck."

Joe, feeling important, nodded without smiling. "See you at Sunday service?"

Youngin' patted his shoulder. "You bet."

Imabelle looked nothing like her voice. There seemed to be a discrepancy, in fact, a disconnect between the way she spoke and her physical appearance. On the phone Joe had imagined her middle-aged, overweight, old-fashioned, and baldheaded--a hippie in colorful robe, stone necklace, and ankle chains. Imabelle was an 80-pound blonde who couldn't be much more than 25 years old. Her knees were bigger than her thighs. Every bone in her body stuck out. Her fat-free flesh appeared stretched to its maximum. She was so tightly wound that you expected her tendons to snap. Her stare was so cold that frost seemed to have permanently damaged her eyebrows. She was dressed in black shorts, a college sweater, and running shoes. Her ponytail and unadorned lips, cheeks, ears, and nails, denoted a no-frills approach to life and business. Disgust twisted her face before she looked away from her plate and her drink. She was here to sell and sell only. So Joe leaned into his seat, crossed his arms, closed his eyes so as not to give in to distraction, and listened to her, allowing himself to be guided by the honey-flavored inflections of her tongue.

"We're a one-stop solution for activists of all creeds," Imabelle began. "Riots on Demand is just a name to reflect the times we live in. We've been in the business for decades, first as a run-of-the-mill K Street lobbying group. For the right fee we'll fight your cause for you. We'll march, we'll protest, we'll sit, we'll go on hunger strikes, we'll raise barricades, we'll burn a couple of cars or trash cans, we'll confront the police, we'll even go to jail. Packages go for as low as $1,000 for a simple half-hour, 15-people demonstration, to well over 5 million dollars for a full-scale popular uprising including armed rebellion, underground cells, pamphlets, government takeover, presidential palace occupation, resignation deals and exile negotiations for the ex-leaders. Our employees aren't actors. They're professional refuseniks, career revolutionaries, political scientists, battle-hardened war veterans. Just tell us what you're trying to achieve and we'll do the work. Protest is our specialty. We do it all the time. We do it well."

Joe opened his eyes. "Why would I pay you when I can do the job myself?"

Imabelle smiled. "We get results. We have a track record. Grassroots campaigning can be lengthy and very costly. We bring your cause to the forefront of public opinion on a one-day notice. We put you in the news. We put you on the map instantly--guaranteed."

A brochure appeared on the table. Imabelle pushed it Joe's way.

"Tiananmen," Joe read aloud. "The Million Man March. 'Save Tibet.' Street protests in Guinea. The toppling of the Berlin Wall. The popular unrest in Nepal. Anti-Coke demonstrations in Bogota to stop union-busting. The anti-police riots in Paris. The anti-sweatshop movement of the '90s. *Mai 68.* L.A. '92...." Joe put the brochure down. "Those were all yours? That's quite a résumé."

Imabelle nodded modestly. "We're especially big in Africa. Just helped the Senegalese president win a second term. Mugabe, of Zimbabwe, is a big client. Somalia's a lost cause, unfortunately. But we're looking into Darfur very closely."

"Do you do sidewalk sign-ups?"

"Absolutely. We have Greenpeace, Children's International, and the Democratic Party on our roster. We know the busiest intersections of every major American city. We'll bring you several dozen new members and their credit card information daily."

"Can you deliver in boardrooms?" Joe asked. "Can

you infiltrate shareholder meetings? Can you heckle C.E.O.'s?"

"Not a problem," Imabelle assured him. "Those are listed on the 'Corporate Harassment' section of our charter. Items # 3 and # 8, if I'm not mistaken."

Joe glanced over the brochure again. "You definitely seem like a step-saver," he admitted. "But I'm still not convinced."

"We looked you up," Imabelle declared. "Your idea is nothing short of brilliant. But you would benefit greatly from a heightened, more focused campaign. The firms you're after are anything but repentant. The crumbs they'll throw your way to silence you can't compare to the potential payoff. Hit them right, hit them fast, hit them where it hurts. They need to understand that, should they refuse to donate to your fund, they run a real risk of being overrun by negative publicity."

"I'm putting all recalcitrant donors on a black list."

"That's a start," Imabelle approved. "But big corporations respond better to unfavorable newscasts and their customers' opinions. All they have is their image, the magic, the halo of their brand. Those things matter even more than the products they're trying to peddle. Taint them, distort them, and the corporations suffer unrecoverable losses. Lafayette Square on a Sunday afternoon is cute. Very cute. It has that spur-of-the-moment thing, the naive but authentic quality of off-the-cuff outrage. But can you do the Nike headquarters in Beaverton, Oregon? Can you do GM and Ford the same afternoon in Detroit? Can you hit Microsoft in Seattle, Halliburton in Dubai? Our office and yours can coordinate attacks: A few days before you start calling a company or private residences in a target area we'll march on that city's streets, we'll flood the sidewalks, we'll put your cause in the local papers, we'll bring it to every TV screen, we'll block that firm's parking garage and that C.E.O.'s heliport, we'll shame the average white man and white woman out of his and her passivity, carelessness, and lack of empathy for black causes, black needs, and black suffering. It'll be quick and efficient."

Joe felt overmatched. "How much is all that going to cost me?"

Imabelle smiled again. "We're aware that you're a startup," she told Joe.

I looked at her eyes. It seemed to me they were turning red in the semi-darkness.

"Bring us onboard as a contractor," Imabelle went on. "No need to pay us upfront. We'll settle for a percentage of your profit."

Joe shook his head. "I'm not alone in this venture. My brother will never agree to anything like this."

Imabelle nodded gravely. "You'll find a way," she intuited as if she knew Joe well and trusted him more than anybody in the whole world. "We already have a contract drawn up. I have it right here with me."

Joe rubbed his eyes before taking a look. Riots on Demand wanted 5%, no less. On the other hand, the service provided could prove priceless. "That's kinda steep. What about discounts? Say, if I supply the marchers' T-shirts?"

"We'll work with you," Imabelle promised. "Such a great opportunity for both our companies, don't you think?"

"I need time," Joe said, backpedaling.

"We understand," Imabelle replied. "Give us a call

when you're ready."

To clinch the deal, she handed him a picture in an envelope as they were leaving. Joe had no trouble recognizing himself and most of his crew standing with makeshift signs a few paces from the White House gates. "Printed from the Talon database this morning," Imabelle informed him. "Nonviolent demonstrations and rallies on national soil are all put on record by orders of the Pentagon's Counterintelligence Field Activity Office, or C.I.F.A. Domestic spying, in short. You don't want to mess with those people, especially with your faith-based grant application still pending. We can shield you from government scrutiny. Let us do the public stuff. We're insured and bonded. Legally, you won't be liable for a thing."

Joe, more than a little unsettled, grunted.

I looked at Imabelle closely as we stepped outside. She seemed unaware of the fact that her joints were creaking. Her whole body appeared inhabited, consumed by something. The more she spoke, the redder her pupils got. She was creeping me out, but Joe was finding it hard to keep his eyes off her. The blonde effect taking over, washing away his preliminary caution. Don't do it, I begged him. Can't you see that something's wrong with the girl?

"Have you considered outsourcing?" Imabelle asked Joe as we were walking toward the church's offices.

"Not very comfortable with the idea," he admitted. "At least for now."

"It doesn't have to be Vish in Bangalore," she said. "Kremena in Sofia can do the job just as well and for a little less."

They looked at each other with the mischievous grin of people who understand each other perfectly.

With the help of Riots on Demand, over $170,000 was amassed in the next six days in D.C. alone, which wasn't bad given the types of obstacles the church was up against. Looking at Imabelle's people in action made a believer out of Joe. They were mostly white. They belonged to all age groups, including a few young children. They appeared very motivated--determined, even. They spoke for him and what he stood for much better than he could have done himself. More importantly, they made the news.

Yet Joe's tone was far from jubilant when he addressed his troops at the end of the church's very first drive ("Always understate the results," Imabelle had advised him). "We'll come back to D.C.," he promised the Grannies and Jay as he pushed the first red tack into the map on the wall. "It was our initial stop and we put up a good, honest fight. Time to move on to Columbia, Maryland. We'll keep the hard ones, like big towns in Virginia, Texas, and the Deep South, for when we're more experienced. The toughest one of all, New York City, we will confront last. Those hedge funds won't be a joke; we'll need to know exactly what we're doing. When we do come back here it'll be in triumph. We'll shame the people who dared turn a cold ear to our demands. We'll bring them to their knees. We'll make them pay."

"Amen," Jay said. "How about some spirituality?"

"How about it," Joe agreed, already thinking of all the things he could buy with the money.

The church's first meeting was for that Sunday, 6 p.m. Joe e-mailed the 529 Internet petition signers. Only 140 responded. 45 cursed Joe out and threatened him for meddling in black people's affairs. 92 wished him good luck and forwarded their bank account numbers. The three who lived in the area promised to show. Joe braced himself for Deadria's phone call, knowing it would come and it wouldn't be friendly. He wondered if he should hire a security company. The church, after all, was dealing in big money. And wherever money was involved, danger generally followed.

Ads had been running for two weeks straight in the local newspapers and on the Internet. The boys and the Grannies invited all their friends and relatives, Maggie excepted. Ahmet promised a caravan of clan members from Jersey City. Brian said he wouldn't miss it for anything in the world. Equipped with two portable metal detectors, Hakim and Claude were going to guard the door. Mofas was on. Nicole and the Happy Cuts ladies had reserved seats. Youngin' was front row pew. Pepsi muscled his way in, demanding two extra spots for his bodyguards. Nasro, to Jay's great chagrin, was out. "Controversy is *haram*," he objected to Jay's pressing request that he attend. "And your church is nothing but controversial, Jay."

"It's a chance to do good work," Jay contested. "You should join."

Nasro, as if suddenly in the presence of the Devil, took a step back "*A unzu lillahi mina seytane rajiim*," he chanted.

"Everything will be transparent," Jay professed. "I have Joe's word. The money will be accounted for down to

240

the last penny. Both Joe and I are on very modest salaries. We'll have the church audited every quarter."

"*Haram*," Nasro repeated obstinately.

"Each check will require both our signatures. Joe can't do anything without me."

"*Haram*," Nasro said again.

"It'll all go into good causes," Jay insisted. "You know how many meals I'll be able to buy? A whole cafeteria worth, daily--that's how many. We'll turn this neighborhood around in no time. We'll bring forth progress for the black community in this town, in this country, in the whole world. We'll offer every white person a chance to make up for the bad things we've done. Just imagine: No more resentment, no mistrust, no hatred between the black and white races. All sins atoned for, all mistakes forgiven, all accounts paid, all debts repaired, all scores settled. Isn't it worth a try? If only to start a dialogue, get people talking, shake things up a little bit?"

"*Haram*."

"God wants me to do this. I told you about that voice. Those dreams. I was born to do it. It's my destiny."

"*Haram*."

"It's all in good faith."

Nasro rolled his eyes.

"We'll go to Africa," Jay, desperately intimated. "We'll buy indentured slaves' freedom. We'll fill warehouses with grain. We'll build schools and bless them with solar energy and cheap laptops. We'll replant the Sahara and the Sahel. We'll equip each hut with a refrigerator, a TV, a fan, a microwave."

Unimpressed, Nasro shook his head again.

"*Haram.*"

"Say something else!" Jay, exasperated, shouted.

"You're lucky I'm not firing you," Nasro shot back. "That's all I have to tell you."

Jay was a wreck come Sunday night. Stage fright had him shaking and retching in the back room despite all the physical and mental preparation. He had been running with Joe on a nearby high school track every morning before work. He had lifted weights. He had grown a beard and retouched his haircut with Nicole's help. He had complied with Joe's demands to try different clothing styles, including a farmer's denim overalls (too prairie), a factory worker's gray cloth uniform (too Mao Zedong), a top athlete's warmup sweat pants and jacket (too street), rock-star leather pants (too Jim Morrison, heavy drug overtones), everyman casual treads (too regular), nature-freak cargo shorts and sandals with matching mountain bike (too green), messiah coverall white robes (too pompous), before they settled on jeans, a white Fruit of the Loom T-shirt, and sneakers, the same outfit Jay had on every day.

So convinced was Jay that he needed to play his part that he even gave passing consideration to carrying the wooden cane that Joe tried to hand him.

"It's not a cane," Joe insisted. "It's the Rod of Correction."

"The what?"

"The Rod of Correction. You're supposed to lead with it. Just like Joshua did during the march to the Promised Land after Moses gave him one."

242

"I'm not walking with a cane," Jay refused.

"It's not meant for walking," Joe refuted. "You hold it in the air and you point. It's a symbol."

"Where did you find it?"

"EBay. I was researching R.O.D., a consulting company I'm considering going in business with. The auction was the first link. Two minutes left and no bidders. I found it ominous. This is the rod Michael Manley used in order to win the Jamaican elections against Edward Seaga in the '70s. It was given to him by a Rastafarian elder. It helped confer him legitimacy in the eyes of the hyper-religious, stoned-out-of-its-mind electorate: Manley was God's--or Jah's, rather--candidate."

"Since when do you specialize in Jamaican politics and biblical references?"

"Since you started quoting the Koran."

"What kind of consulting firm is R.O.D.?"

"Political. They have a vast array of services. Vast. You'd be surprised."

"Don't bring them onboard without discussing the matter with me first."

"I would never do that in a million years," Joe, who had already forged Jay's signature on the draft Imabelle had given him, claimed. "We're equal partners."

"Good," Jay said. "And I hope you didn't pay too much for that stick. Because I don't want it."

"Fine," Joe said. "We'll just prop it on a corner of the stage--I mean, the altar."

"I still don't know what I'm gonna tell all these people," Jay moaned. "Can't you just go and give the speech yourself?"

"You're the guru," Joe refused. "You're the man. They're coming to see you and hear you. This is your movement, remember?"

Jay started to cry. "I've always been scared of crowds, man. Ever since Ma used to lock me up in a dark room for whole days. You know this."

Joe nodded gravely and took his brother in his arms. "I know what you've been through. But now is the time to conquer your shortcomings, Jay. Now is the time to get over all your fears. For God, Jay. For the greater good. For black people. For white people. For all of us. Think of the work you're about to accomplish. You're uniting feuding groups. You're putting money into poor people's pockets. America will never be the same. It'll finally live up to its hype of crucible of all faiths and all origins. You're forcing us to excise the demons from our past. You're showing us how to make amends."

Jay sniffed and looked down. "I'm scared," he said in a small voice.

Joe sat him down. "Let's work on this first sermon," he proposed resolutely. "Think about something you like."

"Music!" Jay said. "Can't we just play something over the system? Make it more like a reception? How about a DJ? We could serve appetizers, let people mingle, and then have volunteers go up there and say their pieces. That's how most fund-raising events are planned."

"We're a church, man. We can't do that. O.K. for the testimony part. But you need to make a speech–I mean, to give a sermon. Everything is on your shoulders. You're the movement's face and its voice. Your every word and action will carry weight. You're a born crowd pleaser, Jay.

If only you trusted yourself."

Jay appeared lost. "I need to see Lisha," he blurted out. "I'm sure everything would be easier if I had her here with me. These past events, man.... That voice waking me up every day. The stuff these kids I care about go through.... Life in the ghetto.... It's getting to me, Joe. Absolutely. I'm lonely."

"I'll find Lisha for you," Joe promised.

"You will?"

"I will. Now about that sermon..."

"How are you gonna find her?"

"Give me her old address. If that doesn't work I'll put Ma's private eye on her trail. That Derek Strange guy."

Jay stopped crying. "Sounds like a plan."

The brothers shook hands.

"For that sermon..."

"Give me a day to think about it," Jay asked. "I'll find a way to handle it."

It was a good crowd for a first. The line snaked around the block. The seats were filled in a matter of minutes. Joe and Jay welcomed the visitors at the door after Claude and Hakim patted them down. They were on the lookout for Deadria, who Joe suspected might show up to make a scene, or lawyers with a cease-and-desist order. Ahmet sold tickets for unspecified upcoming events (at least that's what the $5 coupons he was detaching from a thick roll said: "Upcoming event"). When the people who couldn't make it inside decided to stay out on the sidewalk, Joe plugged the public-address system and installed two speakers by the door.

245

    The atmosphere inside the church was considerably jovial. The congregation's racial composition couldn't have been better handpicked: about 65% white and 35% black. They had the honor of former mayor Barion Merry's presence. An ex-convict and incorrigible crack addict who had taken the city to the brink of insolvency through two very eventful terms, Mayor Merry was best remembered for boosting citywide minority contracting and youth employment and for uttering D.C.'s most famous one-liner, "Bitch set me up!" as federal agents concluding an undercover sting stormed the hotel room where he and an ex-girlfriend were cavorting. Though still active in politics, Mayor Merry was now a prematurely aged man in the grip of substance abuse and narcolepsy. It showed as he fell asleep in his redingote five minutes after sitting down, oblivious to the crowd. "This the Playa's Ball?" a man dressed in black lace and a felt, tipped hat, kept asking, his fingers playing in the long strands of his straightened hair: "Where the honeys at?" Chris was at the right of the altar gossiping with Yvonne. Pepsi and Youngin' fought to sit next to Nicole, paying the coworkers to her left and to her right more than handsomely to trade places with them. They immediately proceeded to put a bug in each of her ears. "I might drop in on you one of these Thursdays," Nicole told Youngin', making my heart skip a beat and Youngin's eyes shine with anticipation. "I wrote you a little poem," Youngin' murmured, unfolding a piece of paper before he declaimed a few very unhappy, very unhappy verses. Looking from the last row, her Nefertiti neck sticking out like a periscope over the uneven sea of heads, Lola appeared anything but amused. "Are they serving anything to eat?" somebody asked. "Vending machines are out back," Joe snapped; "This isn't a cocktail party." "My bad," the person said.

Feeling Maggie's presence, I surveyed the room. She was outside, sitting with Steve in a white Hummer whose ugliness made me want to rush back inside the church. "Can't believe they went along with it," Maggie was saying. "And we weren't even invited! These fools, these imbeciles, these race traitors, these shit-stirrers, these..."

Parked behind her was an unmarked Dodge with three F.B.I. agents in it. They had taken pictures of every attendee walking through the door and they were getting ready to observe the event through the church's de-smoked window and listen to the sermon with a sound-amplifying device.

Behind them were Hank, Chuck, Frank, and Silas--4 sweat-drenched, Copenhagen-chewing, pistol-packing, card-carrying Ku Klux Klaners in a F-150 pickup with Alabama plates. Part of the Klan's cyberpatrol unit, they had seen the Church of Retribution ads on the Internet and they had decided to come check firsthand if this was mere hoax or a true provocation. Four grown men who had nothing better to do than drive for hours looking for trouble to get into. Hank hoped to get in touch with the Klan's D.C. chapter, which had stopped reporting to headquarters more than two decades ago. The four men were a rarity: racists who wore their feelings on their sleeves, hatemongers who were vocal about their opinions, believers in the purity and superiority of white blood who held nothing back. They were as much on a mission to exclude blacks from the national dialogue as the church claimed to try and include them. Unapologetic and ready for battle, they considered themselves the last guardians of whiteness, that most elusive of attributes.

Behind the pickup, lurking in a blue Caprice that looked threatening even as it sat idle in the shadow of tree shadows, was a man who called himself the Unbeliever. Asexual, bland of physique and appearance, relatively young, he was in search of something to stimulate his senses, get him out of his boredom, and hold his interest if only for a few hours. Tonight the Church of Retribution was it. Out of the ordinary, promising, potentially life-changing. Hadn't he been so shy, the Unbeliever would have fought his way through the crowd in order to claim a seat inside. He had seen Joe put the speakers out and he was now waiting for the ceremony to begin. What, exactly, did he expect? He couldn't have said. Salvation, maybe. A flicker of interest. Hope, in the presence of a new kind of message. The Unbeliever--a term he had himself coined--was no nihilist. He was just a born skeptic. He held no faith in God, Man, Nature, or even himself. He lived off the land, robbing banks, convenience stores, gas stations, and the occasional passerby. He had only needs. No wants, no desires, no aspirations. Each morning a roll of the pair of dice he kept in his pocket decided his mind-set and course of action. He was Goetz, the warrior of Sartre's "Le Diable et le Bon Dieu," for whom Good and Evil are equal-opportunity employers. Even number on the dice, the Unbeliever was a model citizen: good deeds, good day. An odd number called for mayhem, murder, and destruction. To anybody wondering why, the Unbeliever would have asked, "Why not?" his pale eyes showing a hint, a very small hint of amusement.

Inside the church, silence was descending as Jay made his way toward the altar/stage, stopping here and there to say hi and thank you for coming and right on, man, shaking hands, raising a thumb, cracking a joke, slapping a shoulder. The contact lenses that Joe had made him wear seemed to work their magic. They weren't meant to help him see better at all, they were there to blur his vision. "If you can't see people they won't scare you," Joe had said to rationalize the artifice. "Aim at the general direction of faces when you look. Folks will feel like you're staring straight into their souls."

And that's exactly how it happened. Jay couldn't make out any detail past complexion and garment color. He couldn't distinguish a smile from a frown. Only Nicole was visible to him, sitting in the front as she was, glowing in all her glorious beauty the way she did--Nicole and Lola Nefertiti, the one giant tree sticking out of the forest.

Silence was complete as Jay grabbed the guitar hidden behind the pulpit. "How y'all doing tonight?" he asked in a clear voice.

"Goooood," the crowd responded obediently.

"Bitch set me up!" Mayor Merry shouted as he woke up with a start and started swinging.

"Gooooood," people on the sidewalk said after the sound delay.

"Doin' a little tune called 'Better Will Come,'" Jay announced.

"Go ahead, brother," was the crowd's response.

"1..." Jay went. "1, 2, 3!"

It came straight out of the old, beaten up 6-string Yamaha, its stickers catching the congregation's eyes, its raw and simple power plucking their nerves, its rhythm pleasing their senses: old Delroy's song.

> *I've been tryin' for a long, long time*
> *Still I can't make it*
> *Everythin' I try to do seems to go wrong*

Why this number when Darondo's "Let My People Go," which Jay had briefly rehearsed before changing his mind, could have worked just as well, if not better? (*Said, you better let my/ Let my people go/ ... I'm talkin' 'bout the bay-bays/ Starvin' to death/ Talkin' 'bout the chirren/ That can't hep theyselves/ Said, let my...*)

You have to be careful with attributions and possessiveness, of course. "My people" could sound a little audacious, and maybe even presumptuous, coming out of a white man's mouth. But I bet that Jay could have gotten away with declaring black people his people and asking Pharaoh to let them go. If anybody could pull that kind of feat it was him. In the end, he went with Delroy because he knew that piece much, much better. He was connected to it emotionally. It put it him in a place, a precise mental spot. It put him square in the zone. Just like keying oneself without the help of drugs.

> *Who God bless no one curse*
> *Thank God I'm not the worst*
> *Oh, my people can't you see*

They're tryin' to take advantage of me
Better must come
Better must come one day
Better must come, yeah!

The people in attendance got right into it. Clapping
hands, stomping feet, swaying, singing along. Better must
come, man. That was the *ordre du jour*, the reason why
they were gathered here today. Better must come. It must
come it must come. It must come and it will, thanks to Jay,
thanks to the Church of Retribution. They were all
underdogs tonight. They had it rough. They had it tough.
They were coming up, they were coming out, they were
asking for theirs. Unhappy with the state of things,
unsatisfied with the world. Ready for a change. Hungry for
a new order and new race relations. Poised to break down
all the remaining walls between men. That song Jay was
singing? They could all relate to it, black or white. It was
about making things right for oneself and for others. It was
about making things better. It was about getting it finally
done. Nothing unifies a disparate group like a struggle, a
shared objective. Prejudice was the common enemy, the
pandemic disease. Whether at the giving or receiving end,
they all suffered from it. We're with you, the clapping and
singing and stomping seemed to tell Jay. Lead. Just lead
and we'll follow.

Jay put the guitar down and wiped the sweat from
his brow. There was no fear in his eyes as he looked each
and every attendee square in the face. Nothing but the
purest of convictions. Never had he appeared so
wholesome, so handsome.

251

The spotlight and overhead projectors went off. Green, black, red, and yellow light beams came out of the floor and side panels. Ahmet projected images and words on the wall behind Jay. Timbuktu, Ghana, Mali, Sunjata, Songhai, Ife, Kankan Musa, tribal dances and ceremonies, slave raids, slave ships, slave auctions, slave masters, slave quarters, slave whippings, slave life insurance policies, chains, cotton fields, overseers, plantations, mulatto slaves, runaway slaves, Kunta Kinte, the Mason-Dixon Line, freed slaves, buffalo soldiers, sharecroppers, burning crosses, General Lee, Detroit, Chicago, Harlem, Emmet Till, Sambo, Uncle Tom, Uncle Ben, Uncle Sam, Amos, Andy, Booker T. Washington, du Bois, S.N.C.C. volunteers, voting rights volunteers, Rap Brown, Stockely Carmichael, Martin Luther King, Jr., Malcolm X, Medgar Evers, bus boycotts, bussing protestors, civil rights marches, attack dogs, billy clubs, bombed churches, Mississippi, housing projects, black children, dilapidated schools, modern-day KDY3 and KDY5. The overlapping images enveloped Jay. They rolled across his body and his face. They subdued the crowd with their sadness, their poignancy, their raw power.

"Welcome to our humble church," Jay began. "I want to thank each and every one of you for your courage, your honesty, your uprightness. 246 years of slavery. A century of continuing oppression. Jim Crow laws, lynching, discrimination, segregation, racial hatred, fear of one another, mistrust, distrust, distance.... We must stop it all. We must take a look at ourselves, take a stand, take a step toward change. I'm talking to my white brothers and sisters. It's true: It's not us who went across the sea and looted and killed and took and brought back. Not us who enslaved

252

other human beings. Not us who denied them simple, basic, innate rights. It was our great-great-grandparents. It was our ancestors. People we remember or think of fondly. They gave us life. They cleared the path. They built this country and made it the most powerful nation on Earth. They made everything possible for us. Yes, this sin committed against the black race, this horror of slavery, is theirs. We didn't start the fire. So why bother, after all this time, putting it out? Why worry about what has passed, what has gone? We didn't start the fire...."

Jay took a pause and looked. The audience was rapt.

Words of encouragement erupted across the floor. "Preach on!" "Get it said!" "Kill 'em wit' it!" "The truth!"

"Why should we bother? Because, my white brothers and sisters, slavery is still with us today. Not only is it still with us, it informs and infects and permeates every aspect of our relations with the offended race. How many of us have black friends? How many ever ate at a black table? How many have shaken, held a black hand? Who among us has never, I say never, felt condescension, paternalism, irritation, annoyance, mere amusement, fear, guilt, anxiety, or repulsion when faced with black problems, black issues, black plight, black people? We all know the stereotypes: promiscuous girl, teenage mother, single mother, welfare queen, fatherless boy, gun-toting kid, heartless killer, rap star, super-athlete, hustler, pimp, high school dropout, absconding father, jailbird, ex-convict, big mouth, drug pusher, drug user, angry youth, hooded robber, loiterer, street prowler, ne'er-do-well, underperforming employee, unskilled worker, untrustworthy businessman, rule dodger, servile old-timer, pitiful bum, pitied loser.... Those impulses, those stereotypes influence our every interaction with members of the black race. They, to put it bluntly, stand in the way. It's not the human being I see when a black man or a black woman and I cross paths: It's the potential menace, the victim, the oppressed, the repressed, the inferior, the joke. Those notions need to be purged. They need to be exterminated. They need to be eliminated once and for all. We must give back what we've taken from the black man: his dignity, his status as a man equal to all men in every aspect. We must ask for forgiveness, my white brothers and sisters. We must, as best as we can, share this wealth bestowed upon us by our ancestors, this wealth built on the back of blacks, this wealth denied to them for the longest time. Let's pay. Let's pay with all our heart. Let's pay without second thoughts or second-guessing. Let's pay to show our support, our solidarity, our contrition, our repentance. Let's tell them, Yes, we understand. We owe it to them. We owe it to history. This debt of our forefathers is too heavy to carry. It poisons the very essence of this country and its ideals. We've suffered long enough from it. Why carry it any further? Why transfer it to our children? Let them come of age with a clean slate, a world where justice is held dear, a world where atrocities and unfairness aren't left for time to mend but are confronted head-on. Let's do it. Let's start today."

Jay stopped again. His face was slick with sweat. His chest rose and came down mightily. The veins on his neck were standing up. His fists opened and closed, opened and closed, as if he was readying himself, steadying himself for a fight. His gaze had a sheen.

Ahmet stopped the slide show and slowly restored the original lighting. The assembly held its breath. Jay raised his arms, taking the crowd into a wide embrace. "To every white person among us, I say, give. Give everything you can. Give without holding back. Give love. Give respect. Give appreciation. But above all, give money. This church will champion your cause. It will accomplish wonders in your name. It will save lives and change lives. It will seal the wounds of slavery, segregation, and discrimination. It will bridge the gap that's been dividing our two races for too long. Starting here, starting today, better will come."

Out came the guitar again. Everybody rose from their seats. Singing, dancing, and shouting, they fell into the arms of one another. Black people, all 35% of them, were in particular demand. They were sought after, they were fought over, they were smothered in comforting hugs, they were mobbed in the name of brotherly love. Wallets and credit cards were pulled out and brandished by whites in newfound--and seemingly sincere--fervor.

Individual testimonies were out of the question for the time being. Joe took control of the microphone and begged for order, terrified that money would change hands before he had a chance to duly register the church's first members. "Close the door!" he ordered Claude. "Let no one out until all the membership forms are filled out and turned in."

Only when all the names and credit card numbers got collected did the euphoric churchgoers file out. The spirit of celebration and communion lasted long enough for Youngin' and Lola to steer a good amount of worshippers toward Macondo's canopy.

"How did I do?" Jay asked Joe after the two of them finished hobnobbing, shaking hands, and walking people to their cars.

"Better than I would ever have," Joe answered, torn between jealousy and self-congratulation.

"Ouch," Jay exclaimed as he missed the door, almost breaking his nose.

Joe wrapped his arm around his brother's shoulders and helped him get back inside. "Time for the contacts to come off," he said.

The F.B.I. agents snapped one last picture and disappeared.

Hank, Chuck, Frank, and Silas pulled away, squinting and bickering over a torn map to find the first of five highways on the road back to Alabama.

The Unbeliever hung around until the sidewalk had cleared. Having identified Jay as the orator responsible for the inspiring song and the rousing speech, he felt a new and strangely exciting stirring in his soul. The man and his movement, he decided, deserved a second look.

Joe lost no time posting Jay's very first sermon on all the major Internet video sharing sites. It was the first step in a long image-building campaign that aimed to make Jay a renowned and beloved figure all over the world. A simple click gave you the song, the speech, and an introduction into the church and its objectives. Links took you to www.churchofretribution.org, where more information could be gleaned, memberships pledged, podcasts downloaded, and contributions processed through Paypal, as well as Jay's own pages on the Web's three main social networking sites. Once those pages started registering enough visits, advertisers would be brought in to generate cash flow.

Joe didn't just rely on the storefront's cameras and DVR for video. Jay's apartment was monitored, and there were the old family tapes that he had rescued from Military Road after the new owner took possession, entering the house with his old key and fighting his way through heavy hashish haze and a couscous-scented cloud. (The winner of the house hadn't been Nepalese or Belgian but one Aziz Bensaoui, a stealthy Moroccan who had waited for the last second to place his bid, making it too late for Maggie to

screen him properly. Because of the eBay terms and
conditions she had preliminarily agreed to, she couldn't
refuse him the house on the grounds that he was from the
Maghreb. Still, it hurt. "It was your idea," she reprimanded
Steve, smacking him hard upside the head. "Now the
enemy lives among us. On our street. In our home. Toting
my ex-husband's guns. Suppose Aziz starts a *madrassa* in
there? Suppose he opens a terrorist camp and the Feds trace
the house and the weapons back to me?")

Joe had an easy time finding the home tapes. They
were where they had always been: in the pantry. When he
watched them they made him--and me--nostalgic. Those
were the times when I had had the time to be a dad. The
35mm camera, a heavy and bulky thing that used to weigh
my shoulder down, had captured preciously rare moments.
Outings at the beach, the mountain, and amusement parks.
Jay chasing crabs, playing in the sand, and learning how to
surf. Joe clowning around in Superman pajamas. Bikes and
electric cars. Soccer games. Birthdays. Grownup parties
where I, Maggie, and our wild friends danced through the
night. The boys used to love it when the curtains were shut
in the living room and images were projected on the wall.
Our own cinema. Our family movies. Our life.

Those tapes weren't put up on the video sharing
sites for the world to see. Joe was planning to keep them for
later, for when everything that could be raked in from
contributions and pledges and donations was raked in and
the time was ripe for side deals with Hollywood and
publishing companies.

The second batch of printed tees included messages
in the same vein as the first: "Pass It on!" "Absolute

Contrition Absolutely!" "One," "Same," "Reconciliation Time," and, of course, "Better Will Come" and "Save the Bay-Bays." Two major differences: Only 100 of each were made, and they weren't free. Stored in the back room and put up for sale on a separate Web site from the church's, they offered a glimpse into what in time would become a full-fledged clothing line called Retribution Gear. The fabric used by Mr. Wang was heavy-duty; the array of sizes, styles, and colors much more comprehensive; the letters weren't ironed in but embroidered, in true street fashion. The shirts were priced very high to confer them and their owners exclusive status. They came in a flat wooden box that contained sheets of untreated cotton, a not-so-subtle tactile and visual memento of plantation days. Unwrapping them was an experience in itself: You worked your fingers, you felt the sun, you ducked massa's whip, you tasted the sweat. Like the $250 "fair trade" and "eco" 501 Levis' jeans made from organically grown denim and all-natural colors, those shirts weren't meant to be worn, ever.

As more and more business ideas started burgeoning in his mind, Joe sought Claude's legal advice. "Do you own the copyrights to those shirts?" Claude prodded him after Joe checked his Howard Law credentials and signed a below-market-rate retainer. "What if Mr. Wang decides to print a few for himself? Do you own the rights to that 'Better Will Come' song? Do you know you can be sued any time, any day, for using it publicly? What about the idea for the Church of Retribution itself? Are you protected against mimics and copycats? What if somebody shows up tomorrow pretending that you borrowed their business model?"

Again, Deadria crossed Joe's mind. Her dreadlocks, her white husband, her reputedly ferocious litigation tactics. "I thought about all those things, but never got around to taking care of them," he admitted sheepishly.

"I can handle that for you," Claude assured him, Chilean shiraz perfuming his breath and seeping through his pores.

They were sitting in Claude's apartment two blocks up from Souk. The place was dark and packed to the ceiling with records. Fire extinguishers hung from nails at 5-foot intervals. Claude, whose paranoia was becoming more obvious to Joe with each passing minute, was wearing a dark-blue plastic suit and the B&L Wayfarers he claimed had been pioneered by Miles Davis on the "'Round About Midnight" cover. The ever-present ascot hid his throat. He untied it once in a while to wipe the sweat from his forehead and his upper lip, the grease leaking from his Classy Curl, and the wine squirting out of his skin. A very sweet smell permeated the air. Joe was feeling ill at ease, whether from the stuffiness or Claude's nervous tics.

"From a first glance at the contract you signed with your brother I'd advise you to never do anything stupid with the church's funds. Independently from the private auditors he requested, you can count on the I.R.S. investigating the shit out of you year after year after year. Every dime has better be going where you say it's going. With the kind of heat you're going to be generating they will want nothing better than to catch you red-handed. The government hates troublemakers."

Joe wrung his hands and moved to the edge of his

seat. "That's why I'm going in business for myself. That salary is a pittance."

"Nothing wrong with making money on the side," Claude proclaimed. "I'll help you set up a separate entity. Watch that Mofas guy and his Houdini tricks. He's an economic hit man. Trust him with your paperwork and you're gone."

"He's what now?"

"An economic hit man. Recruited and trained by the N.S.A. right out of college. Let loose in the ghetto to get as many blacks in financial trouble as possible. Hundreds of agents like him in inner cities. They're doing a great job for their handlers: payday loans, tax-refund advances, furniture and electronics rentals, high-interest auto loans, variable-interest 'resetting' mortgages.... They're destabilizing whole communities from the inside, wreaking havoc on black finances, bringing ruin and desperation."

"Not my Mofas," Joe objected. "He's the sweetest guy. That rent is more than fair. He even lent me his high-pitch machine. And he came to our ceremony last Sunday."

Claude brushed Joe's arguments aside. "They made it easy for you to get that space, Joe. Maybe the N.S.A. wants you here messing with people's minds, talkin' 'bout getting them some retribution money, causin' all kinds of unrest."

"You just said the I.R.S. would love to take me down. So which one is it?"

"Those are two different agencies. And that high-pitch machine? All it did was chase the rats to different digs. They were here a couple of nights ago

261

jumping up and down my kitchen counter and drinking my wine. Even Pepsi's offices on top of KDY3 aren't off-limits. Mofas is making a killing off that machine. Who do you think brought the rats to the ghetto in the first place?"

Joe started feeling dizzy. "Just help me with those copyrights and my businesses," he told Claude. "I'll handle Mofas."

"Economic hit man," Claude whispered as he pushed his apartment door shut. "They're all over Africa, too. Beware!"

The two men steered away from any church-related conversation around Souk, not just mindful of the confidentiality clause but because it had become a sore subject between Nasro and Jay. Nearly overwhelming the church on the Monday after the first gathering, the onslaught of phone calls and walk-ins from people trying to get their share of the donated money right here right now and in cash had tipped over to Souk. KDY3 and KDY5 residents, driven into a frenzy by rumors that the white boy down at the corner store was collecting big money in their name, started hounding Jay. They followed him around the aisles. They stuck their heads between shelved products. They tagged him in the cool box. The stood in his way, preventing him from taking care of his chores. "Wassup with the dough, man?" "You got sumthin' for me?" "When can I get mines?" "I'm here for my slavery money." "I just need a coupla hundreds." "Where can I apply?"

"That's not how it works," Jay explained over and over. "There won't be any individual payments."

"Why not?"

"Too complicated. Who's black? Who's a descendant of slaves? How much should everybody get? How to distribute the wealth evenly? When and where do we start?"

"Every black person in America is a slave descendant. The shade doesn't really matter. We're all entitled because of the 'one drop' rule."

"Can you prove it?"

"My skin is proof enough."

"I know Africans, Latinos, and Indians who look just like you. Then there are true African Americans with skin as white as mine. No, the money will go straight into a bank account. From there it gets invested into community projects. Big things are coming that will benefit everybody: playgrounds, clinics, scholarships, training. It's a nationwide effort."

"How do we know you're telling the truth?"

"Guess you'll have to trust me. I'm here among you, aren't I?"

"White man can't be trusted."

"I resent you saying that. I really do."

"We resent you sittin' on our stash."

"Just wait and see."

"Lemme see everything I need to see now."

"That's not how it works."

"Whatever."

Nasro listened to each exchange with increased impatience. "I'm running a business here," he complained more than once. Jay would have been fired hadn't Hakim and Claude intervened. "The boy is doing good work,"

Hakim, who had been promised a contribution for his mosque, told Nasro. "And I'm saying it from a black man's perspective. The noise will settle soon enough."

"You're only saying that because of your own interest," Nasro countered. "You know perfectly well that his movement is *haram*."

"Not with you on that one," Hakim said.

Nasro turned to Claude. "Can't you see that this church money thing is already corrupting everything?"

"Operations will stay 100% legit," Claude assured Nasro. "I guarantee it. It's my job to keep watch."

Nasro took refuge in silence after uttering an edict straight from Taha's book: "The fortunate ones will learn from the mistakes of others; the unfortunates ones will learn from their own mistakes."

"Not with you on that one," Hakim, Claude, Joe, and Jay reiterated.

Nasro hired the first man who walked in looking for a job and proceeded to cut Jay's hours in half, sending him home at 3 p.m. henceforth. The man was the Unbeliever. He'd followed the dice's counsel and made the day a good day. After Nasro took him in without asking a single question or checking a single reference, Jay started training him. "We got *two* white boys working for us," Riri told the other bay-bays when they came in for snacks later that afternoon. Jay and the Unbeliever, whom they called Un for short, got along fine from the start. They were roughly the same age, and Un's curiosity and eagerness to learn more about Jay made it seem as though they shared the same interests.

Even though he tried to put a good face on his sudden fall from favor, the rift with Nasro weighed heavily on Jay's heart. He had always been one to hate confrontation. He couldn't stand the thought that someone he cared about was disappointed in him or harbored negative feelings. It gnawed at him. It kept him awake at night. It made him uncomfortable. Jay wanted to always be in good terms, to keep the positive energy flowing, to feel appreciated.

Because Nasro was such a moral heavyweight, Jay took the time to rethink the whole Church of Retribution business. He sat on his rug and meditated whenever he wasn't needed at the office. Everything that was happening with the fund-raiser seemed to validate the brothers' idea: White people were anxious to make amends. They were ready for peace and unity. They were digging in their pockets to make up for the past and to help rescue thousands of at-risk black children and adults. It was only going to get better from here. Joe projected that the church would hit the million-dollar and 10,000-member marks by the end of the first quarter. They had already started to scope the area for their very first quality of life improvement project. The bay-bays would soon have a rec center, an after-school destination, a skill-building structure, a purpose-oriented environment. Was there anything wrong with that picture?

The problem with Nasro, Jay decided, was that he was too perfect--something I had been saying all along. Everything was "*haram.*" Everything. The fear of straying from the path kept him from lofty goals, outsized ambitions, or grandiose achievements. There was a built-in remoteness to his demeanor. He showed almost no affection to his wife and daughters, a lack of closeness I'm certain the women suffered greatly from. He took no pleasure in life's little nothings. Work. Pray. Work. Pray. Or maybe it was Taha's assassination and the ensuing persecution of Nasro's fellow Republican Brothers that had dulled his spirit, broken his heart, and made him renounce human ties, deep emotional bonding, social activism, political stances, and the pursuit of justice. He stuck to his almost-free breakfasts and his low prices. He never loaned money or groceries. He didn't get too familiar. He didn't get involved. Jay knew more about the area people after his first 10 days at Souk than Nasro did in 10 years. Perfect people aren't like us.

How could one live his life without combat, without risk, without embracing controversy if only once? How could one not seize the chance to help the multitude? Jay didn't understand. All he knew was that Nasro had given him a job and a place to stay. He held him in high esteem. To be at odds now that he was engaged in the work of his lifetime was very unfortunate indeed. He would have liked to have him in his corner. The old man exemplified many of the virtues that Jay cultivated: discipline, honesty, hard work, loyalty.

Have faith in the future, Jay told himself. Get out there and try to do good. Show Nasro that you are right.

Jay had too much on his plate to let his mentor's defection affect him. If anything, he internalized his feelings in order to give his sermons more punch. Where Nasro shied away from public displays of emotion, Jay reveled in them and knew just how to use them. 6 o'clock at the storefront became the favorite time of the day for registered members and Georgia Avenue commuters to drop in on the church and get an earful of Jay's rhetoric. He didn't always sing a song--jingles do get old a little too quick--but his delivery was always on point, always. Joe and he had decided on the everyday routine after taking into consideration the wholly positive response to the very first Sunday service and the high volume of Internet traffic. There seemed to be a wish, a desire, a hunger to hear the kinds of things Jay had to say, to see the kind of projects that the church had in mind come to fruition. This was a new message, a new direction. America was game.

"One thing about our compatriots ..." Jay mused one day, "... one thing about them is they know when something isn't working. They know, and they aren't afraid to try something else. Racism obviously isn't working. Neither is hatred. To come together, to live as one, to accept one another as equals.... That's what makes a strong nation. That's what solidifies a group. That's what helps conquer any obstacle."

His oratory style greatly improved with each delivery. The contact lenses enclosed him in a friendly cloud. The stage/altar became a familiar stomping ground. He learned to feel the crowd and play its moods. The place, the flock were his. Strolling, sitting, calling, singling members out, invoking the Scriptures, cajoling, berating, conversing as intimately as during a one-on-one.... No trick was passed on.

The floor was opened as soon as Jay was done addressing the congregation for the day. Time for whites to grab the microphone and testify. Most just wanted to formally apologize to the black race. Their soliloquies were tearful, emotionally charged, and cathartic.

"What my forebears did was barbaric," one Michelle M. said from the pulpit. "All my life I've been unable to look a black person in the eye. Today, right here, I feel like I can. Please forgive us for what we've done."

"I sleep better since I've joined," Michael K. revealed. "A big load is off my chest."

"I love black people," Carla D. said. "Always knew it. Now, finally, I can say it."

"My parents taught me to hate and discriminate," Sarah T. confessed. "Superiority was a given in my household. We nigger-bashed and nigger-joked. Prejudice can have catastrophic consequences for one's own development as well as one's behavior. Simply put, it's not a sustainable model. If you go through life thinking you're better than others, you're bound to keep hitting walls. I never liked myself. I used to derive satisfaction from humiliating people of other races and putting them down. They were the scapegoat for everything that was wrong with America and with me. The Church of Retribution is helping me take a deep look at myself and make a change. I take responsibility for my mistakes. I try to be more receptive to different sensibilities and different cultures. Where once stood objects of scorn and ridicule, I now see fully formed human beings. New possibilities have materialized for me. The world has suddenly gotten bigger."

Blacks got to say their word as well. To the white majority's relief, righteous and vengeful anger were set aside. Instead, gestures of acceptance were made. For once an offense has been acknowledged, due regrets expressed, and reparations underway, revenge is superfluous and out of place. "I got no beef with white folks," Leroy S. assured the flock. "Even though I've been spat at and cursed at and passed on for promotions. What's done is done. It's nice of y'all to atone and extend a helping hand. There are many things that we can learn from one another. I say let's start now."

"This country shouldn't have two, four, or six different realities," Raheem W. said. "It's like my world is totally different from whites'. We might rub elbows at work or in the street, but at the end of the day I know they have no clue about what I go through, the way I talk, the kind of music I listen to, the food I eat, the dreams and the thoughts I hold dear. How can we be so close and yet so far apart? How do we make sure that our children don't live in those same parallel dimensions?"

At Jay's prompting, numbers and business cards were exchanged. Members were encouraged to tap into the church's rapidly growing network of professionals and families, and to socialize. Ideas for a Singles Night, a marathon, house-swapping, mixed daycare, diversity classes, and an Adopt-a-Black Day were thrown around.

Jay found it easy to adapt to his role and his new routine. More than that: He was loving it. To wake up early, to go running, to go to work, to sit on the rug and contemplate and prepare his sermon, to deliver it downstairs, to work the crowd, to go back home to a very light supper of pistachio nuts, dried figs, and faucet water, and more contemplation.... He was taking care of his soul. He was spreading love and the good word. He wasn't taking from the earth more than he needed to survive. He was satisfied with the little salary he received from the church.

Low-impact, high-yield: This was the true life of an ascetic, the life he had always wanted. It was hard to believe that only three months ago he was in the throes of a debilitating depression. He felt like he had finally found his calling. This is what the voice and the night creatures had in store for him. This is what he had been put on this planet to do.

Only missing from this perfect picture was Lisha. When the day ended and all the lights went out, when he lay on the rug and propped his head on the book he used as a pillow, it's Lisha Jay pined for. Her face was the last thing Jay looked at before drifting into sleep. Her eyes. Her lips. Her hair. Where was she? What had become of her? Would he ever see her again? What would she do if he just reappeared? What would she say?

"I found her," Joe announced two weeks after his pledge. "Nick Stefanos, Mr. Strange's associate, followed her around for a couple of days. She still lives in that building on 19th Street, but her life has definitely changed."

Jay felt his stomach tighten. "Changed how?"

"She cut all her hair. She's pro-black. She's pregnant."

The last three words were the only ones that registered. Jay felt woozy and he had to hold on to the wall for support. "She's pregnant?"

Joe put his hand on Jay's shoulder. "Sorry."

"Who by?" Jay managed to ask through his tears.

"Stefanos couldn't say. There's a bunch of weird-looking girls around her, but no dudes. Not a single one."

"Got pictures?"

"I do. Sure you want to see them?"

Jay nodded courageously.

Joe handed him a brown folder. He had been just as saddened to learn the news. Lisha would have been perfect as the church's first lady--perfect. Dark-skinned, a body, modest of manners, good taste, nice style of dress, a quiet and serious demeanor, from the underclass but on the road to betterment. Now they wouldn't have a choice but to capitalize on Jay's single man status. Make a side story of the missing piece in his personal life. Organize a nationwide search for his soul mate. Televise the whole thing, of course. Bring in sponsors and marketers. Make the search last for two or three TV seasons. Or they could go the other way: Jay as the celibate prophet, the man who had sacrificed it all to dedicate himself to his cause.

With trembling fingers, Jay opened the folder. The hair was gone, the cheeks were rounder, the belly had quadrupled, the shoulders seemed squarer, the arms much more massive, and the fearsome forehead more convex, but it was definitely her. Carlisha Thomas, 1864 19th Street N.W., Apt 505, Washington, D.C., 20036. Born April 8, 1980, at Children's Hospital. Unwed parents, four sisters, one roommate. Meyer Elementary, Garnett-Patterson Middle School, Banneker High. Social Services major at UDC, senior year. Manager of the Art Supplies Store on M Street. No boyfriend. No driving record. No police record.

271

One credit card. Last year's tax return filed for the amount of $34,476.

Joe handed Jay a box of Kleenex. "Sorry," he said again.

"Not your fault," Jay assured him after wiping his eyes and blowing his nose.

"You're gonna be all right?"

Jay nodded. "I'm a soldier. I can handle pain."

That evening, his sermon, called "Evil," was full of apocalyptic references. Fire, brimstone, the Antichrist, Cerberus, flame-spitting dragons, screeching red-eyed monkeys, bicephalous gargoyles, three-legged beasts, Hell's fork-tailed demons. Evil ruled the world. Evil turned men into puppets and women into whores. Evil prompted entire nations to fight and conquer and slay. Evil sowed hatred and destruction. Evil separated man from wife, father from child. Evil ripped hearts from chests and babies from wombs. Evil ran amok until no living, breathing, and happy soul was left to inhabit the land. Jay prophesied with his arms raised toward the sky, his eyes shut, his fists closed, his body bathed in sweat. He called onto God to cleanse the Earth, he appealed to the sun to destroy all pharisees, phoneys, heathens, hypocrites, and loose women. "The wayward woman," he said, "will be punished. She will be hunted on all four corners of the universe like a leaping rabbit. She'll be made to beg for her life. She'll be forced to repent and renounce her ways. God protects us from the wayward woman, the lowdown woman, the dirty woman, for she has no respect and no regard. She'll take your love and crush it. She'll take your precious heart and

272

use and abuse it like it's made of stone. She'll do you wrong, oh, she'll do you wrong. And Lord knows that's no way to get along."

That being said, Jay grabbed his guitar and sang "Mean Woman," a blues number, a blues so blue that the suffocating air inside the church turned cool. People who had been steaming a moment earlier now squeezed one another for warmth. Breaths drew little clouds. Icicles fell from noses. Tears froze on corneas. The wayward woman became an ice-pick yielding witch, someone to run away from, someone to repudiate and rebuke and revoke. "*Mean woman mean woman/ Meaaaaaaan womaaan.*" Jay moaned and bellowed and kicked and rolled around with his guitar. And when he was finished with that song he got straight into another called "I'm Her Daddy," about a father being kept away from his daughter by a resentful lover for six interminable years.

"What the fuck was that all about?" Joe confronted Jay after the last churchgoer had left the storefront in a hurry, terrified by the end-of-the-world lexicon, dark lyrics, misogynistic rhetoric, kicks, leaps, jumps, and shouts.

"The sorrow in my heart," Jay said as he disassembled the pews to turn the church back into an office. "That's what it's all about, Joe. I feel like I want to die."

"Keep your personal mess out of the sermons," Joe told him, barely restraining himself. "This is business. Do you know how many new members you cost us tonight? Do you know the damage stuff like this can do if it's ever leaked to the press or posted on the Net?"

"This is real," Jay said for his defense. "This is raw.

273

This is life. This is emotions and feelings and expression. The kind of things you want a true guide to convey every once in a while."

"Don't do it again," Joe warned.

Later on, after twisting and turning on his rug for hours, after sweating so abundantly that he felt dehydrated, after pressing his palms against his heart for fear that it would jump out of his chest and start running away, Jay got up, got dressed, called a cab, and left the apartment. He crossed the sleeping town in a cold fever. He tipped the cab driver $50 for listening to his story and playing "Where Is the Love?" "We Both Deserve Each Other's Love," "Don't Stop Your Love," and "Love's Holiday" back to back. He waited in front of Lisha's building until drunk bar hoppers allowed him in. He ran up the stairs on rubber legs and gummy knees.

Marina is the one who answered his furious 3-in-the-morning banging, opening big, huge eyes when she recognized him. "Lisha shan't..." she started to say.

"I know, I know," Jay cut her off, elbowing her aside and charging ahead. "Lisha shan't see me. But guess what, Marina: I don't care!"

He made his way through the stuffy corridor, the dark living room, and as far as Lisha's bedroom. There, as he stood looking for the light switch after pushing the door open, somebody attacked him from behind and knocked him out flat.

When he came to, Jay was tied to a chair. A big, black, tattooed, and baldheaded woman in a white wife-beater was hovering over him, her enormous breasts swinging loosely, her grotesque face inches from his, her nose ring making her look like a pig, making Jay want to reach out and pull on it with his teeth.

"Cracker is waking up," the young woman said in a man's voice.

Jay grunted.

"What you gotta say for your defense, cracker?" the woman went on teasing him. "You don't look so hot right now, do you? You don't look so superior."

"Why did you tie me?" Jay shouted, more frustrated than panicked. "Was it you who hit me?"

The woman slapped Jay. "Why did you barge into this place in the middle of the night?"

Jay tried to kick her. Bound with an extension cord, his feet stayed glued to the chair. "I'm here to see my woman," he declared. "And you better not have hurt her or the baby. Otherwise I'll kill you."

"You got the wrong address," Jay's tormentor said. "Ain't no white girl living here. Just two pro-black black bitches and a menopausal Filipino."

"Where's Carlisha?" Jay shouted. "Lisha! Lisha!"

The woman slapped Jay again. "What do you want with Carlisha?"

"I'm here to get her back," Jay said, anger making his voice raw. "Lisha! Lishaaa!"

"Shut up," Lisha said from somewhere behind Jay. "You've disturbed the neighbors enough for the night."

Spurred by Lisha's voice, Jay almost broke his neck trying to look behind him. "Untie me, Lisha!"

The tattooed woman addressed Carlisha above Jay's

head. "This cracker for real? You know him?"

"He's my baby's daddy," Lisha confessed.

The woman spat on top of Jay's head. "I'll be goddamned," she said, disgust twisting her face into an even more horrible grimace.

They didn't untie Jay just yet. Armed with orange earplugs and the reassurance that Jay's life would be spared, Marina went back to sleep. Lisha and Miki, the baldheaded woman who was crashing on the couch and had mistaken Jay for a white rapist, argued over Lisha's true commitment to their movement, Black Squad 4 Life. Miki seemed appalled that Lisha could voluntarily carry Jay's baby--the fruit of a consensual union, no less. It was a motive for expulsion ten times over. "Wait until the sistas hear this," she told Lisha. "We all assumed that you were just like us, the black single mother-to-be of a black baby, abandoned by a no-good-ass black man, fighting to get your footing in a white-dominated society, ready to defend and uplift the black race. What a shame. What a secret to hide!"

"Y'all wouldn't have understood," Lisha said.

"You're sure he didn't rape you?" Miki suggested benevolently. "Not even once? Not even a little bit? Come on, you can tell me. Don't be scared. We got him. He'll never hurt you again. We can kill him and make him disappear."

Jay's teeth started to rattle.

"He didn't rape me," Lisha affirmed. "We were in a relationship and he disappointed me real bad. I found out after I left him that I was pregnant. I haven't had anything to do with him or any other white person since. My commitment to Black Squad, its ideals and objectives, is real. It stems from what Jay did to me. My repulsion, my rejection of him."

Miki shook her head. "Don't know about you," she told Lisha. "You're carrying his baby. How repulsed can you be?"

"What ideals?" Jay asked Lisha. "What objectives?"

"Shut up," Lisha ordered him.

Miki started to gather her things. "My gut feeling is you'll get banned from the movement," she said from across the living room. "The best I can do is guarantee you a fair trial."

"Forget these black dykes," Jay told Lisha. "You can come and join my church. We're more pro-black than any force, any group living or past. We're the real deal."

"What church?" Lisha asked, moving to face Jay.

"Who you calling a black dyke?" Miki erupted.

"What church?" Lisha asked again, proceeding to untie Jay.

"You!" Jay told Miki.

"I'm gonna hurt him," Miki growled, ready to send Jay reeling into the wall.

Lisha got in the middle. "Out," she told Miki.

Pain darkened Miki's eyes. She dropped her big, tattooed arms. Her breasts started to flatten like twin emptying plastic pools. Her anger vanished, replaced by utter puzzlement--disappointment, even. "Go ahead," she intimated. "Protect your white lover. You're a disgrace to Squad and to all of us black women. A total failure."

Lisha showed her the door. "Out," she said again.

"Out," Jay repeated after Lisha. "Out!"

Miki grabbed her backpack and pumped her fist in the air. "B.S. 4 Life!" she chanted before slamming the door.

"What ideals is Black Squad pursuing?" Jay asked again as Lisha helped him get on his feet. "What objectives?"

Lisha wrapped a handful of ice cubes in a towel and held it against Jay's skull after he went to sit on the couch. "The same old stuff," she explained. "Saving black children. Preparing for the future. Preaching unity. Promoting black values in this hostile world."

"Concretely?"

Lisha shook her head. "Nothing concrete. Almost all talk."

"Google 'Black Squad,'" Jay prompted her.

Lisha shook her head. "Not now."

"Google it," Jay insisted.

She turned on her laptop and typed the search request. The only thing that popped up was Def Squad, the defunct hip-hop act consisting of Erick Sermon, Redman, and Keith Murray.

"Now Google me," Jay told Lisha.

"Holy Mother of God," she exclaimed after complying and clicking on the first link, a video clip of Jay's very first sermon.

"That's Mayor Merry," Jay said, singling out people from the audience. "That's Youngin'. That's Pepsi--he owns the whole neighborhood. That's Nicole–dad's girlfriend, remember her? That's Gypsy. That's Hakim. That's Claude, our lawyer."

Lisha was speechless. Jay took the laptop from her and visited a dozen more Web sites where he was featured, including his MySpace and Facebook pages. "I'll have to update the information ..." he mused, thrilled that he was sitting next to Lisha, his Lisha, wanting but not yet daring to touch her belly and stick his ear to it, "... since I'm about to be a daddy."

Lisha snatched the laptop from his hands. "Not so fast," she said. "You think you can just storm in and make everything all right? I don't care about no church. Did you hear me say anything about forgiving you? How do you even know this is your child?"

Jay's heart stopped beating again. Terror made the blood flee his face. "It's not?"

Lisha shook her head in exasperation. "Of course it is, you dummy! Didn't you hear me tell Miki as much only five minutes ago?"

Jay got off the couch, got on one knee, and took Lisha's hands in his. "I want to apologize to you," he said, locking eyes. "I want to beg you for forgiveness. What I did was wrong."

Lisha snatched her hands back, looked away, and screwed her face. "I'll have to think about it."

Irritated more than he could say, Jay started pacing the living room floor, his hands behind his back. "So you weren't gonna tell me I have a daughter on the way?"

"How do you know it's a girl?"

"I saw the three of us in a dream. You, me, the little one. We were sitting inside an airport lounge. You didn't want to travel with me, but I managed to convince you in the end."

"You had just called me 'nigger,' Jay. Remember? What was I supposed to do? Run back and share the good news? I was completely lost. I was terrified. Do you know how close I came to getting an abortion?"

The thought froze Jay's feet in place. He almost fainted. All his life he had prayed for a child. A little girl, especially. Someone to love unconditionally. "I didn't call you that," he protested. "I was talking about Leslie, the guy who murdered dad. I had never even said that word aloud before. And I haven't said it since. That's not me. That's so not me. Come on. You know that's not me at all."

"It's enough that it came out that one time, Jay. It gave me a good glimpse into your soul. Do you know how it made me feel to hear that? Do you know what it means to hear 'nigger' from a white man's, any white man's mouth? I felt a jolt zap straight through my skull. My heart broke in two. My thoughts were shattered. My hands started to shake. My legs turned into lead."

"You seemed pretty composed to me."

"That's a black woman's pride for you. And stop pacing the floor like a maniac. You're making me dizzy."

Jay came to kneel in front of Lisha again. "That insult wasn't addressed to you. You know it wasn't."

Lisha appeared saddened, and far from convinced. "It's enough that you proffered it, Jay. Think that of one of us, say that of one of us and you hurt us all."

Jay seemed on the brink of tears. "Don't you think I regret it? Can't you see I'm trying my best to make amends?"

An ounce of interest softened Lisha's voice. "With that church?"

"Partly. I'm out there every day preaching the reconciliation gospel."

"Have you apologized to Leslie?"

"No. He's in jail."

"Go visit."

"Why should I? He killed my father."

"Go see him. It'll help you forgive and put it all behind."

Jay relented. "Maybe. Will you come with me?"

"No."

"Why?"

"I don't like jails. Too many deadbeat niggers."

"Why are you using that word?"

"Because I can. I have clearance. Unlike you or any white person."

"I'm confused."

"I know."

Jay took Lisha's hands yet again. "I really miss you," he said. Lisha didn't answer, but it seemed to Jay that her anger was abating. "I could use your help with that mission," he went on. "It gets lonely sometimes."

"Why do you call it a mission?" Lisha asked, stifling a yawn.

"There were signs," Jay announced mysteriously. "The path was drawn out."

"You're still having those strange visits at night? Those dreams?"

"Not in a couple of months. Not since Joe and I founded the Church of Retribution."

Unable to restrain herself, Lisha laughed and laughed and laughed. "That's a crazy name for a church.

You realize that?"

Jay started to laugh, too.

"Am I forgiven?" he asked after a little while.

Lisha hesitated. "It's not that easy," she finally said. "I really do have to think about it."

Jay's eyes filled with clouds. He wanted to kiss Lisha. He wanted to touch her belly bad. He wanted to never leave her side. "Can we talk? Can I call you every day? Can we do stuff?"

"I have to work," Lisha said. "And I'm still going to school. But we'll see. Consider yourself on probation."

"Thank you," Jay said. Then, emboldened, he kissed her on the lips.

Frowning in disgust, Lisha jumped back.

"What's up with the hair?" Jay asked, pretending not to notice her reaction. "Why did you cut it all?"

"It's a Squad thing," Lisha said. "You wouldn't understand it."

I know, I know, I know
I know, I know, I know
I know, I know, I know
I know
I oughta leave the young thang alone
But ain't no sunshine when she's gone

Leaving the boys and Maggie to their own fates, I hung out with Nicole as much as I could for the next week or so. If stress from my wife's behavior and my sons' endeavors was killing me, it was loneliness that was getting to my former lover. Though she hadn't given in to either Youngin's or Pepsi's outlandish solicitations, I felt her to be more and more receptive to the older suitor. There seemed to be a pattern here: My baby liked them middle-aged and experienced. (Men who are over the hill take their sweet time. They ease into things rather than jumping the gun. Not at their physical best, they're less likely to pound-pound-pound and tear something in the grip of carnal passion. They're easier to manhandle should a confrontation arise. They're not inclined to want children.) And what was that Amateur Night thing if not an attempt to seduce Youngin' and have him eat out of her hand? Nicole pretended to do it for me--that's the way she explained it, or I should say justified it, to herself. But what did I need her to get on Macondo's stage and shake her body-body for? No, that dance was more of a device to let me go, kick me to the curb, kick me out of her mind and out of her heart. A trick to claim her independence and her freedom. A way to assert control over her life and her body, that phantasmagoric work of science and its most formidable asset, Mr. Butt. Two birds in one bold stroke: I was out; Youngin' was ushered in. Nicole, my Nicole was ready to move on.

And what a succession ceremony it was. She stayed in Happy Cuts after closing time and got dressed by candlelight to set the right mood. She listened to Blue Magic, the Miracles, the Stylistics, and Teddy Pendergrass on the "Quiet Storm." She curled her hair, painted her nails, and did her face. She polished every inch of her body and made it shine. She kissed my picture as I looked on and smiled, feeling happy, feeling proud, feeling blessed. She stretched her muscles and rehearsed her routine. She said a little prayer. She walked into Macondo wrapped in nothing but a full-length, diamond-studded Rock & Republic gala dress, clutching a Rock & Republic diamond-studded gala purse. The band hit the "Darlin' Nikki" theme when rumor spread that Nicole was making her way through the crowd, which was denser than usual thanks to Ahmet and his "upcoming event" tickets. Youngin' himself escorted Nicole backstage, taking her hand and shoving Lola out of the way when she objected to the breach of protocol. Five whole minutes the crowd waited in perfect obscurity and complete silence, anticipation making the rowdiest of patrons hold their breaths. Everything stopped. Not a cough, not a laugh, not a stir--only the beating of our expectant hearts.

Finally, Nicole unzipped her dress, dropped it, and pushed the curtain. People couldn't yet see, but they could sense and they could hear, and what they heard set their imagination on fire. I walked onto the stage right behind her, ready to watch the show up close--me and Mr. Butt. "This is for you, Ben," Nicole murmured right before the orchestra attacked the prelude to "Miss Black America." The spotlight revealed her to the world--no word of introduction, no announcement, no hype. Just Nicole, her high heels, the stage, and a pole.

> *Stepping so proud*
> *Mother Nature's only godchild*

Arms outstretched in offering, Nicole walked toward the edge of the stage. The audience let out a collective gasp. There was such a thing as perfection after all. It existed. It inhabited a human body. It was here in the room tonight, walking and standing just a few feet away. An ideal magnificently fleshed out. Femininity incarnated. A dream designed, contracted, given shape, and paid in full.

Nicole stopped, put her hands on her hips, and unashamedly basked in the crowd's admiration.

> *Society salutes you today*
> *And we'd like to say,*
> *God bless Miss Black America*

Watch over
Miss Black America

Nicole turned around. The sight of her walking away would have been enough to seal the night. Mr. Butt had us beat, whipped, whooping, whacked, trumped, madly in love. Much like I remembered, it rippled and jiggled, it bounced and stretched and snapped, it expanded and contracted, it spread and came back, spread and came back, spread and came back....

Our hearts went wild. We were on our feet, shouting and whistling and clapping and jumping in place. Men and women, young and old, the alive and the dead, patrons and workers, tourists and locals, regulars and first-timers, the black-and-white spillover from tonight's Church of Retribution sermon. Flashes burnt brightly. Lighters were held up. Hands shone behind the blue, red, green, purple, and orange glow of cellphone screens and keypads. We were all fitting to be dazzled, and goddamn it Nicole didn't disappoint. This was something else. Something out of the ordinary. Something unbelievable.

Worldwide admiration
From nation to nation
They love you,
Miss Black America

Nicole, who was far from finished with us, grabbed the pole and went all the way up. One after the other, she seamlessly executed some of the most difficult figures in pole dancing: P-Poppin' (pussy in your face), Bottoms Up (head down, ass in the air, may be complemented by individual motion of each butt cheek), Wink-Wink (now you see it, now you don't), Deep-Sea Diving (holding oneself with one hand while suspended head first, the feet acting as propellers), the Helix (rotor-like motion of the whole body executed at the very top of the pole), the Grind (freestyle using the pole as phallic object), the Drop (going down suddenly and very fast), the Lock (abrupt stop, completes the Drop), the Twirl (legs mimicking a majorette's stick), the Fireman's Slide (self-explanatory), the Flag (another one-hand figure executed at the very top, requires turning and holding the legs at a 45-degree angle), the Dragonfly (very similar to the Helix, with variations in altitude), the V (so hard to accomplish that only the very fit and best-trained dancers can attempt it: back turned to pole, both hands holding firm, legs open toward the audience, rotation of the thighs added for more points), the One Hand (self-explanatory), the Scissors (chopping the air with one's legs), the Door Peep (showing just enough to entice), the Boa (dancer and pole are perfectly entwined).... Nicole smiled, slipped, shook, glided, and undulated. She tilted and pulled her head back and offered her throat, her breasts, her belly, her toes. With only one of her legs clutching the pole she lay in midair, arched her back, and stretched her arms. She completely let go at one point, executing a daring flip before catching herself at the last second.

A shudder rippled through the crowd. It was too much. Much too much. Some people fainted, crushing tables under their weight as they went down. Some gouged their eyes because, after tonight, they had seen everything on Earth worth seeing. One man cut his chest open and

287

ripped his heart out, throwing it at Nicole's feet. Another proclaimed his love by kneeling and banging his head on the carpet.

Slightly out of breath, validated by the reactions she had elicited, Nicole bowed gracefully and retreated toward the curtain. She had held herself up to the collective mirror of our eyes and our senses, and our verdict, a unanimous "Prettiest of them all," seemed as pleasing as it was reassuring.

She cries tears of success
We wish her long happiness

Elated, Nicole took Youngin' home that very night. He popped a Viagra before leaving the club, knowing that by the time they got to her pad he would be ready for the boo-tay. I watched them leave with no regrets or bad feelings, having made my peace with Nicole's search for a new love, having seen how miserable she looked when the time came to shut Happy Cuts' door lately, having witnessed how she pressed her employees for happy-hour martinis and margaritas and appletinis so as not to face the prospect of a lonely dinner, a lonely apartment, another lonely night.

Treat her right, I begged Youngin', a bad premonition dogging me all night. Treat her right because deep down inside she's really sweet and insecure as you couldn't guess and wouldn't believe. Don't let the borderline exhibitionism and big-girl antics fool you, Youngin'. Don't think she does this all the time. It's a precious lucky few who've gone up into the Condo in the

Sky and tasted Nicole's love. You're a member of a very select group.

But I doubted that Youngin', Viagra in his bloodstream, would heed my prayer.

So I worried. And worried. And worried.

When Nicole didn't show up the next morning I knew something serious had happened. Happy Cuts was her life. She never missed a day and she never forgot to call. Cherie, her closest assistant, opened the shop with her own key.

Calls to Nicole's cellphone and to her home remained unanswered. 911 directed the girls to the Coroner's Office. They tried all the hospitals and the morgue, fear numbing their fingers, dulling their brains, and freezing their tongues. Nicole was like a sister. She was such a big part of their everyday that they couldn't picture her gone. Such a beautiful girl. Such a wonderful, wonderful human being. Who would want to hurt her? What could have happened? Did she have an accident? Was she driving the 650i too fast? Who had seen her last? Was it a medical emergency? Had one of her artificial body parts detached itself? Was she lying somewhere leaking to death, waiting for someone to find her?

Word of Nicole's performance at Macondo reached them around 11. The girls ran to ask Youngin' a few questions. Of course, the old man was nowhere to be found either. Lola, in a head scarf and sunglasses, was trying to gather Macondo's herd. Her dancers had quit en masse after seeing Nicole work the pole last night--they knew they couldn't compete: Nicole, with her savoir faire and workmanship, had raised the bar way too high and pretty much killed it for every D.C. girl in the profession.

Confronted by the Happy Cuts crew, Lola looked at her watch and smiled a contemptuous smile, the giraffe deigning to pay attention to members of a more lowly, earthbound species. "I don't know where that little *puta* is. In jail, I hope. Youngin' is on a gurney getting his dick reattached. The girl and he had a little argument last night. Things got out of hand, as you may say. I hear he messed her up pretty bad, too. More trouble than that face and *nalga plastica* are worth, if you ask me. Fuck silicone."

Lola wouldn't say more. She slammed her office door and got back to cajoling her troops out of hiding. I could have slapped her myself.

"We'll open Happy Cuts and honor today's appointments," Cherie decided. "Let's just act normal and pray for the best." The crew group-hugged, held hands, sent a quick but heartfelt plea to the Lord, lit candles in front of the big mirror, and got to work, Nicole in their thoughts and Nicole in their hearts.

It's Jay who heard from her first. She called Souk a little before 3 and asked to speak to him. After he hung up, Jay handed his apron to Un and rushed out to her in Nasro's car. He, too, had heard about last night's show.

He was ready to chastise Nicole for worrying all of us so much, but one look at her face stopped him cold. She was all pummeled and bruised, her lip busted, her nose askew, both her eyes blackened, her hair missing in spots. Jay almost burst into tears at the sight.

Man up, I prodded him.

Man up, he prodded himself before taking Nicole in his arms and holding her close, keeping her against him as she sobbed uncontrollably.

We sat on the couch. The Condo in the Sky was still my favorite place on Earth--she hadn't touched a thing. White on white on exposed brick. Plush. Orderly. Quiet. Framed mirrors. Same giant pictures of herself on the wall. Flowers. Plants. So thoroughly Nicole.

Jay held her hand as she spoke, her pretty little hand with its scratches and broken nails.

"I miss your dad," Nicole told Jay for the thousandth time, making me cry, making Jay fight hard to keep control. "I miss him so much.... None of this would have happened if Ben were with us still."

"He's here," Jay affirmed, pointing to where I was sitting. "He's right here with us."

Nicole looked straight at me and smiled through her tears. "I know it sounds crazy," she went on. "I know nobody can possibly understand. But Ben made me feel comfortable. I didn't have to do anything but be myself. No role-playing, no second-guessing, no tentativeness.... I was free."

"That's him," Jay echoed. "That's the type of guy he was. Easy and relaxed."

Guilt-ridden, I got up and wandered around the duplex. I couldn't stand looking at Nicole's face, seeing what had been done to her, surveying the damage. I hated Youngin' for what he had done. I hated myself for not being alive. I hated fate for what my people were going through.

I didn't have to wait for Nicole to start explaining

291

what had happened in order for me to know. The memory, fresh and bloody, played in her mind as she sat next to Jay, her speech interspersed with silences that he took great care to respect. I saw it as clearly as she had lived it, and immediately realized that my assumptions were false: Youngin' hadn't attacked Nicole after getting enraged by a post-coitus heart-to-heart about her sex change. In fact, they never even got to that point.

Youngin' was on fire all right. The dance, Viagra, the euphoria, the rush he got from getting so close to Nicole after hunting her for so long.... They walked into her place and he got right down to business, groping her, pushing himself on her, his hands everywhere, his breath hot on her skin, his crotch heavy and itchy. Nicole wanted to take her time. She wanted to kiss and neck and maybe dance some more. My baby is no cold starter, see. She's got to feel you, captivate you, entrance you. A private striptease, flavored condoms, glow-in-the-dark intimate jelly are a must. They're part of her M.O., her mating ritual. She derives joy, an extra reward from her partner's desire, her own assessment of her ability to please and satisfy. Not so much sex as the idea, the sublimation of sex. Nicole is a woman's woman.

Youngin' had no time for such intricacies. Viagra had him hot and he wanted to stick it, do it right away, do Nicole right, do her on the floor, do her all night. She tried to put a drink in his hands. She tried to grab the pole and do a repeat, a recap of the whirlwind of less than an hour ago: the Drop, the Flag, the Helix for Youngin's eyes only. My man wasn't having it. Dance? Enough for the night. A pole? He was sick of poles. He knew everything there was to know about poles. He saw poles every day at work. Collapsible, telescopic, self-cleaning, heated, platinum, gold-plated poles--you name it. His insurance premiums were off the charts because of poles, because of lousy girls breaking their necks when they fell off poles. And poles were all over the place nowadays, the "cute" factor dwindling because no custom-built home was complete without one. And to top it off Youngin' owned stock in Vertical Hold, the company outfitting the whole D.C. area. "Stop foolin' around," the 60-year-old bull moaned. "I've got your pole right here in my pants. And baby, it's achin' for your scratchin'."

Nicole pushed Youngin' away, laughing nervously.

Youngin' slapped her, undid his belt, and freed himself.

Nicole ran inside the kitchen and grabbed the biggest knife she could find.

Youngin' followed her and hit her again.

The knife slipped.

Nicole dove for it.

"It's not grief that's holding me back," Nicole told Jay that afternoon. "It's my anxieties. I was, much like you, Jay, but for very different reasons, persecuted by my mother. I was the fag, the mistake, the freak, the sissy. Couldn't do anything right. Mom had me under her thumb. My dad, God bless his soul, wasn't in a much better predicament. We're Haitians. They came here together and made it big together. One thing my mother forgot to leave behind was that superstition shit, that voodoo shit. My condition wasn't genetic, physiological, hormonal, developmental, or psychological: It was a curse. It was something someone back in Port-au-Prince had done. A hex, a charm invoked by her 'enemies' to affect me, her son, her only child. It's not acceptance and understanding and affection that I needed: It was an antidote, a counterpoison, an exorcism. The jinx had to be fought. If need be, it must be whipped and lashed and beaten out of me. My mother terrorized me, Jay. She took me to strange places to see strange people who did all kinds of strange things, things you wouldn't believe take place here in America. Blood, chickens, roots, leaves, liquids, mud, smoke, powders, horns, dried skins, mummified animals, needles, nails, a monkey's skull.... It was all paraded before my eyes. I was made to wear amulets, bathe with nasty stuff, swallow potions, and chant Creole incantations. I was forced to lie down without moving while people walked around me, pushing crosses into my face. I ate manioc and I drank ginger, manly foods and manly drinks. I inhaled the smoke of burning baobab bark. All I wanted was to become a girl, Jay. To wear pink dresses and carry a little purse. To play with dolls. To let my hair grow. To be left alone. To be in peace."

Jay nodded. He understood. Of course he did.

"It got better after mom died. She'd never once told me she loved me, but I felt free. Clothing, hairstyles, manners, behavior.... Everything changed overnight. I blossomed. My dad helped me make the transformation permanent--or at least as permanent as we could make it--when I became old enough.

"So here I am. A full-fledged woman who, at some level, feels like a fraud. I'm not the real thing. I'm not the authentic article. I'm not 'made in heaven.' No period. No babies. No man of my own. Danger and heartbreak behind every encounter because of course you have to be honest, you have to tell them the truth about the goodies before they learn it from someone else. Ben was my one success story. Now what? Stay alone? A quarter-million-dollar body and nothing to do with it. Always things coming loose, stuff to touch up, parts to reattach and rebuild. Old age is going to be a bitch, I can feel it. How do I fend off moral anguish, suicidal thoughts, the uselessness, the futility of this all? I have to find some kind of direction before it's too late."

Jay cleared his throat. Nicole's confession was touching him in a deep, deep place. It wasn't just about empathizing, walking in her shoes, treading the same waters. The fact that she had called him, of all people, in her moment of need, humbled him. He was on top of his game lately, what with the semi-reconciliation with Lisha and the baby girl on the way. His heart was full of compassion. His tongue was as sweet as honey. His speeches were right on the money. Evening after evening he had the attendees on their feet, jumping, shouting, hollering, laughing, embracing one another. He had never felt such confidence, such sense of purpose, such conviction.

He took Nicole's chin between his fingers. He looked into her eyes. Like doves taking flight, appeasing words flew from his mouth. "You're no victim," he told her. "You're no loser. None of us can tell why we're here, why what happens happens, why we're going through what we're going through. All we can do is do our best, try our hardest. So we can say at the end of it all that we didn't flinch when life was beating us up, that we put up a good, honest fight. That we never ran from our responsibilities. That we're leaving the world, and the people around us, in a better shape than we found them. That we took our God-given capital and did something with it."

Nicole smiled.

"You're beautiful," Jay told her. "You're beautiful and we all love you."

Nicole went back to work the next week, bruises and black eyes and all. Youngin' was out much, much longer. When he did reappear it was in a wheelchair and with a full head of gray hair, testimonies of his life-changing ordeal. In a brazen yet very American attempt to cash in on the sympathy induced by his uncommon injury (less than 150 such male genitalia sectioning reported nationwide annually), he set out to write his memoirs and an accompanying dating guide called "Things Not to Do When You Want to Do IT." Nicole declined to press charges, preferring to put the incident behind.

Jay got her more and more involved in the church's life. She helped supervise the installation of a foundling wheel after they started to find abandoned babies at their door every other week. The wheel came with a heated cradle and a sensor connected to Joe's pillow. Nicole helped care for the infants and took it upon herself to navigate the city's child services office on Jay and Joe's behalf. If Jay was the church's figurehead and Joe its eminence grise, she became its spokeswoman and goodwill ambassador.

Her charm did wonders in securing the required permits for the brothers' first undertaking. Named ARCH, it was slated to go up on the no man's land between KDY3 and KDY5 by the end of the year. Getting city permits was a walk in the park compared with obtaining Pepsi's authorization. He wanted nothing to do with improvement projects. The chaos and blight afflicting the neighborhood suited him just fine. What would the future hold for his business if everybody suddenly got their stuff straight? How would he make money if nobody did drugs, if his addicts got clean and his drunks got sober, if young thugs learned skills and earned degrees and clinched jobs that were more stable, safer, and better paying than what he offered? If the kids he groomed to stem the never-ending flow of fallen street soldiers grew up wanting nothing to do with the game? If desperation became a thing of the past?

"These brothers are proving to be a major pain in the ass," Pepsi complained to Nicole. "I didn't mind them being here at first. But between the rats, the congestion on Georgia Avenue come sermon time, and these utopian projects, I'm really beginning to wonder."

"They're all about the bay-bays," Nicole assured him. "They just want to make it better for all these kids. It's their mission, in a nutshell. That, and bringing the white and black races together."

Pepsi couldn't have cared less about kids and peace on Earth. He throve on mental confusion, slashed opportunities, compromised futures, wasted chances, ignorance, doom, gloom, and ruin. If he relented in the end it's because he didn't think ARCH would get anywhere. One more bubble inflated by white men and offered to black people as a hot-air balloon to Freedomland. If it didn't explode on its own it could be brought down at a moment's notice. The disappointment that would follow would be even more crushing to the Kennedy Street residents. More dashed hopes, more need for dope. "Go ahead," Pepsi told Nicole. "But I want you to keep me in the loop."

"Absolutely," Nicole said.

She was good with Lisha as well, helping her, to Jay's great relief, nurse her mowed-down hair back to health. They shopped together. They talked. They hung out after Lisha, at Jay's insistence, stopped working.

Not that things were all lovey-dovey between the parents-to-be. "I have no desire to come live with you in that ascetic's cave," Lisha told Jay when he invited her to move in with him above Souk. "We're not back together. I don't go with you. I'm just trying to be nice because I'm having your child."

"You have to forgive," Jay pressed her. "Otherwise it's gonna poison you. All that negativity. Think of the health risks."

"I'm still mad at myself for trusting you," she said. "I should have known better just from taking a look at history. I'm paying for my own dumbness. All the brothers out there waiting to be saved by a good black woman and I chose to mess with you."

"You can't put all white people in a bag. That's generalizing. That's profiling. Some of us are genuine. A few of us are genuinely good."

"All of y'all got racism ingrained in you. It's always

there, waiting for the right time to come out. I don't think you can help it, Jay."

"I know I can," Jay affirmed. "I'm doing it as we speak. There's not a single racist bone in me any more. I beat the odds. I'm squeaky clean."

"Until next time."

"No next time."

"If you ever call my daughter 'nigger' I'll kill you."

"Why would I call her 'nigger'? She's my daughter, too."

"One never knows with white people."

"Black Squad brainwashed you."

"Whatever."

"You have to let go," Jay insisted. "If you stay angry, if you keep this ugly thing in your mind it'll destroy everything we're building. It'll win."

"'Building'? Who's building anything with you? Building what?"

Jay tried to take Lisha in his arms. "A family. Something I always wanted. Do you know how long I've been praying for a wife and a daughter? Do you have any idea? I always thought you could be the one, Lisha."

Lisha pushed him away. "You're out of your goddamn mind, man."

Day and night, he pursued her: "Let it go"; "Let it go"; "Let it go." Lisha wouldn't relent, though it seemed at times that she wanted to. Jay, who sometimes thought himself unworthy of affection because of all the stuff with Maggie, didn't believe that Lisha had stopped loving him. There was definitely something there, remnants of the passion that had them stealing kisses in Cairo's aisles and Cairo's basement, and sneaking in and out of his Military Road room. He knew that disappointment wasn't the only problem at hand. The product of a broken home, Lisha had her own trust and neglect and abandonment issues. Her reserve, her independence, her self-reliance were proverbial.

Give up? Out of the question. This was a new Jay: A Jay who roused all kinds of emotions in his followers; a Jay who could play a packed hall just as well as his Yamaha; a Jay whose conformance to the beliefs and courses of action etched out by himself for himself gave total conviction.

So he did the one sensible thing that came to mind: He got in front of the flock on a Sunday and asked for Lisha's forgiveness. Humbly, simply, honestly. He recounted the events leading to his outburst, that one fatal insult in Cairo. He brought in officer Melvin Lee to testify in his defense. He got his black Facebook friends, all twenty-five thousand of them, to drop by or write notarized affidavits or phone in a good word during the marathon session (Joe approved the personal tone of the proceedings. This was good news and excellent business for the church. This, in fact, might represent the "tipping point," the Holy Grail of marketing concepts according to Malcolm Gladwell, Joe's new marketing guru).

Jay got on one knee and bowed his head. Crying like a baby, he begged not only for Lisha's clemency but for her hand, popping the question in front of all those people and live on the Internet. "I don't have a ring for you, my dear. I don't have a thing to my name. I'm a man of little means. An imperfect man. My only wealth, my only treasure is the love I once called mine. Your love, Lisha. Not any love. Not an easy love. Not a shoobedoobedoobop-shoodoobop kind of love. We never got it made in the shade. You know this. We faced all kinds of barriers when we started. In a sense, we still do. The world isn't kind on people like us, relationships like ours. The world scoffs. The world shrugs. The world smirks. We're doomed. We're dumb to even try. We're sick. 'Jungle fever,' they call our affliction. Little does the world know, this thing is real. It's real, it's strong, it lives. It's bigger than us, Lisha. It's you, me, and the little one. It's sharing and giving and enjoying every passing moment. It's having your hand to take, your eyes to trust, your beauty to behold. It's having an ally, a partner, a sister, a friend, a companion for the road. It's making something out of nothing. It's taking a leap together, not in blind faith, but with the conviction that your heart will be cared for, your needs fulfilled to the best of my abilities, your feelings honored, your life held up high. You, Lisha. You, me, and the little one."

Sobbing out of her mind, Lisha flung herself into Jay's arms. She had just recently started to show, and, boy, that belly was growing fast and big and beautiful.

I was just as excited as them. Excited for them. Excited for me. Grandpa Ben. Check that out. What a joy. What a blessing. Thank you, Lord. For Your infinite kindness, we thank You. May You shower a heap of blessings upon this young couple. May You grant them a long, bountiful, peaceful life. May You bestow wealth, good health, and good fortune upon my daughter Lisha, my son Jay, and my yet-to-be-named granddaughter.

And while I'm at it, Lord, let me pray for my wife Margaret and my son Joe, two very misguided souls. Maggie is going crazier and crazier by the day. She got a house on Maryland's Eastern Shore, a place called Bel Air, and turned it into an S&M dungeon complete with a waterboarding room and antique torture rack. Her live-in partner Steve works on his drones out of a workshop outfitted with a sliding roof. They roam the countryside in that monstrous Hummer looking for yet more antique torture instruments. I would go and visit them more often, impatient as I am to be near the water, except there's something malefic about that house--forgive me for saying so, Lord. Something sickening. Something definitely out of place. Maggie is far from happy that Jay and Lisha are expecting. Her bouts of rage are increasing in frequency and intensity. It's getting to be too much: the Church of Retribution, her good name associated with the goo Joe and Jay are up to their necks into back in that black town named Chocolate City, on that black block, with all those black people. Maggie has stopped taking phone calls from our relatives and acquaintances. She says she's tired of feeling apologetic. Tired of fielding questions. Tired of dodging rumors. What worries me, Lord, is that smoldering anger of hers. Maggie is like a ticking bomb. All her pent-up emotions are slowly making their way to the surface. On a bad day she'll ride all the way to D.C. just to park in front of the church and watch the show come 6 o'clock. How she rejoiced when she caught a glimpse of Nicole after her fight with Youngin'! How she laughed!

Then there's Joe, Lord. He and that Riots on

302

Demand lady. That Imabelle. They've quickly become an item. They don't see each other much, busy as they are with their respective jobs. And they're trying to keep their fling secret. Imabelle moves in the shadows required by the very nature of her job. To her superiors Joe must remain a simple account, albeit a growing one. They talk on the phone. They visit furtively, always at night. They kiss, but they never make love. Imabelle is as averse to physical contact as she is to feeding herself. Nothing touching, caressing her bare skin. They tried once, on the immaculate bed of the immaculate bedroom of her immaculate house, after she had made Joe take four showers in a row. It proved hard enough to hold her still during foreplay. When he entered her she bucked, barfed, and ran to the other room in tears. So Joe knows not to start anything. He knows to ignore the call from his loins and to focus on what he and his girlfriend do best: plot, strategize, come up with the blueprint for the perfect business, a perpetual-motion moneymaking scheme. The Church of Retribution is at 5 million dollars and 33,000 U.S. members three months after its inception. Out of a storefront with a handful of aging employees, a couple of Web sites, and a self-styled high priest. Never mind the death threats, the controversy, the uproar. Joe and Imabelle are visualizing hundreds of millions of dollars and a few million more paying members. They're planning for unchecked growth and huge returns. They're conceiving a graft, a side business just as juicy and profitable. They're giving birth to Retribution, Inc.

So protect us, O Lord.

Joe contacted Sally Harris, the Washington Post reporter responsible for a brief column on my death back in August, and told her of his intention to go visit Leslie with Jay. Sally, an ambitious junior writer, was on hand with a photographer come that afternoon. She was herself a rags-to-riches story in the making, a local girl who had been through her share of rough patches. Out of school at 14, pregnant by 16, on welfare at 17, addicted to hard drugs for a couple of years afterward, she had completely turned her life around by the time she hit 20. "Shine Eye Girl," the book she co-wrote with her Somali husband Mo to relate her formative years and the story of their hard-time tough-love relationship, had been well received and still generated respectable sales on Amazon. She was smart, edgy, and tough. She kept it real and really gritty. She knew her streets as well as the Post's newsroom.

The brothers secured a special authorization from D.C. Jail and conducted the meeting in a private room. Inside the prison's derelict halls Jay was stopped every few steps by beaming young prisoners who recognized him from Kennedy Street and Souk, the same toughs who acknowledged him around the neighborhood but wouldn't be caught dead attending service. Jay wasted no time enrolling them into the church's outreach program. Sally was intrigued when a few of them asked for his autograph. It looked like something straight out of her favorite movie, "Coming to America."

Leslie, who seemed more than a little confused by the fuss, took advantage of the opportunity to proclaim his innocence one more time for the record. "I'm thankful for y'all to forgive me and everything," he told the brothers, "but I had nothing to do with y'all's father's death. Nothing at all. I was just passing by and I saw him lying there. My mistake was to stop and take a closer look. The other two strikes against me were being black and being homeless."

Sally, who had read Leslie's indictment papers, sighed a here-we-go-again sigh. The correction officer overlooking the scene sucked his teeth and patted his club. Joe suppressed a smile. Jay, who was feeling ill at ease, shook his head the way one chases away a bad dream.

Leslie was small and round. His speech was slow and deliberate, as if talking didn't come naturally, as if there were a disconnect between his thoughts and his tongue. His slightly bulging eyes were perpetually on the brink of tears. He had the toughness of a sheep, the hardness of a just-baked peanut butter cookie--a real sweetheart of a guy. It was next to impossible to imagine him inflicting pain on a fly, let alone murder a burly, 6-foot-1, 250-pound Vietnam veteran.

"We're here to tell you that we harbor no hard feelings," Joe declared. "We pray for you every day."

"Every day," Jay echoed.

"We invite you to join our church," Joe went on.

305

"Www.churchofretribution.org. Daily Mass at 6. Feel free to call us collect whenever you need to talk. We'll send you canteen money, sweets, and a few personal effects once a month."

"And you guys are welcome as well," Jay told Sally, the Post photographer, and the guard.

They got up for the photo op. Leslie was summarily sandwiched between the brothers, who each wrapped a protective arm around his shoulders. He had the conflicted air of a man unable to excuse himself from a bothersome and superficial social function. His hope was that, once published, the article and accompanying picture would help promote his cause: Maybe a pro-bono lawyer or one of those Innocence Project kids would take pity on him.

Joe and Jay managed to look both serious and humble. Joe was there only to advance the church's agenda, to give Jay some exposure. He cared nothing about Leslie and he wasn't seeking closure, having long ago accepted--not to say embraced--my death. Jay was trying to cleanse his heart of the hatred he felt toward Leslie. His thoughts kept coming back to that August night, that wretched alley. The fact that Leslie was still refusing to confess bothered him. Jay carried my memory like an open wound.

"Victim's Sons Forgive Perpetrator" read the title of Sally Harris's piece the following morning. The article included a profile of each brother along with a recap of the murder, Leslie's arrest and his quick conviction by a predominantly white jury. Officer Lee was quoted. The reporter dug deep, to my surprise, making up for the hasty treatment she'd given me the first time around--two lines buried in the "Metro" section. This time Sally Harris went as far as unearthing my military record. She spoke with Seymour Hersh for background information. She interviewed Harold and Reggie, the army buddies who had showed up at my funeral.

"It appears that Mr. Benjamin Wilson was a hero in his own right. He earned a Silver Star in Vietnam for saving dozens of lives in what could have become another My Lai. A member of a LURP, a long-range reconnaissance unit based in Danang that went on search-and-destroy missions that could last for weeks at a time, Mr. Wilson happened on a hootch in a seemingly deserted village early one afternoon. As his comrades began poisoning the village's well, killing the animals, shooting inside the structures and setting them on fire, Mr. Wilson entered a hut and found a large number of children and elderly people huddled together. 'Ben shot the top of that hootch,' Mr. Harold Gibbs, a fellow unit member who witnessed the events, recalled recently. 'That's the way we did those things, you know. We're so far from base, how are we gonna hold any prisoners? So we enter a village and we shoot the tops of the huts first thing. Any VC hiding in them will drop. Then we shoot waist-high. Then we pull out the Zippos and torch the whole thing. You didn't go inside those huts. You didn't so much as take a look. Especially on that day Ben saved all those people, all those bunches of kids and old men and old women. We were fired up. A sniper had got two of us less than an hour before. So we're looking for the rest of them. We're ready to burn some stuff down. We're wound up real tight. That hut Ben went in must have been a school or something. It was big. Nothing dropped when he squeezed off his initial round. Instead of reducing the whole thing to a heap of pail, he stepped inside and found the villagers and got them out. Some of us still wanted to kill those kids and old people. Said it's useless, they're all VC anyway, let's put them in a ditch, spray them and call it a day. Ben wouldn't have it.'"

The article also featured a section on the Church of Retribution, "which, despite its name, is a hub of good faith, communion, tolerance, and racial unity in the heart of the nation's capital. A one-of-a-kind philanthropic endeavor, a dynamic grassroots organization focused on the Herculean task of obtaining a formal apology as well as financial restitution for all African-American descendants of slaves."

Though by far not a definite endorsement, the piece generated many phone calls, e-mails, and letters of inquiries. Sally's editor gave her the green light for a second, 5,000-word article to be featured in a future Washington Post Sunday edition.

It was her first big assignment. Granted unrestricted access, she started spending time at the church and at Souk, taking turns tagging Joe and Jay, interviewing members, scribbling furiously on her notepad as she sat in the last row (Joe, a big fan of NanoSnitches, insisted she ditch the notepad and try his), her eyes and ears open, decorum, moderation, and professional detachment not preventing her from occasionally joining in the good cheer. She shared tea and cookies with the Grannies and she sat in on a couple of phone calls. She scoured the church's Web pages.

She witnessed Glaxo's capitulation a mere 24 hours after it made its appearance on the black list, which, with its sister the "white" list, represented the church's shrewdest and most effective tools when it came to scare corporations into digging in their pockets and coughing out the reparations dough. (In a twist straight out of Joe's twisted mind, companies and individuals who had, in fact, made a contribution, appeared on the white list; the black list compiled people and organizations that hadn't donated to the church, either because they had refused to do so or had yet to be solicited. The black list was a list by default. Its wording had been carefully examined and approved by Claude, which explained why the lawsuits threatened by berated C.E.O.'s and PR campaign managers failed to gain substance. For better or for worse, the church had positioned itself as the emerging champion of black causes. In a market-centered and perception-driven society, companies ignored its requests at their own peril.)

Sally made the trip to Houston, Texas, for the very successful fund-raising blitz that followed a very successful Riots on Demand campaign. One of the protesters-for-hire, a young white mother, impressed her to no end with her fiery brand of activism, her seemingly spontaneous dedication to the reparations cause. She wore an American flag bandanna and she had applied war paint to her cheeks as well as her baby's. Local TV stations and newspapers had been covering such demonstrations for a few months now. So far the incidents had always been presented as isolated, a fact that the Riots on Demand people and Joe sorely lamented but couldn't do much about short of filming their own promotional piece and providing it to the media. The marchers typically made the 5 o'clock flashes of very small stations and the middle pages of even smaller newspapers. Whichita's KPNW was no CNN. The Abilene Herald was no USA Today.

It's Sally who connected the dots and proposed to bring the church's name to the nation's attention. She made the most of her research. The story was big enough to make her, and it was one that deserved to be told in the first place. Sally couldn't have guessed that the protests were coordinated. She saw an authentic and quasi-spontaneous openness to making amends among a growing and diverse segment of white America. In her view, the brothers' genius resided in their ability to harness the current for atonement that seemed to run deep within the white population, and to transform it into projects that were inspiring, concrete, redemptive, healing, and helpful all at the same time. The Church of Retribution's success was proof that times were changing. This was indeed a new era. Reexamination of America's troubled past, reconciliation, and justice were triumphing in the face of cynicism, mass consumerism, individualism, and indifference.

If Sally made much of the difference in personalities and approaches between Joe and Jay, she downplayed their character deficiencies. Judging the rape accusation against Joe inconclusive from a review of the case and a one-on-one with the victim, she only mentioned it in passing. "The real truth," Rebecca had confessed, "is complicated. Did Joe roofy me? I don't know. Were we both drinking? Yes. Did sexual intercourse occur? Undoubtedly. Was it consensual? I'm not so sure. Why did I file a complaint? The guy's a total asshole. There."

Jay's depression, hallucinatory dreams, and incursions into Jamaican patois were described in a favorable light. He was a mystic; he was a shaman; he was exotic; he was quixotic; he was eccentric; he was debonair; he was "connected." Sally respected his wish to keep the abuse he'd suffered secret. Maggie refused to be interviewed face-to-face or on the phone. Her name was on the black list, a fact that Sally did point out.

All said and done, the Wilson brothers were regular people. People capable of good and bad, people who were far from perfect, but who tried their best and gave their best.

Sally asked all the right questions. What was this new inter-ethnic faith that was taking root in the ghetto? Who were its adherents? What drew them to its philosophy and its guide? Were the brothers for real? Sally looked for paternalism; she sniffed for wrongdoing; she dug for slush funds, lies, and conflicts of interest.

In the end, she didn't smell a hustle. The church's operations appeared completely transparent and completely legal. Claude showed her the numbers, the permits, the registrations, the projections, the certificates, the commendations, the copper plaque presented by the Brightwood Park Business Association, and the many children drawings depicting Jay as an angel complete with wings, an aureole, and a cross inside his heart. She and Claude walked around the ARCH site with Jay and Joe every day, wearing hard hats and steel-toed boots and carrying rolled blueprints, reveling in the noise, the activity, the dream being erected. Sally met Hakim, Nasro, and Ahmet. Un confided his own transformative story, common

311

among the congregants. He was now one of the church's most devout followers. His zeal, his faith in the movement and its prophet were boundless, if not outright fanatical: "The church has come to mean everything. I was lost and now I'm found. I had no soul and it gave me one. Today I have a purpose. I feel love in my heart. I feel alive. All this, I owe to Jay."

(Isn't it Barbra who first deemed him to be a little too creepy, a little too intense? Like Jay, Un lived very simply. He slept on the floor of a rented room. He barely ate. He practiced yoga and controlled breathing. He hung around the storefront whenever he wasn't on Nasro's time, lending his services anywhere they may be needed. Mostly, he stuck close to the leader, whose aura he seemed eager to share, whose teachings he was anxious to absorb, whose gestures he was quick to replicate. Un dressed like Jay, talked like Jay, moved like Jay. "Given the chance," Barbra remarked to the other Grannies, "he's gonna want to be Jay. Mark my words.")

Jay's appeal was plain to see. He had become one of those persons you always want to be close to and close with. He exuded goodness like some do cheap cologne. He was helpful, open, good-natured, patient. He preached by example, getting things done without having to utter a single word. He took nothing and gave much. He had very little needs.

To be honest, it was his face that first drew people to him. Seldom did you find one that looked so kind. Harmonious without being too soft, beautiful but not intimidating, striking yet far from arrogant. The shoulder-length blond hair, the limpid blue eyes, the fleshed-out lips, the straight nose, the high cheekbones, the scraggly beard. His voice could persuade, pump up, entice, electrify, seduce, massage, enrapture, or condemn. His frame was lean and muscular. His back was always straight. He wore his jeans like a cowboy and his sweat pants like a track star. Jay's walk was purposeful, even if he was only going as far as the Safeway to fetch sour pickles and ice cream for Lisha.

Public as his life and actions were, unclouded as his vision might appear, relaxed as his body language may seem, nobody knew what was going on inside his head unless he expressed it. Jay could revel in the crowd's attention one moment and completely isolate himself the next. Solitude seemed to be something he craved but rarely found the luxury to dwell in. And sticking to his shadow like very old friends were seriousness, sadness, and gravitas, the quality of hurt so essential to Joe's purposes, the quality separating Jay from the common of mortals. Whether carrying his own pain or that of the whole world with him, Jay was a burdened man.

Sally spent more than 45 days following him around, watching him meditate and eat pistachio nuts, hearing him deliver sermons, seeing him perform baptisms and weddings; she accompanied him as he tended to his Kennedy Street flock and witnessed the tender relations he entertained with Lisha, his "backbone." He was a whirlwind, an energetic guru, an indefatigable priest.

"Why pistachio nuts?"

"They're easy. Nuts, figs, dates, raisins, bird seeds,

313

fruits, bread, water.... I like easy stuff."

"What flavor is that incense in your upstairs quarters?"

"'Blue Nile.' I burn it in tribute to a man called Taha."

"Why do you sleep on a rug?"

"It keeps me humble. Plus it's good for the back, you know?"

"Does Lisha sleep on the floor with you?"

"Are you kidding? Lisha's a comfort creature. A pregnant one at that. We just bought her a bed, living room furniture, and a TV."

"What gets you going? What makes you wake up every day?"

"Injustice. I want to fight it everywhere I see it."

"There's a glow in you most of us only dream of possessing. You seem content."

"I'm about to become a father. I'm flying on the wings of love."

"The church is growing exponentially. Do you ever get weary and resent your mission? Do you feel like priesthood is taking up too much of your life? What happens to Lamaze classes, baby baths, and quiet evenings at home when one must heal-heal-heal?"

"Priesthood is my life. It's what I was born to do. But I would never let it come between me and my family."

"It's a balancing act that many mighty figures have failed to strike."

"Tragically so. Just look at the King and Shabbaz kids. I read somewhere that Che's wife had to borrow money to supplement her husband's government income."

"Speaking of money: I've seen your pay stubs. The church's coffers are full and getting fuller, but you live on chump change."

"The coffers aren't mine. And yes, it's becoming a challenge to stretch that stipend now that I have two more souls to provide for. But God will make a way. I'll work even harder. We won't beg, we won't steal, we won't borrow. 'Rasta no pickpocket. Rasta no run racket.'"

"Because of the controversial nature of your message, death threats are a fact of everyday life. Are you prepared to risk it all? How do you justify exposing your family to such hardships, such risks as harassment, potential bombings, assassination attempts?"

"Men will always fight you when you try and make men change their ways. I and I refuse the status quo. I and I shake up the tree. I and I dispel the lies to make room for Jah light. I and I roam the Earth. I and I conqueror. This is important work. Me cannot stop because someone somewhere feels they have fi hurt me, bring harm pon me. Me simply cannot stop. Me no deal with fear. Me no check fi that."

"Are you afraid of anything?"

"Yes: Being afraid."

"What's your idea of fun?"

"Escape for a couple of hours and walk the downtown streets with Lisha. Shop for old records. Pack up a huge car and go to the beach. Most of all, I'm looking forward to holding my daughter in my arms."

"What are you and Lisha calling her?"

"'Kaya.'"

"Sounds like a Marley album."

"Precisely."

Sally felt that the article was providing her with a once-in-a-lifetime opportunity. Something was going on. Something special was in the air, and if you listened carefully you could hear. Things were not the way they used to be. Things were happening that hadn't happened before and would never happen again. These weren't your average people. These were far from your everyday, middle-of-the-paper events.

The time came to inaugurate ARCH, an honor the church gave Mayor Barion Merry in support of his long-shot bid in the upcoming municipal elections for a seat on the city council as Ward 8's--the town's blackest and poorest--representative. Mayor Merry fell asleep on his feet, shouting "Bitch set me up!" right on cue every time someone nudged him awake. But he managed to cut the ribbon with shaky hands and a crooked smile at the very first try, co-opting with that symbolic gesture the retribution movement, the church, the streets, and the bay-bays to jump-start his controversial return to D.C. politics. Pepsi, who had grown up in Clifton Terrace, the same housing project that had almost taken Sally Harris under, watched the events from a rooftop, surrounded by dogs and a phalanx of bodyguards--a man on the outside wishing for once that he could show his face, feel the love up close and personal and join in the good spirit and the good cheer. "Motherfuckers don't know that nothin' would have been done without my consent," he complained to Pain, his bodyguard closest to earshot. "I'm the nigga they should be thanking and shit. I should be the one cutting ribbons. It

316

should be my name on that wall. What the fuck do 'ARCH' stand for anyway?"

"That white boy Jay think he Noah," Pain advanced with a shrug. "The black race is going extinct and he's coming to save us all." Turning toward the rest of the crew, he shouted, "Help is on the way, y'all!"

"Noah had an 'ark,'" Pepsi corrected. "'Arch' is the top part of a structure. Something that bridges two points. Something that supports the weight placed above it. You fool."

The men and their pit bulls doubled over and laughed themselves to tears. When they managed to stop laughing five minutes later, they doubled over and laughed some more.

"Brothermen Gonna Work It Out," one of the bodyguards joked.

"Black Power!" another chanted with mock-conviction.

"Black and Proud!" Pepsi chimed in.

"We Shall Overcome!"

"I Have a Dream!"

"Young, Gifted, and Black!"

"Someday We'll All Be Free!"

On and on they went.

At street level, followers, well-wishers, and revelers were streaming in by the hundreds. Not sure that refreshments would be served during the building's dedication, they stopped by Souk on their way in. Nasro and Un were helpless in containing the flow. They got confused from following so many movements; their ears burned from hearing so many voices; their muscles ached

317

from ringing up and bagging so much stuff. All the shelves were picked clean. The hordes left not a single wretched item behind. Stuff that Nasro had carried for years and despaired to ever be rid of found buyer that day. It was eerie. After the last person left, Un and Nasro turned off all the equipment, swept and mopped the floor, hauled Nasro's safe to his car, shut Souk's door, and lowered the curtain. "Good luck to you, my brother," Nasro told Un as he pushed a pile of cash into his hands. Bewildered, Un was able to assist to the ceremony.

One wondered who had warned all those people, what they were doing there, how they even knew to show up. Leroy Hutson's "The Ghetto" played synchronically from Cadillacs, Chevrolets, Lincolns, Benzes, Rolls-Royces, trucks, vans, cargo buses, Winnebagos, scooters, and motorcycles. Playas, playettes, pimps, hustlers, squares, Africans, Jamaicans, shopkeepers, day laborers, housewives, politicians, babes, babies, old men on walkers, crackheads on the lookout, prostitutes on the job marched in procession toward ARCH. Afros and weaves and waves and braids and plaits and pearl-studded dashikis were spotted by the dozen. It seemed as though black folks were playing at being themselves, overdoing it oh so slightly. White donors and white sympathizers from the city's upper crust and the airy suburbs were embraced and carried on shoulders. Less welcome were people from the Talon database; Maggie and Steve in their Hummer; Hank, Chuck, Silas, and Frank in the dusty Alabama pickup.

Ahmet, in a chef's hat and chef's apron, manned a smoked-rib pit. Claude looked in vain for Nona Hendryx. Hakim networked with city officials and directed the

318

movements of his brand-new phalanx of Ninjas for Islam
security officers, having anticipated the church's need for
protection services and won a two-year contract from Joe.
Youngin' plugged his dating guide and distributed
Macondo flyers from his motorized wheelchair. Four news
crews vied for antenna time with Jay and Nicole, who had
been made ARCH's C.E.O. in order to free the brothers
from daily involvement in the center.

The ghetto had never seen such a thing. The
modular structure that had been slapped together in an
impressively short amount of time looked fantastic inside
and out, what with a computer lab, Olympic pool,
basketball court, tennis court, indoor football stadium,
classrooms, nursery, playroom, Ferris wheel, weight room,
legal clinic, health clinic, rehab center, day care, dry
cleaning and full laundry services, electronic arcade, movie
theater, free cafeteria, workshop, repair shop, skateboard
ramp, 50,000-volume library, and Joe's personal addition: a
Quiet Room. Every single component and feature of the
multimillion-dollar facility had been offered free of charge
and logos by a major corporation (Nike and Under Armor
picked up the tab for the athletic fixtures and gear). ARCH
promised to become a haven not just for KDY3 and KDY5
children but for senior citizens as well. Connecting those
two generations was an objective actively pursued by the
church in designing ARCH's services and its schedule of
activities. Seniors screened and hired by Nicole would
supervise the center. Each would be assigned a group of
children to mentor. Lay workers would all be from
Kennedy Street or the surrounding areas.

"This is how you reconstruct a social fabric," Nicole

said at the press conference as she faced the cameras, flanked by Jay and a snoring Mayor Merry. "This is how you rebuild a village. This is how you revitalize a people. This is how you breathe new life into a culture. *Amandla!*"

"*Amandla!*" the crowd chanted in response, pumping fists high in the air.

Flags were floated: Empire's blue, red and white; D.C.'s red and white; the African liberation movement's red, black, and green; the Church of Retribution's own black and white.

"Hail to the Retribution Brothers," Sally's photo-peppered 5-page article, ended on the cover of The Washington Post Magazine. It did more than propel the church to the forefront of a slow-news summer week: It was a blast that resonated far and wide in the country, got picked up internationally by several wire services, and was widely circulated on the Internet. All of a sudden the movement became a household name, its members enlightened and wizened denizens, its supporters fearless trailblazers of cutting-edge social activism, its contributors model citizens, its founders instant celebrities. Pushed despite himself into the limelight, Joe promptly retreated back into the shadows befitting his role. Jay was left alone to handle the curiosity, the hype, the scrutiny, the ill will, and the adulation. He did an excellent job fielding the questions that started pouring in from all over the world. With Souk closed for an indefinite period of time and Nasro impossible to find, Jay had the leisure to humor all the interview requests. He smiled benevolently for the cameras. He patiently explained the church's mission. He carried the torch. He preached the gospel. He did Elle and Vogue spreads without smiling or taking his hands out of his pockets. "With this face and style and grace," read one unhappy caption, "who needs game?"

One of the shows that came knocking was "Democracy Now!" Amy Goodman and Juan Gonzales welcomed Jay in their converted firehouse studio in New York early one morning. He felt he had found kindred souls as they broadcast live on radio and TV channels across the nation. "Democracy Now!" was a hotbed of activism, a bastion of alternative news and countercurrent views, a sizable staple of the informed man's diet. Jay listened to it every day on his computer. Amy and Juan relentlessly pursued the truth. They were Empire's archenemies and freedom's most passionate defenders, exposing government lies, treachery, corruption, and coverups. One feared for them as they pursued the most dangerous stories: the mercenary armies doing the dirty job in Iraq and Afghanistan, and, maybe soon, Iran; the private contractors bilking billions of taxpayers' money; the vigilante posses at the Mexican border; the push for the reopening of civil rights-era murder cases; NYPD's abuses of power. "It's an honor to be in your company," Jay told his hosts.

They had thought that the tumult would be short-lived. They had believed that past the initial moment of surprise and spike of interest the public would get bored and move on. This was a self-absorbed public, a divided and inattentive public, a public that looked the other way while Empire roamed the Earth committing all kinds of misdeeds in its name--a hedonistic, jaded public. But the

321

more the world learned about Jay, the more it seemed to want to learn. The Web sites crashed under the strain of traffic. The video clips and free podcasts of his sermons were downloaded millions of times into portable digital music players and mobile phones. His speeches were put to techno music, burned on CDs and played at raves in trendy clubs and abandoned silos. His effigy began to appear on T-shirts and products that hadn't been sanctioned by the church. Jay was in. Jay was cool.

Underlying the novelty aspect, carrying it, was the triumph of an extra-temporal idea. The concept of paying retribution for slavery, segregation, and discrimination was finally taking hold. It called for contrition on the part of whites and forgiveness from blacks. Beyond that, it forced people of different origins to look into themselves for unifying threads, common beliefs, shared values. The past could be beaten. It could be excised. Victory was suddenly at hand. Victory, unity, equality, a new social contract, long-lasting peace, a new day. No invisibility. No scorn. No supremacy. No tension. No chips on shoulders. No superiority or inferiority complexes. Just men dealing with men with respect, civility, and dignity.

After breaking it to the world Sally became the movement's official chronicler, its embedded journalist. She could be spotted at Mass several times a week in the company of her son Eli and her husband Mo, himself a novelist who had written extensively about the Soul and its disappearance many, many years before James Brown's death.

Starting with the second quarter and right on the

footsteps of Sally's noise-raising article, Joe stopped taking prisoners. He went with all guns blazing into a branding, marketing, and promoting offensive. Imabelle, on consultation with Korean "comfort women" of the Second World War locked in a fight to wrangle apologies and payments from the Japanese government, phoned in judicious pieces of advice from Seoul.

Joe organized a bus trip revisiting major sites of the civil rights struggle. Arm in arm, followers reenacted the March 1965 march from Selma to Montgomery, Alabama, among other things.

As he walked across the Edmund Pettus Bridge on a Sunday morning, cameras rolling and flashes flashing, Jay felt like an usurper. He couldn't stop thinking about what Reverend King and his troops had faced, the savagery and brutality that had met their own peaceful protest. Then, while visiting the tombs of bombing and lynching victims in Mississippi, Jay experienced his first pang of guilt since the inception of the movement: What was he doing? What right did he have to appropriate those people's lives, their pains, their tragedies, their dead bodies?

He tried to open up to Joe about his misgivings. Joe, of course, felt no qualms or uncertainties about anything at all. "Suffering is universal," he told Jay. "It belongs to no one and to everyone. We're the next generation. We're the continuation. We carry the torch. Far from using the Freedom Fighters, the S.N.I.C., the S.N.C.C., or the N.A.A.C.P., we took on their struggle, we're building on top of their gains."

They saw their first cotton fields. They visited the Jim Crow Museum of Racist Memorabilia in Grand Rapids,

Michigan. They toured post-Katrina New Orleans and prayed on top of "repaired" levees. They witnessed poverty unseen and unheard of in America: Trailer-park, compacted-earth, no-running-water, no-electricity, no-hospital, Third-World poverty. They drove through all-white towns and all-black towns. Some of the latter, like Allensworth, California, were early-20th century colonies that had been formed to offer their settlers a semblance of self-rule and dignity, a haven from the pitfalls, tribulations, and hazards of racial hatred.

Wherever they went, the brothers Wilson and their flock were received with open arms by some and they were booed and pelted by others. They were saluted as liberators of blacks and belittled as traitors to their race. It was like taking a risky act on the road--you didn't know how it would play out in front of such a diverse array of sensibilities. "Go back to where you're from," an old white farmer told them. "We sure don't like your kind around here."

It was an emotionally mixed, bittersweet journey. Jay longed to go home to Lisha, whom he phoned every day. He wished only for the simplicity and directness of his storefront priesthood. "You're doing the right thing," Lisha kept assuring him. "I believe in you."

Back from the trip, Joe burned a makeshift cross in front of the church in the middle of a sweltering night. It was an ugly and evil thing, but one that generated a lot of attention while the firemen were hosing it and after they took it down. The charred symbol remained on the sidewalk long after daylight, long enough for commuters, passersby, homeowners, journalists, and everyday people to see it and bear witness. The bay-bays frowned, shook their little heads and pinched their little noses. Jay turned pale. Lisha was hysterical. Nicole and the Happy Cuts girls were shaken. Pepsi was pissed. KDY3 and KDY5 residents caught a whiff of what their ancestors had gone through. Claude stopped coming out and started to get his wine delivered by the truckload. Hakim organized sidewalk vigils and prayers. His Ninjas for Islam started providing the church with round-the-clock security. Un assigned himself to Jay's detail. Armed to the teeth, his flat face devoid of any color, he kept guard over the leader and his companion without a single minute of rest, a single second of sleep.

The bulk of churchgoers wasn't deterred from attending the sermons and participating in group activities. Everybody made a point to go on about their business, to come and go as usual, to keep a smile on their faces and a spring in their steps. It was too early for a sense of persecution or victimization to settle in, but it seemed that a line had been drawn in the sand: There was an enemy; some people out there deeply resented the Church of Retribution, its credo, its actions. It wasn't just bomb threats and insults and false alarms any more.

"Let's not go into full-scale war," Jay reasoned from the pulpit. "Let's not heed the provocation. Let's keep our cool, our clarity of vision, our dedication to the cause. This is proof that we're on the right path. This is vindication. This is a sign that our adversary is feeling cornered. Victory, my brothers and sisters, is drawing near."

From the Texas golf course where he was vacationing, the president called the crime heinous, vicious, and one that wouldn't go unpunished. The public was riveted, especially after a group that professed close ties to the Klan claimed responsibility for the act on a prerecorded message sent to newspapers and TV stations. Hank, Chuck, Frank, and Silas felt a surge of pride and no small measure of admiration toward the sleeper cell. Those guys were smooth. Those guys were ruthless. Those guys were front-page material.

Last but not least in Joe's push to manufacture news and stoke the nascent groundswell of public sympathy toward the church was an assassination attempt on Jay's life that took place the following week.

Kaya had just been born. Jay was coming back from the hospital with Un at two in the morning when three unmarked Riots on Demand cars boxed their van in at the Georgia and Irving traffic light. A masked man jumped out and sprayed the side of the vehicle with an assault rifle. Un undid his belt and dove on top of Jay, who was sitting frozen in place. The noise was deafening. Bullets tore through the metal, shattered the windows, zoomed around the huddled shapes of the van's occupants, and punctured the tires. By the time Un forced Jay under the dash and reached for his weapon, the attackers were gone.

No friend of the cops because of numerous brushes with the law in his former life, Un left the scene before they and the ever-present reporters showed up. Jay appeared on TV and in the papers every day for the following month. Footage of the bullet-poked van--a nonpolluting hybrid thing that bore the church's name on its sides--was looped endlessly on every major station.

Once again, donations poured in. Kaya, who had been born the night her daddy almost died, and Lisha, whose courage and stoicism in the face of adversity were in the tradition of, say, a Jackie Kennedy, became the world's new darlings. Jay's popularity reached new heights. He was now on a first-name basis with most media workers in Washington, Maryland, and Virginia. He was mugged whenever and wherever he appeared. To touch him was to share into his blessings, his--in Nasro's word--"*baraka*." To hear him was to be transported into another world. People inside and outside the church hung on to his every edict. The sight of him was precious. Who knew how long he had to live? He was a man among men. He was an endangered prophet. He was a doomed messenger. He was a revolutionary who had withstood the ultimate test of bravery.

Joe distributed flak jackets to the Grannies. Dirty Maggie told the brothers that she wished they were dead already. Detectors were installed at ARCH and inside the church. They became standard in every building the movement erected across the country, every structure it stamped its name upon.

Jay's life insurance policy was revoked overnight. Lisha took shooting lessons. Claude took the insurance company to court and won.

Un's profile within the rank and file soared. They couldn't thank him enough, for he had saved the guide's life. His weirdness was forgotten, his creepiness set aside, his Ugly Duckling ugliness forgiven. For the very first time in his life he was made to feel not only that he belonged, but that he was appreciated. He and Jay became true friends. The former couldn't remember ever feeling such kinship. The latter was still reeling from Nasro's disappearance, though their relationship had long ago stopped being what it used to be. Jay found it extraordinary that another human being would jump in the line of fire to protect him. In a sense, it was.

Not all the changes were for the better. Not all the attention was welcome and well-meaning. Paranoia ran high for a while, fueled by the agents provocateurs and the spies who infiltrated the congregation. The Talon people became omnipresent. The phones were tapped. The walls were bugged. The vehicles were tagged with G.P.S. transmitters. The I.R.S. raided the office early one Monday morning, seizing files, computer disks, and hard drives. A man called "Reparations" Ray, claiming he had been in the retribution business for over 30 years, publicly accused Joe of hijacking the movement. "I was at it before you guys were born," he told Joe at the National Black Church Convention in Atlanta a little before the brothers Wilson were due to be honored with yet another award. "You're misrepresenting yourself, you're bastardizing the movement, you're spoiling its spirit! You should be ashamed. One day African Americans will wake up and find their dream of reparations gone. Gone!"

"Do you own the copyright to 'reparations'?" Joe asked him. "Have you ever 'repaired' anything? What have you done to advance black causes aside from carrying that cute moniker?"

Ray was booed and stripped of his surname. He was accused of sowing the seed of infighting, divisiveness, and parochial envy. He was ostracized at the reception. He would have been kicked out of the conference grounds if it hadn't been for the prevailing Christian spirit. "That's what's wrong with black people today," he complained to everybody who gave him an ear. "They don't have an ounce of fight in them. They'd rather a white man do the job. They allow themselves to be blinded by the crumbs thrown their way."

Deadria Farmer-Paellmann, the one person whose challenge Joe dreaded more than anything, remained conspicuously absent from the debate, which was now raging nationally thanks in no small part to the Church of Retribution's sudden rise to prominence. New polls showed that a little over 65% of the country's white population was now favorable to an official government apology and payments to descendants of slaves. Among blacks, the percentage was a staggering 99%.

When "60 Minutes" and Spike Lee called asking respectively for an interview and the opportunity to film a documentary, Joe knew they had arrived. "Your boys did a great job," he, mindful of phone taps, told Imabelle.
"Just like we knew they would," she answered.
"Miss you," he said, kissing the phone.
"Miss you, too," she cooed. "What did you tell Spike?"
"I told him no. We might consider him when the time comes to film our own movie. I told him we're keeping all the rights."
"Knowing him, he already has a working title."

"Of course: 'The Great Black Hope.'"

They laughed and cooed some more. Joe relished the moment. Imabelle and he had never achieved romantic bliss. Theirs was primarily a work relationship. Imabelle still balked at anything more profound than a fleeting, tentative, hands-off tenderness. The subjects of sex and food were still taboo. Tough as his position was, Joe saw no immediate way to improve it. One, he loved the girl; two, therapy wasn't an option because of the nondisclosure clause in Imabelle's contract with Riots on Demand; three, he wasn't about to start cheating or find solace in the arms of prostitutes. As the church's Number Two and the prophet's brother, Joe had an image to maintain and assets and achievements to protect. Gold diggers and paparazzi were constantly on the prowl. How many people out there were waiting to see him stumble? How many wanting in?

Needless to say, sexual frustration drove Joe crazy at times. He released it on his old high school's track, on the phone, and on the drawing board. Growth was his new mantra. Growth, growth, growth.

Joe looked up and down Wisconsin Avenue for the P-Funk bum whenever he was in the area. The man was nowhere to be found, confirming my notion that he might well be one of the Devil's minions. His deed done, he had disappeared into the fold. Joe often imagined meeting him at the most impromptu moment. He wondered if the man had heard of the church and made the connection. He saw him showing up one day to ask for his share. "You owe me some dough, white boy."

Another documentary that Spike Lee wished he could have made was "American Gypsy." It created a sensation when it opened at the National Geographic headquarters on 17th and M, showcasing Ahmet's adaptability, his toughness, his inventiveness, his handicraft, his struggles, his street smarts, his work with the Church of Retribution, his indoor tent, his polygamist lifestyle, his crooked smile, and his humility. The audience lapped it up, amazed to find right here in our midst a man who lived from his wits, a man who looked and talked almost exactly like you and me, but whose origins and daily acts and motivations were so completely removed from ours as to appear foreign and novel. Ahmet, much like Jay, became an instant celebrity. Budding ethnologists marveled that the camera was able to capture ethnic traits that were so exotic, so remote from those of mainstream America. Young single women found his ugliness utterly cute and oh-my-god awesome. Parents wanted to take him home, put him in a cage, and let their children pet him. Montgomery County briefly considered a repeal of its much maligned No Palm Reading and Other Divination Devices Law on Ahmet's behalf.

The ensuing question in academic circles was how

would Ahmet be affected by the fame, the acceptance, the embrace, the clout: Would he settle down and renounce his nomadic ethos or would he gut the inside of a Chevrolet Suburban and move, roll on to another state, another country? Wasn't America, in its infinite diversity of peoples and places, the unexplored territory par excellence? Where else to go? What else to discover? America had it all: Eskimos, Harleys, Manhattan, Las Vegas, Chaka Khan, Wattstax, Apple Computers, desert lands, raging rivers, mountain ranges, valleys low.

Ahmet surprised the world by choosing assimilation: He put his hustling ways behind and boldly enrolled himself and his wives into an English program at the University of Maryland, a decision that rippled all the way to Baku, Azerbaijan. The purists at National Geographic lamented that one of the last authentic cultures on Earth was being corrupted. The Gypsy Council of New Jersey banned from its ranks Ahmet, his wives, and his children for showing such total disregard toward values and traditions as old as time itself--what was next: a house in the suburbs, a steady job, the public repudiation of chiromancy?

Ahmet was defiant to the end. Not only was he going to learn how to read and write, he planned to sign up for a four-year degree at Maryland, authenticity and clan loyalty be damned. The world held its breath.

Ahmet's newfound riches didn't prevent him from giving a hand for the Church of Retribution's move to its new home on 16th Street, smack in the middle of Worship Row. Much like he had done for the storefront, Gypsy

332

wired the place for audio, sound, and light. Only this time it took extra help to complete the job given the size of the edifice, the amount and the sophistication of the equipment involved.

Sudden and subdued as it was, the move was justified. The church had long outgrown the storefront of its humble beginnings. It was now a powerhouse in its own right--more than 100,000 members worldwide, millions of dollars in contributions, a dozen concurrent ARCH projects in as many states--move over, Hubbard. Attendance had been put on rotation, with a lottery allowing no more than 77 followers inside the small space at any time. It had become next to impossible to see the messiah and receive his precious teachings and his blessings in person. So the exodus to 16th Street was more than overdue: It was mandatory. Coming on the heels of the assassination attempt on Jay, it took a meaning of biblical proportions. This was a persecuted guide leading his persecuted people across the Red Sea. This was a thriving congregation flexing its muscle. "Move!" Jay shouted from the stage, leaping high in the air, his arms outstretched, a crazy look in his eyes, his head flashing dreadlocks he didn't possess. "Move through Creation, y'all!"

Who cared if the new house of worship was a defunct Ethiopian Pentecostal outfit that had been on the market for years? Who cared that Joe and Mofas had found it on Craigslist? The price was right, the location a dream come true. Both Jay and Joe experienced teary eyes and a trembling heart when they took possession of the cavernous edifice. Dusty and damaged as they were, the nave, ribbed vault, pillars, bell-tower, pipe organ, and Rose-window

333

infused them with a sense of the Sacred. They thought they were in the presence of God. Me, too. They felt both humble and proud. So did I.

The renovations took about three months. Most of the building was left intact. The yellow paint was replaced with a sober gray. The altar was turned into a concert-hall stage replete with orchestra pit, walls of speakers, pyrotechnic hookups, and a jumbotron. The ceiling was equipped with a battery of lights. The pews were dismantled and rebuilt. The bells were brought back to life. The floor was carpeted. A brand new air conditioning system was installed. The confessionals were turned into recording and broadcasting booths. The Sunday School, nursery, kitchen, and cafeteria were modernized. The state-of-the-art foundling wheel could accommodate triplets.

The church built upon its gains, taking in a fresh influx of donations and financing more projects all over the country. Armies of missionaries roamed the inner cities in an outreach effort whose stated goal was to get as many kids off the streets and inside Church of Retribution satellite units as possible. The volunteers were at every corner, playground, pool hall, mall, jail, and video arcade. The first charter school sponsored by the church was slated to open its doors in Washington in the fall. Its endowment placed it above the fray, providing it with a level of education unmatched by public schools. The church sponsored enrichment programs and life-skills workshops for struggling students. Churchgoers were encouraged to become active in their respective communities.

The shakeup was internal as well: Dipping into the congregation's talent pool, Joe put in place a corporate structure responsible for all the financial operations, from fund-raising to investment to procurement to disbursement. He delegated all his day-to-day functions, trading his position for that of general manager. Jay remained in charge of Spiritual Affairs, his status equal to Joe's. Directly under the brothers was the new C.E.O., Donald Sylvers III, lured from a moribund N.A.A.C.P. by the dual promise of top pay and free hands right after the organization honored Jay with one of its "Image" awards. The Grannies saw their number increase tenfold. Nicole was given national oversight over all ARCH and self-improvement venues. Investment bankers, lobbyists, and marketing specialists were brought onboard. Claude was dismissed in favor of an established K Street old-boy firm. The saber-, throwing star-, and nunchaku-wielding Ninjas for Islam were replaced by Blackwater mercenaries, the same people who fought Empire's wars side by side with career soldiers. They were famous for skimping on operating costs after all the government contracts had been signed and advances duly pocketed. They had recently been convicted of killing scores of innocent civilians in Baghdad. Some of their own men had been sent to their deaths, out on missions with compromised data or faulty equipment, a fact that had the ex-soldier in me going berserk, a fact that Jay didn't miss to point out.

"Blackwater are profiteers riding the corporatization of war," he told Joe. "I was happier with the Ninjas."

"The Ninjas didn't look serious," Joe replied.

"Nunchakus are banned in several states. That's a lawsuit waiting to happen. Blackwater is the way to go. They learned a lot from Iraq and Afghanistan. Their motto went from 'Who's your Baghdaddy?' to 'Uzi does it.' I trust they'll do a good job."

"Bigger and meaner," Joe said to describe the new Church of Retribution.

"That's us," Jay acquiesced.

They moved to separate homes belonging to the church. Jay's was in Chevy Chase, ten minutes away by way of Rock Creek Park. Joe chose a bungalow in the Palisades section of town. The houses shared three eminently desirable traits: they were highly valuable, in excellent condition, yet understated.

The brothers gave themselves their first raise in over 18 months. "We're still very far from what our counterparts are making," Joe remarked. "And let's not even compare our meager earnings to what we're paying Donald and Nicole."

"We're not in it for the money," Jay reminded him.

"A man still has to make a living, Jay," Joe, who had his eyes on that Potomac mansion, added with a sigh.

Jay thought he understood what his brother was getting at. "Nothing keeps you from doing your own thing," he professed. "The church pretty much runs itself at this point. You're free to use your time and your energy as you wish. As long as your activities don't implicate us...."

Joe nodded. "I've been thinking about going into business."

"What kind of business?"

"Commercial ventures."

Jay nodded in turn. "You go, Villanova Boy."

They laughed.

"What about you?" Joe asked.

Jay yawned at the thought. "It'd be a disaster. You know I'm not business-minded. I might go back to school and complete my computer science training. Lisha's getting her degree online. I don't want to be the one uneducated adult in the household."

"Where will you find the time?"

"Good question."

Jay's life was full enough without the prospect of school. His days had stopped belonging to him. He was dedicating himself to a grueling schedule of in-house speeches and sermons, public appearances, interviews, photo-shoots, and excursions on the lecture circuit. "You're never here," seemed to be the only words in Lisha's mouth. Truth be told, he never was. He rose at 4:30, jogged with Un, prayed, meditated, read, wrote, ate breakfast with his family, left at 7, came back late at night, read some more, and poured over his own papers. He missed so much of Kaya's development that the thought of her was enough to make him shudder with guilt. First on his list of to-do things was "Learn how to cook," for his dream of domestic happiness started, quite literally, with putting food on the table. He wanted to complement Lisha in every way, to help around the house, to be so close to his wife and daughter as to become an unbreakable unit. He aspired to make of the union a resounding success. No ladles, no fights, no insults, no manhandling the kids, no hunger strikes, no closed doors, no withholding sex. Above all, a good environment for Kaya, the childhood he himself had been denied, freedom from fear and parental abuse. He wanted his baby's laughter to fill the house. He wanted her room to be full of toys. Sunshine in their lives. Nothing but the brightest, warmest sunshine every day.

It was a victory of sorts just to be here together. So deeply ingrained were his boyhood traumas that, even back when he was longing desperately for a family, Jay didn't really think that it'd be within his reach, his capacities. It was paradoxical that the man who had come to represent such a lightning rod for audacity and courage in the eyes of the hero-starved multitude should struggle with self-confidence, self-doubt, feelings of inadequacy, and limitations real or imagined. Jay truly believed that Lisha and Kaya were a God-given gift.

So his intentions were nothing if wonderful. But it seemed the church was always calling. It needed him. It was lost without him. He who had promised Sally never to sacrifice his loved ones to the cause began to despair that he could reconcile work with the demands of family life.

In a sense, that's what things became for Jay after the move to Worship Row: work. Gone were the fun, the intimacy, the urgency of the first days. In their place were a routine that felt more and more cumbersome with each passing day, distractions like PR meetings and made-for-cable-TV harangues, responsibilities that were heavier and heavier. As the flock grew, so did Jay's burden. Sometimes the most pressing question in his mind wasn't "What would Jesus do?" but "Why in the world would

Jesus do it?" Was it ever O.K., he wondered, to put down the cross if only for one relaxing minute?

"As a G.M. you don't spend more than two hours here each day," he finally complained to Joe. "And most of that time is devoted to coffee-and-donuts brainstorming sessions with Donald. I put in 90-hour weeks. How did I get stuck with Spiritual Affairs?"

"You're the guru," Joe countered. "You're carrying all of us on your shoulders. This house would crumble without you. We appreciate your dedication. You know we do."

Inevitably, the church's focus shifted a little as its base started to broaden. Elements of religion now suffused Jay's sermons. Universal propositions such as morality, ethical conduct, respect, charity, compassion, honesty, civility. He spoke of God often, a God who was good and merciful and powerful but not interventionist, not manipulative, not meddling. Issues of concern weren't just black or white any more: They were broadly human.

Joe wasn't enthralled by the new direction. "You were doing good with your guitar and your sweat-and-tears act," he told Jay. "That's what you're known for. That's what people have come to expect. Don't go and make it too complicated."

Jay disagreed wholly. "We have members from all around the world: Sao Paulo, Sanaa, Stockholm, St. Louis, Samarkand. Have you looked at the new faces among the crowd? Retribution may be our bread and butter but it's a song that's getting old, Joe. People want to hear about the wars, about ending all Empire's expeditions and bringing our soldiers home. They want to hear about health care, immigration, globalization, the minimum wage, human rights, AIDS, Darfur, Palestine, and greenhouse gases. They're tired of corporations running their lives. They've had it with corrupt politicians. They're hungry for a philosophy that'll guide them through these crazy times, Joe.... People are fed up with the same old Black/White rhetoric. Those aren't the only two colors in the palette."

"Keep it simple," Joe repeated stubbornly.

"It used to be simple," Jay said. "Not any more. We've outgrown the reparations outfit. People now come to us for enlightenment. People of all creeds, people of all colors and provenance."

Joe shook his head, appalled by what he was hearing. "It's a big mistake, Jay. I'm telling you. Our mission is the black man. Saving the black man. Helping the black man. Nothing less, nothing more."

In his heart of hearts Jay was still doing it for the KDY3 and KDY5 bay-bays, though he wasn't around them or their mothers any longer. He was convinced that somebody, somewhere, was calling him a sellout. Kevin, Mashey, Riri, Shawn, and them. Where were they? What was happening of them? It's in vain that he searched for their faces among the 16th Street worshippers. He thought of calling, stopping by, checking on them, making sure that they weren't on some dope corner pushing Pepsi's stuff. But where to find the time? Jay's only consolation was ARCH, the gleaming structure the church had erected-- ARCH, whose clones were starting to dot the country's urban landscape faster than new Wal-Marts and Starbucks, and were to become, in time, just as ubiquitous. Multiple Church of Retribution charter schools and vocational training centers were right behind. Every bay-bay in every American city would soon have a blueprint for success--decent learning environment, a surrogate father or two, tuition assistance. Sometimes you had to cut back on one-on-ones and take the whole group into consideration. Sometimes you had to overlook the tree and mind the forest.

"The forest, my brothers and sisters, is getting bigger and bigger. It started in a storefront on Georgia Avenue. It moved right here to 16th Street. Tomorrow it'll be all over the planet. We'll keep growing and growing and growing ... until we fill the whole universe. Why? Because ours is a message of inclusion. A message of peace. Like-minded souls need not hesitate: Come join us. We welcome you with open arms. You belong. We'll pick up your load and add it to ours. We'll etch your complaint into our platform. We'll graft your voice to the ensemble's. We'll weave your dreams into ours. We'll go and ask that man in the White House when he's gonna do the job we sent him up there for. We'll go and tell Big Money he can't keep plundering the planet for his profits. Stop poisoning our children's minds! Stop denying us our rights! Stop dividing us!"

Maybe Joe saw the fracture first--maybe he understood just how deep it would become with time. Maybe the moment had come for him to focus on his true motive for starting the church: Milk the game for everything it was worth, go for his, create and accumulate wealth. (Not to say that he didn't care about the church. It was his creation. He was proud of it, as proud as an artist or an inventor can be of breakthrough work. Joe had made something out of nothing. He had invoked this behemoth out of empty air and given it shape and breath.) Great movements make for great opportunities.

Joe pulled a tearful and resentful Claude out of retirement and rehired him as his personal attorney.

"Why did you abandon me?" Claude cried from the bottom of a magnum of shiraz.

"Your ties with the church had to be severed before you and I could pursue a private relationship," Joe explained. "I never meant to do you harm."

"What are we doing?" Claude asked, floating to the top of the bottle.

"Setting up a holding: Retribution, Inc."

Claude cracked a smile. "I'm in. As long as you keep Mofas away from me."

"Still think he's an economic hit man?"

"More than ever. Same way I know Pepsi is the Devil's son, Nasro is back in Sudan after finally making his pilgrimage to the holy city of Mecca, and you're about to become super-rich." Claude smiled, adjusted his Wayfarers and his ascot, dabbed his forehead with his hankie, and rubbed his chin. "So where do we start?"

"Retribution Gear," Joe announced decidedly.

Claude unveiled small, tainted teeth. "Sounds good to me."

Joe reintroduced the T-shirt catalogue and completed it with jeans, shorts, sweat pants, armbands, headbands, wristbands, and sandals. He struck a manufacturing deal in China and a distribution deal in New York. He took out ads in youth-oriented magazines as well as more serious publications like GQ, Cosmopolitan, Vanity Fair, and O, Oprah's monthly showcase. The focus of the line was Jay's image as a pioneer of human rights, a freethinker, a rebel, an antiestablishment public intellectual, a healer, a gatherer of men, an engaged citizen, a crowd mover, a leader.

Kids on every continent hungrily went for it. Joe doubted that most of them had a clue who Jay was and what he represented. Such was the state of fashion: A face and fame for the sake of fame carried you a long, long way in the clothing business. Further, in fact, than quality, durability, or dependability.

As soon as sales passed an acceptable threshold, Joe licensed the brand to a Hong Kong buccaneer who started to crank out everything from bed sheets to tablecloths to home furniture bearing Jay's likeness.

Joe muscled Jay's fondness for running and his wholesome appearance into a one-year, one-million-dollar endorsement contract with Nike. He forged Jay's name on a power of attorney affidavit, signed all relevant papers without informing him about the deal, and pocketed the checks. "You need Jay," he told his Nike contact, "you call me. I'm his agent." Jay's house was inundated with package after package of Swoosh-stamped stuff after Joe e-mailed his measurements. So abundant was it that Jay had little choice but to wear it all the time. The Nike people never got to meet him in person, a fact Joe explained by Jay's very busy schedule. Jay himself never suspected a thing.

Next was a venture with Sierra Nuts Corporation, a one-man processing, packaging, and distribution outfit operating out of a small warehouse in Rockville. Sierra products were largely out of sight in Washington, where Barcelona reigned unchallenged, but they were renowned in the suburbs for their freshness and tastiness. Every gas station on 355 North had them. The roasted almonds were the best around, period. Habib, the brand's Lebanese owner, was famous for handpicking fruits and nuts as far out as California. "I'm looking to market a trail mix called 'Retribution,'" Joe told him during their introductory meeting. "I want nothing but the best organic stuff in it: cashews, peanuts, raisins, apricots, bananas, dates. Suggested retail price of $1.99 for a 4-ounce bag. We cut the profits 60-40."

From organic trail mix, Joe moved to organic iced tea and an energy drink. The Retribution Brew and Retribution C beverages were both bottled by Honest Tea, a Maryland startup that had just gone through a very successful I.P.O. The drinks were "only a tad sweet." Their wrapper was stamped with sermons and Jay's effigy. "Simple Goodness" and "The Taste of Truth" were the gimmicks.

Joe took advantage of the arrival on the retail market of the first generation of 3-D printers to make Jay Wilson action figures in his garage. From a scanned picture and an array of anthropomorphic data he was able to produce 10-inch dolls with an uncanny resemblance to the real thing. Dressed in mini-Retribution outfits for cross-branding purposes, the little Jays used recent advances in nanotechnology: A NanoSnitch no bigger than a pin's head allowed them to blurt out "Better must come!" every time you shook their right hand. Joe made only a dozen that he took around town, eventually selling his patent to Mattel, whose engineers improved on the original design and created an accompanying fantasy world and cast of characters much like Barbie's. It became one of the hottest toys come Christmas, especially after the "Better Will Come" ringtone for cellphones was introduced.

No craze was too new or too marginal to ignore. When Joe noticed a surfing and skateboarding revival, he contacted a leading board maker and sold him Jay's image and a couple of his most famous speeches. General Motors paid big money to win the rights to name the hybrid version of the resurrected Camaro after Jay. Yamaha rolled out a limited-edition line of Jay Wilson acoustic guitars. They were preprogrammed to play "Better Must Come." Joe convinced the Ben & Jerry's ice cream company to name their new vanilla-chocolate mix "Simply Jay-Lishious," after the world's most visible mixed couple.

Joe became a millionaire ten times over in the span of four months. Revenge was sweet to Villanova Boy when the man who had expelled him from his campus fraternity called long-distance begging to become his business partner. "At this point in my life," Joe told him, "you'd only become a liability."

Joe went into real estate with Mofas despite Claude's repeated warnings about the jackal/economic hit man. "His hustling skills are precisely what I need, Claude."

"He takes from poor people, Joe. Black people. He gets them up to their necks into debt and then he abandons them."

"I'm no different," Joe shrugged, giving Claude a glimpse into his soul.

Claude looked at him quizzically.

"A pigeon is a pigeon," Joe explained. "Rich or poor. Black or white."

Mofas and Joe set up two structures aiming to cash in on the booming subprime market. Retribution Loans offered a line of credit to minority borrowers with weak earnings and a nonexistent or shaky FICO score. The interest rates on the loans--under $300,000 on average--were several digits above market rate and they were adjustable, shooting up (resetting) over a certain period of time. After they were issued the loans were securitized, insured by A.I.G., stamped with AAA rating, and sold to investors with a no-buyback clause guaranteeing that they never came back to bite Joe. "My exposure," he liked to tell people, "is close to zero."

The second company, Retribution Homes, bought and sold distressed properties in the city's far-flung and poverty-stricken bastions. Those were houses seized by banks after the original owners fell behind on their mortgage payments. They were likely to be in serious need of repair, stripped by crackheads and petty thieves of carpeting, appliances, and plumbing fixtures. Joe bought them from a handful of banks without even looking at them, sometimes by the dozen, mostly for no more than $4,000 each. They were resold "as is" at very affordable prices, often with a zero-down, interest-only loan from the financing arm of Joe's holding. Even with the ensuing high default rate and foreclosures Joe made a killing, recycling the same seemingly endless stream of properties. His clients all belonged to minority groups. They were for the most part recent arrivals desperate for home ownership, that overhyped steppingstone into the American Dream.

When a buyer complained about finding a dead porcupine in his living room, Joe was quick to reuse Mofas's line: "I threw that in for free."

Last but not least, Joe invested in Bloodline, a tech firm whose specialty, DNA genealogy, was becoming all the rage. It was an opportunity nearly missed, for Joe had heard that the truths revealed by DNA analysis weren't always pleasant, and definitely not the ones anticipated. When it came to ethnicity few people found themselves to belong as fully to a certain group as they had assumed, a resounding corroboration of the notion that all men share common links and a common origin. "Black" genes, for example, were commonly found in Caucasian and Asian subjects. Pure bloodlines were the exception, not the norm.

Such a discovery was vast in its implications. It should have, in a reasonable world, a world where good faith and goodwill were destined to prevail, put an end to racial disparities, mistrust, and conflicts. Why hate, fight, and be afraid of one another if we have so much in common? If, behind our physical appearance, we're really all the same? In a reasonable world people would have finally taken heed of the obvious and put down their arms. Peace would have covered the Earth. Men would have embraced one another. The Church of Retribution would have been effectively and definitively put out of business.

Preaching equality would have been akin to selling the oxygen in the air.

Joe betted on the fundamentally devious and inherently evil nature of man when he bought Bloodline shares. After missing out on the Google bonanza when the company went public, he was determined not to be left out of the next big thing. Bloodline licensed him a portable genealogy test kit that he was able to market as part of a package offered by yet another one of his spanking-new companies, Retribution Travel. The kit decoded your DNA from a sample; the sample was entered in a database; a match reunited you with long-lost family, say, the offspring of the slaveholder who had raped your great-great-grandmother; a name and an address were provided; tickets and hotel arrangements followed; legal services were made readily available for anyone intent on suing for reparations. It worked the other way, too: White folks who suspected the existence of a black side to their family could provided their sample, hope for a hit, and go down the willy-nilly road of discovery.

The kit was a success, but not other services and products offered by Retribution Travel, such as slave safaris including reenactments of manhunts in the West African bush, voluntary overnight captivity in preserved slave holding forts like Gorée Island off Senegal's coast, transatlantic trips on replicas of slave ships, and educational summer camps on the grounds of old Maryland plantations.

Mofas scouted the Bible Belt for, as Joe put it, "land big and cheap enough to accommodate a theme park, sort of an all-in-one educational and entertaining experience centered around the lives of slaves." The effort fell short after Mofas's inquiries in rural Tennessee provoked an uproar. The small town's homeowners posted "No Slave Park in My Backyard" signs and petitioned their congressman to block the land deal.

To Joe's disgust, relatives on different sides of the color line fell into each other's arms soon after they were reunited by DNA tests, like this one white Texas rancher and his "cousin" the black music teacher from Harlem. They saw only the things bringing them together: the physical resemblance, the similarities in character and personality. They compared notes and retraced steps back to their common ancestors. It was a pretext for giddy, We-Are-the-World happiness, for bringing together that which had been pulled apart. Not, as Joe had hoped, a cause for bitterness, resentment, recrimination, court proceedings, and retribution fees. "I looove my master"? No. Your master loves you.

Joe made his money all the same. More than he had hoped for. More than he knew what to do with. And it made him truly happy as only true money can. He bought everything he had ever wanted, things he hadn't known existed until the day came that he could afford them.

First was the house in Potomac, where the region's rich, famous, and powerful cavorted--athletes, team owners, music moguls, media barons, finance captains, foreign investors, international crooks on the run. Joe's property was gated. It had an infinity pool and a splendid view of the river. Inside, the displays on his walls were digital: immense screens tapped into the world-renowned Getty and Microsoft databases of images and showed revered

349

paintings, famous photographs from around the world, real-time NASA and Google Earth snapshots of the planet and the stars, or computer-generated patterns--you never saw the same thing twice. Ahmet wired the house for technologies and gadgets that had yet to be invented. The master bedroom was as big as the entire Military Road ground level. Its glass walls opened onto a Japanese garden. Joe could make the sun shine on yet another giant screen behind his headboard.

Just as outlandish were his cars. I had betted that he would go back to his first love and snatch a low-mileage 1960s Nova, Chevelle, or Camaro from eBay, but no: Joe went foreign on me, buying two Lamborghinis and an Aston Martin back-to-back. One of the Lamborghinis had a glass panel in lieu of a trunk, allowing for a breathtaking view of the breathtaking engine. I personally had never seen anything like it. Joe took to running all three cars at the same time, reveling in the growl, revving them up one after the other, inhaling the burning gasoline as if it were the most powerful drug. It was like being in the company of wild animals--lions and cougars and leopards. Joe's basest instincts were pleased, and profoundly so. Prophecy fulfilled. This was what he had always wanted. His reward. The fruits of his labor. Finally.

I can't lie: It was a gas to ride into either one of those things. It was a gas-gas-gas.

Joe didn't bother trying to hide his new wealth. He felt invincible. Why apologize for who he was, what he had achieved, what he owned? Prudence and decency were thrown to the wind. Never mind that Jay still toiled in relative indigence. Never mind that Joe's every action was associated with the church, want it or not, admit it or not. Never mind the paparazzi who made a big deal out of the big house, the cars, and the blondes who started appearing at Joe's side the longer Imabelle stayed in Seoul. Never mind the "Jesus Saves. These Guys Withdraw!" scathing City Paper article about the Wilson Brothers. Never mind the public opinion backlash, the grumbling fomented by agitators and saboteurs, the rising outside opposition to the movement, the early defections, the schisms brought about by secessionist fractions. Never mind the purity of the cause. The time had come to get rich.

To appease the flock and quell the rumors, Jay had the church audited from A to Z. No siphoning of donated funds, no diverting of investments by either Joe or Donald Sylvers III were found. Jay never caught whiff of the City Paper piece. He didn't suspect that Joe was behind the nebula of businesses and parent companies grossing millions and millions in his name--everything from the dolls to the ringtones was blamed on those bootleggers, rogue capitalists and modern-day pirates: the Chinese. The priesthood had effectively isolated Jay from reality and disconnected him from the pack. "I'm doing good on the stock market," was Joe's explanation for his fattened pockets, and the siblings left it at that. Jay preferred to assume the best when it came to the people in his life. Joe was his brother, wasn't he? He had changed for the better, hadn't he?

If anything, Joe's success made Jay strive harder to

achieve his own. He wanted Lisha and Kaya to be safe. He wanted them to be free from the grip of material need should the worst occur to him. Alive or dead, he didn't want the fortunes of his family to be tied to those of the church. A man has to make his own way in the world. God bless the child that's got his own, that's got his own.

Quietly, Jay resumed classes in computer programming, sharing car rides with Ahmet to the College Park campus of University of Maryland. Code writing, which had been his career of choice before he dropped out, wasn't so big any more. Game developing was where it was at. It appealed to Jay with its demands on both sides of the brain. Most of the work could be done on a laptop from anywhere in the world at any time of the day. It required team play or outside input only toward the end, when all the different bits and pieces were being brought together. Last but not least, there was a real potential for a financial windfall.

Jay could definitely see himself creating engaging story lines, fantasy worlds, and fun and endearing characters. Just don't ask him to come up with the next shoot-'em-up flick. (Violence, real or imagined, wasn't his thing. He detested it all the more now that it had almost felled him. At times he could feel it enveloping him in a dark cloud. It was in a stranger's eyes on the front-row pew; it was in the headlights tailing his vehicle as Un dropped him home; it was in the death threats phoned at 4 in the morning; it was in a heckler's voice interrupting his speech in a faraway college auditorium; it was in the vicious attacks from members of his own church accusing him of trivializing the civil rights movement and patronizing blacks.)

With that purpose in mind, Jay's enthusiasm for college knew no bounds. His motivation, this time around, was cranked all the way up. He lost no time gathering the tools and the knowledge required. He felt no qualms asking questions, sending e-mails to professors, and contacting fellow creators and aficionados. Here, too, a difference with the past was perceivable. Gone were the shyness, the reserve, the inhibitions, the reluctance to compete, the fear of failure. Jay gave free rein to his hunger. As his expertise in game-making started to grow, so did his ideas.

When a big-name New York publisher approached him for a book deal, Jay didn't hesitate. He had been waiting for the right contract for quite some time, unwilling as he was to end up on the same roster as the authors of such page turners and literary touchstones as "Sheisty," "A Gangsta's Wife," "Charge It to the Game," and "Still Sheisty." Grove Press seemed like the perfect fit from day one, having decades ago and in a similar sea of controversy taken a chance on the manuscript of Malcolm X's autobiography. Jay's only conditions were that all advances and proceeds from the book go to a trust fund controlled by Lisha, and that he have the ultimate say on the designation of a co-writer. His choice eventually rested on Mo, Sally's Somali husband.

Mo was between projects and more than willing to dabble into a little ghostwriting. His first question to Jay was, "How honest are you prepared to be?"

Jay sat and thought hard about it. How honest, really? What to say? What to keep hidden? What to leave behind? Was image more important than the truth? Were certain revelations essential to the public's grasp of his personality, his motivations? Were they even necessary?

He didn't mind disclosing the big depression of a couple of years ago, the sleeping spells, the mistakes, the soul-searching. Everyone was entitled to gray zones and weaknesses. Central to Jay's psyche was everything that had happened with Maggie. The blows, the insults, the dark rooms, the neglect, the shame, the terror, the conditioning, the timorousness, the timidity, the bed-wetting, the bloodletting. If anything had been instrumental in shaping him it was those things, those facts, those events. People who saw him preaching from the pulpit only got half the picture. Those who knew his sermons by heart and hung his photograph on their walls knew next to nothing about the real Jay. Should he keep it that way? Should he leave them in the dark?

He wished Nasro were around to help him make up his mind.

He conjured the spirit of Taha.

He asked for my guidance, hoping that I'd appear to him in a dream. It's your decision, I whispered in his ear. Your call. I'll support you whatever you choose.

He discussed the subject with Lisha, the one person around him who seemed to remain herself despite the overblown fame, the fishbowl that their life had become, the maelstrom of public attention. "Honesty should always prevail," Lisha told him. "Describe things as they happened, as you lived them. For history's sake."

In the end, Jay decided to leave nothing hidden.

"I'm going to put it out there," he warned Maggie over the phone. "But understand that I'm not trying to get back at you in any way. I forgave you a long time ago. Grove Press is paying me to tell my story. Millions will read it hoping to get inspired. The church might not survive either me or Joe, but books live forever. I just want to describe everything as it took place. To do otherwise would miss the purpose entirely."

"Bullshit," Maggie answered, and Jay knew that, had they been in the same room, fists would have started to fly. "You want to destroy our family. You want to put me on the spot. Both you and that ghostwriter of yours are muckrakers."

"Not at all," Jay protested, feeling like a 5-year-old caught in the middle of some not-so-innocent mischief. "I looked deep into myself before making that decision. I know for a fact that I'm not doing this out of grudge or a wish to grab attention--I mean, how much more famous can I become? I'm just as scared as you, Ma: Who knows how people will react to the story? How they will look at me afterward? But honesty is its own reward. Lisha told me so just the other day."

Maggie scoffed. "I'm not scared. I'm just mad at myself for letting you live. Now the world will know me as the mother of the biggest rat on earth.... That is, unless I shut you up first."

Jay's blood ran cold. "Are you threatening me? Is that what you think? That I should be silenced?"

"You're a telltale, aren't you? It's you making a big deal out of things that happened almost 30 years ago. A grown man crying because he got pushed around a little when he was a child.... You have no shame, Jay."

Jay took a deep breath. "Did you do those things or did you not? I mean, am I inventing stuff here?"

Maggie laughed. "I did them all right. No denying that."

Jay's tears started to flow. He made no attempt to stop them. "Why?"

Maggie shrugged. "Because some of those same things had been done to me. I wanted to hurt you. I wanted to hurt you bad. And whenever I did, it felt good. It came--how can I say it?--naturally. By the time I caught myself the damage had been done."

"I don't remember anything that happened before I turned 6. I just know it was pretty bad. That whole period is covered in darkness. I blanked out on it. But each of the times you punched me afterward is engraved in my memory."

"You were a good little boy. Never ran to tell your daddy."

Jay wiped his face with his sleeve. "You never apologized to me," he said, as encouraged by Maggie's confession as he was repelled by it. "That's the one thing that would make me keep all this under silence. If you show some regret ... if I know for a fact that you admit being wrong."

"That won't happen."

Jay remained silent for a few seconds, hoping his mother would change her mind, praying that the words he was waiting for would come. "I love you." All Maggie needed to say was, "I love you."

"Are we done here?" Maggie railed.

Anger chased Jay's sadness away. He squeezed the phone hard enough to crush it. "I gave you the heads-up," he said, fire in his voice. "So be prepared. Don't say I didn't warn you when your evil deeds stare back at you from the middle of a page."

"I'll kill you before any of that happens," Maggie snarled back. "Mark my words: I put you on this earth and I will be the one taking you out."

"God is great," Jay proclaimed, putting the phone down.

I shook my head, just as heartbroken and exhausted as he by the exchange.

The phone chirped.

"You're so quick to judge," Maggie said sweetly. "Wait until you get the impulse to bash the head of that half-breed you call daughter against the wall. See how well you fare controlling that type of urge. Then you can talk."

"The 'half-breed' is your granddaughter," Jay reminded her. "Her name is Kaya. And I'm glad you chose to stay out of her life after all."

"Tell me you never feel like beating her to a pulp," Maggie teased. "Tell me the sight of her blood doesn't fill you with the most delicious sensation."

"Never," Jay affirmed, his heart rising in his chest. "Never.... The cycle stops with you."

357

Both the Church of Retribution's finest and darkest hours came a few weeks later in New York City during a one-night fundraising event that collected dozens of millions in donations. Joe, Nicole, and Donald Sylvers III went after the town's biggest equity groups, hedge funds, investment banks, and consulting firms. They invited this crème de la crème to a fabulous white-tent, long-gown and white-glove evening presided over by a handful of opportunistic movie stars whose adoption of the restitution cause was as much a publicity stunt as the alternatively-fueled limousines that ostentatiously chauffeured them in.

The night was aglow, the city abuzz, the food first-rate, the champagne abundant, the speeches short, the women elegant, the stakes high, the competitive spirit at its fiercest, the adrenaline unbelievable. Robin Fickle, the first white singer to ever reach #1 on the R&B charts, performed a salsa version of "Gross Without You," his breakaway hit. Donors outdid and out-pledged one another under crystal chandeliers, in front of cheering flashbulbs, and amid countless toasts and congratulatory accolades. The year had been a record one for fund managers, brokers, deal makers and investment bankers, if not for their clients. Wall Street was awash in bonuses. The church's timing couldn't have been more perfect in the sense that hedge funds, the biggest players in this outsized field, were now anxious to shed some of the secrecy surrounding their activities. What better night to present their genteel side to the world? What better cause than that championed by the brothers Wilson? What better occasion to don the mantel of civic-minded philanthropists? What better way to pile up much-needed tax deductions?

Many records were set that night, the one in hypocrisy not the least. Joe was in 7th Heaven, hobnobbing, schmoozing, exchanging stock tips, collecting business cards, generally talking equal to equal with the world's most ruthless 3-and-30 managers, its brightest executives and its most famed C.E.O.'s, half of whom were there hoping to win a consulting contract from Retribution, Inc. should the rumors that Joe was about to take it public be confirmed. The other half wanted to buy Joe out outright and add his umbrella of companies to theirs, allowing him to cash in while keeping full operational and decisional prerogatives. Let the young ladies and the journalists in attendance rush Jay and crush him under autograph requests: The people who mattered were well aware of the hidden importance of the gathering. Those sharks of finance were vying to win Joe's favors by giving so generously to his pet project. Few of them, caught up in the trappings of their success and blinded by hubris, suspected that they were living the last months of the second Gilded Age. Fueled by bad loans and unchecked speculation, the real estate bubble was close to burst and help drag the world's major economies into a recession of cataclysmic proportions, a shakeup during which institutions that once seemed impregnable and all but venerable would be swallowed whole.

If no contracts were signed right then and there, contacts were made that would prove invaluable in the near future. This was, definitely, Joe's time to shine.

"I'll let you fly back on your own," he told Nicole, Donald, Un, and a bored Jay. "I'll charter another plane in a few days."

"Why don't you just come back with us?" Jay asked.

"A couple of business meetings," Joe disclosed rather mysteriously.

"Fine," Nicole told him before absentmindedly kissing him on the cheek. She was, as usual, dazzling. Her hair was worked into an elaborate chignon. Her dress was stunning in its simplicity. The People Magazine poll taken at the soiree's conclusion had found her "best dressed" and "most charming" on the red carpet. To the trophy wives who discreetly and not so discreetly approached her asking for her surgeon's name, she'd invariably responded, "Honey, I had a whole list of them," before obligingly directing them to The New Yorker's archives, now available in a DVD box-set and a mini-external hard drive ($299 plus applicable tax. Free engraving. 2-day shipping).

So we left Joe behind and flew the rented jet to Reagan National. Un buried his nose in "How Europe Underdeveloped Africa," a book recommended by Jay. Donald fell asleep before takeoff. Nicole kicked her shoes off and thought about the work awaiting her the following week--two new ARCH dedications and four schools in five different states. She was sick of traveling and sick of hotels. She wanted to switch gears, adopt two or three or six of the motherless children she encountered every day, and become a stay-at-home mom. Only the fear of letting Jay and Joe down was stopping her.

Jay folded his arms, looked out the window, and let his thoughts wander. He'd wanted Lisha to attend the gala with the baby but she'd laughed him off gently. "Me? With Robin Fickle and all those stars and moneymakers? Come on now!" He was anxious to get home. The glamour and hype of the dinner were already behind him. He'd been in a deep morass, lately--something he could not shake. A fatigue both mental and physical was sticking to his shoulders--the corollary of his conversation with Maggie, among other things. The collaboration with Mo was going well, the manuscript taking shape amazingly fast. But the difficult memories being called to life, the emotions being stirred added to his overall lassitude. Maggie was right about one thing: the stuff was muddy and nauseating. Once you started stirring it and digging in it, it splattered everything around and took a life of its own.

Next to my Nicole I was brooding for the duration of the whole flight, occasionally leaving the group to go sit with Maggie and Steve in their Hummer. Maggie's eyes had turned red the last time I was in her presence. I knew what she was getting ready to do, and it worried me to no end. As the church's team flew through the starry night, a plan was being hatched back in Washington to rid my ex-wife of the two persons she hated the most on this earth: Jay and Nicole.

"Is everything ready?" Maggie asked Steve for the 10th time.

"We're good to go," Steve assured her.

"Check again," she prodded him.

"Okay," he obeyed diligently.

Jumping in the back, Steve inspected the C4-laden drone resting on a small launching pad where the truck's extra two rows of seats used to be. Too bad this baby wouldn't come back home with them. Had Maggie given him more time, he would have mounted long-range killing devices on the underbelly--mini-rockets or armor-penetrating projectiles--allowing the drone to fly safely back into the Hummer after annihilating its targets. "Three weeks? I don't have three more weeks!" Maggie had shouted. "I want to kill both of them now. It's long overdue. If I see one more pint of Jay-Lishious ice cream or another 'I Brake for Restitution' bumper sticker I'm going to go nuts. Nuts! So get that thing ready. Make it blow everything up. Make sure that nothing gets traced back to us. Can I trust you with that much?"

"Check," Steve said, leaving the drone to jump back into the front seat.

Next, he opened the Hummer's sunroof, enlarged to allow for the drone's ascension. The glass glided noiselessly, revealing a sizable chunk of sky.

"Such a beautiful night," Maggie mused.

"Check," Steve said again.

Finally, he seized the drone's remote, pulled the antenna, and flicked the controls on and off. "Ready," he told Maggie.

"Good."

She looked at her watch. They were idling behind the church's limousine in the airport's hourly parking lot, waiting for the jet to land and its occupants to file out.

"Now it's just a matter of seizing the moment. Remember: I don't have a beef with Joe other than the black list thing. We can spare him this time around. Two sons on the same day might be a bit too much. It might attract undue attention."

"I know," said Steve, who was thinking of ridding himself of Simone, the most useless and drugged-out of his two useless, drugged-out, boomeranging daughters.

They relaxed in their seats. Steve tried to focus on the mission. He couldn't wait to get back to the beach house (they had named it Calypso after a failed dream of his to join the Cousteau team on its very first exploratory travel across the seas). Maggie was worked up. Steve was sure that should the plan be executed without a hitch she'd reward him accordingly. A few days ago she'd surprised him for his birthday, peppering their torture session (they were using the John C. Yoo memo on executive powers and the "Iraqi Insurgent Handbook") with French curse words she had been learning on the sly. She'd called him *pédé, pédale, pétasse, pêteux, poltron, peureux, Pied-Noir, petit juif, salaud, salopard, salope, saligaud, enfoiré, andouille, enculé, trou du cul, bougnoule, imbécile, tête à claques, tête de con, connard, couillon, couille molle*--things his mother used to call him, things he hadn't heard in years. Steve had cried warm tears that night. Birthday tears, tears of gratitude and intense happiness.

My only prayer as the Church of Retribution plane

363

began to descend toward the city was that Un would be wide awake and quick to shoot.

Maggie nudged Steve out of his reverie. "Here they go! Great, Joe's not even with them."

Nicole, Un, Jay, and the limo driver were coming out of the terminal and crossing toward the parking. Steve straightened himself and grabbed the remote.

Maggie slapped him upside the head. "Not here, dummy. We wouldn't make it out of Virginia. Don't you know how deep security forces are around airports? Don't you listen to the news?"

Steve dropped the remote back in his lap. Looking up, he caught a glimpse of Nicole in her heels and strapless Isabel Toledo evening dress. The sight froze him in place. Never in his life had he been around such a beautiful woman. She shone from far away. She walked without touching the ground. Her stomach was impossibly flat. Her shoulders were a kissing field. Her breasts stood firm and full. Her hips swayed this way and that. She was a flower kissed by the breeze. She eclipsed the moon and the stars. "*Putain qu'elle est bonne la noire....*" he blurted out.

Maggie slapped him again. "Don't be looking at that tramp."

"I'm gonna have to look at her if you want me to kill her," Steve demurred. "You're making this more complicated than it has to be."

"Just do as I say," Maggie barked, easing the Hummer out of the parking lot right on the limousine's tail.

I teleported frenetically from one vehicle to the other for the next 20 minutes, trying to get a handle on the unfolding situation. Lord, I prayed, please let no one be hurt tonight. Please repel Satan in his harvest of evil actions. Please don't allow this ignominious act to be committed. These are good people, O Lord. Good, decent people. Their work here on Earth isn't done. They don't deserve to die in such ugly fashion, by the hand of such tortured souls as Maggie and Steve.

I prayed and I prayed. What else could I do?

Nicole dozed off during the short trip to her 19th Street loft. Jay thought about Lisha, Kaya, the autobiography, the church, and the video game that was starting to take shape in his mind. Un thought about all the books he needed to read before he became as smart and as informed as Jay. Donald Sylvers III mentally reviewed the blueprints for the renovations on Progressville, his civil rights-inspired second home. Mitch the limo driver focused on the road. Steve promised himself he would get a good glimpse of Nicole before he blew her to pieces. Maggie held on tight to the Hummer's steering wheel, giddy with anticipation. This was fun, this was edgy, this was action, this was living life to the fullest, this was following no rules but her own.

I held my head in both hands, weary to no end.

"Hit them as soon as they park," Maggie instructed Steve.

"What about the chauffeur, the important-looking black dude, and the bodyguard?"

"Collateral damage," Maggie said. "Better yet, wait a little. I'm sure Jay will walk the tramp to her door. You can drop the drone at their feet. That should do the trick."

365

Steve took the remote and flicked all the levers on. A green dot appeared on top of the square box.

The limousine stopped, with the Hummer hugging the curb only a few feet away. There had been no other place to park, 19th Street being always packed even this late into the night. I knew that firsthand, having had to leave the Eldorado in the alley behind Cairo whenever I visited Nicole.

"You're too close," Steve informed Maggie. "The fallout might endanger us. Debris will be flying everywhere."

"Never mind that," Maggie replied. "I want to see them go. Watch the blast from front-row seats. Why else do it in person?"

Steve shrugged.

I flew into the limousine and yelled at Nicole and Jay to stay inside, hide, run, call the cops, call Homeland Security, call the F.B.I.--all to no avail.

Nicole yawned and kissed Jay. The sonorous mwah! mwah! she planted on his cheeks left me uncharacteristically cold. "See you tomorrow."

"Let me walk you," Jay proposed.

"You don't have to," Nicole told him.

Un dropped the Walter Rodney book and took his gun. "I'll come with you."

Mitch stepped out to open the rear door.

Jay came out.

Steve made the sunroof slide and started the drone's engine.

Un stood on the sidewalk, looked around, and thought nothing of the white Hummer.

Nicole's legs emerged from the limousine. The Toledo dress revealed vertiginous lengths of skin and the highway, the superhighway of Nicole's thighs.

Steve stopped breathing, opened his eyes wide, and licked his lips with a parched tongue.

Nicole took Jay's hand gracefully, landed in the middle of the asphalt, yawned again, and stretched her arms. Her breasts seemed ready to take flight. She was the Winged Victory of Samothrace.

Steve sighed and gave one of the levers on the remote some pull at the same time that he tried to devise a way to spare Nicole, at least until he found out if she could work a whip. He wanted to get next to her. There weren't two like her in the whole world, of that he was sure. There had never been talk of he and Maggie getting married--they had both learned their lesson--so he felt no qualms entertaining the thought of leaving her for Nicole, *oui oui tout de suite*, he'd give it all up for her.

The drone climbed out of the Hummer, hovering noiselessly a few feet above.

Steve watched Nicole walk toward her building, flanked by Jay and a very alert Un. The street was theirs. Only a few lights shone upper head. *"Putain qu'elle est bonne,"* Steve said again, finding it hard to keep his eyes off Nicole's chignon, her almond shape, and Mr. Butt, the tantalizing Mr. Butt.

Maggie punched him across the jaw. "Give me that!" she shouted, snatching the remote.

"Give it back!" Steve said, diving across the seats.

They struggled briefly, their grunts filling the truck, their fingers knocking the remote's levers on and off.

"Let go, fool!"

"You let go!"

Steve yanked the remote from Maggie's hands. It slipped from his fingers and crashed into the windshield. Steve's face turned ashen when he realized what he had done.

Like a free-falling rock, the drone dropped back into the Hummer. The C4 exploded when it touched the launching pad, blowing Steve and Maggie to bits, engulfing the truck and the adjoining cars in a white-hot ball of flame.

Nicole and Jay turned around, their ears whistling, fear in their eyes.

Un pushed them behind a parked car and pointed his weapon toward the burning carcasses. Thick smoke rose above the trees, hiding the moon and much of the sky.

I can't remember what I was getting ready to do before my surroundings faded and everything became dark. Huddle with Jay and Nicole? Wait for the police, ambulance, and fire engine whose sirens could already be heard approaching?

Before I could collect my thoughts and gather my senses, Maggie appeared in front of me. "You?" she said.

I looked at her. Bewilderment and consternation tugged at my brain 10 different ways. System Error, System Error. Disbelief strained my voice. "You?"

It was Maggie all right. Or her ghost, rather. A few pounds lighter, a few years younger, dressed a little more conservatively, her hair brushed back. Death was easy on our bodies, apparently. (She'd confirm later that I, too, looked better than during the last years of my life.) I wasn't thrilled to have her company, accustomed as I had become to roaming this little dimension alone. But I didn't think I had a choice, and neither did she. The last time I'd talked to her was on the morning of my last day on Earth, as I was hauling my duffel bag into the Eldorado, effectively leaving the marital home. "Go. Go to your nymphs," she'd lashed out in her slippers and hair curlers. "Oh, I'm going," I'd answered with much joviality. "Soon I'll be swimming in a pool of love."

We picked up on the same tone, getting into it five minutes after she joined me in the afterlife.

"You don't seem too sad I'm dead."

"Sad? Why should I feel sad? You were off kilter, man! Way off! Killing Nicole and our son? What were you thinking? Better you than them. You have nothing to offer the world. Here at last you're harmless."

"What's 'here'? Where are we?"

"Purgatory. Although with you it'll start looking like Hell pretty fast I'm sure. Pain in the ass in life, pain in the ass in death."

Maggie ignored the quip. "Purgatory? How do you know? Somebody told you?"

"Nobody told me anything. I'm assuming that's what this is. They're taking it easy on the eschatology but it's Purgatory all right. I've been waiting since the day I died."

"What for?"

"We're being judged, Mag. Not just on our actions but those of our children as well. They're our responsibility. They're what we left behind. Everything they do and say reflects on us. It's all taken into account during the final

369

weigh in."

"You mean we have to stay here until Joe and Jay die?"

I shrugged. "Who knows how the stuff is being computed? Maybe this is one big bureaucratic apparatus with millions of files and long lines. Maybe our own parents had to wait for our cases to be settled. Maybe something will happen that'll free us to go one way or the other: The kids can do enough good or enough bad that our fates--and theirs--will be sealed for good."

Maggie laughed hysterically. "'Enough good?' Joe and Jay? Have you seen what they've been up to? That church? All that noise? The robocalls? The TV sermons? The blackmail? The galas? They had the nerve to set up shop in the middle of 16th Street! Jay is some sort of pastor now. And Joe got rich behind some kind of funny scheme. If those two are what's keeping us from eternal fire we're as good as gone, Ben. As good as gone!"

"I have hope," I told Maggie. "Joe's definitely iffy, but I'll take my chances with Jay. The boy's not done surprising us. Plenty of room to grow. He's working on a video game that'll revolutionize the entertainment industry."

Maggie shook her head. "All that nigger stuff. I'm just as glad I'm dead. It was driving me straight to the grave."

It had been a long time since I'd heard the word, and it jolted me. "I'd watch my mouth if I were you, Mag. The movement started in good faith. As far as Jay is concerned anyway."

"It's like you weren't even killed by that black bum.

Instead of doing the right thing and staying away from those ... those murderers, our sons go and embrace a whole heap of them. A whole country worth!"

"Y'all got it wrong," I informed Maggie. "It wasn't Leslie who shot me. It was Vladimir, the Ukrainian kid from the flower shop next to Cairo. Everybody went for the black suspect, even the black detective."

Maggie frowned. "Vladimir? Why?"

"Trying to rob me. He thought I was taking the day's receipts home every night."

"You fought him?"

"I did," I admitted sheepishly. "I recognized his voice and tried to pull his mask. The fool fired."

"That's what you get."

It was true: That's what I got. Easy to explain my state of mind that evening. Easy as 1-2-3. I had my head full of Nicole. She had me flying high. On my way to her, on my way to the Condo in the Sky. We would go to sleep and wake up together. I would finally get to see what she looked like in the morning. I was unstoppable, that night. Unstoppable.

Maggie looked around. Sadness was hunching her shoulders. Or was it fear? No one else but us, nothing to do but watch and wait, the restlessness of a charged conscience, the confusion of a transitioning soul, the flesh turning into spirit, the spirit struggling to make sense of it all.

I almost felt like taking her in my arms. What a shock it must be. Everything gone: Hummer, house, lover, Amore cookies, Rod Stewart concerts, money, plans, good health, time, the remaining years. On top of the world one minute and stuck in barren ether with your dead husband the next. Confinement before judgment, the possibility of eternal punishment. Above all, the realization that one might have lived erroneously, followed the wrong path, embraced the wrong beliefs. So life on Earth isn't it. There is a God. There is something bigger than us. I should have paid attention, your mind goes. I should have listened. I should have seen the signs. I should have walked the straight and narrow. I should have lived righteous. It was all a test, dammit. It was all a test and I might just have failed. Is it really my fault? Now we're moving to the next level. What will happen of me? How fair is this?

I broke into my breakdance routine to lighten Maggie's mood. "Remember my back pains? Gone, baby!"

Maggie barely smiled.

"You can teleport," I told her, eager to show off the perks of our condition. "You can follow Joe and Jay around, but not at the same time--no ubiquity, it sucks, I know. You can see and hear them, they can't see or hear you. Might feel your presence, though--someone as perceptive as Jay especially. You're never hungry or thirsty or tired or sleepy. Emotions are the same but with no physical side effects, and I find that truly rewarding. Stress can't kill you or make you lose your hair. Boredom is the thing to watch out for, really. Days are extra-long when everything is slow on Earth. And then there's the unspoken code: Don't peer too much; respect people's privacy."

Maggie seemed in the grip of unbearable torment. "Where's Steve?" she asked, her voice breaking. "What about Steve?"

It had all slipped by her, my little speech. In through one ear, out through the other. Steve. I felt almost jealous. A part of me had just started to awaken with her arrival--the part in each of us that only exists through communication--the social animal part. So she loved her little Stephane after all. She truly loved him. That nerd, that freak, that geek, that doormat--forgive me, God. "Steve is not family, Mag. Just somebody you were having fun with. Now he's in his own continuum, awaiting his own final decision. Unless they sent him straight on down for that triple-homicide attempt--infanticide plus double murder for you."

"Go ahead and make fun of us," Maggie said. "You cheater. You liar. You unfaithful husband."

"I meant to thank you for that Costco casket," I said, hitting her real low.

"Costco was the way to go," Maggie retorted unapologetically. "You barely left me enough money to bury you."

"I left you a lien-free home, a very valuable car, two beautiful sons, and a thriving business," I countered. "Your pettiness and narrow-mindedness know no limit. You had to exact revenge on my corpse. You had to go after Nicole, who's never done anything to you. You had to try and murder Jay, who's the sweetest guy you could ever meet."

"I took my kicks where I could," Maggie admitted. "Does that make me a bad person?"

"Your kicks were a little extra, Mag, you'll have to admit. Just a little."

"Tell me you never sinned."

"I sinned plenty. I also did plenty good."

373

"Like what?"

"Those people I saved in Nam."

"That's right," she nodded sarcastically: "Your own little personal My Lai. Think sparing a bunch of rice eaters will get you to Heaven?"

"I think I'm a pretty good candidate overall, yeah."

"Do you even know what you're talking about? How can you believe in something you barely understand?"

"I don't have to understand all of it. Nobody ever does. It's enough to feel it in your heart. 'Faith' is what it's called. You should try it sometime."

Maggie hung her head. "Doesn't seem like I'm gonna make it, does it?"

"Repent," I urged her. "Repent in your heart. He is most merciful. God is."

"That would make me a hypocrite."

"What, you feel no remorse at all? Not even for hurting Jay?"

"No," Maggie affirmed.

"No?" I asked, incredulous.

"No," she repeated. "And you know what? God made me this way. So how can He punish me for being who I am and doing what I do?"

"That's a weak line of defense, Mag. Very weak. I'll concede that your background was problematic.... You didn't have the best parents. But there's a statute of limitations on childhood traumas. Adults can't point to their genes or families to justify personal shortcomings past a certain point. It's up to us to work on our problems. We have a choice. We have free will. That's why I'm so proud of Jay: He's soldiering on despite everything. He's more

374

than making up for his handicaps."

"That stuff is built-in," Maggie insisted. "I didn't have it in me to change. And how can one prepare for life after death when one doesn't have a clue of its existence, its realness?"

"Faith," I said again. "You believe in something and you live your life accordingly."

Annoyed to no end, Maggie looked around, for her ladle perhaps. "Spare me your dime-store philosophy, Ben. You know no more about these things than I do."

We argued for days and days, until the time finally came for Maggie's funeral. We reconnected with the living world, assisting to the ceremony in the same way that I had been present for my wake, and then Arlington. Maggie and I, sick of each other by then, went our separate ways, much like we would in the following months. If she tagged Joe, I stayed with Jay. When I wanted to see what Joe was up to, she went somewhere else.

The kids didn't go cheap on her at all, even though much confusion surrounded the circumstances of Maggie's and Steve's deaths. Joe hooked up with Simone, Steve's daughter, the druggie from across the street who had never held his attention until she dyed her hair and eyebrows a pale yellow accentuated by heavily made-up eyes and an assortment of tattoos and piercings. "Curious how I never noticed you before," Joe told her during the inquest, knowing damn well the reasons behind his interest (Simone a seemingly easy and vulnerable brand-new blonde; Imabelle still in Seoul; Joe's own aching loins). Maggie's remains barely filled a lunch box, but her casket was topnotch. I had to laugh when I found out that the service was being held at the Church of Retribution. This was the brothers' response to the barrage of unanswered questions, official and unofficial, authorized and unauthorized. A terrorist attack had been suspected at first, the version of the explosion still favored by a White House in desperate need of homeland security breaches and homeland security threats to feed the public's anxieties, distract its attention from the Middle East fiasco, and prepare the terrain for another GOP handoff at Empire's next presidential elections. Claims were made and maintained that an underground cell had flown an undetected armed drone above Empire's capital. Aziz Bensaoui was dragged in chains from Military Road live on TV, promptly declared an "enemy combatant" and shipped to Guantanamo, where he disappeared never to be seen or heard from again, joining the legions of innocents whose basic rights were being trampled by Empire's big blind feet. The F.B.I.'s discoveries at the Eastern Shore property were downplayed, though agents privately informed Joe and Jay of the probable plot against their lives concocted by their own mother and her lover. Luckily for the boys the torture equipment was seized and the house sealed, sparing them the more sordid details of Maggie's indulgences and her sexual explorations.

Still, the affair left a bitter aftertaste. Jay remembered the threats professed by Maggie. She had promised to kill him, hadn't she? What was she doing in front of Nicole's place at 3 in the morning? What else but carrying out a botched hit? Why had Joe stayed behind? Had he been aware of her plan? Was he like those 4,000

LeRoi Jones Jews who had purportedly received secret directives to not report for work at the World Trade Center on September 11, 2001?

"Of course not," Joe defended himself. "I stayed in New York to network. 25 business meetings in three days. I have an I.P.O. coming, in case you forgot."

"I can't stop believing that you knew something," Jay insisted. "You and Ma were always so tight. You were her favorite."

"That was before the church. In the end she hated us both equally."

"Maybe you're scared of this upcoming book of mine, too. Maybe you guys reconciled behind my back. Maybe she told you what she was about to do and warned you to stay away."

"I'm not scared of your book. Just don't publish it before I sell my shares."

"I'll publish it when it's ready. And thanks for offering me part ownership."

"You don't want anything to do with this business, believe me."

"Money," Jay said. "That's all you care about."

"That's what makes the world go round. Not people. Not pussy. Money."

The rift between Joe and Jay grew unchecked. They buried Maggie distractedly in the first plot they could find, along Riggs Road near Adelphi, under a hybrid poplar tree. Beautiful as it was, the place drove Maggie to tears. "I wanted to get cremated!" she shouted, jumping in place.

"Now you know how I feel," I told her.

Steve was disposed of more matter-of-factly. His ashes were dispersed from atop a cliff overlooking the Atlantic, though Simone would claim for a long time to come that she'd mixed them with coke and snorted them during a week-long binge. "People more famous than you have bragged about similar stuff," a doubtful Joe commented.

Joe picked JPMorgan to guide him through his public offering, one of the very firms so lambasted by the Church of Retribution for its ties to slavery. The buzz surrounding the proceedings on Wall Street promised to make it the most successful stock launch since the I.P.O. craze fueled by the technology boom of the '90s.

On the personal side, things were starting to get out of hand. The combination of easy money, thrills, greed, grief, sex, and quick access to drugs threw Joe for a loop. He woke up some mornings with the feeling of being the sole passenger of a high-velocity train that he didn't know how to stop, watching helplessly as his life flew by. Cocaine was taking over his life, sadly and rapidly. He did it in the morning. He did it at night. He did it while fucking Simone on the see-through trunk of the running Murcielago. He did it on his iPhone's glass screen between calls. Cocaine. Cocaine. Cocaine. Running around his brain.

Never one to be happy with nickel-and-diming since he had made it, Joe struck a deal with Pepsi to purchase, have delivered, and store in his mansion 50 pounds of pure coke.

"Why so much?" Pepsi asked out of sheer curiosity.

"Just because I can," Joe answered. "My girl and I, we want to roll around in it. Have it all over our bodies. To see what it's like."

Joe had never forgotten the first time he'd tried snow. Having a drink with Simone, sitting in the booth of some cheap Chinatown pub she frequented. They were just getting to know each other. She proposed him a line. He said no. She pulled her sweater up, pushed her bra aside, took a pinch of the stuff, rubbed both her nipples with it, cupped her breasts, and invited him to suck on them. He blushed, looked left, looked right, latched on, and made her laugh.

"Your problem," Pepsi said neutrally. "Long as your money's good."

Joe flashed a fiendish grin. His eyes, too, were turning red on me. "Oh, you know it's good."

They made all the arrangements on a rooftop overlooking Kennedy Street. If the Church of Retribution was making any difference in ghetto people's lives it barely showed here. Crackheads darted around every corner like hyperactive ants. Dope boys held their spots. ARCH shone resiliently two blocks away, full of well-tended bay-bays, signaling a still-possible, still-reachable future.

Pepsi's demeanor denoted nothing less than a business-as-usual approach. "Does Jay snort, too?" he inquired when Joe and he were finished cutting their deal.

"Jay doesn't do anything," Joe replied with something akin to disgust. "Jay is as pure as a white sheep. And Jay is almost as dumb."

Pepsi shook his head. "The boy is drug-free and

here you are buying blow by the truckload. Sounds like he's the smart one to me. No wonder he's such a star. Everybody loves him around these parts. Jay this, Jay that. Kids swear he's their father. Girls want his baby bad. Only white man on living room and bedroom walls apart from Che Guevara. I'm almost jealous. The day the 'hood starts showing me this much love I'm running for president."

"Che's Hispanic, not white," Joe corrected Pepsi bitterly. "And Jay ain't shit."

Pepsi looked up, amused. "Word?"

"I've been pimping him from day one," Joe added rather imprudently. "He's still on church salary while I'm getting ready to become a billionaire. So how smart is he?"

Pepsi raised an eyebrow. "'Billionaire,' huh?"

"Billionaire." Joe motioned toward the beast parked on the street below. "You see my whip, don't you?"

Pepsi sneered. "Lambos ain't shit. They're all over the Internet. I have a neon-green one that I only drive around the race track."

"That's because you'd get stopped by cops every other block if you used it in the street," Joe said. "My stuff is legit. I have all my receipts. My name is on everything I own."

"That's because you're white," Pepsi retorted. "They're not gonna profile you like they do me."

Joe extended his hand, feeling a rush of sympathy for the guy. "Come hang with me," he said. "I might show you a thing or two."

Thus began another one of Joe's strange associations, after Mofas, Ahmet, and Claude.

"So how does one become a billionaire?" Pepsi asked, he who, though he had assiduously studied the lives of famed entrepreneurs as described in their own self-authored self-help books, was still struggling to break the 100-million-dollar mark.

"Easy," Joe answered. "You take an original idea, finance it, leverage it, and take it public."

Pepsi shook his head. "Me at the Stock Exchange? They'd just laugh, call me a 'nigger' and hand me a broom, a mop, and a shoeshine kit."

"They would. But who cares? You'd be richer than most of them. Eventually, you'd belong. The money club is colorblind, P. Everybody's green."

"I'm a drug dealer," Pepsi said. "What do I incorporate and leverage? What do I take public?"

"Let's look at your business model," Joe proposed. "You're pretty much a household name around town. Good product, flawless supply chain, firmly established retail spots, dedicated employees, a captive market. What you want to do is go vertical, spur growth, stave off complacency. Become a one-stop shop. I won't even state the obvious: private coca fields, processing facilities, distribution routes and networks.... Let's go beyond that. Customers should be able to come to you for anything related to their primal need to get high. Not just a $10 rock but a pipe, a lighter, matches, a chaser--beer or weed--a syringe, a rubber strap, vitamins, maybe even a place to use the drug discreetly. So invest in paraphernalia under the same name brand and integrate all your products. Make it known that addicts can enter your retail space and, for a nominal fee, get an all-around experience.... Then there's the whole issue of R/D."

"'R/D'?"

"Research and Development. You deal in mind- and behavior-altering substances. People might get tired of the same old trips. Put chemists on your payroll. Hire a dozen Johns Hopkins graduates, rent them a lab--that guy Mofas can help with that--and sponsor their research. Create sample and control groups. Organize contests. How hard will it be to find volunteers for your experiments? Imagine if you discover the next crack and flood the market with it."

Pepsi seemed blown away by the world of possibilities flowing from Joe's mind. "Legality," he stammered. "That's what I really crave. I want to be able to live in the open. I want to break free from these chains. I want to stop looking over my shoulder. How easy do you think it is to launder all this cash coming in? Much as I long for it, money always equates problems."

"I have one word for you," Joe told him: "'OxyContin.' Purdue Pharma marketed it as safer than other painkillers knowing that oxycodone, its active ingredient, is a narcotic, an opiate capable of inducing a high as powerful as heroin. All OxyContin users had to do was chew the pills or crush them and snort the powder. Purdue Pharma trained salesmen to overcome reluctant doctors' objections. Sure enough, OxyContin tore the Appalachia apart. It was called 'Hillbilly Heroin.' It brought in 2.8 billion in sales. The company only paid 600 million in fines when the F.D.A. caught up. No jail time for any Purdue Pharma executive. You do the math."

"So white-collar crime is the way to go?"

Joe nodded. "Absolutely. Fuck Horatio Alger

382

achievements. That's good for people like Jay."

"How do you stay motivated?" Pepsi, whose temples were burning with fever, asked. "I get lazy the more I make. It stops being fun."

"Think of all the things you desire and can't get yet," Joe proposed. "Me, I want me a yacht, a plane, and a private island in the French West Indies. Have you ever been to St. Barth?"

Pepsi shook his head.

"My eBay 'Wish List' is full," Joe went on. "Whenever I get unfocused and restless, all I need to do is log on to my account to motivate myself. It reminds me what I'm fighting for. It gives me that extra push."

"Those are things worth giving your all," Pepsi nodded. "And remember to always be grateful for what you have."

"True. We are blessed."

The two men truly bonded when Pepsi confided how misunderstood and under-appreciated he had always felt. "People think I got it made. They think I like to be mean and kill so much. They don't have a clue what I go through."

"Let them walk in our shoes," Joe commiserated. "And see if they can handle the pressure."

It was the beginning of a long and beautiful friendship, cemented on Joe's side by the fact that Jay and he were growing apart, their goals as different as day and night, their aspirations irreconcilable, their characters treading different paths.

Jay's proselytizing was becoming somewhat

redundant to his own ears. Even the much-publicized appearance of Hank, Chuck, Frank, and Silas--the Klan boys--into the church's fold didn't hold his attention for long. (They had tried Retribution Travel's genealogy kits in a moment of boredom, found out that they were all at least 25% black, and decided to throw in the towel.) Sometimes Jay wondered if the loud marquee out front --"30 Million Saved!"--was anything but a lie. Just the other day a middle-aged brother called Young had approached him after the evening sermon and shared his vision of things. "Blacks should drop the 'black' thing," Young, himself an African-American man, had told Jay. "They should just try to be. Part of our problem is we're dying to recapture something that doesn't exist any more."

"'Just try to be,'" Jay had repeated slowly and thoughtfully. "How is that possible? Why would the world ever let a black man forget that he's black?"

"I've been to Africa several times," Young said. "There's nothing there for us. Heck, there's barely anything there for Africans."

"So the solution is to be white?"

"The solution is to be. Just be."

Attacks started coming from all fronts. Joe had used Bloodline to make a very special gift to Oprah, Jesse, and Al--the black luminaries: He had researched their family histories, discovered who owned their ancestors, and presented them with the results as a goodwill gesture. A prankster applied the same formula and found people whose forefathers had been owned by Maggie's side of the tree. No DNA matches were discovered between the two lines, thank God, and the concerned family, well-to-do blacks who, coincidentally, lived on the stretch of 16th Street called "Gold Coast" right here in Washington, D.C., expressed no interest in getting to know either Jay or Joe. But much was made in the press of the fact that, despite all that they so relentlessly preached, the Retribution Brothers had neglected to sweep their own porch, an oversight whose attribution was bitterly debated between Joe and Jay.

When Al Sharpton invited Jay to his radio show, Joe begged him not to go. "Every single white man who accepted Al's invitation never made it back," he assured him. "That show is a trap. You go to apologize or clarify a racially-charged situation and you disappear. Do the names Michael Richards and Don Imus ring a bell?"

"No."

"That's because Al finished them. Don't do it, man. It's dangerous."

Jay went anyway. Al hammered him, as expected, his graying James Brown perm shaking with righteous anger under his huge headphones. One felt he had been waiting for the face-off opportunity for a very long time. "You had no right to appoint yourself a black leader," he told Jay, jutting a menacing finger across the table. "You misrepresented yourself."

"Who's black?" Jay asked him.

"Not you," Al retorted.

"We're all black," Jay asserted, answering his own question. "What happened to the 'one drop' rule? Aren't you keeping up with progress? Don't your people brief you on sensitive matters? Science itself is saying so: We all came out of Africa. We all share a common ancestry. So what's the bickering about?"

"You're a fraud!" Al shouted.

"And you an ambulance chaser," Jay attacked back. "I've put my life on the line. I've worked my ass off trying to foment change. I took great pains to stay away from consulting jobs and public panels so as not to infringe on your territory. I let you and Jesse split all the high-profile cases. So what's the beef?"

"Black people don't want a white man handling their business. We don't need your type of help. It sends the wrong kind of message. It tells the world we're not mature enough, we're not organized enough, we're not angry enough."

"What's your track record, Al?"

"You're nothing but a crook," Al went on. "You and your brother. You stole Sister Deadria's idea and took it straight to the bank."

"Sister Deadria doesn't mind us. She knows we're pursuing her work, bringing it to fruition. We carry her torch. We're her spiritual heirs."

"The only reason you never heard from her is she feels too disgusted to even intervene. She very narrowly escaped a nervous breakdown. You rascal! You profiteer!"

"Bring me proof," Jay asked. "Anything substantiating your claim."

"The constellation of businesses surrounding your so-called church is proof enough. Not a day goes by without some Retribution gadget appearing on store shelves. They can't get shipped out of China fast enough!"

"I don't have anything to do with that. Find any instance of wrongdoing inside my temple and I'll act upon it myself. My hands are clean. Let's see yours."

"Clean?" Al objected. "You're playing with fire. How can your hands be clean? Racially motivated attacks are up 10% since you started your false preaching. More arson, sexual assaults, beatings, insults, and vandalism. Do you even monitor those things? I do. There's a direct correlation: You've provoked prejudiced people all over the country into showing their teeth. They're going out of their way to prove you wrong."

"I've seen the numbers," Jay interjected. "Those attacks are the last shudders of a dying breed, the growls of a cornered beast. The spike will be followed by a long-lasting decrease."

"What of the pain? The tremendous amount of pain felt by every victim of racism, every person of color? You gloss over it. You minimize it."

"Pain? I know everything about pain. Bessie Smith ain't got nothing on me. I am the blues!"

"Fine," Al said. "You want to be a black leader, you go ahead and be one. But don't start crying when somebody pulls an Audubon Ballroom on you."

"I'll take a bullet," Jay proclaimed defiantly. "Hell, I'll take a whole hail of them. Wouldn't be the first time. It's an honor to follow in the footsteps of Malcolm. What greater man to emulate?"

"You're no Malcolm," Al said derisively. "And you're no Martin."

"The same goes for you," Jay said sweetly.

Forays into overseas missionary work were only mildly rewarding. The field was crowded with philanthropies, foundations, doctrines, and uncooperative governments. It had become impossible to give any more. You couldn't just take your money and do something good with it. The wish and the means to help weren't enough. What lacked was coordination, common sense, honesty, and peace. Just like Mr. Young had intoned, Jay and Lisha found Africa much troubled. War in Congo, Chad, Somalia, and Sudan. Political strife in Kenya. Famine and cholera in Zimbabwe. It wasn't clear whether mosquito nets, grain, $100 laptops, microloans, and generic AIDS medicines would make much of a difference. Nasro stayed on Jay's mind throughout, especially after our group met the Aga Khan and his delegation of Ismailis near Kampala, Uganda. They had favored for-profit ventures over donations as a vessel for economic development in sub-Saharan Africa for decades, an approach that, though slow to take off, seemed to make all the difference. "It's not about handouts," the Aga Khan told Jay, echoing Nasros's teachings. "These aren't children. Provide them with opportunities and a stable environment and watch them make a go of it."

I was happy to discover that part of the world. We had to skip a much-anticipated stop in Darfur due to restrictions imposed by the authoritarian government in Khartoum.

Back home white supremacists marched on the church, picketing its facade. Jay was called everything from the usual "traitor to the white race" to a coward. A stuffed doll with his picture tacked to its head was theatrically hanged at the end of a stick before it was set ablaze. Hank, Frank, Chuck, and Silas watched those antics with heavy hearts. It could have been them on the other side of the

388

fence, channeling pure hatred through yells and pumped fists.

Black supremacists marched on the church, picketing its facade. Wearing berets, boots, fatigues, gloves, and dark sunglasses, they formed a line and chanted "Jay Wilson Go Home!" and "Church of Destitution!" for three long hours.

From his rehab ward, the musician Gil Scott-Heron sent Jay a bitter postcard whose only inscription was the title of one of his earliest pieces: "Who Will Pay Reparations on My Soul?"

And what to make of the Retribution Brigades, an armed movement that claimed ties to the church and pretended to push its mission one step further by arming itself and taking the restitution fight to the streets? Jay didn't know. As for Joe, he was busy with Simone and his I.P.O. The Brigades stated that all they were doing was bringing a different, tougher approach to the cause. They were hardliners, youths who had been standing on the fringe of the movement ready to fractionalize and radicalize it.

Only Un was supportive of their intentions, he who took self-indoctrination to extreme levels. The reparations credo was getting transformed into a more and more abstract ideal in his mind, one that suffered no deviation or dilution. For a long time he had looked for something to believe in, something to give him worth, something to keep him going. The concept of restitution, with its promise to unite the country, was perfect in its beauty, its simplicity, its reach. It was a dogma worth fighting for. If people everywhere didn't adopt it as gleefully and as wholly as they should, wasn't it all right to force them? The end justified the means. Ideals needed to be imposed at times. The restitution movement was perfect. It is men who were weak.

It was hinted by many that the church was losing steam after the N.A.A.C.P. landed a neat coup by publicly burying the N-word in a Chicago chapel. The ceremony was attended by many. Bill Cosby and Maya Angelou each said an eulogy. Prominent rappers, not ready to put the word to rest, boycotted the event en masse. "I don't care if the stunt reeks of made-for-TV opportunism," Joe proclaimed. "I don't care that the N.A.A.C.P. lost all relevance long ago. We should have thought about it first."

Adding insult to injury, Henry "Skip" Louis Gates, Jr., the eminent Africanist and Harvard professor, wrote a column for The New York Times in which he lambasted the Church of Retribution for never acknowledging the notion that, when it came to slavery, Africans had their hands as dirty as Europeans and Americans. Slavery, he wrote, was no stranger to the continent. It was a fact of life long before the first white man arrived on African shores. African rulers had aided, abetted, and profited from the transatlantic slave trade from the first day. In that line of thought the Church of Retribution's reason for existing became nil, its crusade nonsensical, its founders uninformed naifs at best, dangerous hypocrites at worst.

Jay shrugged the whole thing off. Joe was livid with rage, foaming at the mouth. "Traitor!" he yelled.

Time came for another audit. Unable to get in touch with either Joe or Donald Sylvers III, the head of the crew of accountants sifting through the mountain of paperwork contacted Jay about, among other questionable items, the Riots on Demand contract. "All I see are monthly statements and payments," the young bespectacled man declared. "No invoices, no actual list detailing the services provided. These people have been claiming 5% of all your revenues practically since day one. It hasn't happened yet, but the government will wonder what, exactly, they do for you. At the very least you might want to renegotiate--the fees seem pretty hefty to me."

Jay remembered a conversation with his brother about a consulting firm around the time of his very first sermon at the Georgia Avenue storefront, but he doubted having ever signed the contract standing before his eyes. Since the line of communication with Joe wasn't what it used to be, he took his doubts to Sally Harris and asked her to investigate.

"My signature was forged on all the binding documents," he told her. "Who is R.O.D.? Why did Joe establish a relationship with them behind my back? Why hasn't this come up before? What else is there that I need to know?"

Sally went on the hunt. What she uncovered was big enough to scare her to death and have her watch over her shoulder for years to come.

The first person she encountered when she ventured inside R.O.D.'s discreet downtown Bethesda office was the young woman she had interviewed two years ago in the middle of a protest in Houston, Texas--the one with the Stars and Stripes bandanna, the war paint, and the war-painted baby. She was sitting in front of a computer at the information desk, the only employee in sight. "Have we met before?" Sally asked her.

"Not that I recall," the woman answered with a straightforward smile. "But I grew up around these parts."

Sally's subsequent questions were stonewalled just as nicely and skillfully. R.O.D. didn't do walk-ins. All media inquiries were handled by a PR firm whose representative described the company to Sally in very vague terms, repeating "consultants" over and over. Not much luck on the Internet, either. Direct searches brought little to no results, which was weird for people who had been in business for a very long time. R.O.D. was privately held. It provided no information about its goals, its figures, its organizational chart. Sally hit a wall, dusted herself off, and went back to work.

Weeks of research yielded few clues. The Beltway insiders who knew anything about R.O.D. appeared reluctant to discuss it.

"It has government ties," a Hill staffer nervously told Sally after making her promise that he wouldn't be quoted.

"C.I.A.," a retired cigar-chewing general whispered with a wink before following the arc of his golf ball above a flawless Fairfax course. "At the very least a shadow contractor since the Colby days."

"Even if their work goes against the official line?"

"It all depends on who gets to them first. Or which side has the bigger pockets."

"Can you tell me more?" Sally pleaded.

"Not if you paid me a million dollars and put me in a lifelong witness protection program," the general said.

Sally's break came when she stopped nosing about R.O.D. head-on and followed the bandanna girl's lead instead. Going back to the Church of Retribution early days, she poured over the tons of photographs, news clippings, and recordings of pro-restitution demonstrations widely available on the Web. Though hard to recognize at times, Bandanna Girl was all over the place. Her hairstyle had changed with locations, she had never worn the same outfit twice, she had gone from campus activist to pregnant woman to breast-feeding mom in a 20-month period, before dropping from sight altogether. But it was her all right.

Sally studied the documents day and night, looking for more identifiable faces. She found a grand total of eight. Not merely enough to shout conspiracy--those could be serial marchers or dedicated protesters--but more than enough to suggest foul play. Bandanna Girl denied having ever been to Houston, Texas, though face-recognition software matched frames of her downloaded from the Internet with the picture Sally secretly took using her cellphone during a second visit to R.O.D.'s headquarters.

Slowly, a pattern of activities emerged. R.O.D. had

hit towns and raised awareness about the restitution cause a mere days before Joe's people came to hold their fundraising or flooded the area with calls. When the town was swept clean the partners moved to another one. Strong-arm tactics were used to mollify the most recalcitrant big business donors as well. Flash mobs showed up at mistresses' homes, spoiled Sweet Sixteen parties, egged boats, and ruined Hamptons vacations.

"Nothing illegal so far," Jay remarked with something akin to relief before Sally finished sharing her findings in a quiet Ethiopian restaurant in Adams Morgan. "Debatable, morally questionable, and distasteful for sure. But not illegal. Joe felt he had to use those people to promote our cause and to help disseminate our name. He knew I wouldn't go for it and so he hired them alone and signed all pertaining documents himself. Those were the beginnings. We don't have to resort to those means any more, thank God."

"It doesn't stop there," Sally said. "R.O.D. is behind every big demonstration, every spontaneous mass protest, every significant popular uprising of the last century, foreign or homespun, government-backed or antiestablishment. You see the same operatives demolishing the Berlin Wall, deposing and then reinstating an anti-American general in Venezuela, burning oil fields in Nigeria, and attending Vietnam-era Jane Fonda rallies. They're a secret protest industry all by themselves, a manufactured, transportable, for-hire popular movement, the most influential company people have never heard of."

"That has nothing to do with us," Jay, still in denial,

asserted.

"It has everything to do with you," Sally said. "Because it's only a matter of time before R.O.D. is exposed. And when they finally fall the history of many movements will be rewritten, including yours."

Jay looked deep into Sally's brown eyes and shivered. System Error. System Error. His mind was telling him to disconnect, and fast. Lose himself in Sally's pretty face, her reddish complexion, her flat nose, her juicy lips, her ponytail, her golden hoops, her short nails. System Error. System Error.

"Are you listening, Jay? You need to cut your ties with them. Distance yourself from your brother as well. Make it known that he signed your name on that contract. Otherwise everything you've built, everything you've accomplished will be lost."

Like a killer wave washing through, acid filled Jay's stomach. He winced and pressed his palms against his belly. "My brother? I can't turn my back on Joe! We're tight. We're super-close."

Sally sighed and slowly shook her head. Pity softened her next words. "You've been misled, Jay. I hate to be the one breaking it to you, but..."

Jay's heart started to bleed. He found it impossible to lock his gaze into Sally's. His voice, when he spoke, was almost a murmur. "But what?"

"He's been using you for years," Sally went on gently, cautiously, but firmly. "Joe has. There are talking action figures designed after you out there. All kinds of stuff bearing your name and likeness: shoes, jeans, ringtones, vacation packages, energy bars, granola mix, juices ... even ice cream."

Jay's mind blanked out. System Error. System Error. "Ice cream?" he repeated weakly.

Sally nodded. She was accustomed to delivering news good and bad, bringing it raw to an unsuspecting public, telling it as it was. It was her job. She did this every day. "People have been talking for months, Jay. Some think you're trying to cash out. Others believe you're the biggest fool on this face of the planet. Most love you enough that it doesn't matter to them one way or the other--they'll give you the benefit of the doubt until you prove them wrong, and even then they'll be quick to forgive you. Sorry."

"Fool?" Jay mumbled like an old man. He had trouble focusing, suddenly. All he wanted to do was to lie down and go to sleep for a long, very long time. System Shutdown.

"So you see why it's important you take action," Sally prodded him delicately, as if she were talking to her son Eli. "This is your movement. This is what you'll remain known for until the end of time. Action, inaction, hesitation ... everything will be etched in stone. There's a philosophy, a legacy to protect. People count on you, Jay. They look up to you. Don't allow crimes to get committed in your name. History doesn't stop here. It's still being written. Don't let it tag you as a dupe."

Jay's eyeballs lost their luster, traveled around his sockets, and disappeared. "Tired..." he whispered before collapsing on the table, his forehead sending speckles of tomato sauce and chunks of *injera* flying everywhere.

Weakened as he became by the shock stemming

from Sally's revelations, Jay recovered long enough to confront Joe in Manhattan on the eve of Retribution, Inc.'s I.P.O., and to deliver a bewildering 2-part speech entitled "Universalism/Got to Get Away" immediately afterward in Washington.

"What does it matter that R.O.D. did a little pre-market work for us?" Joe argued from the balcony of his pied-à-terre overlooking Central Park, his head full of coke, contempt dripping from his voice. Black-clad, toned, tanned, gelled, and pomaded, he was as physically perfect and morally corrupt as a modern-day Dorian Gray--you half-expected to stumble upon a hidden portrait detailing the progress of decay on his handsome face.

Maggie and I were both present, pretending not to see each other as we, the two coaches from la-la land, each stood near our respective favorite son.

"We got what we wanted," Joe went on. "And we got it fast. There was no better method. And I don't believe we did anything wrong. This is how elections are won nowadays. This is how markets are conquered. Crowd control, spin, and influencing the public's opinions and its political leanings go hand in hand with data mining, consumer behaviorism, and microtargeting: Find out who people are and what they want through information-gathering and polling; create a need where none exists; play on your target's fears or aspirations; tailor your delivery, whether message or product, down to the household level. Nothing is a guessing game any more, Jay. Pointillism and accuracy are what we strive for."

Jay smirked. "You've come a long way, Villanova Boy."

397

Joe crossed his arms. "Spare me your sarcasm."

Jay thrust his shoulders forward as he went on the offensive. "Why did you breach our agreement?"

Joe looked him in the eye and spoke evenly. "You would have never accepted to hire R.O.D. I know you. Always worrying about doing things the right way. We would still be sitting in that rat hole on Georgia with four old ladies working the phones. R.O.D. is the single best damn investment I've ever made."

Jay shook his head. "We had a deal, me and you. But it was all about money, wasn't it? From the first moment."

Joe shrugged. "Of course."

"Do you even believe in the concept of retribution?" Jay asked.

"Only as a moneymaking device," Joe answered frankly. "I would have shown the same amount of enthusiasm peddling encyclopedias door to door."

The declaration seemed to sadden Jay. "Why drag me into this?"

"I needed your face," Joe confessed. "It's more trust-inducing than mine, apparently. You were perfect for my plans, come to think of it. You're big with blacks. People from all walks of life dig you--don't ask me why."

"So it was all just a game?"

"Not at all. By this time tomorrow I'll be rich, at least on paper. So could you, too, if you wanted to. Instead of playing gadfly with Sally and Mo, try to focus on putting something away for your old days. You have a live-in girlfriend and a baby daughter. Nobody's in a better position than you to profit from the church. Get yours."

Jay smiled ironically. "With dolls and endorsements and a sandal line?"

"You can laugh all you want. Those sandals sell out quicker than Air Jordans. The whole world is buying my stuff. Wall Street is showing me much love. Brokers and fund managers recognize me everywhere I go. They call me the Man and give me hi-fives. I'm the new Gordon Gekko."

Jay sighed. "Did it ever occur to you that I knew what you were up to? Don't you think I've seen through you long ago? I figured you would make your move at one point or the other. I didn't need to know the details. I didn't have to ask a single question as long as I thought you were making your money honestly. I understand how material wealth is important to you, Joe. We all have our thing. I don't look down on you for wanting sports cars and big houses. You're my little brother. I raised you. I was there when Ma gave you your first bath. I got you ready for school every morning."

"Why didn't you stop me, if you knew? Why go along? Why allow me to use you?"

"Because you're all I have left, Joe. You're my blood. What's money? I had been waiting for such a long time to have a good relationship with you. It was killing me that we could never get along until that day we sat down and talked about the church. Finally there was the chance to set things straight. We could repair everything that had gone sour between us. We could work as a team and do good, help people...."

Jay's voice trailed off. Childhood memories were dancing before his eyes, crowding his head. "That's why I did it, Joe: Out of love, pure and simple. Love for you, my brother. Love for others. And to be completely honest, your offer came at a decisive moment. I was lost. I was hurting. What better opportunity to put my life back on track and redeem my one big mistake?"

Joe laughed long and hard. "You sincerely believe that you owe black people something, don't you?"

"Of course."

"Why?"

"Slavery, segregation, discrimination--all the old reasons. And my own racist thoughts and racist ways and racist comments. We white people owe something collectively and individually."

Joe pointed a reprimanding finger at his brother. When he responded, anger lifted his chest. "Let me tell you something, Jay: Unpleasant a truth as it is, we're superior. The white race is."

Startled, Jay looked up. "What are you talking about?"

"We're superior," Joe repeated. "Nature made us so. We run this. White people do. Everything worthwhile on this Earth was conceived, created, and implemented by us. We're smarter and stronger--I don't care how many guns-germs-and-steel theories you invoke. The world is ours. We don't have to apologize for the order of things."

Jay stopped breathing. The pain he had felt in his stomach during his conversation with Sally resurfaced. Acid, acid everywhere. He considered Joe as if Joe had suddenly turned into a complete stranger. "Is that what you truly think?"

"Of course."

"Then you're seriously misguided."

Joe shrugged. "Everybody thinks the same. They just won't admit it. Life is open competition, Jay. Nothing more, nothing less. Blacks need to stop passing themselves off as victims. They need to stop expecting a preferential treatment. Justice Clarence Thomas has been saying it for years: 'Let them compete!' 'Let them compete!' But nobody's listening."

"Justice Thomas is no kind of example," Jay countered, incensed. "He's a basket case who benefitted from those same Affirmative Action measures he's so prompt to vilify. Everybody knows the man has issues."

"He's one of them," Joe ventured. "He should know what he's talking about."

"How do you compete when the field isn't level?" Jay asked. "How do you shake 80 years of legalized oppression? What kind of start do you have in the race when you and the people before you were stripped of rights, possessions, dignity? Things should be so it doesn't feel like a miracle when a black child beats the odds and makes something of himself. They should be so the same amount of effort delivers the same results across the board. Give black people and all minorities a fair chance. Only then can you praise or attribute blame. Only then can you judge in complete fairness."

"You're only proving my point," Joe said. "Blacks lost a big one. It's their responsibility to stage a comeback. Let them prove their worth. Why should we fight their battles?"

"Ever heard of the 'white man's burden'?"

"Another politically correct concoction. There's no lifting these people from the state they're in, Jay. All the

401

time we've spent out there representing them, collecting money in their name, funding all kinds of crazy projects.... We showed more motivation, more dedication, more clarity of vision than any of them and their so-called leaders. We obtained more tangible results. We contributed more to their advancement than any organization or person dead or alive. Two white middle-class kids did this with no prior training or experience in less than 36 months, Jay. Where's the outrage? Where's the outcry? Where's the self-respect? Where's the fighting spirit?"

Jay started to feel tired again. Sleep as heavy and dark as the blackest cloud was creeping up on him. He fought to stay awake. "What about doing the right thing?" he proposed in conciliation. "What about doing God's work?"

Another bout of sudden hilarity shook Joe.

Floating in Joe's corner, Maggie turned her head, appalled.

That's your boy, I told Maggie.

"God who?" Joe exclaimed. "What God?"

"The mission," Jay reminded Joe, perplexed. "The dreams both you and I used to have. What gave us our sense of purpose at the very beginning."

Joe searched his pocket and pulled out a small object. "I got your dreams and sense of purpose right here," he announced before throwing the NanoSnitch at Jay.

Jay caught it midair, examined it, and hit the Play button. "Work for me!" the voice that had disturbed his sleep many nights above Souk pressed him like a recurring nightmare. "Work for me!"

"What in the...?"

Joe considered his big brother with the pity one feels for certified fools. "I'm your 'God,' Jay. You shall look no further for guidance and enlightenment. All I need from you is to keep quiet and play your part. Leave R.O.D. alone. Those are people you don't want to cross. Their henchmen won't miss you on purpose next time around. Understand?"

Jay stormed out of the apartment and took a cab all the way back to D.C., making it to the church right on time for the 6 o'clock sermon. Un, who had been warming the crowd, barely had a chance to introduce Jay before he pushed him out of the way. Sensing something amiss, the flock rose to its feet. Jay was disheveled and out of breath. "Crazed" is how many who personally witnessed his last moment with the church described both his appearance and his performance that evening.

"Go away," Jay told his followers in a seething, soaring voice. "Get out of here. Let's give it all up and call it a day. Let's turn off the lights and shut the door. Let's hang the 'Closed' sign on the window. Let's put this building back on the auction block. It seems brotherly love is a dream. It appears that most of us only pay lip service to the ideal of oneness. It feels like nobody truly believes in fraternity."

Jay shook his head. Gasps provoked by his harangue could be heard here and there. Eyes were considering him with horror. Mouths were agape. Hearts that had been ready to rejoice were now hurting with him, hurting for him. Jay was poised to lash at all misconceptions and expectations. A storm was suddenly gathering inside the nave. Nobody was safe. Nobody dared escape. There would be no call-and-response tonight. No singing and hand-clapping. No oh-yesses and amens.

Jay raised his hand. The crowd, subdued into immobility, froze. "Why are you here?" Jay asked. "What do you want? What do you care? Why waste your time? Let humanity regress to the Stone Age. Let us go back to the caves, the clubs, the tribes, the 'us' and 'them.' We'll never make it further than that stage. We're not built for cooperation. We're not built for civility, respect, warmth, peace, spirituality. We're worse than dogs. We fight, we raid, we kill, we conquer, we take, we pilfer, we rule. We see no further than the satisfaction of our vilest instincts. There are days when I'm ashamed to call myself a man. Men are liars. Men are hypocrites. Men are no good. Men will betray men for money. Men will stab their own brother in the back."

Jay turned and spat in the direction of Un, whom, in his deranged state of mind, he believed to be in collision with Joe--hadn't Un pretended to save his life during the staged assassination attempt?

The crowd reeled from the shower of accusations.

"You believe in restitution no more than you trust in a Higher Power," Jay went on, simmering in an all-consuming anger. "You'll pay your tithe and wear the T-shirts and put the stickers on you bumper but that's it, that's where it stops. Not one of you will give his life for another human being, especially not a black, red, or yellow human being. Not one of you thinks blacks and whites are truly equal. Not one of you cares about what happens outside your door. As long as your belly's full and you got

404

you a job with health benefits and vacation time and your kids are cared for and a nice car is in the garage, you're content. Never mind that your schools, your neighborhood, your own city are segregated. Never mind that integration is still a dream. Never mind that the rest of the world is crumbling. Never mind that your comfort is taking so much away from the environment. Never mind that two-thirds of the human race lives on one-tenth of your entertainment budget. You just got to have it. You just have to live life your way. It's not your fault that others don't have enough to eat. It's not your problem that children are dying. There's nothing you can do about your own armies going abroad to seize oil wells and kill at will. You'll sign a check and feel better about it. You'll come to service and appease your conscience. You'll wear pink and yellow and march on a sunny Sunday before stopping at your favorite hangout for a hearty brunch and mimosas."

Jay stopped for a second. What came next was the icing on the cake: "You, my white brothers and sisters, are full of shit."

Ears started to burn. Faces reddened. All heads hung low. Tears began to flow. The flock braced itself for more.

But like the wind shifting without warning, Jay's tone turned appeasing. "There should be no need for a retribution campaign. There should be no reason for a restitution movement. Each one should be able to look into his heart and know the truth. Each one should be willing to take action. You quiz your soul, you understand what's right, you go out into the world and do it. That's the way. One by one. Every day. Every moment of the day. Don't think you're better than others. Don't look at them with suspicion. Don't stop at the color of their skin. Don't pay so much attention to their ZIP code. Accept in your heart the principle of equality. Embrace it. Cherish it. Nurture it. For you are one of many. You don't hold the secret to life. You don't hold the keys to the Kingdom. Only charity and humility can take you there. Charity, humility, and love."

Sobbing like the chastised bunch that they were, the Church of Retribution members, in full attrition mode, embraced one another. Much like he had stormed in, Jay stormed out never to be seen inside the building again. The jumbotron had never looked so empty and gigantically useless.

Jay went to bed that night and stayed asleep all through the seven following months. Lisha dismissed the stretch as fatigue-related. She spoon-fed Jay at regular intervals, washed his body with a warm sponge, shaved him, cut his hair, flipped him to avoid bedsores, and hushed him when he cried for Joe in the thick of nightmares. She turned off the house phone and canceled all of Jay's appointments. She quieted baby Kaya whenever she got too loud. "The leader is resting," is what she told anybody who inquired. The paparazzi stopped hiding in the bushes and peeking through the backyard fence. Jay had stopped being news.

The church scrambled to fill the sudden void. Joe briefly considered picking up the challenge. Stage fright and the massive influx of I.P.O. cash held him back. He was rich. He had made it. What did he need to strut a stage and address a gathering of docile imbeciles for? The movement, having served its purpose, was becoming an afterthought. Joe was in such demand in financial and cultural circles that his frenzied brain was finding it hard to keep up. Work, people, ideas, ventures, travels, toys, cocaine, Simone--he was caught in a maelstrom. He shocked me by investing deeply in startups dedicated to the development of sources of alternative energy--Joe, my Joe, Joe Babylon, pro-environment? But the one thing I found truly funny was his incursion into the world of philanthropy. Solicited by such bedrock institutions as MoMA and the Met, Joe came full circle by becoming a big-time sponsor of the arts as well as a contributor to an array of causes celebrating diversity. But nothing he did seemed to satisfy him any more: Not the round-the-clock plugging of all his senses, not the crazy things he bought and the servile cast of characters he surrounded himself with. He found Simone boring, million-dollar cars passé, happiness elusive. It seemed the more he owned, the more he had to lose. He could never completely relax. His mind was never at ease.

Un, who had been waiting in the sidelines for such an occasion to push himself to the forefront, seized the moment. He knew not when the transformation in him had taken place that turned him into an aspiring minister from an obedient gofer and a steadfast bodyguard. But here he was, all of a sudden: At the helm preaching the gospel, collecting the now-mandatory membership fees, outlining new goals, imposing a redefined direction. His voice replaced Jay's. His image filled the jumbotron. His sinister and coercive presence hovered above the crowd.

It took him a while to find his own style, and his speeches were never as rousing as, say, "Better Will

Come," but he more than made up for his lack of experience by a hard-charging pursuit of the retribution agenda. "There's talk of corruption. Of low morale. Of waste and loss of clarity. Of widespread abuses. I've come to shine the light. I've come to pick up the pieces and rebuild the house. Our house. Hotel America. The line is clear and we won't stray from it. We'll impose our will on the greater group; we'll guarantee payments for every member of the African-American community; we'll force blacks and whites into an union of races; we'll defeat discrimination single-handedly; we won't rest until peace and cooperation take hold into the heart of every man and every woman in this country, on this planet. This we will accomplish by adhering to the letter of our mission, the core of our constitutional charter. Doctrine is everything. No interpretation of the message will be tolerated. Deviation will be punished by expulsion. We must live, eat, breathe retribution. We must achieve our objective come what may. We must arm ourselves and fight whoever disagrees with us. We must win!"

Un's usurpation of the leadership role introduced a new era. Where the brothers Wilson had attempted to smoothly usher in a world of social entente and cohesion, his firebrand's rhetoric divided would-be sympathizers into two camps. If you were white you were either for reconciliation with the black race and in favor of monetary compensation for all slave descendants or against. There was no middle ground, no soul searching, no maybes. Un revived and polarized a debate that had all but softened in the past couple of years. His utopian dream of a mixed society found a lukewarm reception in the public. In the mind of the majority, it was the natural order of things that should decide if Earth was meant to become the stomping ground of a uniform and composite race of mulattos. Un's belief that he could intimidate Caucasians into opening their hearts, paying blacks, and accepting them as equals was deemed ludicrous. Such feelings and decisions were personal. Jay's message of gentle persuasion had been received with warmth and goodwill. Un's tactics and his veiled allusions to an all-out war promised to antagonize even yesterday's hardcore fan base.

In his rush to gain his stripes and radicalize the movement Un went further than anybody before, including Deadria Farmer-Paellmann: He attacked the federal government, filing suit in order to obtain an official apology for slavery, segregation, and discrimination, as well as an unspecified financial allotment. Though his own battery of lawyers and lobbyists deemed his chances of success dubious at the most, Un charged ahead, accusing Uncle Sam of harboring double standards and violating the Constitution.

Un was saying nothing untrue or unfounded. It was the way he said it that drew the White House's ire and brought it to place the Church of Retribution under intense scrutiny in the following year. One sensed that the days weren't long before the organization would be declared an enemy of the state.

Internally, Un shook the status quo. Softies were singled out and forced to leave. References to Jay, verbal or physical, were proscribed. His picture was erased from the Web site. Purges rid the congregation of yet more nostalgic followers. Every remaining member was required to take an oath of loyalty. Training in weapon handling was provided. Events like the annual Race for Restitution around downtown streets were revived. Focus groups were tapped to see if economic vessels such as the still much talked-about microloans would work for black America. At the top, Donald Sylvers III was pushed out following Nicole's voluntary departure the week after Un's takeover. Joe more than happily signed away all his rights and claims in exchange for the files detailing his involvement with R.O.D. "My portfolio is choke-full of investments," he told Un. "It was a fine and fun project while it lasted. With the direction you're taking, this church is becoming more of a sinking boat by the minute. You couldn't pay me to stay one more day. Good luck, bud."

Worried as she was by Jay's condition, Lisha lost no time crying over Un's betrayal, he who had slept on their couch, eaten at their table, studied in their basement, and held Kaya in his arms. She correctly anticipated the vendetta against Jay and moved her family out of the Chevy Chase home before marshals came to reclaim it in the church's name. She used Jay's book advance to purchase a property in faraway and quiet Charles County, where she hoped that all the controversy of the recent years would slowly fade away. Nicole helped transport Jay from the old bedroom to the new. Not once did he wake up during the trip.

The retreat to the Maryland countryside did all of us much good in those uncertain times. Even Jay's sleep seemed more peaceful. I enjoyed being in the company of Lisha, Kaya, and post-ARCH Nicole, who visited often. It was a pleasure witnessing my little granddaughter's first wobbly runs in the wide-open backyard. It was a joy swimming alongside Nicole in the pool, dreaming of all the children she now felt free to adopt. It was heartwarming to spend rich hours in the kitchen with Lisha, who was growing into her responsibilities. It was instructive to sit with her, Mo, and Sally as they put the final touches to "Jay Wilson," the much-anticipated and much-delayed autobiography.

"Will Jay ever wake up?" Mo asked. "How should we end the manuscript?"

"We leave the final chapter open," Lisha instructed him. "We make it clear that the story's not over."

"Do we include all the last developments? Even his sleeping sickness?"

Lisha nodded. "Everything. Jay was adamant that nothing be sugarcoated, his own failings included. He believes in telling the full truth. And yes, I have faith he'll wake up soon."

It took another pre-dawn dream to pull Jay out of his spell. The same dream that had gotten him out of his Military Road depression: the white Caprice, the female cop, the house, his Syrian friend Awazen, the voice inside his head calling Jay "Believer." Jay opened his eyes after the voice shouted the epithet seven times. "Believer!" "Believer!".... He sat up and stayed up, unable to go back to sleep no matter how hard he tried. Lisha wrapped her arms around him, covered him with kisses, carried him to the bathroom, scrubbed him from head to toe, dressed him, and sat him at the breakfast table. Kaya jumped on his lap and said "daddy" for the very first time.

As soon as he felt strong enough to walk on his own Jay searched the bedroom for a concealed NanoSnitch. "Joe never set foot in this house," Lisha assured him. "No cable or phone guy came by--I haven't had either service installed. I didn't hear a thing as I lay next to you last night. Nobody spoke to me in my sleep. Your dream was real and it was yours only."

"What do you think it means?" Jay asked.

"Everything will be revealed in due time," Lisha, who had never appeared outwardly or outrageously religious herself, affirmed. "Have faith."

The doorbell interrupted their conversation. They looked at each other. It was only 7 o'clock.

"It's Nasro," Lisha announced, preceding Souk's old owner into the den after letting him in.

Jay rose. The two men embraced with much emotion. Nasro had aged a lot since the day he disappeared. The mustache was gone. Worry circles shrouded his eyes. All his hair had turned white. He wore a simple tunic, a fez, and slippers.

"I kept having visions of you riding a white thoroughbred," Nasro told Jay after refreshing himself with a glass of mint-flavored water and a handful of pistachios. "You were fighting human-shaped creatures with red pupils and slaying more than your share with skillful swordplay, using both hands and both sides of the brain. Though they didn't participate in the battle, angels were at your side. The horse, a magnificent animal, was covered with graceful Arabic inscriptions. What a stunning pair you made! I left my retreat 200 miles from Khartoum and came back to America looking for you. It took me seven days to find you."

"Those inscriptions," Jay asked, "what did they say?"

"I am to instruct you in the ways of Islam," Nasro revealed, his eyes moistening. "You are a true believer, a chosen one. You hold a special place in God's plans. You are a Muslim."

"*Alhamdulillah*," Jay, who wasn't aware that he knew the expression, murmured.

Nasro nodded, got up, and pulled Jay by the arm. "Are you clean?"

"Lisha just bathed me."

"You must pronounce the *shahada* at once," Nasro urged. "You must repeat, 'I attest that there is no God but Allah and that Mohammed is His Prophet.'"

Jay sat back down. Hesitation dulled his face. His blues eyes turned cobalt-blue.

Lisha looked at him with renewed apprehension. "What's wrong?"

"I'm not sure I want to go down that route," Jay said dreamily, as if he were alone and talking to himself. "All my life I've tried to do good, be good, be there for others. Look where it got me. I almost died of grief. I went out of my mind. And for what?"

Lisha knelt by his side. "You were right from the first moment," she assured him. "Good is the way to go. You're generous and brave. You've been pursuing worthy ideals. You've always lived according to your beliefs. That's what makes a man. That's what makes me love you more each day."

Jay shook his head. "I almost died," he repeated, looking past Lisha, past the wall, past the house. "I need to stop being a fool. I need to stop worrying so much about others, the world, things I can't change. I'm tired of giving everything I have and everything I am to people who don't care. They'll just keep taking and taking and taking until I have nothing left. Why should I let myself be used and abused?"

"Well," Nasro intervened, "it's a choice. Consider this your own personal crossroads. The signs are clear: those voices, those dreams.... The true God is calling."

"Is He, really?"

Lisha nodded. So did I. So did Nasro.

"Why is the path so hard to follow, then? Why the confusion? Why the suffering?"

"The suffering made you who you are. It's thanks to what you went through as a child that you can connect with other human beings. You know pain. You feel pain. You fight pain. You heal pain."

"It's so hard," Jay said again.

"Of course it is. Just like anything worthwhile. Where would the challenge be? Where, the difficulty? It's always harder to be good, to do good, to do the right thing."

All three of us looked at Jay intently.

"You have to believe in your dreams," Lisha added. "Literally."

Kaya, who had remained silent the whole time, approached her father. She stood in front of him, she smiled, she raised her arms to get picked up.

Jay got on his feet, scooped her, and pressed her against him. Kaya threw her arms around his neck and buried her head in his shoulder, still smiling.

Jay let out a deep, heartfelt sigh. "I attest that there is no God but Allah and that Mohammed is His prophet," he declared firmly.

Overpowered by emotion, Nasro and Lisha and I embraced him.

A sense of peace descended over Jay after he recited the words.

I felt inexplicably elated, me who knew nothing about Islam and even less about what was taking place.

Maggie, snooping in on us, burst into tears as she caught the oath-taking.

415

"What's your problem?" I prodded her.

"I don't know," she said. "Those people scare me. Those Muslims. They worry me to death. I never thought I would come to count one in my family."

"Don't be ridiculous," I scolded her. "Please."

"What kind of Muslims are we?" Jay asked Nasro on the first day of his instruction, which took place in the hut the two of them built in the backyard, promptly calling it a *madrassa*.

"We're Sunni," Nasro told him. "We adhere to the *shahada*. We pray five times a day. We fast during Ramadan. We give away a percentage of our income in alms. We make the pilgrimage to Mecca if and when we have the means. We're mainstream, moderate, tolerant, open-minded, and respectful of the laws and traditions of the country in which we live. We mingle. We socialize. We promote peace and understanding. We call nobody 'infidel.' We stay away from *fatwas*, be they issued out of Al-Azhar. We don't pay or charge interest, we don't engage in usurious practices. We respect women and grant them equal status and equal freedoms as men. We avoid vile thoughts, vile acts, vile deeds. We fight injustice, we help the poor, we protect and defend the weak. We live simply and humbly and honestly. We prepare for the afterlife. 'Islam' means, above all, submission. We accept God in our hearts and we do our best to live in accordance with the precepts of our faith."

Jay's education took the better part of the following year. He proved an apt and eager pupil, just like Nasro

416

proved a patient and knowledgeable teacher, or *ustaz*. Jay learned all the Koran's *suras* by writing their verses on a wooden tablet with an old-fashioned stylus, reciting them aloud until he knew them by heart, washing the tablet with water, and moving on to the next verse. Apart from the fundaments of *iman*, the faith, they studied *hadiths*, the collection of the Prophet's edicts meant to guide adepts through everyday life, as well as rudiments of *fiqh,* or Islamic jurisprudence. Lisha and Kaya often attended the daily sessions, which started after the dawn prayer and ended before lunch. They all shared Lisha's simple and tasty *halal* meals in the main house afterward. Afternoons were dedicated to work. Nasro tended to the vegetable garden he had planted in the backyard. Lisha researched wedding dresses, wedding cakes, wedding venues, and wedding singers on the Internet. Jay either met with Mo or completed his apprenticeship of C++, the intricate game-writing software.

Thoughts of the church often crossed Jay's mind. "I miss it," he told Lisha once. "And I miss Joe. Why did he do me like a dog?"

"Joe doesn't know any better than to do people like dogs," Lisha soothed him, marveling at the resilience of Jay's affection for his brother. "He'll come around. You try and forgive. Rid yourself of all negative feelings. As for the church, better let it go. Your work is done as far as it's concerned. That part of your life is over."

Jay nodded silently and took Lisha's advice to heart. "You never steer me wrong," he told her. "I can always count on you. How lucky I am to have you."

"I'm lucky, too."

Jay thanked God for Lisha and Kaya. He prayed for Joe and for the chance to see Joe again. He prayed for the church and for true reconciliation between black men and white men. He prayed just to pray. It felt natural. It felt good. It calmed him.

Insert "happiness" here.

The road was clear, at last. No more uncertainty. No more doubt. The comfort of religion. A key to reading the world and understanding life. Overall, Jay felt better than he ever had. God, a family, a home, a guide, health.... What more could a man ask for? He had truly found himself. He wasn't Che. He wasn't Malcolm. He wasn't Gandhi. He wasn't Bob. He wasn't Jesus. He was finally the person he was meant to be: Jay Wilson. Nothing more. Nothing less.

His wasn't an all-encompassing, on-all-the-time or shine-through-everything faith. Jay wasn't immune to doubt, maybe because he never heard the pre-dawn voice again, maybe because the change was so big and so new. Darkness still descended on him at times. It came from the outside, from forces every man has to reckon with in his life. It came, mostly, from the inside. Jay fought it. He fought it hard. Never again would he give in to the temptation of sleeping for days on end. Belief is a constant struggle against oneself. Constant.

"True knowledge is the knowledge of self," Nasro taught him. "True wealth is controlling your life. The place where you live, the people around you, the type of work you do, the amount of hours you work, the quality of the services you have access to. Success means nothing without peace of mind. Unless you're solidly grounded it'll carry you like a strand of straw in a raging stream. 'Round and 'round and up and down you'll go. And where you stop, nobody knows."

Jay wrote the final chapter of his autobiography himself, dedicating the last pages to his newly found faith, which provided the book with that Holy Grail of literary projects: an open ending. Grove Press rushed the book out. The reviews were mostly favorable. The public, far from holding Jay's conversion against him, embraced him anew. Americans loved nothing better than big comebacks, tales of spiritual awakening following years of hardship and extreme abuse, fraternal rivalries, and celebrities who kept reinventing themselves. People bought the book not to read it (they knew a big-budget movie wasn't far behind) but because it was a necessary thing to possess, absolutely. The paparazzi reappeared, snapping pictures of the *madrassa*. Jay finally made it to the "Oprah Winfrey Show," basking in the tear-jerking and praise-showering attention of the feel-good diva and her hug-hungry audience. He professed his love for Lisha and Kaya, who joined Oprah and him on the signature cream-colored divan. Jay confessed missing me, his dad. He publicly forgave Maggie for her unjust and brutal treatment of him. He pronounced himself open to a reunion and a reconciliation with Joe. The audience was understandably disappointed when Oprah announced that her producers had been unable to convince Joe to appear on the set. "He sends his regards," Oprah read from a cue card, "and expresses deep regrets."

Oprah took care not to mention the Church of Retribution during the taping of the show, but in people's minds Jay was still associated with the now-failing movement.

Un's novelty had come to pass. He had never been able to shake the copycat image attached to his persona and to capture the imagination of the multitude the way Jay had and still did. Not even the publicity campaign based on Un's name ("Un-breakable," "Un-touchable," "Un-mitigated," "Un-surpassed") succeeded in swaying the general mood in his favor. He didn't have the golden touch, the Midas touch. Something was missing and he didn't know what. He never inspired so much as intimidated. He never galvanized so much as dominated. Feeling rejected, he ventured deeper and deeper into open provocation, paradoxically preaching confrontation as the fastest mean to achieve his stated goal of everlasting racial peace. In yet another unfortunate move, blacks were barred from the church that was supposed to fight on their behalf. Though the ARCH network was to keep providing the full array of services defined in the organization's charter, 16th Street became off-limits. "First we find ourselves as a people," Un declared to the benefit of his now all-white congregation. "Then we open our doors and spread the love around."

Adding to the confusion, his sermon "Black Danger?" painted a dire picture of race relations in the event of America's failure to improve its integration record. "This is the age of radicalism," Un declared. "Of Improvised Explosive Devices, roadside bombs, suicide bombs, hijackings, and Quassam rockets. We all know what discontent breeds. We see it every day in Iraq, Afghanistan, and Pakistan, and we'll see again it when

Empire finally invades Iran. Black people live right here among us. They've penetrated every nook and cranny of American society. What if they harden their stance? What if they modernize their struggle? What if it becomes an armed and open rebellion? What if they embrace terrorism? Imagine: Black babies, black mothers, black youths strapped with bombs and suicide jackets. At your mall, at your office, on your street, inside your plane! They play with our children. They prepare our food. They run our mailrooms. They mix our drinks. They run the few factories we have left. They staff our hospitals, our poultry farms, our tomato fields. They're everywhere. Each one of them a possible recruit, a soldier, the enemy within! Every day can become a Bomb-a-White-Person Day!"

His was a house of controversy, a theater of the absurd. Loyalists began to openly question Un's sanity, going as far as looking for clues to his madness in his appearance and his personal life. Why was Un's face twice as long as it was wide? Why did it seem that blood never irrigated it? (Rumors that Un might not even be white despite his proverbial pallor had started circulating. What if he was a black man masquerading as a white man to lead white people into embracing black people?) Why didn't Un have a companion, or even friends? Why was he obsessed with guns and street fighting? Why didn't Un have a family history? What to make of his rap sheet? Why did he carry a pair of dice wherever he went? Who was that alter ego called Goetz Un so often mentioned?

Defections became massive. Massive. Membership and attendance fell respectively 30 and 55 percent when a

421

tabloid falsely reported that Jay was about to start a new movement. Un began to resent Jay a little more each day when Jay's book was published and he reclaimed his spot in the limelight.

Things worsened when Un took his cause to the United Nations a few months before the courtroom showdown with the government was due to begin. In an attempt to reclaim the initiative, Un turned his combat into a human right issue by lobbying the council of nations for a solemn condemnation of Empire's treatment of black Americans. Un aimed to get that centuries-long treatment classified as genocide, a measure that would force the U.N. into a set of actions whose nature, framework, and timetable were as yet unspecified.

It was a risky gamble, if not a very original move. No country was more powerful than Empire at the U.N. table. China and Russia briefly expressed interest in Un's motion, but solely in the ultimate goal of using him as a pawn during negotiations on unrelated issues. He went as far as presenting his case in front of the Human Rights Comity.

Un's dangerous alliance with the Retribution Brigades left him open to Empire's counterattack: Using "secret" evidence and citing the severity of the Brigades' acts of sedition and their impact on national security (they had spray-painted a few area highway signs and public monuments), the government classified the Church of Retribution as a terrorist group and moved to freeze its assets. Overnight it became illegal for American citizens to belong, donate, or otherwise associate with the church.

R.O.D., having already been contracted by officials to bolster street-level pro-government support, refused to organize pro-Un demonstrations.

Un was jailed and released on bail pending his trial. His name was added to the no-fly list. His passport was seized. He was barred from making speeches.

The jumbotron was, once again, turned off indefinitely. The 16th Street worship house was sealed. The ARCH buildings and church-mandated charter schools, free clinics, and training centers passed under government control. The movement was, for all intents and purposes, finished.

The church's most ardent followers, people of good faith and good intentions who had stuck with it through thick and thin, quickly rose from their slumber after an initial period of discouragement. They carried on the movement's work and its core message of peace, tolerance, and integration in a loose network of mushrooming underground churches that became known as the Resistance.

The public quickly lost sight of the bigger issue: Empire's stubborn refusal to deal in a reasonable and just manner with the reparations problem. It seemed blacks would never get their due.

"One only hopes," Jesse Jackson declared during a triumphant press conference, "that the demise of this so-called Church of Retribution will send a clear signal to all the other would-be champions of the black race: We can take care of our own, thank you very much. Don't fight our battles. Don't appoint yourself a black hero, a black revolutionary. You haven't earned that right. You haven't paid for that privilege in blood, in sweat, in loss immeasurable, in heartache. So don't worry about us, mister. We'll be fine."

But things, of course, were far from fine. They reverted, in fact, closer and closer to the pre-Retribution Brothers state of affairs with each day that the movement stayed away from the news and people's minds. Only remained T-shirts and other memorabilia, general goodwill, and nostalgic Internet films. The latest polls showed a waning interest in the issue within the white segment of the population. Most considered reparations a case closed: Hadn't they apologized? Hadn't a lot of money been donated? Hadn't some measure of healing been brought?

Among blacks division reigned supreme. Some argued that, despite all the noise, the effort had felt way short of their expectations: Where was the improvement? Where was the money? Nobody could agree on a future course of action. No one stepped forward to pick up where Joe and Jay and N'.C.O.B.R.A. and N.A.P.O. and the U.N.I.A. and the New Black Panther Party and Deadria and the Kwame Ture Institute had left things. For all their bombast, the true black leaders didn't know what to do with the issue, either because they weren't true black leaders or because the issue was a non-issue. In the words of Mr. Young, the old man who once told Jay that blacks needed to "stop being black and just be," perhaps the solution was to forget about the whole reparations business and focus on more pressing needs--the antipoverty fight, public education, the health care debate, corruption, graft, gun violence, the ballooning budget and trade deficits, the environment, the auto industry, the guest worker program, the rise of the neocons and the religious right, the housing crisis, and Empire's unchecked imperialism among others. Not just black needs--American needs, human needs, global needs.

But that, too, was easier said than done. Children of the African disapora know that a great sin has been committed against them. Their whole life, the place where they live, the way they are in the world are one big consequence of that sin. In America, not a single black person doesn't get reminded at one point or another of the purported inferiority of black skin, black intelligence, black history, black culture.

Is there a single way for whites to apologize and make up for their crimes? Does the burden to forgive and move forward fall upon black people? What to make of, how to go beyond the barriers of ignorance, prejudice, and self-hatred? Blacks and whites. Whites and blacks. We're forever linked by the aftermath of slavery, colonialism, segregation, and discrimination. Forever linked by our ability, or inability, to find a solution to our one big problem.

If Jay felt any sadness that the edifice he had helped erect crumbled so rapidly and so definitively, he didn't show it. Islam was helping him abandon all his intellectual and sentimental connections to the church. He did draw a quick balance sheet in his mind upon hearing the news. Had the adventure been worth it? Yes. Had Joe and he accomplished anything? Yes. Was the world better for their actions? Yes. Had they been instrumental in promoting peace and understanding between the black and white races? Yes. Was the specter or racism banished forever from human relations, human interactions, and human hearts? No. Were there ways to keep the struggle alive? Yes.

One such way was "Mankind: The Game."

It had taken shape in Jay's mind over the years, going through several incarnations even as he lay asleep for the past months. In its final conceptual stage, MTG, as it became known long before it was officially launched, was a fine role-playing video game that took aficionados young and old through a set of virtual undertakings as close to real life as possible. It was a game of gigantic reach and proportions, meant to be played exclusively on the Internet by several million users simultaneously connected through computers, smartphones, yet-to-be-invented tablet PCs, or one of the three main gaming platforms: Sony Playstation, Nintendo Wii, or Microsoft Xbox.

MTG stuck close to the notions, rules, and forces guiding human life. You were randomly assigned an avatar the first time you logged on. A pull-up menu explained who were your parents, what was your family background, what culture you were born into, your ethnicity, the customs and traditions of your country, the particulars of your household. The outcome of your first years of development (two hours in real time) and a big part of your early identity depended on the way you were brought up and treated by your parents (two real-life gamers following their own arcs). By the time you reached your teens (the four subsequent hours), the formative criteria shifted beyond environmental and familial circumstances to encompass your reactions to various stimuli meant to mimic the temptations, pleasures, and pitfalls of adolescence. Choices, chance, interactions, encounters, random events in the larger community determined what "worlds" you moved into next, what level of the game you accessed. Crossroads were constant. You were asked to make potentially life-changing decisions every 30 minutes in real time. At the age of 20 your avatar could find himself in college, backpacking across Europe, working in a car shop, running the streets, doing nothing at all, or fighting a war. At any given moment your financial situation depended on your station in life. Did you take out a student loan? Were you being fully supported by your parents? Were you drawing a salary? Were you involved in illegal activities? Every choice had repercussions. Every action, inaction, or hesitation had consequences. By 25 (two more real-time hours) you were considered an adult and held fully responsible for your decisions. The compounded choices you made throughout brought you from one point in your virtual life to the next.

And what virtual life it was. The worlds were as beautiful, rich, and diverse as the real thing. The background music was constantly updated thanks to a link to online music services. You shopped in painstakingly rendered malls. You chose how you looked and the way you dressed. You talked with other players inhabiting your sphere through Instant Messaging or a Bluetooth connection. You associated with them, hanging out in cool spots, skateboarding downtown, playing pickup basketball, starting companies, running a gang. You had your fun or you proved to be the serious type. You got high or you

427

stayed away from drugs. You met and hooked up with girls or boys. You had protected or unprotected sex. You got pregnant, got an abortion or kept the baby. You got married or you absconded. You did the family thing or you kept living the single life. You had affairs or you stayed faithful. You provided well for your loved ones or you thought about yourself first. A home or a brand-new car? Private or public schools for the kids? Anything in the savings account? You worked hard or not at all. You volunteered at the local soup kitchen or you stayed clear of community service. You crossed people or you played by the rules. You took care of your parents as they got old or you never looked back once you left home. You loved your siblings. You had no siblings. You used your siblings. Religion played a part in your life or none at all. You were agnostic or atheist. You were Muslim, Christian, Hindu ... you were nothing. You lived day by day. You lived for the future. You lived until you died (24 real-life hours that could be spread out at will). You lived only once.

MTG's attractiveness came from the fact that it very closely and very cleverly simulated the human experience. Random, unexpected, and uncontrollable as character-changing events can be, in MTG as in true life smart choices, good decisions, hard work, and a little luck made all the difference. Past the childhood stage, decision-making affected each new step. Part of MTG's appeal was that it was meant to be played in absolute concentration. You had exactly one chance. You were born, you grew up, you lived your life, you checked out. There were no winners or losers. Points were assigned starting with the adolescent stage. Actions with positive

428

consequences brought pluses. Minuses came into effect every time you were unkind, didn't show compassion, mistreated your pet, neglected to help someone in need, lied, cheated, stole, killed, raped, etc. You reaped bonuses for overcoming handicaps and hardships, showing courage and integrity, living ethically. Coefficients were applied to pluses and minuses: Deeds, good or bad, weren't of equal importance. The objective of the game became apparent at the moment of your avatar's death, when totals were tallied. A positive balance got you in Heaven (the darkness of death was progressively replaced by a golden light. A door appeared. You leaped through it and became one with the light). A negative balance sent you to Hell (the screen that had turned blank at the moment of death stayed that way, becoming more and more opaque).

MTG's detractors made much of its use of religion, spirituality, morals, and the social conventions generally accepted by the majority of western cultures. Some went as far as to call it "TGG"--The God Game--or, even worse, "GGG"--Goody-Goody Game. Others simply found it dull--here was, after all, a game that had no nudity, graphic sex, or shoot-'em-up sequences except for the occasional act of violence. Positive thinking, collaboration, civic involvement, and the expression of one's feelings were prized over cold calculation and ruthlessness. And the dizzying array of choices proposed every 30 minutes broke the flow, especially at the beginning of the avatar's adolescent life. You had to constantly think about your next move, manage your time, allocate your resources judiciously. Decisions made at each stage narrowed future perspectives. You found that as your life progressed the options became less and less abundant but proportionally weightier in their consequences. You were rewarded for meeting expectations and fulfilling obligations, especially where matters of faith and work came into play. As you joined a corporation or organization, secular or religious, you were informed of your duties and judged on your subsequent performance. Help was peppered along the way, in the form of advice from experienced players or wildcards (angels who appeared at crucial moments). MTG, in other words, relied heavily on the notions of Good and Evil as the main forces underlining the human condition and shaping human endeavors. Not everybody was O.K. with that.

End-users were also frustrated by their inability to play the game more than once. Some never got the chance to pass the first developmental stage: They were killed by a car accident, a collective catastrophe, their parents, a disease.... It made no difference to them that it meant guaranteed Heaven. Some would have liked to come back reincarnated. Some would have liked the chance to live a full arc as an avatar.

But to most, MTG came to represent the ultimate. The concept was thought-provoking, the graphics beautiful, the interactions with other gamers fulfilling, the suspense constant. Early adopters had the privilege of roaming a pristine, not-so-crowded Earth.

The very first person to log on was a cancer-stricken 13-year-old from Cincinnati named Philip. His avatar Eddie had no parents. He ran away from his foster home, hitchhiked his way to California, became a surf champion and a guitar hero. Philip found MTG so engrossing that he regained his fighting spirit and his appetite for life. His cancer went into full remission. Jay categorically forbid his marketing people to claim responsibility for the cure.

Everybody felt compelled to play MTG. It was like a dry run, a preparation for the actual thing. The situations encountered could very well pop up in real life. When the screen went blank everybody waited for the door to appear and the golden light to fill the screen. It was an intensely rewarding moment. At the opposite end, the downer induced by the blackened screen of Hell forced gamers across all demographics to reevaluate themselves, their values, and their lifestyle. 24 real-time hours from beginning to end. A lifetime's worth of lessons.

Sensing that time was of essence, Jay sold his patent to Electronic Arts, the giant game publisher, for $2.4 million. Mo's agent Nicole A. helped negotiate the deal that allowed Jay to retain full creative control. A team of 15 developers was mobilized. $5 million were poured into the project. The software used real locales, up-to-date and fact-checked data. With young adults in mind, the educational aspect was emphasized. Since chances were you wouldn't share a background with your avatar, you had the opportunity to learn about other races, other cultures, other countries, and other customs as you played. Upgrades and debugging were made easy by the fact that MTG was Internet-based.

When it was unveiled less than a year later, MTG became the first game to make use of advertisers in a sweeping and systematic fashion, helping the publisher reap great profits. Just like in the real world, firms were invited to plug their products and sell them. Avatars saw billboards. They watched television. They banked. They bought houses. They got dressed, they drove cars, they went on vacation, they snacked, they went out, they paid for lattes and haircuts. Trips to virtual stores or shopping centers were converted into real-world sales. It became chic for young men and women to closely resemble their online personas.

Jay and Lisha changed nothing about their lives. Hard as he worked, Jay always made sure to put his family first. It's in that measure that he felt truly rich and doubly blessed. His heart sang every time he thought that Lisha and Kaya were beyond the reach of need, that should anything ever happen to him they would be cared for. He felt he was fulfilling his role as a man, a husband, a dad.

But the work wasn't done. It was, in fact, far from finished. When news broke of a strange, possibly racially motivated abduction case in a small southwestern West Virginia town called Big Creek, Jay felt compelled to intervene. Six people had been arrested and charged with sequestrating, assaulting, raping, and wounding a young woman during a week-long ordeal inside a trailer and a nearby shed. The perpetrators, three men and three women, were all white. The victim, Marianne Johnson, was black.

The moment he heard about the crime, Jay felt a shiver run through his spine. He hadn't thought that such things, such horrors were taking place in today's America. Marianne had been lured to the trailer by someone she knew. She had been made to drink toilet water, eat dog feces and rat droppings, and lick blood. She had been beaten and forced into sexual acts repeatedly. Her tormentors had called her "nigger whore" and "nigger bitch." "You're going to die," they told her. "The Church of Retribution can't save you now."

Tipped anonymously, deputies showed up at the trailer and rescued Marianne. She was now recuperating in a hospital bed, her mother at her side. The mainstream TV networks and newspapers that mentioned the crime played up its sensational and bizarre aspects--the accused were related; they had a long history of trouble; they were poor; the trailer itself had seen its share of death and violent acts. It surfaced that Marianne had befriended at least one of the defendants prior to the current events. She was said to suffer from minor disabilities.

Jay's first instinct was to add his voice to the outpouring of outrage rippling though black television, black radio, black print outlets. Black America wanted the offenders to be punished. It wanted the kidnapping to be classified as a hate crime. More importantly, it wanted it to be known that racist attitudes and mind-sets were still on the loose at the beginning of the 21st Century. It wasn't safe out there for children, women, and men of color. Bad things could happen anytime, anywhere, to any of them. Empire was no Rainbow Country. It just wasn't safe.

Jay refrained from speaking publicly, fearing that it wasn't his place to do so. Marianne's tragedy touched him acutely, but he understood the necessity for the black community to close ranks, form a common front, and show support for one of its own. For the first time in a long time, Jay felt his whiteness. He felt a profound sense of shame. No amount of jail time could make up for what had transpired in that trailer. No apology, no sum of money could compensate Marianne's family. The girl was marked. Time itself couldn't erase this stark reminder of deep-rooted racial hatred.

Jay asked Lisha's permission to travel to Big Creek.
"What do you have in mind?" she inquired.
"I just want to be there," he answered.
"Go," she told him. "And please be careful."

434

He and Nasro drove down to Logan County. They didn't stop to snack, and by the time they arrived both were pretty famished. Jay didn't think he'd be able to swallow anything for a while. He was way too upset. "Is it *haram* to go on hunger strikes?" he asked his mentor when they came in view of the sordid trailer and the shed at the end of a dirt road.

"Nothing is *haram* if you're using it to fight injustice," Nasro replied. "But stay clear of vanity."

"I don't know how else to show solidarity," Jay explained. "I have no other way to condemn this act, to take responsibility, to show remorse. Something needs to be done. Otherwise more resentment, distrust, and intolerance will spring forth."

Nasro nodded. "Follow your heart."

They set up camp on the trash-strewn patch of grass in front of the beige-and-brown mobile home. Newborn pups were sleeping near the shed, protected by their mother. Police tape was dancing in the wind. The nearest house was 200 yards away. The surrounding forest was a buffer from the rest of the universe.

"Shouldn't we do this at the hospital or in front of the girl's home?" Nasro asked.

"Too disruptive," Jay said. "I don't want to burden the family."

Jay lost no time rolling out his prayer rug, kicking his shoes, and kneeling in his jeans and T-shirt. The thin rug let him feel every bump, every pebble on the ground. He went from upbeat to tired and disoriented to upbeat

435

again in a few hours. Nasro protected him from the elements with a blue tarp stretched over sticks. He acted as Jay's spokesman and fielded the inquiries from the police officers and the reporters who came, alerted they didn't know how. "Jay is asking you to respect his vow of silence," Nasro relayed to the press. "Anybody entering the site must do so quietly. Feel free to join the strike."

The reporters, conscious of Jay's position as the public's enfant chéri, agreed. Lights illuminated the scene at night. Cameras rolled from a distance as townspeople joined Jay into his fast on the third day. Jay himself didn't know how long he would last. Most of the time, he prayed, sat in peaceful contemplation, or slept. His hunger tore at his insides. It filled his whole being. It seemed to feed upon his body. It induced a certain lightness, an euphoria, a strange sense of elation. Mineral water was the only thing he allowed himself. He missed Lisha and Kaya. He wondered if what he was doing made any sense, if it would have any impact, if it would matter beyond the point of making him feel better. Would people understand?

Marianne herself came to relieve him from his self-imposed act of contrition. She came straight from the hospital and sat beside Jay, a tiny little thing in a yellow dress with still-visible bruises and a gigantic cast around one arm. "Thank you," she whispered before feeding Jay a handful of dates.

Jay went home to Lisha and Kaya, Nasro driving all the way. Lisha cleaned him, shaved him, and fed him some more. Though they stopped short of calling his West Virginia excursion a template for future interventions in the country's civic life, both understood that Jay would answer the call of duty wherever it proposed to take him. A packed suitcase was kept at the ready. Their life together promised to become one of active citizenry.

"Will mentalities ever change?" Lisha asked Jay.

"They already have," he told her.

"It seems everything the Church of Retribution did was in vain," she went on.

"It wasn't," Jay insisted.

"How can you be so sure?"

"The police were tipped of Marianne's presence in the trailer. A few years back nobody would have placed that call, the cops wouldn't have showed up, Marianne would have died, the case wouldn't have been tried, outrage would have been limited to the black part of town."

"Think we'll live to see a black president?"

"Probably not. But one can always hope. It would be something, if that happened. Real change. A change we can believe in."

The day to get hitched came. Lisha tracked her father down all the way to a basement in Queens. Both her real mother and Marina were also at hand. Joe was invited, though it wasn't sure until the last minute if he would come. The religious ceremony was held at the Islamic Center at the end of Embassy Row in Washington. Nasro officiated (the couple's presence is not required at the mosque) before running back to Charles County to double as Jay's best man.

Bride and groom exchanged vows in the intimate setting of their own sunny and airy living room. "You shall now kiss Lisha," Marina announced without skipping a beat after Jay and Lisha slipped on their wedding bands. Kaya clapped with glee from the cradle of Nicole's arms. Champagne started to flow. Everything was perfect except for one thing: Un was among the small crowd, boiling with visible jealousy and barely contained hatred in a corner. It was Jay's idea to have him, the same way he had invited Joe, Ahmet, Claude, Hakim, and Barbra, the one surviving Granny.

"I'm not feeling Un," Lisha told Jay at one point during the reception. "He looks like the Devil himself. See how fast he's been knocking back cocktail glasses? He's working himself into a stupor."

"He's fine," Jay assured him. "The man's on his way to jail. He's all messed up in the head. Cut him some slack."

Joe showed up almost toward the end, Maggie in tow. He had debated if he should come for days and days, only to find out at the last moment that he couldn't stay away. So he drove all the way down to southern Maryland in a white Phantom (his most inconspicuous car), bringing with him many gifts but looking hesitant after he parked and got out, almost tempted to go back to New York.

Jay welcomed him at the door, hugging him silently, holding Joe's chin up when Joe found it hard to lift his head and meet his eye.

"Good to see you," they said at the same time.

I wiped a discreet tear. So did Maggie.

Ahmet got the party going. Jay sang "I Choose You" acappella and gave all of us goose bumps. First dance was, of course, Delroy Wilson's "Better Must Come." Everybody jumped in for "Always" and "Ribbon in the

438

Sky," the following numbers. We knew just then that
Marvin and Chaka weren't far behind. Claude led the long
and winding Soul Train line.

Nobody paid attention to Un. Nobody except Joe,
Maggie, and me. Joe because his heart was too full to join
into the good cheer and because he knew his face would
turn red as soon as he kicked a few tentative steps. Maggie
and me because we had just found out Un had come to the
house for one thing only, and that one thing was to kill Jay.
Now the hair stood on the back of my neck every time I
looked at him. I had no doubt that he would go for it. What
did he have to lose? Empire was on the prowl. Empire was
all-mighty. Empire let no one stand in its path. Un knew he
was on his way to Guantanamo. He knew he didn't stand a
chance.

Maggie and I huddled near, shaking with
apprehension.

Nasro popped the cork of a bottle of apple cider,
making us jump.

Looking as pale as a ghost except for his red eyes,
Un fished a gun out of the folds of his white robe shortly
after the cake was served.

Unaware of the danger, Jay was approaching Un's
corner, holding Lisha with one hand and Kaya with the
other, waltzing effortlessly, floating, beaming all the way.
They were caught in the moment, the happiest time of their
lives. They were oblivious to the world. "Heaven Bound"
was the song.

Un pulled his gun all the way out.

A few paces from Un, Joe was lost in thought.
Something had changed in him since Jay had forwarded the

invitation to his wedding, he now realized. "I don't care what happened between us," Jay had scribbled inside the engraved card. "You're my brother and I'm getting married. You need to be here." Joe had considered the note for a long time. Marriage was so Jay. Joe had made fun of the whole thing before feeling disgusted with himself, his excesses, his out-of-control life. Simone was long gone. He was too paranoid to trust anybody new and too weak to be alone. So there was a different girl in his bed every other week. Marriage would never happen to him, let alone fatherhood (Joe had enough sense to understand that he was one of those people who would be no good to his own children). Exciting things or concepts or people were few and far between. You had to chase kicks all the way to the moon--literally (Joe had signed up to become a space tourist on a Russian rocket and he was already wondering what to do next). He hung out with top-seeded athletes, going as far as renting their time for one-on-one sessions. But even skateboard tricks on a mega-ramp with Bob Burnquist and motocross backflips with Twitch only held his interest for so long. Sometimes he thought about giving up his whole fortune to start all over again just for the fun of it, just to see if he had it in him to do it twice. Sometimes he wanted to kill himself. He'd heard about MTG before it hit the stores, of course. One of those foolproof investments he wished he could have thought of himself. He'd been one of the first to play it. Unlike Philip from Cincinnati, Joe took all the wrong turns and ended straight in Hell, and fast. His screen stayed pitch black for so long that he thought something was wrong was it.

     Un took aim.

Bang! the gun went. Bang! Bang! Bang!

"Did I really do that?" Joe wondered aloud after joining Maggie and me in Purgatory. "Did I jump into the line of fire?"

"You did," Maggie assured him.

"You sure did," I echoed.

"But why?" he lamented. "I had so much to live for."

"You couldn't help yourself," I suggested. "You didn't have it in you to let Un wipe out your brother and his family. You're a better person than even you thought."

Joe, feeling trapped, started to jump in place. "Damn! Damn!"

"Watch your mouth," Maggie and I shouted at the same time.

Joe, shaken by an intense regret, wouldn't shut up. "I sure didn't mean to do that," he said again. "All that stuff I left behind. The houses, the cars, the money.... I was about to fly into space."

"Forget all that," Maggie said.

"Can't take it with you," I added, stating the obvious.

Joe managed to remain silent for only a brief moment. I had my own fears of being stuck with him and Maggie for many more years to come, though the latter seemed to have been mellowed by death. We were almost friends now.

"What happens next?" Joe asked.

"We're being judged," I told him.

"They're tallying our stuff," Maggie explained, as if

she knew what she was talking about.

Joe turned pale. "Who's 'they'?"

Maggie shrugged. "Whoever does the work around here. Your father and I are betting on supercomputers, just from the number of cases and the amount of data."

Joe tried to loosen his collar and found out he couldn't. The collar, his shirt, his suit, his socks, and his shoes were an integral part of him. "So we're in Purgatory?"

Maggie and I nodded.

"Praise the Lord!" Joe exclaimed.

Maggie and I laughed our heads off. We laughed for the first time in months. We laughed and laughed and laughed.

"You shouldn't be mocking me," Joe scolded us. "I'm sincere. I was just about to change my ways and redeem myself. God knows what's in my heart. He knows."

Maggie and I looked at each other and roared. The kid was impossible. The kid was something else. The kid was a riot.

"Anybody knows what took place after I went down?" Joe inquired after our hilarity subsided.

"Hakim, Jay, Ahmet, and Nasro subdued Un," I told him. "Nobody else was hurt."

A smile covered Joe's face. "Then I'm glad," he said.

We exchanged small talk for a few more minutes, Maggie and I giving Joe a tour of a ghost's powers and limitations: teleporting, levitating, reading thoughts, crossing walls, the code, the lack of ubiquity.

Out of nowhere, a door appeared. More like a frame, really. A glowing thing made of pure energy that seemed to be a passageway beyond which a blinding light awaited. Slack-jawed, we considered the pulsating wonder. We had never seen anything like it.

Joe broke the silence first. "What's this?"

"This is new,"Maggie answered.

"It's the Gate of Heaven," I told them. "Just like in Jay's game. He got it right. A door. God awaits. The ultimate leap of faith. You jump through."

The three of us looked at one another.

"Yes!" Maggie exclaimed.

"Yes!" Joe shouted.

"I knew it!" Maggie added.

"What did you know?" I asked.

"That everything would be all right. Jay ... Jay is connected."

I shrugged. We had made it. It's all that mattered. Joe and Jay had done enough good down there that we were safe from Satan. The rest of our little clan down on Earth would be fine, too. It came as a big, big relief. Only now could I begin to realize how heavy the experience had been.

"Shall we?"

We locked arms. Sandwiched between Maggie and Joe, I gave the signal. "*Uno. Dos. Uno, dos, tres, cuatro.*"

We started to walk toward the frame. As we got near, it widened to accommodate us. The golden light warmed our hearts and shone on our faces. Love. All-encompassing love. Love everlasting. "God," I murmured before all three of us jumped. "Here we come."

ACKNOWLEDGMENTS

Special thanks to Marthe, Issa, Nathalie, Ngone, and Paul Lo; Vieux Lo; Gustave Lo; Ngone Diallo; Khoudia Diouf; Ieasha, Isaiah, and Anthony Morris; Susan, John, Johnny, and Katie Palmont; Keith Johnson; Florence Duarte; Abdou Diagne; Helene Sow; Ousseynou Fall; Oumar Ba; Bath Sylla; Cecile Sow.

Many thanks to Madieyna N'diaye, Erica Meade, Sally Ginsburg, Chai Woodham, Jacek Niecko, Kilcha Menser, Bobby Kim, Ingrid Groller-Lane, Stephen Schwartz.

To Chester Himes, Cheikh Anta Diop, Mariama Ba, Ousmane Sembene, Ferdinand Oyono, Michel Deon, Souleymane Faye, Hampate Ba, Tierno Bokar Tall, Walter Mosley, Joseph Kessel, Georges Simenon, Bob Marley, Curtis Mayfield, Bill Withers, Delroy Wilson, Gil Scott-Heron, Quincy Jones, Marvin Gaye, and George Pelecanos.

Cover design by Erica Meade.
Photography: Camille Mosley-Pasley.